Mary Fatima Cyr

ALSO BY DAVID ADAMS RICHARDS

FICTION

The Coming of Winter

Blood Ties

Dancers at Night: Stories

Lives of Short Duration

Road to the Stilt House

Nights Below Station Street

Evening Snow Will Bring Such Peace

For Those Who Hunt the Wounded Down

Hope in the Desperate Hour

The Bay of Love and Sorrows

Mercy Among the Children

River of the Brokenhearted

The Friends of Meager Fortune

The Lost Highway

Incidents in the Life of Markus Paul

Crimes Against My Brother

Principles to Live By

NONFICTION

Hockey Dreams

Lines on the Water

God Is.

Facing the Hunter

Mary Cyr

A NOVEL

DAVID ADAMS RICHARDS

DOUBLEDAY CANADA

Doubleday Canada and colophon are registered trademarks of Penguin Random House Canada Limited

Library and Archives Canada Cataloguing in Publication

Richards, David Adams, 1950-, author
Mary Cyr / David Adams Richards.

Issued in print and electronic formats.
ISBN 978-0-385-68248-0 (hardcover).—ISBN 978-0-385-68249-7 (EPUB)

I. Title.

PS8585.I17M37 2018   C813'.54   C2017-904879-1
                                               C2017-904880-5

This book is a work of fiction. Names, characters, places, events and incidents are either the product of the author's imagination or are used fictitiously. Any resemblance to actual persons, living or dead, events, or locales is entirely coincidental.

Jacket design by Rachel Cooper
Jacket image © Ilona Wellmann / Trevillion Images

Printed and bound in the USA

Published in Canada by Doubleday Canada,
a division of Penguin Random House Canada Limited

www.penguinrandomhouse.ca

10 9 8 7 6 5 4 3 2 1

 Penguin
Random House
DOUBLEDAY CANADA

My daughter-in-law, Keltie McCarthy,
My goddaughter, Ellie Carleton,
My rebel-in-arms, Sara MacDonald,
And my dear friend, Jessica Davidson,
This book.

"Let me tell you a secret: her courage came from her being not just English, but Acadian. It was not something she wasn't proud of; it was something you yourself tried to wrest from her soul."

—Perley to his mother, Nanesse, June 2008

I wouldn't want to be a saint. They burn saints, don't they?
> —Mary Cyr, speaking to John Delano, July 1979

She's as sweet as Tupelo honey
She's an angel of the first degree
> —Van Morrison

And what a wonderful though tragic task this is—to tell this to the people.
> —Dostoevsky

PROLOGUE

New Brunswick, Canada

WHEN THE SECOND WORLD WAR ENDED, COLONEL BLAIR CYR, through a variety of organizations, helped to bring Dutch, Polish and Latvian families to Canada. There was much red tape that he knew how to ignore and families in his care were processed quickly. Blair Cyr tried to keep in touch with as many of these people as he could. On occasion, out of the blue, someone would get a phone call, and Mr. Cyr would be on the line.

Blair Cyr was a known benefactor, though he never spoke or took credit for it. Neither for the most part did his sons, or his grandsons. Thirteen Dutch families benefited from his kindness.

A Dutch family, the Vanderflutin, immigrated to Canada in early 1947, one family in a group of thirty-one. For a time the father, Dug Vanderflutin, became somewhat of a fixture in the lives of the Cyrs.

He was, as the expression goes, a wheeler-dealer. In fact he had managed to immigrate to Canada with a good deal.

Dug Vanderflutin tried to open up companies in the States, tried to buy and sell gold, even tried to find the fortune at Oak Island, where one of his colleagues was killed. A Mi'kmaq worker he had hired to help build a tunnel to the gold—or where he thought the gold should be, with the map he had. Dug Vanderflutin made it back out, but his Mi'kmaq friend did not. It was one of the unfortunate incidents in his life.

In 1960 he told Mr. Cyr he had some paintings. One was a Matisse, and there were two Picassos and a Monet.

"I am broke," he said. "If you can help me with this, I'd be grateful—"

Mr. Blair Cyr bought them for a lot of money, and donated them to the newly opened Beaverbrook Art Gallery. With those funds Vanderflutin opened a mining operation in northern New Brunswick, against the wishes of almost everyone.

He did not understand mining. There were strikes, one lasting almost eight months, and by the late sixties the talk of shafts and blasts and tailing ponds infuriated him, and he moved on.

It seemed the whole thing went belly up, though he held on to it as best he could. Then he tried a shipping venture to and from Venezuela, but he needed the docks of Saint John, and there was certain trouble with the port authorities over the tanker *Caracas Albión*, which dropped anchor in 1968 and never left port for over a year, with many of the sailors, Filipino and Chinese, complaining of beatings and asking for asylum.

Dug moved on to other things. He tried farming in Saskatchewan—a farm of 160 hectares, much of it useless, and one of the first to attempt canola, which lamed out with blackleg; his last venture was importing jewellery from India, which he sold to immigrant stores in Montreal. Still, he was a mover—and as a mover, he always moved on. In a way he had abandoned his wife and child in far-off Saskatchewan in order to be adventurous. But, perhaps in a more secretive way, to escape his past.

At the last of it, he was tired, overweight, drank to excess in bars in New York, and by the late sixties was rumoured to have something going with running guns to the Irish Republican Army from depots in Sweden.

Still, Blair Cyr forgave him the rumoured IRA business and would often say: "He was a saboteur in Norway to help British shipping in 1942 and '43, and he blew up depots, so you have to think of it that way, I suppose."

There was, however, something Mr. Cyr did not know. That is, it would take time to discover who this Vanderflutin actually was, where those paintings actually had come from. That there was in fact another Vanderflutin from the same Dutch village, whom Blair Cyr had confused with this man.

This Dug Vanderflutin died suddenly, alone, almost broke and fairly forgotten in 1971.

The son's name was Ernest. Blair Cyr wrote to him, informing him of his father's death. They offered to buy his father's assets if the son did not want to continue with them.

The son wrote back, that he was still in university, still finishing his doctorate, but would think it over:

"I will bide my time and look for the right buyer——" he wrote.

They wondered, since they had floated many a loan, why they were not the right buyer. But he was young and full of green, and they never responded.

Still, the offer remained open, and it seemed though Ernest looked in many places for another offer, he did not find it. There was only one family interested enough in the ore mine in New Brunswick to make an offer.

So finally this Ernest Vanderflutin went back to his father's old friends.

The Cyrs came forward and bought the mining company and folded it into their mining concerns called Tarsco—this company owned the iron ore considerations of New Brunswick, a potash mine in Nova Scotia, a gold mine in northern Ontario—and almost as an afterthought, with the purchase of Vanderflutin enterprises, a small out-of-the-way coal mine in Mexico.

Ernest never knew his father's dealings—his trafficking in gold and his search for treasure at Oak Island. But the offer he got from Cyr, and the offer he had to take, was far less than he assumed it would be. He felt cheated out of a fortune by the Cyr family. He was bitter about this, and about how much he was paid when he sold it to them.

Oathoa, Mexico

MINER NUMBER T-70909, PEDRO SONORA, COULDN'T SAVE ANYONE. After the bump he ran up the rail past the elongated drift that they called "the sky is falling" toward the lanterns pitched and dangling, broken on the side of cracking timbers. He was fifteen hundred feet away from safety, a small feeble light the colour of soft tin, way, way up in the tunnel.

He heard something like shovelfuls of coal falling around him. Confused, he thought men were still throwing shovelfuls of coal into the railcars at the side of the drift. Then down the side tunnel he could hear men shouting. Someone—was it Jorge?—carried another man on his shoulders, but then fell to his knees, and was covered above his head in ten seconds, with his hands in the air, all his fingers extended so one could count out loud on them, and his helmet light still glowing while the man was being buried.

Then there was a sudden silence—almost an awesome silence—and Pedro could hear someone, whoever, saying a prayer to Our Lady of Guadalupe. There was a shrine in the mine, at the cross-section of tunnels, where people put in money on their way deeper, and blessed themselves on their way back up. Those who forgot or did not, then worried about bad luck. Now Pedro thought, someone had not blessed himself, and a bump had come.

It was Pedro's oldest son's fourteenth birthday today. He had bought him a little tape recorder because his son liked to go into the woods and record birds and sell the recordings to American tourists. Pedro had given it to him just before he entered the shaft.

And he had said:

"*Cuida de tu hermano—esta noche tenemos una fiesta.*"

Take care of your brother—we will have a party tonight.

Pedro was forty-three years old. His wife had died of cancer two years before. They were people who had lived simply, attended Mass, worked at jobs, worried about crime, and did all they could to be decent.

When his wife was dying, she was rag and bag of bones, and sat on the steps outside their apartment to get fresh air. That is where, when lifting Florin to sit on her knee, she fell over, bled from the mouth, and was carried into bed. Victor, her oldest, ran to get her a glass of water. And then the priest. She died that night, holding prayer beads in her hand.

His two sons were all he had, and he loved them dearly. He loved them more than dearly. He loved them with all his heart.

Pedro would someday be known as the hero of the Amigo disaster—he would be written about. He would be the one great moment in their darkest hour. That is, he would be like the First Servant, in *King Lear*, the kind of man C. S. Lewis wrote about, who didn't have great plans about great things but did his duty come what may. That is, Pedro didn't pretend to know how the script of his life was going to turn out—he only did what he could to honour it.

But this was not for Pedro to know.

He would be stuck in a pocket of air for eight days.

The mine's owners would call off the search after three. At that time Pedro and twelve other men would hear the bulldozers closing off the opening three hundred metres above. They would look at each other—with their feeble lamps still glowing.

When the Mexican families became outraged that their loved ones might still be alive—might still be praying to be rescued—the Mexican government was silent. Then the government became very angry. They sent the army in to bring discipline back to the town. How would these people—these ignorant people—know anything about a coal mine?

After two weeks of outrage Señor Carlos DeRolfo, Amigo's president and CEO, supervisor and co-owner, said he had done all he could. No one looked more sorrowful than Mr. Carlos DeRolfo at this time.

The international investor still owning part of this mine's enormous debt was the Canadian company Tarsco. The Mexican company was called Amigo. The Amigo board of governors had been extracting far too much coal, leaving the air saturated with methane gas. But there was a secret Amigo's owners had not revealed to the Mexican people: Tarsco had assumed the greater part of this debt so Amigo could refurbish and reinvest in safety. More than assuming the debt, they had given Amigo another fourteen million dollars in order to upgrade standards. They had then closed the mine down in 2001 until these upgrades were completed. After the new upgrades were completed with this fourteen million, and a list of upgrades was sent off to the mining authorities, the mine was allowed to reopen.

However, Carlos DeRolfo, his wife and other board members had secretly spent most of that money on themselves—that is, the entire fourteen million—thinking not only that they would not be caught but that what they did would be considered legitimate if they had the right paperwork in place. (They had been robbing this mine, and misappropriating the legitimate offers of financial assistance, for years.)

A man named Hulk Hernández oversaw this transfer of funds for them into certain bank accounts, and became the chief inspector of the mine. The people of Oathoa relied upon him to tell them the truth, and Mr. Hernández did.

What was in their favour was this. The transfer of money had happened a few minutes before 9/11. It was wired from New York, and any record of it was probably lost. Warren, the oldest grandson of Blair Cyr, and the man who had wired these funds, had died in that attack as well. Days and then weeks passed, and no one knew about this transfer, and how much money was actually given.

DeRolfo had a new indoor-outdoor swimming pool and had built his wife her own chapel, where he had the local and quite pious priest come to say Mass. He had a stable of eight Arabian horses.

Once a day, after the implosion, Mr. Hernández held a press conference, where he read from a chart. He showed the routes the rescuers took, the impediments they had to face, the damage that supposedly had been done.

A few weeks after the implosion a safety group was formed to look into the cause of the disaster. It had many people in the town involved. They were to recommend changes to mining and decide who was responsible. They were also going to decide who would receive the majority of the compensation that the mining company said they would offer. Carlos DeRolfo's wife sat on this board, along with Hulk Hernández. She told them of the amount of safety measures they had installed, the work they had done—and her suggestion was that if anyone was at fault, it was the international company Tarsco, which wanted too much coal extracted from the mine. She blessed herself, and cried when she spoke.

"Thousands of tonnes of coal," she said.

However, all during this time, all during the days of agony just after the collapse of the mine, during those days of prayers and masses after this implosion, Carlos DeRolfo and his wife were hoping to locate one small boy, a boy about fourteen years of age, named Victor Sonora.

Carlos went to the school to find him, but the boy did not show up there.

"*Hijo de puta. Hijo de puta*," he would repeat.

Son of a bitch.

Carlos would tell other children:

"It is not important, but if you see him, and he is available to see me, tell him I am at home." And he would look rather fatherly at the boys he spoke to. Especially the boy's best friend, Ángel Gloton, who Carlos had a managerial interest in as a young junior lightweight.

He took Ángel Gloton aside and said:

"Tell our friend Victor I have a lot of money for him—if he wants to see me. I want him to know I am looking out for him—he is an orphan now, and has lost his father, and he has a little brother."

But the truth was much, much different. Why Carlos wanted to see Victor Sonora was because Victor had recorded something on his new tape recorder. Something that proved the men were still alive when the search was suspended. This would become known, but it would take time. Victor had been sitting on the steps of the old school, playing with this tape recorder, when the accident happened, and like so many he had rushed to the mine. Later that day he turned his tape recorder on, to keep a record of the rescue. And a sound was recorded that proved men were calling for help.

Twice Victor had tried to get this tape to someone who would listen—and twice he realized that the policeman Erappo Pole was waiting for him. Why? He did not know, but he believed something was not right. In fact was terribly wrong. So not able to go to the police he would hide, with the tape recorder and his little brother, Florin, and wonder what to do. When Ángel saw him, and told Victor that Carlos DeRolfo wanted to speak with him, Victor knew he was in trouble, and the tape he had on him was a dangerous tape. He finally decided to take it to a tourist, and believed that would save his father.

Then a strange event happened. Young Victor Sonora was found dead in the bedroom of a Canadian woman's villa.

And Mary Cyr, the granddaughter of Blair Cyr, found herself in a Mexican jail in that small town of Oathoa; a woman who on paper was partial owner of this mine.

PART ONE

1.

WHEN JOHN DELANO FIRST SAW MARY CYR, IT WAS ABOUT FIVE that evening. She was sitting in the cell. The early darkness seemed uncomfortably solitary, while life echoed down the hall, the smell of coffee and beans and supper. He could see words on the side of the far wall: *¡Viva Cristo! 5 mayo 1922*. John later heard some priest named Father Ignatius had scratched them there. This priest was hanged on International Workers' Day.

For what it was worth to ten thousand prisoners, *¡Viva Cristo!* was still legible after eighty-six years.

There was dust everywhere because of the white unpaved road that ran to the north of the jail. A field of scrub bushes was to its left, and here a solitary donkey grazed and now and again looked up at a passerby with its filmed pussy eyes. The dust came up around the solitary donkey as well. Far away huge hills lay quiet and restrained in the silent evening air; hills that were made of grey rock, and bush. A car sped down the hill and disappeared. Across from the jail a confectionary shop that sold tortillas and tobacco and cola and beer. Or at least, that is what John could make out it sold.

A man in a white suit jacket, with big white buttons—one sewn with black thread—walked by carrying some kind of outboard motor toward the garage that John had seen on the way in.

That is, John noticed as much as he could. It was his job.

"Welcome to the black hole," she whispered to him. Then she said excitedly: "I knew if anyone would come to save me, it would be you. I wouldn't have anyone else!" Then she added: "All those others are nothing to me now!" This was a comment said to mollify any tension they might have—saying that now the others—those lots of others she flaunted in front of him were nothing to her now. So one might ask, had she flaunted them? Well of course she had.

He had come to save her—but he wondered how to. Though seemingly taciturn and offstanding, believed by the press to be both a misogynist and a misanthrope, he was perhaps as good a detective as there was. Still, he was very aware this was not his playing field, not his country; he had no jurisdiction, not even the right to question people.

Her wonderful eyes looked out at him. Mexican people were wonderful too, as wonderful as anyone. But if you got into trouble real or imagined while down here, you were on your own.

Nothing ever levels the playing field quite as much as sin. And she was taken to be wealthy. That is, they had just realized a day or so before he arrived who exactly *she was*. They had taken her passport away, and it did not bode well. Some officers looked at her so sternly she shook. Well, they said she did. And smiled about it. But perhaps she did not shake as much as they wanted.

She did not know why this sudden hatred had flared up when her name was revealed. The biggest bullying officer had spit at her. But the idea of even saying this was ludicrous. So she said nothing.

They had closed her cell door with a clatter and walked away.

He had not seen her in over three years. It was, seeing her again, as if he had found an alien sea creature among the shore rocks on an October Sunday afternoon. But she noticed his appearance too, and it was drawn and thin. He was ill and had been for months, and the dust and the heat of the small town had done nothing to alleviate this.

But what struck him too was its beauty—the beauty of the town was almost too much to bear; you came around a nondescript corner and saw a remarkable fountain spouting water against a palm tree square—and yet beyond the fountains and the coloured stones was another world. They had built the railroad across this part of Mexico, from coast to coast, back in the fifties, to transport goods for the United States. The track was rusted and torn apart just to the north of the village, but a new line had been made parallel to it for the transport of coal. That too was now unused, yet the rails still gleamed in the sun. A signal to those above about the tragedy that had happened to those below. And life, Carlos DeRolfo said in his statement, would go on.

"*Más grande y mejor*," he said.

Bigger and better.

They still had gorgeous festivals—and multicoloured adobes, and small donkeys too. For the *turistas* and the children. They had some twenty-nine bars along the streets above the jail—and they, being a backwater 145 kilometres off any main route, had no real drug problem. There were some problems, of course, but not in the way of the cartels. John realized this could be a liability for her. That is, at the moment she seemed to be the only game in town.

Her fingers were purple and bruised from having banged them against the metal door when she asked to be let out, because for a long time she had no idea why she was locked up. They told her if she did not stop, they would put her in a straitjacket. And by now the word was out: the crazy rich lady had committed a crime—a terrible crime—and people shuddered at it, and came to stare at her as if she was a trapped animal. Some just gloomily looked at her. Others glibly glanced and looked away. More gathered every day, as who she was became known.

"*La mujer es viciosa*," mothers told children. "*Señorita Cyr demonia.*"

The woman is vicious . . . demonic.

"Certainly somewhat exaggerated," Mary said. "At least a little."

This anger at her had nothing as yet to do with the coal mine disaster—that would come, and build exponentially. This rage had to do with another crime she was accused of.

This is what John had heard before he reached his room on the second floor of the resort. His room, or three rooms, was called *una vista de tomar aliento.*

A breathtaking view.

It did have that. On one side there was the sea, and to his left mountains. But it was a stale, sad place, really; full of second-hand furniture. Probably the same thing existed in her rooms. *Una vista* as well.

Mary Cyr was now left staring out at a half-blind donkey.

This was the idea of rumour that he realized had plagued her since she was a child. Now she was just the crazy rich lady—a kind of emblematic old woman (though she was not yet forty-five), with greying hair. Still and all the features were classic. That is, as far as he could ever tell what classic was. How could he even pretend to know one way or the other? It was left to other men to talk about classic beauty. It was up to other men to finish university, take history courses or poli sci. But, my god, she was beautiful.

They had not seen each other in years. And the fact was, she was worth millions only if her family decided. And they were back in Canada. Garnet was the head of her side of the family. The other, more prosperous and even more secretive, side had parted ways with them. There were the newspapers and oil, and lumber, and business ventures of Blair Cyr's three sons. But her father and mother were dead, and she was in the newspaper section. That is, she and her cousin Perley and her uncle Garnet. Garnet might not be on her side, since she had accused him of many things—including murder, which she later confessed was a slip of the tongue.

Her cousin Perley had spent much of his childhood brought up by maids. His favourite was Flora.

After a while Flora went away. He wrote her a letter, asking if he could go visit, for she was much like his mother. He got an answer, which he kept in his locked toy box at the end of his room. Flora said she would come and see him someday, but she never did.

Mary had herself been left alone, an orphan without being called one. She had flaunted her freedom and her money too often in too many places. John knew this as much as anyone.

John had come here on a moment's notice without thinking much of what he was doing, or how he was going to get her home. It wasn't even his duty to do so. There were clothes hanging in another cell, and a radio playing. There was laughter farther down the hall, loud and racked by coughing that sounded obscurely fitting for an evening after five. Just as in some places one might think of having a drink before dinner, now coughing and hanging clothes seemed to be entirely appropriate.

There was the smell of cigarettes everywhere; the stench of harsh black tobacco. Along with the smell of cooking oil. There were two women cooking french fries in the corridor between the cells; the back door was open, so the women could easily have walked out.

But Mary could not.

Her family had called on him two days ago.

So he had come carrying his clothes in a black bag. He had gone in the darkness, and in winter, to travel God knows where. If at night a traveller, he thought.

He arrived from Phoenix earlier in the day.

He waited at the small airport, took a car down the inland highway, passed derelict adobes in the sun.

He was let off at Bruno's Tea Room, a small restaurant up the way from the resort he was to report to. There was a cactus plant against the side wall, and a porch light shone at noon. He stayed there an hour, drank a cold beer, bought another for his journey, picked up his black shoulder bag, and trying to remain focused in the awful heat (it was already 85 degrees) set out on foot, the dust of the roadway coming up his legs. He walked where whitewashed walls towered on his right, behind which dogs would on occasion bark. He walked downward toward a spot of granite that opened at a turn and partially showed the blue sea.

The small town with its wonderful fountain became visible after twenty minutes. The cobbled square, the centre stone laid by a dignitary in 1922, the glass windows of dress shops and antiques—the Bank of Mexico, a local casino, the resort with its colourful flags shining. A dead cat lying in the weeds.

He reached the square and sat near the fountain and milled about in a place he was unfamiliar with, a northern man in the middle of Mexico, until he saw the jail itself. It was at the top of a hill, surrounded by a half acre of dirt. There were nine graves just at its border. Two of them were the priests hanged years ago. The others were the people whose lives John had not heard about. He walked toward the jail and saw just up a side lane a sign that said POLICÍA.

"*Sí*," said a youngster he asked.

So he walked toward it.

It was murder; the Mexican policeman told him after he introduced himself as a policeman and a representative of the family in Canada.

He was stunned into silence, though he tried not to show it. He thought it might have been anything, from refusing to pay a bill to a traffic ticket, being inebriated in the square. Anything could land you in jail here.

"Murder," Constable Fey said, looking down at the indictment as if he was himself surprised by it. He raised his eyebrows and looked up and gave a slightly guilty smile that seemed to become infused within the sunlight. He was tall, thin and young—and the policeman John would end up dealing with. It was as if at this moment he wanted to impart some knowledge, but hesitated. John at least saw something of a hesitation; a Hessian hesitation, he thought.

So after a time, when it was late afternoon, he walked to the jail to visit her. He crossed the road, the dry cement walkway, and could smell sewage from somewhere close by. He was led in through to her by a policeman named Erappo Pole—who seemed slightly amused with him and his demeanour and seemed to be slightly—just slightly—drunk.

Erappo Pole pointed, shrugged, turned and left him.

The jail had long corridors and grey walls. As he walked toward her, he had to keep reassuring himself that he must show a happy face.

The Cyr family had restructured, having sold many of its holdings. Garnet, seventy-seven years old, was the head of her side of it.

Perley, his son, would take over, but people knew he was overshadowed by his cousin Greg, and overshadowed too by Mary Cyr. But a few days ago Perley had told his father that Mary was in trouble again and they had better see to it. So his uncle called the Mexican embassy, then the Canadian ambassador, and then decided to send someone down. Perley said he would go; it was his duty. But his father was adamant that they send someone else.

Although Perley in his hapless way had tried to keep it quiet, it had already made the papers—even their own papers, albeit on page eight.

All of this must have made their enemies jubilant. Mary Cyr had lived with them as an orphan. But she had never felt comfortable being called, for appearances' sake, "Garnet's daughter." From the age of eleven she was solitary. She said she was often locked in her room—and left without toilet paper. This was when she was twenty-six and trying to sue them for what she called "her money." She knew the only friend she had had within the family was Perley, but she had attacked him viciously also, and spread rumours about him. People claimed that she told his girlfriends that he had herpes, and not to try to get to second or even first base with him—unless they wanted it too. Then she would take it all back and tell him she had not spread rumours—it was terribly unlike her to do that. (In the end she admitted that she was trying to protect him from gold diggers—but he said, and in a way rightly, she had no right to do so.)

Garnet had disliked her for how she had attacked his son, and his wife, Nan, calling her French—which she was, but something that if said by Mary Cyr might have meant something else entirely.

"I only said she was French—I said nothing at all—intimated nothing whatsoever about the Frenchiness she displayed to lord over and browbeat and try to destroy my English mother—for instance, I never said a disparaging thing about frogs—or even pollywogs—or losing wars to the Germans on a fairly regular basis—how they all ran away in the Second World War. I simply said—well, she was French. She was French—and she said I was French and that started it—because Cyr can be French—but we are not—she is."

"We damn well are French."

"Just a tadpole's worth!"

"No one ever said a mean thing to your mother."

"You called her British."

"Well dear, she is."

"And Nan—my aunt is, how do you say in *anglais*—French!"

This would be precocious at twenty, and was said when she was thirteen and her mother was still alive but no longer living with them.

She would not apologize. She would not say sorry—there was sorrow in her—a great masterly whirlwind of sorrow she had to deal with, confront every morning when she woke, like a giant weight upon her—but would not say sorry.

Only Perley stuck by her, the boy she tormented to distraction, and the boy she teased and even seduced at seventeen, one hot summer afternoon for something to do; and then when he was in his underwear trembling, she simply turned and left the room. (Or this is what the rumour stated.)

She left for years. Lived here and there after her son, Bobby, died. But then people lost sight of her. She became wise and earnest and wanted to help—things like Greenpeace. Stopping whatever oil pipeline she could, even while living off assets that came from oil pipelines, thrusting down now from Alberta.

So she was a very rich woman living off of many assets she deplored, and, like certain of her friends in the Kennedy family, who she had met as a child, she never seemed to see the contradiction. Well, it was the problem of most moneyed leftists. But fortunately, or unfortunately, she herself wasn't leftist—not really in the slightest. But she was Mary Cyr. So then they could take her to be anything, use her for any cause or scandal, and then leave her be.

From the childhood escapades to the university and charities and African diplomats she dined with because she had just turned up there. To the atrocities she spoke about in *Maclean's* magazine, with a picture of her reading a university brochure as if she really wanted to go.

"I am against all sorts of atrocities—I could pick out quite a few I am against—most of them, really—except a few of the sillier ones—you know at times some people just get a notion in their heads—and run amok."

Then she would write a note to Perley saying, in her queer but rather handsome handwriting:

"As you can tell I am—getting most of the publicity."

That she was getting more publicity than either Greg or Warren.

"And by the way—those newspapers are really mine, so when you print something about me, make me sound clever."

2.

BUT WHAT PERVADED MARY CYR NOW WAS REALLY WHAT HAD pervaded her always, an aura of sudden (sudden) tragedy in a dark cell with brown eyes searching John for his soul, and a smile on her face—there was bravery in this, if nothing else. The Cyrs knew how to be brave. Her father did too know how to be brave; out of that wilderness of temperament he fashioned his own illusive flights, and destroyed himself, but not without courage. So John now thought. Her father was a Spitfire pilot in the Second World War, was in the Sinai with an Israeli forward tank position in 1967 and was the first journalist to report that the Israelis had smashed through and were destroying defensive positions, that their air force had destroyed Egyptian planes on the ground. That is, the first Western reporter to see it first-hand. Why John thought about this was that there was bravery in her sudden smile if nothing else.

It had been three or four years since he had heard a word from them. They had become in his own lore simply the really rich family he had once dealt with. In fact they had turned their back on him when he got into trouble in his own department. Though this could not really be said, for the rich act with a kind of impartiality and dismissing someone was not really a betrayal to them. That sounds like a cliché, until one has spent time with the rich. No matter how close you thought you were to them they could always fall back on the employer-employee ratio. Of course they could be so generous at times it astounded you. And John never knew really why. That is, why he was astounded, or what the motivation was they had for certain kinds of kindnesses. Garnet too had moments where he showed this side of the dynasty. Perley, he had always felt, was the most subjected to belittling and the most human.

But now with that phone call, it was as if their treachery never mattered. That they had almost four years ago simply told him to go away did not seem to be remembered. When he had stormed into the cottage looking for her (trying to protect her—he had forgotten from what) and they were sitting having drinks with former prime minister Mulroney, who stood politely to shake his hand.

John was ushered through the front porch and into the side kitchen, where he was given a large glass of pure orange juice—almost as if this was the main reason for his visit. They stood around him watching as he drank it. Then they took the glass away and washed it.

Then they asked him what in hell he was doing there. He begged to see her, to see if she was okay, but they said he could not. He was let go—calling the reason for his dismissal his emotional attachment to her.

"You have a rather deep emotional attachment to her," Garnet said.

Yes—he had. So he was let go. And they did not contact him again.

That is, they could scorn you, not lift a finger to help, let you walk through the desolate ages alone, time and again, and then suddenly in the middle of the night the phone doth ring:

"Hey, John—this is Garnet Cyr. How are you?"

It was as simple as that.

"Mary—what happened to her? What's wrong?" he asked, looking through the night table drawer for a match to light a cigarette while he heard the storm ascending outside against the planks and boards of his motel room.

"Well, she's got herself into a world of trouble, John—we thought she was back in Toronto but kept phoning her the last while with no answer—so what we were thinking is—"

"This is an unlisted number—how in the world did you get it?"

They did not even have to answer that.

"When is the last time you had any contact with her?"

"Oh, months and months—over three years ago."

So he went in the night to find the woman (perhaps the only woman he ever really loved and was never allowed to) behind a scarred metal door. She was so much younger and so much richer than he was.

He was staying at Los Marinas Resort—the place she had been staying. His villa was called the Beautiful Vista, or the Wonderful View—or something. Hers, across the way, was a two-storey villa with patio and stairs, it was called Ángel de la Mañana.

Angel in the Morning, or Angel of the Morning.

But both these villas had seen better days. The whitewash was faded and so were the small plants that bordered them.

There was some terrible heaviness come over him because of the ruined and seedy place, a smell of displaced human eroticism; a sad, languid sunlight.

A place for refugees, some might say—or middle-class working people taking their first and only vacation south; but not a place for her. How in hell did she end up here?" Of course he was being exclusive for her sake, and he knew it.

3.

HE WAS PUT IN A SMALL VILLA WITH A FEW SIDE WINDOWS, a faded potted plant and small velvet Mexican paintings of bullfighting. The shadows of the sun lingered there and then dissipated and went elsewhere. It reminded him of a Robert Mitchum movie somehow. He loosened his tie and opened the second beer he had bought. Then he looked through his pockets for the pills his doctor had given him. He held the bottle out at arm's length to study what it said, with an inquisitive self-depreciating look. And shrugged.

His breathing was more laboured than it had ever been. But down in Mexico the heat was already oppressive and his chest was sore again. He sniffed and looked through some papers where he had written down the constable's name, the name of the jail, the name of the town Oathoa; a town of 1,800 people. He was continually losing what he had written down—not like his friend Constable Markus Paul, who seemed to have a wealth of notebooks, filled with information.

John had a few scribbled notes. And the resort brochure. He flipped it over and read it as if he was interested:

LOS MARINAS—a small, private resort tucked away in Oathoa, charming, out of the way and modern—with panoramic views of the Sea of Cortez. Feed the dolphins, visit the principal ruins of the Lost Tribe of the Jaguar. Listen to the music of the mariachi, dine on the beach with tuxedoed waiters. Swim in the sea, walk along our golden sands, explore the jungle, the splendorous Cave of the Crystals. Visit our licensed casino or just relax in your own Jacuzzi.

It said the same in German, Japanese and Spanish.

Lady Mary Cyr had been running from something. He wasn't sure what. But she had entered Oathoa almost a month ago.

She was called "Lady Mary" because her grandfather Blair Cyr had become Lord of Doak in 1986. He was reviled for taking a lordship, and giving up his Canadian citizenship; she, for calling herself "Lady"—and for fifteen years insisting on it. This imperial strain in her was nonsense and John knew it. Now everyone in her family was pretty well dead, except for Garnet and young Perley (who was in fact forty-six). Not on the other, more important and richer, side—that is, Lady Mary Cyr, for all her wealth, was a poor relative.

She was one of the few family members to attend Blair Cyr's funeral in 1997. (The idea that he had died in the Bahamas and she had brought his body home sitting up in a private airplane was fodder for jokes by academics in the universities here, and others too, none of whom, as Mary said, would ever themselves give up a seat on a plane.)

By that time (he had lived too long) his empire was taken over by Greg and Donald Warren Cyr, Mary's other cousins, who she hardly knew. She saw pictures of them in Canadian newsmagazines, being compared to young Kennedys. That might be true, except they were far richer than the Kennedys.

"Where's my money—I want my money" was one of the headlines in one of the papers that the Cyrs did not control, showing Mary Cyr on a balcony overlooking some ocean. (She was in Brisbane, Australia, at that moment, John discovered later.)

She was on an allowance. She would receive the greater portion of her finances on her birthday this year: that is, in six months as the crow flies. But there was a certain catch—it stipulated this largesse of many millions of dollars be given to a woman who had "retained" herself. This was a strange word, one inserted into the equation by lawyers eight years before, who, abrupt, bright and at times abysmal in their dealings, decided it was a way out for her family. That is, if she was examined—people are always examined—and found to be incompetent—then she had not retained herself; and she would be kept on a sizable allowance.

At that moment, in a jail cell in Mexico, Mary did not know of the word *retained* or what it would suggest to others.

Had she retained herself? That would depend, John knew now, on him. (John had been informed of this for some reason. He asked in a halting voice—feeling like a snoop—how much this money, her inheritance, was to come to. And the lawyer said: "Perhaps seventy-eight or eighty million.")

"Who is she?" one of the bony porters at Los Marinas had asked him, an elderly man with emaciated wrists and a boyish, hopeful smile, a smile that lit up his ancient face, as if he was just about to skip school, or at its worst learn an unsavoury secret about a teacher, and who pointed at that day's paper. "People say she is from the United States." He smiled as if being from the United States was part of the scandal.

"No, she is from someplace else. How long have you been carrying bags for people?" John asked, pulling out some bills the value of which he did not know, and handing them to him.

"Sixty-four years." The man's smile changed to indicate a kind of jubilation at his longevity.

"Did you know her?" John asked.

He nodded.

"And did she do the least thing scandalous?"

The porter shook his head. "But," he said, "she is the coal lady—so we can't let her go."

Mary Cyr did not know this yet—or if she did, she did not let on. She attracted attention even when she was trying not to. And now this attention was the worst of all. It was her great crisis, the public eye. The family had hired a lawyer. A brilliant young lawyer named Xavier Santez. The cynics would say it was just for family honour. No, it was much more. It was in spite of her dishonour. That is, no matter what this present charge was, Mary would say she was guiltless, and just might be guilty.

But if the old porter called her "the coal lady," everyone in Mexico already knew who she was.

4.

JOHN KNEW THAT PHOTOGRAPHERS HAD COME TO THE JAIL TO take pictures. One was from the local paper; a young woman with her head shaved and a nose ring. That was already four or five nights ago, John realized. He studied the paper—just to get the date, not understanding anything but the picture of Mary Cyr. No, of course he understood more. After the recent trouble at the mine, this was going to be a real problem.

They had just started to discover the enormity of exactly who she was. And this boded very poorly for her.

Mary Cyr was both wealthy and spoiled; and worse, thought to be English, even with a French name. She had cursed everyone—had laughed at everything—had stolen husbands. Or so they said. That is, the reporters and certain writers who once were her friends. There was a picture of her tossing a gold necklace over Niagara Falls while a young woman looked on in disbelief. (But she could, she said, explain it all. And John had discovered years ago that it was not gold, anyway.)

Stifling in the background, filled with soot and dust and the tapping of tin cups in the hope of rescue that did not come, were the miners who some few weeks before had worked for Amigo Mining and Coal.

John was told this by Perley as he was being driven to the plane a few days before.

"There might be something to that," Perley said, looking at him with a kind of knowing and bewildered, shocked face.

The thing about Perley is that once in his mid-thirties he too had taken up the Oak Island mystery and tried to find the gold. One of his partners told him that the secret of Oak Island could be discovered by reading Shakespeare—so now Perley had read almost everything Shakespeare had written, and could quote whole sections of plays, off the top of his head, but had never discovered the gold. Mary Cyr never went on a trip without coming back carrying something written by Shakespeare or on Shakespeare to give to her troubled cousin.

Now she was in jail, and there was a book coming on her.

"A book?" John said.

"A book," Garnet's lawyer had told him before he left. "A book about Mary Cyr—that someone she knows is going to write for some publisher—perhaps it is already written. Well, you know."

"No," John said. "You tell me."

"Well, it could be about anything, but it might be about Bobby—but there are things on the internet as well. Pictures and things—one or two of her half naked—and you know with something in her hand—people can be cruel."

"I will go down tomorrow," he said. "And try to help if I can."

"Good—look for Perley to drop by and drive you—you of course will be flown by us to Phoenix—and we have another plane waiting—"

"It is easy to talk about us," Perley said, whispering to him as he shook his hand. "So much of what you might hear about her—is like a mirage, it has not really happened. It is like a gigantic fantasy."

"I know," John said, almost hopefully. But then he knew her uncles fired men at their pulp and paper mill for lighting a cigarette at the wrong time of day.

He thought of better things on the flight down.

One where Blair Cyr openly took on Bernard Shaw and his obsequious trip to Stalinist Russia when Cyr was a young reporter.

One when Blair Cyr insisted that Beaverbrook still publish Winston Churchill in the *Evening Standard* in 1938—something that Beaverbrook fired him over, and then rehired him.

No, these things would be forgotten.

He thought about Blair moving with the Canadian troops into the Netherlands and coming under fire and delivering shoes to children; fighting against German and Dutch SS officers. He thought Blair Cyr's heroics would not come into play. His money, his takeover of papers, his lumber assets, his steel assets, his ship-building contracts with the military would.

Blair had made it a point to rescue people from the Netherlands after the war. Mary, when she began to feel like an out-and-out outcast, often claimed that one was Garnet's mother. That is, Mary Cyr was sure she had seen a picture that for the life of her she could no longer find. She had it confused, of course, but what she was remembering was not completely untrue. It simply was not Uncle Garnet or his mother. That, however, did not deter her from saying it was.

But John knew some of it was true. There was a family named Vanderflutin—in the end it is why they owned part of Amigo Mining. The elder Vanderflutin had helped ship art to America early in the war—before the US entered combat. He supposedly did not do it for himself, but after the war he claimed it for himself. For years no one—except little Mary—questioned it.

The elder Vanderflutin always hoped Mary would warm up to him, but she did not.

Then she got a bump on the head, in her grandfather's library one day—and people said it changed her personality. She was never quite the same after. Some said it made her crazy; others said it made her brilliant.

Afterwards Mary maintained she had seen a picture in a book of Dug Vanderflutin in a German uniform, standing beside Kurt Meyer. No one ever believed her. (Because she was a child, and would not have known who Kurt Meyer was at that moment—yet she said his name and was adamant it was both he and Vanderflutin.)

Every time Dug Vanderflutin came to the house with his expansive tales (which is how she thought of him) she hid behind a chair, so that only the top of her head was visible.

Now and then, as he spoke, she would clear her throat, or rustle a *MAD* magazine.

Then she met his son, Ernest, and something made her dislike their family forever.

But—what had happened to her in those intervening years? Those years he had lost sight of her?

He wasn't too sure.

She had gone to Buenos Aires and learned the tango. She had taken a ship to the Falkland Islands and put flowers on the grave of an English soldier. (Her mother's youngest brother, who was killed in 1982.) She had supposedly had an affair with an Argentine poet.

"Of the Che Guevara–Fidel Castro stamp," she wrote him once. "Always devoted to a cause—just like the best of us should be."

Then she came back to Canada, and tried to fit in. But with whom, John no longer knew.

5.

SHE LEFT JOHN'S PROTECTION SOME YEARS AGO, AND HAD MET many Toronto activists. Could one of them be writing against her? Perhaps all of them. Her gay friends she did not like anymore, her former allies in Greenpeace she refused to give money to. It could be anyone. She was now called among other things "anti-gay."

"I'm supposed to like gay men," Mary wrote. "But I find a lot of them too fruity—and don't talk to me about being self-righteous; they have that up the ying-yang."

That is, in this world there were things one was required to like, or at least to accept. Mary Cyr did not seem able to do that as well as most. Nor did she seem to care. But John now knew she was only turned to anger when someone attacked her or her loved ones first. And her statement about gays came he found out because someone in that community had used her kindness once too often.

"People mistake activism for morality," she wrote to him some years before. "And are disgusted by morality that shows activism for what it really is."

She once wrote him that she knew many of the male Canadian writers. Two had dedicated books to her. She had even asked John to allow himself to be interviewd by one of them.

"A Nova Scotia genius, a Percy rock of a man who bagpipes his way along the crags of Cape Breton."

Not too long afterwards she had argued with that certain genius. Not too long afterwards she had hidden his bagpipes, and not long afterwards she threw a bottle and cut him on the cheek. She was fined and made to go to anger management classes. She would phone John about the course and how well she was controlling her anger.

Yes, some writers were great, grand people she wrote, from one end of the country to the other. Her favourite was Jack Hodgins. But some she told him, were unconsciously shallow. That is, she said, there is no one so transparent as certain Canadian writers who want to prove themselves by protecting the rights of women. Those were the writers, unfortunately, who had befriended her for a few years in Toronto.

You could smell them a mile away. "They are," she wrote to John, "MPPFs."

Then she put in brackets: *mincing, preening, pandering fucks.*

Trouble was, she never seemed to recognize them at the time. She had always wanted to be an artist and to be accepted. After her falling-outs, she sounded vindictive—perhaps jealous. But in a certain sense, John realized, she was right. So often these people had used her to benefit from her grandfather's publishing house, and to get nominated for the literary prize given annually by her family. Many of them guessed she had something to do with both. And many times she never caught on.

So what she said always had a reason behind it that was more complex and far less self-serving than her outbursts suggested.

Mary's antics and her statements began to appear in papers here and there. Once she was considered an enemy, women disparaged her and men made up stories about her sex life—or her lack thereof—and the trap of fame began to close about her. A boyfriend was furious he had not won her grandfather's literary award and told her so:

"I hung around here for months—months—for what?" he said. Looking at him with a bemused smile she realized he hadn't caught on to the rapaciousness of his words.

So she had simply telephoned John one night and left a message on his phone that said:

"I've caught on."

Then in final defiance she turned away from professors and established literary men, and women, and what was surely fashion-conscious sycophants more than a few after her for her money, and came to Mexico—but why? What was the reason?

John dropped the bottle into the trash can at the end of the bed. And took out his puffer and inhaled. He looked over a list of her Canadian and American friends. (That is, some were very influential and he had jotted some names down.) Of course he hated them all—why shouldn't he? They had more than hated him. Where were they now when she needed them?

Well, wherever they were, they were not in Mexico campaigning for her freedom. Some were writing about her family being industrial monsters.

He tried to catch his breath as he looked over his notes. He looked too over the doctor's prescription.

It was reported in two papers she was American. Her British mother had lived in Roanoke, Virginia. John was not at all cynical, but if a movie was made, they would need her to be American. Hell, the Americans could do anything. They could revise anything.

And that was a danger too.

Anyway, Mary had always considered herself Canadian. Up until two weeks ago, who she was or was not, American, Canadian, British or Australian, would have never mattered. Two hours after a young boy was found dead in her hotel room she was brought to the small police station at the top of the hill, handcuffed and leg-shackled (Why? John had asked the constable seven times already, but both knew why—it was the novelty—or *júbilo*), surrounded by arid sand and weeds, followed by a dozen curious people, some tiny women, Mexican Maya and a few local officials, very stern and important, one policeman eating his lunch, a *bocadillo de lomo*, who turned to wait for the photographer to take pictures. This seemed to be the main point—that is, the heat, the dust and the pictures, with her trying to manoeuvre in leg shackles, looking back over her shoulder. It was that picture alone that convinced John she was innocent.

Then they took her into a room, searched her, kept her without charges, and at some point were about to let her go. But then over the hours things changed. They looked terribly disappointed in her. They had found out she was Mary Cyr, whose family owned Tarsco Mining.

At night in their beautiful seventeenth-century village, vampire bats, with their flat pig noses, skirted the air, looking for blood.

Already two or three local women couldn't help but go to the cell window.

"Hey, lady—you want to be my *amiga?*" one laughed. This was Lucretia Margarita Rapone, who was reputed to be scandalous. (At least, the porter told John this with a smile that seemed to suggest Mary Cyr was now in for it.)

"Could you please stop being idiots?" Mary asked, clutching a cigarette in her bruised hands. "I have done nothing—except, well—you see, if you think about it long and hard, I came here to save you from yourself. Other than that I have done *nada de nada—¡no mia melesto!*"

Nothing at all—don't bother me.

The most spectacular picture of her was in the back of a black Mexican police car with a yellow stripe along the roof, taken at night by that young woman with the nose ring, showing only one part of Mary's face illuminated in a tragic glance over her shoulder. That was the picture that made it look as if she was fleeing.

"*Dama Mary Cyr,*" it proclaimed. "*Trabaca de murte.*"

The picture would be published in the next day or two all across North America.

The rumour said there were other cases.

"*Trabaca de murte.*"

Dama Mary Cyr worked a murder. The picture had been asked for in Mexico City, Montreal and New York.

"Why New York?" Mary said, trying her best to remain light-hearted. "I've done nothing there except shop—"

It took Mexico to catch her; for they were brave enough to stop this behaviour.

Tomó México para atraparla.

That is what people in the town of Oathoa were now so proud about. Especially people like Lucretia Rapone, who lived with her older sister, Principia Gloton, and Principia's two children, Ángel and Gabriella, both of whom had lost a friend when Victor died—and both of whom went every day to search for the smaller boy, Florin. Ángel was not just angry he was sickened by all of this. He walked about as if he was in a daze—

The women who looked at her from the cell window—taking turns standing on a garbage can—said:

"All of us know what it is like to bleed and suffer, and you do not—but you will."

6.

MARY MANAGED TO TELL JOHN THAT IT WAS AN ACCIDENTAL meeting with that boy Victor two short weeks before. She had turned to go to a restaurant and lost an earring among the cobblestones. She bent to look for it just after dark. And there was Victor, a cute little slavishly nice boy who helped her find it.

"Well, maybe *slavish* is the wrong word to use," John cautioned.

"Yes, perhaps."

He was with a group of other boys.

"What other boys?"

"Oh, those kids, young boys and girls, who were selling lotto tickets—they come every couple of days. Sometimes he liked to sell tapes of birds."

She said Victor came the next day and asked if he could run any errand, or be her guide for two dollars a day. (She gave him twenty dollars and bought him dinner at Restaurante Polo.) Yes, he looked at the twenty dollars as if he had just won some gold.

He took her to a ruined burial ground, and an old village made out of falling stones. They hacked through the trees and saw howler monkeys.

He told her about Jaguars and she told him she drove one. There was a moment when she was overcome by his determination to be the best guide she had—and he was earnest and purposeful, arriving always at nine in the morning in a faded white shirt and grey trousers—and trying his best, she noticed, to hide his desperation—his poverty. His wrists were almost black with dirt. Or no—in a way, he didn't know he had to hide it. Then she discovered something else: he did not arrive at nine—he arrived as early as seven, and waited outside the foyer of the resort, pacing back and forth. Then, after the mine disaster, something happened. He was more uncertain. He told her he would give her a tape, but he never did. She was, she said, ready to go home, when they found him in her spare bedroom. He was dead.

John asked her if she noticed anything else.

"He wanted to hide—he was hiding—from someone—he wanted to give me a tape—but he said he would give it to me only when I was leaving. I thought it was twittering birds, because he had a lot of tapes of them. Twice he went to get it—and then came back and said he didn't want to give it to me yet."

"Why?"

"I don't know—but I should have left sooner."

"He had to trust you before he gave it over—and he had to make sure you could get away with taking it—he was probably worried about you as much as anything."

"Other boys came searching for him—two or three times."

"I see," he said. "He asked to sleep in your spare room—or did he?"

"No—I was too stupid to ask him to—I certainly didn't think he was there that night—I asked him three times what he was nervous about— why he was scared—but he didn't tell me. I am sure he would have given me that tape if he had a chance. But he was scared of me—it was as if he wanted to be certain he could trust me—because he did not really trust anyone."

"So there were two beds—or two bedrooms."

"Bedrooms?" she said.

"Yes—and where did he stay if he was not staying with you?"

She shrugged.

"Somewhere near the Calle de Republic—but you see where is his tiny brother, Florin. I am worried about him."

"Well, I will find that out."

"Okay—find out why it happened—please."

7.

IT WAS ONCE SAID ON CBC RADIO BY A PROFESSOR FROM OTTAWA that she had met the poor, but she had never really known them. But that was not true about her—John believed it was what was said about her by the middle class, who pretended to know everything—in fact she had met the poor everywhere and was more knowledgeable about them than were a host of devoted middle-class activists that he himself had met over the years.

But once she had met activists and doers, she was encouraged to think of the poor as "something else." That is, not as poor but as *underprivileged*. Oh, there was a vast difference in those words. One said what was: the poor were poor. One said they were not like you and me.

Before, when she was spoiled, she had been far too clever to have causes. "I shouldn't have come on this trip," she told him. "But I had to prove something to myself—finally."

"Well, that is for another day," John said. "My main concern is to keep you safe, and to get you the hell home."

"No one wants me home," she said.

"That is not true at all—Garnet and Perley both do—very much."

"Back to a snowstorm," she said, "blizzard-like conditions—white-outs on the bay—eating a plate of smelts—that would be fine!"

John had been her unofficial protector since her father had died when she was twelve, and he slept in a trailer on their back lot for weeks during the summer when she was home. Always taking his vacation to coincide with her arrival. In that way he watched as she grew up. He loved her—but he knew she had opportunity with a hundred other far more important men. (One was almost a goddamn prince.) She knew movie stars and premiers, prime ministers and famous hockey players, could make them fall for her with a glance of those beautiful brown eyes, and he had succumbed too—and he was no different. Well, after she was herself twenty-five.

"Yes, I am old enough to be her father—so what?" he would say to himself as he drove the highways at night. But to him it would have been a betrayal of the family to act upon it.

The pill made him tired. He went back to his room. He felt the night coming on, and his room little by little darkened so the cheap frescoes and cheaper furniture could not be seen anymore.

The next morning he woke, sweating and dizzy, and rose without remembering exactly where he was. His face was thin and pale. He was not well now. He knew it—but he kept it, like so much else, to himself. Or in most ways, from himself. That is, he had had a heart attack the year before and was on various medications. He was trying to get off booze but as yet hadn't. He had not informed the Cyr family about any of this.

He remembered the sunlight and how it hurt his eyes. He fumbled for his sunglasses, and searched for the pill to help him breathe. He had to do something. He had to go out again, and follow the street past the jail. It was now after two in the afternoon and it got dark early. He supposed Mary wanted to see him too. And he wondered about bail for her—though he was sure her lawyer had already tried.

John had already solved some of it.

Victor must have known something or seen something about the mine—he must have come to her with a tape of someone saying something, perhaps—and was worried. Why? Because he hid Florin. Why was it older people or an older person he worried about? Because he did not go to the police, so it had to be someone with some power. And why did he want to tell Mary Cyr?

Because his father worked at the mine? Because she was an American (he would think) who could help him?

And why did he not tell her sooner? Simple. Because he had something to give her and was continually being watched, and he did not want to put her in danger. His little life was heroic.

At first John had speculated that the reason the boy was killed was that he sold lotto tickets and there was a fight over this—that is what the old porter told him Victor did. But now he felt the boy had been beaten and left near the villa, not to have the death blamed on Ms. Cyr but to have it blamed on the boys he was in competition with. (That is, a fight among boys, which John had first suspected himself.)

But Victor had managed to make it back to her place, and what followed was the result.

This is what John already knew.

He went to the restaurant and had cereal and *café con leche*. He went to the reception desk and asked for a map.

Mary said that Victor lived somewhere near the Calle de Republic. So that is where he would go. But she got the name wrong—slightly; it was called the Calle Republica.

Mary had told him that Victor's mother died and his father was killed in the mine explosion. She said she asked him three times about the tape he wanted to give her, and he said one night, "*No más me molestes,*" and looked about as if frightened, so she nodded and did not ask him again.

"Ah," John said.

"Ah what?" Mary said. "Ah yes or ah no—I think it is an ah yes."

John shrugged and for the moment said nothing else. That is, John did not think he was waiting for Mary Cyr specifically—but she was one of a dozen tourists he might have approached. John was also sure he would have given the tape to her if he had not been worried about his four-year-old brother, Florin.

So in a way it was accidental that this had happened.

But John knew already that this would only be if you discounted the input of Mary Cyr herself—the idea that she met the boy accidentally, and did not have some other plan. In his entire life John had never seen her without another plan—a secondary road on which she travelled parallel to the road bystanders believed she was on. So she might very well have sought Victor out by the dropping of an earring onto the cobblestones. She might have badgered him to give her information about the mine disaster, told him who she was (or he found out from others that she was the coal lady), and he just might have worried that he could not trust her. When he realized he could, it was too late.

The more John thought of this, the more he came to this conclusion. So he tried to decide if any other scenario worked. No, not really.

8.

HE FOLDED THE MAP OF OATHOA AND PUT IT IN HIS POCKET. IN the late afternoon he found his way over to the back part of town with small haciendas and *apartamentos*—old stuccoed apartment buildings of three or four storeys, with their windows opened blankly, and grapelike clustered dark wires leading to and from them in the warm late-afternoon air that smelled suddenly of smoke and rain.

He walked his way behind seven streets filled with skinny angry dogs and blind dark windows with small cafés, along back cobblestone streets to the out-of-the-way Calle Republica, where that same sewer that ran by the jail ran too. It was desolate, this street; the buildings were small and haphazardly constructed, with corrugated roofs and fences and on a few roofs large, old satellite dishes.

It was now 85 degrees. Looking back, he could see the jail in the distance. He watched as some people loitered outside the woman's cell window. John counted five, and more gathering. They gathered there because they were women, and she was a woman who had done a terrible thing, using her womanhood to do so. Often we need people to fall beyond us, in order to refrain from grasping the hand they hold out in order to be saved.

Last evening he had gone into the church to say a prayer. (In fact, he did that often wherever he was.) The church had pictures of the thirteen men from Oathoa who had died in the mine disaster, along the left wall near the fount of holy water. He looked at all the names—there, second from the end, was one Pedro Sonora. A small man with tousled black hair, a weathered face and a grin.

LA MINA HA MATADO A ESTOS HOMBRES, a plaque stated.

The mine has killed these men.

And the priest, who was deeply embedded in the political ramifications of the mine disaster, knew who Mary Cyr was. And though he should have told these women not to go there, he gave them Communion each morning and watched as they traipsed down the street to the jail being led there by Lucretia Margarita Rapone, who, the old porter told John with a slight grin, was *"una bromista."*

And John did not know what that meant, but standing off to the side was a German fellow in a wide white hat, with a bandana around his thick neck and a very expensive watch on his right wrist.

"He says she is a—prankster—charlatan—something like that."

John thanked him.

Something like that.

And then he left to find out what he could.

The farther John got along the desolate road, the less the village looked like anywhere a tourist would ever want to be. The road became narrower and overgrown with weed, and intermittent rocky yards and fields spread out. A small white burro passed him, with a sore on its back. Far away, across a number of small fields, he could see the hills where the Amigo mine had been sunk. He kept walking, looking up at the giant head frame, desolate and peering out like the ghost of some terrible sick giant.

Now and again an SUV raced by, first slowing down, then speeding up after it passed him. The dust was white and came drifting up on his legs, and caused him a kind of spasm, suddenly. But he stopped walking, and waiting until he regained his strength, continued. He took a shot of nitro—just a short one.

A corrugated tin door shut closed. He passed a garage where he noticed some boys, and the man in the white suit jacket he had seen yesterday—the man with the motor, who was now working on a car engine, looked back at John curiously. The SUV pulled into that garage and a man got out. He looked at the man—knew him emphatically as a gangster.

Inspector de operaciones mineras was written large on the back window.

The inspector of mines.

This man, he would come to know as Hulk Hernández. He would begin to see him at various places almost every day. And Mr. Hernández would make sure John saw him.

The idea—or the worry—the corroborating specialist had in Halifax was that if John was working on a case too strenuous, he would have another heart attack, a big one. But he had no idea he would be working on this case four nights ago.

He came to a road—left led back around to the main square and centre of town, and right led to the lower, even dimmer and more cluttered, part of Calle Republica. There was a sign in Spanish, a bronze plaque with a man on horseback. Two legs of the horse were raised, so the soldier had been wounded. A soldier who had fought for the city 180 years before.

He went right.

Here he saw many dark little cubby doors into small white houses with black kitchens burned into the cliffs, the smell of kerosene. Behind all of this was the panorama of the sixteen-acre municipal dump, where bright pieces of cloth moved under the glare, and a man in a tractor pushed garbage ahead of him. John realized these were people scavenging, and he became aware of what the old porter had tried to tell him:

that Victor had likely lived in a shelter constructed in the dump itself. Vultures circled high above—still, the night was quiet and it was growing later. From this part of the road he could look down in the other direction and see the enormous villas, and vistas of the rich.

John walked back over the mounds of dirt to the road. Then he walked back along the streets he had come until he came to a familiar-looking fountain. Across the street there was a sign for a bar. Two of the young men who had been at the garage had followed him at a distance of about fifty yards, smiles on their faces, as if they were sharing a joke about his gringo stupidity.

He walked over and stood at the bus stop. A bus would take him back to Los Marinas.

The Sea of Cortez shone in the distance. Glimmered. The doctor told him his years of struggle and intensity had allowed his body to now turn against him, to cause it to fight against itself. This is what caused the illness. The doctor had even predicted another heart attack unless he retired.

And in a way if he did not watch it, it might cause something as bad.

"And what is it called?"

"Autoimmune."

"I have heard of it."

"I think you might have the beginning of it. Stress will kill you."

"Thanks for the information. But don't tell that to anyone else."

"Why?"

"Because I have to work."

The bus manoeuvred its way back over the streets in the evening. Lights were coming on; the motor scooters sounded lonelier as the day wound down.

Where he was staying was a sad affair—a derelict resort with one of the two pools closed. Of all the resorts, why had she picked this one?

Of all the towns too, he thought. This was, it seemed, the end of the line for her, in one way or the other.

So why?

To disappear, of course, and to pretend that she was useful, for so many had called her "useless." She was going to prove herself to the Toronto crowd, or to her family; start an orphanage and "get on *The Oprah Winfrey Show.*" This is what she told people.

But now—well, it might be true, that she would be mentioned on that show—but not for the reasons she supposed.

Or did she suppose—perhaps there was another game she was playing; perhaps she knew exactly why she was here.

Her family had tried to protect her. But maybe in doing so they were protecting themselves. They had sent her to a physiatrist when she was fifteen, and put her on medication.

She got off medication, and began by seventeen a regimen of something else: gin and tonic. She was a pianist and had a good grasp of the art—so she told John. She held a Stradivarius in her hand, but did not play the violin, and had met those who did hold one in their hand and did play. But then it started—after so many years; her dislike of being followed, and being watched. So she kept sliding away from him.

"I have changed," she said the last time she saw him, almost four years ago, inviting a dispute, "And you have not."

She was in with the Toronto crowd; one who was teaching a course called "Diversity Awareness, Societal Change and Sensitivity Training for White Males." Ah yes—white males needed most to be sensitive. In many white intellectual minds, the only white males allowed in the coalition of the dispossessed were of course themselves.

"No—I have not changed," he said. She could be filled with a kind of naive intellectual disappointment, and she showed it. She had taken a trip to Africa—or as she said, in a scathing tone, "Almost two trips to Africa—almost two of them—well, I could see Africa from where I was the second time—and I have seen things over there. Little black boys and girls—have you ever seen them?—perhaps not."

(That he had seen them and had seen them massacred in Rwanda, and had nightmares over it, is something he did not mention. Still, there was a moment when a smart person—and John was very smart—understood that she knew and wanted you to catch on that she was being affecting.)

She was always triumphantly imperial over the smallest things—like the first time she helped hay a field in back of her grand cottage. She telephoned the editor of one of her grandfather's papers and said:

"Just to inform you—I too have hayed a field."

And lo and behold it made the front page of the paper. Her grandfather was furious that it had; but the poor editor thought he was supposed to acknowledge the event because she had phoned him. What then was he supposed to do?

They found her in a smelt shed out on the bay when she was sixteen, smelts freezing on the ice about her, and the elderly Micmac Amos Paul helping her learn.

"I have learned," she said, "how to smelt fish—name ten women who can do the same."

Now she teetered on the brink of despair, the crust of earth under her feet giving away to where small troubled lanterns shone in the depths below.

The Mexican was just a boy. She was now almost forty-five. If he could get her out of here—and convince her family that she had "retained" herself, she would inherit seventy-eight to eighty million in six months.

"That's a lot of dill pickles, Mr. Man," she once said to him about her money. "If you marry me, I will give you some."

The idea among the population of Oathoa now becoming clear to him was the depraved motivation of a kind of older, wildly sexual predator with hordes of money, coming down to Mexico to look for pleasure—with a young boy.

"This is what you get for not marrying me," she said to him today, and then smiled as if it was a joke. So, on the blogs that now followed her endlessly, the rumours abounded, and it was now murder. The act was, in the blogs, more and more sordid as more time passed. Though John never read them—and in fact reading anything about her in the past twenty years gave him a shock and pain, a prolonged sense of waste. But now the line "This is what you get for not marrying me" made him realize why. If he had married her—in spite of all objections, his own included—perhaps she would never have found herself in a Mexican jail.

9.

"YES, MURDER—OF A YOUNG BOY."

So said Constable Fey, who had a grim, determined look when he spoke. And he spoke with a certain moral conditioning that he exhibited toward Americans (and by proxy Canadians), which was reflected in his impeccable demeanour.

Fey's national pride allowed his mistrust of her, and there was a very delicate encouragement for John as a common man and a fellow policeman to understand why. But John refused to succumb to this psychology, even though it might have brought him closer to the constable.

"I cannot see her killing anyone," John said, "ever."

John knew that in Mexico it might have been a dislike based on how she dressed and carried herself. Because Fey must have seen in tourists this same duplicity of warmth and superiority—and Fey was protecting national honour against the conceit of so many from the north.

The secret was: A case of rape of a Spanish tourist had been reported in this town just two years before—and it cast a dark shadow against the lawns and buildings about the old square, the gated resorts, the mist across the golf courses, and meandered into the conscience of citizens who were told by the foreign press that they were unkempt and brutal. So this now was their turn. That is, John sensed in every fibre of his sick body the hidden—deeply hidden—delight that this now was their turn. It was now their turn to be morally outraged; and they would be. Not to be would be unthinkable for them. This is what he had already seen in Lucretia Rapone.

And in fact this is what Fey now confirmed:

"Why did she come here?" Fey asked. "She is . . ." Here he hesitated and looked at some papers and held them up, to make the papers launch his remark. "She is a very—well, sexual woman, people say."

"That is what they say. But I think there is a more innocent explanation, maybe?" was all John said.

The constable paused a moment, and then answered.

"No—she killed him. They overheard the argument."

"Only one?" John said.

Fey countered with:

"He said to her one night, '*No más me molestes.*'" That is what they do, these fading American beauties—come here looking for boys—you must know that. That's their new liberation—"

"Well, some of them, perhaps," John said. "A few, maybe—but not Mary Cyr. And I know why he said that—"

"Oh, you know why he said that?"

"Yes—it was because she was asking about his father."

"But I don't believe that," Fey said. And his refusal to believe was impeccable, and therefore unshakable.

So John shrugged and said nothing.

It was already too hot, and his head ached; his eyes too were sore. So was his throat.

Three days before, he was sitting in a motel room where he had lived after leaving his wife, Jeannie. He had loaded his revolver. What if he had not picked up the phone as he did? In fact over the past year he often had the phone cut off for lack of payment, but he had it reconnected last week, so in a way these things were out of his hands.

Little Mary Cyr was once again sadly enough in them.

That picture of her in the car that said POLICÍA could be spotted here and there on the third page in certain papers of the world. Most of the world did not know her. Yet. The policemen here were so sure of her guilt they had a dismissive but paternal attitude toward him. They were so sure of her guilt they did not mind him asking questions, for they felt (or Fey did) that a Canadian connection in the investigation did add some weight and fair play.

"The coal miner's daughter," they joked. This had gone from lip to ear to lip throughout the poorer district of Oathoa, where many of the miners' families lived. Everyone wanted to line up to see her.

"*Ponemos en mejoras de carácter grave, pero no nos dieron dinero para poner más.*"

That was the statement from Carlos DeRolfo. John asked at the desk for someone to please translate it for him. It said something like this:

We put in major upgrades, but they wouldn't give us money to do any more—

He went on to say this is why the bump happened.

When they asked him if those upgrades were actually done, he said solemnly:

"*Sí, en la tumba de mi madre.*"

Yes, on my mother's grave.

Besides, he said, you could see them as soon as you entered the mine.

"Then why did you continue to mine if you wanted and needed a better infrastructure?"

"*Habíamos planeado para este mes.*"

We had planned to stop this month.

So with all of this, and Mary Cyr in a cell, they knew they had a very big fish.

"Tell them I am just a little fish—almost no fish at all. Much like a guppy—only a small guppy at that."

That is why people were now gathering about the cell. It is why other tourists were sitting in the cafés gossiping. It is why the archaeological expedition was interviewed about a cave Mary had visited. (Did she plan to take the body of Victor there?) And all the statements gathered were put into a giant folder tied with blue ribbon and kept in secret, even though everyone knew what was in it. And Constable Fey had this blue-ribboned folder and looked at it with a great deal of concern. As if his expression was not suitable to match his anguish over what she had done. (This folder would be transferred to the prosecutor's office within the next few days. The well-known, *importante* Isabella Tallagonga.)

10.

SHARON DEROLFO HAD ALREADY SNAPPED NINE PICTURES OF Mary in the cell, and was trying to sell them abroad. A few weeks ago Sharon DeRolfo had thought of moving to Mexico City with her girl-friend—now it was the most fortuitous thing that she was here. DeRolfo dressed as if she was of the people and poor. But that was not really the case, and even a casual observer would notice the bling of a watch and ring, and a diamond nose stud that glittered when she spoke.

And John had already noticed that when looking at a picture—and he had too noticed her last name was the same as Carlos DeRolfo's, part owner of Amigo. So, John thought, she went to fine arts school—became a photographer, is rebelling against convention but in a safe, tolerant way. No, there was nothing at all wrong with that, he decided.

But that he knew this already would have somewhat amazed Fey.

In Mexico, Fey gravely reminded John Delano, one was assumed guilty until proven innocent. You could not look upon her as innocent once the cell door was closed. Up until that time she might be presumed innocent—but you see—once the door closed—well—the door closed.

Poison over a number of days, Fey said, raising his eyebrows slightly, as if nothing was more insane or grave. He did not have to add, he simply took it for granted that both knew; women were noted poisoners. The young boy, he whispered, was found without his shoes and socks.

John asked if he could speak to someone else—the captain here.

He could not. John asked where would she ever get this poison or even want to? Why would a woman who was in a campaign with Princess Diana to stop land mines suddenly go for the gruesome poison? However, John himself could be cynical enough to know that that was more than possible.

Fey shrugged as if it wasn't up to him where she got it. Fey became more and more certain of her guilt the more he discovered how infamous she was. Her son had died when he was seven years old.

The Brits had given her the title "Lady" because of her grandfather's money? So how well would that sit with her many debunkers now? And besides, she went to lay flowers on her British uncle's grave after the Falklands War. (That too was in the papers filed on her.) That did not sit well with Fey.

Fey made it clear—as he read over her file, sitting behind the large desk—if the situation warranted, and she became too much of a nuisance here, she would be transferred to the women's federal prison near Mexico City. This of course was not up to him at all. It was up to the federal police. But it did display—even though he tried not to show it—how a conviction was a necessity. And this is what John knew in his gut.

The women who crept up to the cell window at night told her she was going to go to the Prisión del Rayo—and never be seen again. They would kill her in that prison, just to make a name for themselves. One was Lucretia Margarita Rapone. The other was her sister, Principia. John had asked the porter their names, because both their pictures were in the paper. Principia looked the most distraught—but John was unsure of their connection to the boy.

Lucretia was much more sensational. She carried a picture of Victor around her neck. She continually went to the cell to look in, in a kind of nosy, boorish way, as if it was not only her right but also her obligation. Lucretia had been in this excited state for a while now.

It was amazing how many friends Victor had now—one was in fact the local prosecutor who had been briefed on Mary Cyr. Ms. Isabella Tallagonga. She had already met with Lucretia; Lucretia who asked her questions in an inquisitive, combative manner—hoping for restitution for the family. But there was no family left unless she herself claimed that status. Then there might be some money.

"*Ah—sí—mi familia,*" Lucretia said.

That is, she said Victor was her family. Yet everyone knew Lucretia was childless and Victor's mother was dead.

All were now caught up in this brilliant farce. That played out in a brilliant way on televised programs across the state.

No one five days ago knew who Lucretia Rapone was.

No one five days ago knew the gravity of the situation.

Now:

"Murder," Uncle Garnet said. His voice was weak; he was not in good health. "How in God's name can that be? I mean murder—you know as well as I she's a pumpkin head, an empty- headed girl—how can that be?"

"I don't know," John answered, "We will have to wait to find out."

Garnet too was ill, and at the last of his life was seeing how wealth and power meant nothing when it came to scandal, and how in fact scandal was enhanced by wealth and power. They could not have trouble now, with the oil pipeline ready to move through from Quebec. Greg, her cousin from the far side of the family, needed Garnet and his son, and Garnet and his son couldn't have anything untoward happen. The pipeline was a touchy subject with the Micmac and Maliseet, the Cree and the Algonquin. And now Mary might have thrown a wrench into it all.

Empty-headed girl.

"She is innocent of all charges," John said.

John of course knew much about this empty-headed girl. He had loved her most of his life, like a father she never had and the daughter who had escaped him. Or if he was truthful—a lover he never managed to have. She had asked him to marry her when she was eighteen and went over the embankment in her car:

"Marry me and we will be happier than anyone else in the world, forever—if not, both of us will be miserable and never find love."

Of course he said no. And when she closed her eyes and pouted her lips to kiss him, he simply kissed her cheek and put her in the patrol car.

"I will never forgive you for saying no," she said, "never, never, never, never!" And perhaps she hadn't. No, she hadn't, and perhaps he was somehow in hindsight at fault.

It was prophetic. For both of them had in fact been miserable most of their lives.

So now he knew these things:

She had been accused of murder.

She did not commit this murder.

She was said to be a sexual predator.

That too was bogus.

The state things were in these charges would be almost impossible to disprove.

He had supper about eight that evening. There was a singing trio in the bar he went to, and he drank four tequilas.

Later on, he followed the road toward the hill, and made way, past the jail, beyond the donkey, to the old mine shaft in the dark.

When he came to the yard, piles and piles of coal lay about him, railcars sat orange or rust-coloured and all of them silent, tarps sat still. The three-storey cement office was padlocked. Someone had planted a cross on the hill beyond the shaft.

He knew he was being watched—he felt it.

11.

PEDRO WAS THE ONE BANGING THE TIN CUP. HE BANGED IT against the tin plate. His fingers were bleeding. It was the plate they placed their coins in, in front of the statue of Our Lady when going down into the tunnel. Now he banged his tin cup, which had been attached to his belt against the side of this plate. His blood fell on the little statue, and ran down her face.

Of course Pedro had written letters that were never answered. And he had shown Victor these letters, about the conditions of the mine and the lie that was in the papers that they had done millions in upgrades. They had wanted rid of Pedro.

Now the others kept telling him to stop banging, there was no use. But Pedro was in something of a trance and could not stop. He even began to sing.

The mine was open seven months when Pedro Sonora left his donkey in the hovel by the jail and went to help his friend fix his outboard motor. His friend worked as a mechanic at the local garage, and told Pedro that he could work there too if he wanted.

As Pedro was helping take the housing off the engine, his friend's wife said they were hiring men at the mine. She brought her husband's coat to him, with the button she had just sewn on with black thread.

So after Pedro fed his donkey a big juicy carrot he walked up the hill toward the mine office. His friend started to, but then got to the top of the hill and for whatever reason turned back.

"I don't like those people, the DeRolfos," he said. "Besides, I have a job."

So Pedro went on alone.

And that is how Pedro became a miner, in a cumbersome hat and a pair of big yellow-and-black rubber pants, walking around 300 metres beneath the ground—right into the deepest part of the hill.

That day, as he banged his tin cup against the Virgin's plate, he could hear men shouting far away. Those near him spoke of other disasters, where people sent a pipe down and water and food—and then a two-way radio.

But up on the surface things were very different.

Knowing they had done nothing to implement safety measures, Carlos and his wife were panicked. If they tunnelled down, the safety regulators out of Mexico City would certainly find out. There would be dead bodies and a structure that had not been secured in thirty years. The money they had stolen would somehow become known. Besides, Pedro, who they detested for complaining about conditions, was one of those trapped miners.

So he and his wife—pretty but a little obese—devised a plan. And they believed it too. They talked themselves into it, fidgeting and muttering and eating croissants. Pondering too, and eating steak and eggs.

And then they came up with an idea.

"They are dead," Señor DeRolfo said. He wanted to close the mine, cover it all over twenty-one hours after the bump, because they had been digging up to 175 tonnes of coal a day—much more than they should have—for the profit. And they had lied to Tarsco about this. They had done upgrades to the front of the mine.

Not a timber or a light had been replaced deeper down. But it wasn't his idea to call off the search. No, Mr. DeRolfo got a call.

"Close the mine off—they are dead—that's all there is to it. We don't want investigators poking around down there." The man who called them was Hernández. A nice-enough man, sweet and gentle for the most part; but a killer, of men, women and children.

No queremos husmear por ahi.

Instructions like this are always said with a certain amount of clever principle.

Two days after the bump DeRolfo truly felt the men were dead anyway. He had talked himself into it. No one could have survived such an explosion.

His wife stood beside him wringing her hands, a silver cross on her neck and big diamond on her fat left hand, and looked suspiciously at the cameras.

"They are all gone," she said to the priest. "They must be—so pray for them, Father!"

Pedro was banging his tin cup for another six days.

The owner spoke to his daughter about his nightmares, and his loss of appetite.

But the wife was not satisfied. She did not feel safe at all—not with a boy who said he had a tape recording from his new tape recorder with sounds from below.

"Send that boy of yours, Ángel, to search for him," she said. The idea of federal prison was terrifying.

But Ángel said he could not find him.

She and her husband drove around in their two Mercedes, and found the child and his little brother. Victor made a mistake—he did not think that anyone would harm him if a woman was with him.

"We have come to get the tape," Gidgit said, with surprising assurance, "and take it to the police."

He edged toward her as she smiled at him, the car idling almost silently, and as he moved toward her, Carlos came up behind him.

It was Carlos who killed Victor, by crushing his windpipe, but it was Gidgit who much later in the evening, not knowing what to do, finally in a fit of exasperation stabbed the little child. They put Florin in the dump—wrapped him in two garbage bags, and said a prayer. That he would not be found.

With Victor it was different. They threw him from the car, thinking he was dead and thinking he would be found in the morning on the road. But he managed to crawl away. And managed to get into that woman's villa and into the spare bedroom, where he died.

Now Victor was dead, and who would feed his donkey? Maybe Gabriella. Ángel Gloton, the young junior lightweight with the incredibly heavy punch, couldn't—he was too busy, he thought, working for Mr. DeRolfo, trying to solve the murder of Victor and trying to find little Florin.

12.

VICTOR WAS IN THE MORGUE. BUT JOHN WAS NOT ALLOWED TO see the boy's body. He was allowed to see the doctor if he went and requested it.

She was there when he entered. Her dark hair was long and clasped with a brown plastic hair broach behind her, and her face was exquisitely dark. She wore a small golden crucifix on a chain around her neck. She waited with her hands behind her back and said nothing to him. She was short and her white coat came down to her ankles. She was wearing sneakers. When he glanced at her, she maintained a professional inexpressiveness, yet her eyes caught his once and were slightly mirthful. Then she handed him the autopsy results.

The preliminary test said arsenic, she told him.

"Was there anything else—any sign of a struggle?" he said.

"It was poison," she said, more certain than defensive. And then, "Mexico has always been blamed, but not this time."

"No one is meaning to blame Mexico—"

"Ahhh," she said.

He had to wait two hours, and then went to see Mary.

"It is unfortunate, but I wasn't allowed to see the body—they are not going to let me trudge through their investigation, and I did not think they would. Would we allow the Mexican police to do it at home?"

But then she wondered about something:

"I think someone set me up," she whispered.

"Of course," he said.

"Who?"

"Well, start with who filled out the autopsy report," John said.

Already John understood that the reason they had taken Mary into custody—that is, the argument that was overheard a few nights before the boy's death—had nothing whatsoever to do with the death of the boy if it was from arsenic over weeks. He also knew that saying Victor was poisoned over two weeks was very convenient since she had known him for two weeks.

He knew just by this that she was completely innocent.

When he mentioned this to Constable Fey, Fey simply said:

"Yes, it has to be two weeks—you are right—because that's how long she knew him—so it stands to reason!"

But of course Constable Fey knew Mary was innocent. So, John suspected, did the prosecution. But that did not matter, for now she was in a cell, and therefore she was guilty. Which was a peculiar flaw in the Napoleonic Code.

The one thing he was beginning to suspect was the subtle nature of the dialogue going on between state and federal police forces, and that so far Isabella Tallagonga was winning because murder was a state crime.

John also suspected that it was important for someone in Mexico City to have her on the case. So that meant she was ambitious and certain people were ambitious for her in the country's capital. That also meant, quite naturally, that she had enemies. But his main concern was Mary.

She was too small to have beaten Victor to death, so they had to say it was poison. Even if that was ludicrous. That meant if there were marks on him, someone much larger might have killed him. To say poison was in fact to weaken the charge.

This is what John reasoned. It had to be an adult, and he suspected marks on the body. So he suspected within a few hours that it was probably an adult male who had killed the boy.

13.

SHE, MARY, SAT IN THE CELL IN A SMOCK, SMOKING ONE cigarette after the other. For the first time he realized her knees were knobby.

The thing she told him on this second visit, as if it was a secret:

"There are bats that come in at night. And I am thinking—if they can so easily come it, maybe I can get out—hmm?"

He told her he was contacting a lawyer in Mexico City that her family had acquired, and the lawyer might be here in a day or so. He was a Mexican lawyer of Spanish descent, one of the best. Then he whispered this: The American side of her family had been informed, and had informed the American embassy. That was all to the good. For, he said, Mexicans like Canadians but do not fear them. They do not like Americans, but I tell you this—they fear them.

Mary listened to this and nodded quietly. The worse thing she did say was that when she peed, a male policeman sometimes watched her. So she tried not to have to pee.

"Erappo Pole is his name," she said.

"I see."

"He is no gentleman," she said. She had tried to put a blanket over the bars, but he insisted for her own good she be in plain view.

"Suicide," she sniffed. "There is the idea that I am ready and willing to bludgeon myself, as long as I can find a bludgeon to do it."

"Keep the blanket over you when you have to go," John said, "and run the tap water too."

"Ah, tap water—but where is that?"

What he did love about her, and always knew it, was how restrained she could sometimes be in a crisis involving her own safety.

Suddenly now, out of the blue, she asked John to find Plu. That is, her childhood comforter—her blanket.

"You brought Plu?"

"Of course," she said, wringing her hands and smiling, and then tears welling in her eyes. "It's tucked under the bed—so it looks like part of the bed. But tell them you have to go into my room to find it, because—"

"Because what?"

"Because I have hidden my diary in it—you keep the diary, but I want Plu. I just pray to God they do not find my diary—but maybe they have already!"

"Well, I will look."

She had had Plu (named after Pluto) since she was four years old.

He said he would see to it.

"Yes—I will owe you big-time if you bring me Plu," she said.

So he went out into the sun and bought himself a Corona beer and sat down to relax.

Mary had asked continually where the little child Florin was, and if she could see him. She had asked the guards, but they did not answer.

"Victor had to take care of him, by himself," she'd said almost in a daze. "I gave him—he had on him forty dollars—I gave him two twenties the last two days—was that found?" she said. Then she gulped to keep back tears.

John didn't answer.

Later that afternoon when he spotted the boy he had seen the night before he asked the porter his name.

"Ángel Golon," the old man said. "Why—do you want to talk to him?"

"No—not if I don't have to." John smiled.

"He was Victor's best friend—really—he wouldn't have hurt him—"

"Well, someone did," John said, "and I will tell you one thing."

"What?"

"It wasn't Mary Cyr."

PART TWO

1.

MARY CYR WAS THE FAVOURITE GRANDCHILD OF NEWSPAPER
baron Mr. Blair Cyr himself, amasser of millions—no, billions—of dollars.

The man who had been on the one oil tanker that made it to Malta,
so the Brits and Canadians could fuel their Spitfires in 1940. He walked
the open deck when it was under attack.

Blair Cyr was with the Canadian troops on D-Day, and rode with them
in Holland. In a way he was Hemingway without having to be him.

He was there when the Canadians disarmed the Germans, and the
Dutch celebrated their liberation by piously shaving the heads of
women collaborators they had caught and blamed. He brought Dutch
men and women out to Canada. Just as Lord Beaverbrook had done for
the Dutch queen in 1940. One was a Dutchman named Dug Vanderflutin.
He had a wife and young son, named Ernest. Cyr was very fond of the
older Vanderflutin, because he had been an adventurer in his younger
years. He had been in the Far East as part of the merchant class of
Dutchmen.

Twice Dug had to be bailed out by Cyr because of financial difficulty.
Then he took a trip with a Micmac man to find the treasure at Oak
Island. A scheme that was very in vogue at the time, among dreamers
and schemers. But he came back alone some weeks later—and only
months after he came home did the truth come out: that this Micmac
man was lost in an attempt to dig a parallel shaft to where they believed
the great treasure was. The RCMP questioned Vanderflutin—and
during this questioning and subsequent investigation a little-known fact
emerged. There was, or had been, another Dug Vanderflutin from the

same town in the Netherlands. There was some conflicting information about their identities, which was left unresolved.

All of this happened about the time Mary Cyr herself was born, and Vanderflutin hoped to be her godfather, which Mary discovered in a letter written to her family in early December 1963.

When Vanderflutin died, the Cyrs had to decide what to do with the mine, which they had floated for a long time. Mary was about nine or ten at that time, John thought. Did they want it or not—not really—but then, they decided to buy it all as they said, *lock, stock and barrel*.

The man's son, Ernest, who had studied political science at the university and wrote articles mainly about the dispossessed First Nations, wanted to sell it. Though he lived on a cattle farm out west, he wrote about the dispossessed natives; though he had never been in the woods, he wrote about their prowess. In fact at this time, this was quite fashionable for middle-class boys who had attended university to do.

So he came east to sell the mine.

Then this happened: Mary's own father died in a plane crash at the age of forty-nine, flying to inspect the shafts of the New Brunswick mine to see if they should remain open or be flooded.

After all was said and done, they ended up with the iron ore mine, and incidentally the major part of Amigo, the coal mine Dug Vanderflutin had bought while in Mexico. It was just a small part of their financial empire, and Amigo was almost never thought of. It was shut down and reopened on a variety of occasions, and ownership changed hands. Finally it was owned in part by a former top government official, Carlos DeRolfo, and on two or three occasions Tarsco fed it money to keep it afloat.

But back to Mary.

After her father died, her mother was alone. She travelled. She drank—she was celebrated as a worldly socialite. She died.

For some reason, putting it all together, with the premature deaths of both parents, Mary hated the mine, and decided it was a very good idea to hate the Dutch. And just maybe everyone else. And she did so for a long, long time.

2.

THE FIGHT OVER MARY CYR AND WHAT SHOULD HAPPEN TO HER began when she was about twelve years of age.

Mary became the orphan of the family. She loitered in the great smoky rooms of her grandfather or uncle, sat in chairs in huge offices in downtown Toronto at midday, was left in the huge cottage on the Miramichi. Sometimes by herself. She was forgotten. When she was thirteen, she set out on her own with a picnic lunch to find her mother, and made it all the way to the main highway before she was spotted. She was picked up and taken to the RCMP headquarters, and sat on a hard bench in the midnight humid air, trying to look at the bottom of her big left toe, which was cut. It was the first of many calls that came to John Delano because of her.

"That young rich girl you know—Mary Cyr is here—should we put her in a cell, or take her home? I am not sure?"

"For God sake don't put the child in the cell—I will come and get her, and take her home."

People believed she was daft because she had been hit in the head by a book and had fallen off a ladder in her family's library. But John believed, if no one else did, that she was far closer to brilliant than stupid, and knew every nuance of what they did say concerning her and realized she was a burden to others by the time she was thirteen. Her eyes would brighten when she heard her name, and she would stop running or walking—at times remaining in the curious position of motion without moving, clandestinely waiting just beyond view to hear what was being said. Then she would continue as if she had not heard a thing. What they were trying to decide is what part of the fortune would be hers without ever saying it.

It was not that they did not care for her—they did. Perhaps as much as anyone. She knew that someday come what may she would have much money at her disposal. So she refused to speak to them. She took to disliking Garnet, and saying he had killed her father.

Garnet never answered these assaults. But Mary Cyr believed she had good reason for saying what she did. It had all started, she felt, at a dinner party the night before her father died. Everything that would happen to her that was bad had started then. Certainly something traumatic had happened. The death of her father came the night after.

John discovered that that was the night she decided to side with her English mother rather than the Irish or French sides of her family. That is what it came down to.

In a clumsy way she told John why that had to be, a few years after that night—the summer she was sixteen.

"Why? Well, simply because you do not make fun of my mother," she said. "I hardly remember it—but Daddy was away, and my mother was being made fun of because she was British. She had been before this, but this was a bigger case. A Dutchman came into our house thinking us French and Irish, so he started to insult the English, yet when he made light of my English mother—I became British at that moment to protect her." She shrugged, looked at him, sighed, and her shoulders sank. "And I would do it for anyone I cared for. Even if they were Dutch."

"Who was this man?"

"Ernest Vanderflutin, the lanky, bony, skinny son of the other fatter, flabbier Vanderflutin—the one we bought the mine from."

"Who?"

"The older Vanderflutin—and I found out."

"You found out?"

"When I was seven or eight—I told them I had seen a picture of the older Vanderflutin—no one paid me the least bit of attention—but he— the older Vanderflutin did—he paid attention. You could see he was worried. I saw a picture of him at a Nazi rally."

"You are sure of this, Mary."

She simply looked away.

So John waited a moment—not knowing whether to believe her, and then asked:

"And that's what happened? I mean between you and the family?" He did not know if she was delusional or not, for so many people simply assumed she was.

"Yes. Then my daddy died, then my mommy died last year—and I guess I will have to fight them all!"

John felt that she took solace in the fact that she was alone, and believed she would be alone always, and by this loneliness would sooner or later—she did not know when—come virtue. She did not know how she would live life until this virtue came, or in what way it would show itself—but she felt it as a second layer under her thought—that someday even for one brief moment she would be virtuous, and this came primarily because she was as she was, alone. She was always alone—or nearly always alone—except for that one thing in her upstairs rooms that everyone told her she should never have had.

The idea that she was delusional, or as the girls on the beach often said, "a wack job" because she had fallen and hit her head when in the library that day, infested the thoughts of dozens of people who had to deal with her. But it also made John want and need to protect her.

3.

SOMETIME AFTER HER DAD DIED, AND HER MOTHER HAD travelled alone to Dénia, Spain, Garnet—on the urging of his wife, Nan, who was six years his senior, bolder and more brazen, and hated the wealthy, and therefore took it out on her niece (conveniently forgetting she had married into improbable wealth)—sent Mary to a convent in northern New Brunswick to study with the nuns of Notre Dame. Nan decided that Mary could be drawn to religious orders—and she was prepared to help her do so. It would, Mary thought later, be advantageous for Nan to have the heiress who was worth more than Perley in a convent taking the oath of poverty. (Or this was the reason Mary later believed.) But there was even a more insidious reason. Mary Cyr had proclaimed herself as English to protect her mother; Nan insisted that the Cyr girl be French. She was partly French—Mary never denied it. She simply chose her mother's identity as a choice of loyalty.

Mary at first seemed ambivalent about going. Her father had died and her mother, never comfortable in the family, had gone, believing at least for a time that Mary would be better off with her father's family. When she changed her mind, she was too drunk and it was too late.

So Mary Cyr went to the convent at the age of thirteen, packing her lipstick, her rouge, high-heel shoes, her Plu and some arrowroot biscuits. The lipstick, rouge and high-heel shoes were taken away. Her Plu was allowed; the arrowroot biscuits were shared.

As winter came, she felt more and more trapped. Especially in the cafeteria, among all the other girls.

"The nuns," Mary Cyr wrote John, "they act so strange they must be religious—besides, all their heroes have been chopped up or boiled in oil—one was even roasted on a grill—please confirm to them that I don't even like a toothache."

These pleas were written in childlike handwriting and had the ache of loneliness and childhood in them. But the idea of being roasted on a grill gave her horrific nightmares for years. The idea of fire terrified her.

And then a week later she wrote:

"I want to come home. Mr. Delano Captain, Sir, you are my only friend and I really, really like you—"

John took his own money and time and visited her. The convent was off the beaten path—behind a small village near the open bay. In the frigid months, a blue icy haze surrounded the third storey, and wind echoed and moaned—the trees' icy branches snapped, and in a gale sounded like a vise was being closed on a head. There was the smell of soup and darkness and porridge all at once. She was forced to converse in a language that up until the first semester she had never spoken and did not know.

She was suffering under the agony of being an English girl—even though her name was Cyr—in an unfriendly French school. They called her *anglaise* and teased her about it—about her wealth. It was all done on the sly—a note here, a pinch there, a kick under the table. A heavy crosscheck during floor hockey. And a smile when she fought back and got caught.

Pretty little Acadian girls whose boyfriends were just starting to grow their inestimable goatees.

She made a phone call to him, collect from a pay phone at Pizza Delight.

"Is that you, Mr. Captain Constable—is that you? You've got to save me, Sergeant Captain Delano—you have to kidnap me, and take me away. I am restive."

"You are restive?"

"Well, you pick the word—that's what I've become."

You could tell she was holding her mittened hand up to the phone and whispering into it.

"Are you still there—are you, Sergeant, my best friend? Well—" she whispered gravely. "Listen up!! Whatever I mean, it's what I am. I am living in Mother Superior's office—" (pause) "—because I am sent there at least three times a day—and three times a day—" (pause, coughing) "—Mother leaves me there kneeling in the corner, praying, while she makes her rounds—my knees are getting all red and rubbed off. Besides, she delights in speaking French—so there is definitely something wrong with her."

Time and again she told him she was brought to the Mother Superior because it was said she, Mary, started fights. She had a bruise on her face—up near her eye. But she would not tell who did it. She was in fact honour-bound, as her grandfather had taught her to be. She would sit in the principal's office on a chair with her hands folded, staring glumly and silently ahead, and refraining from speaking against the accusations piling up against her.

Knowing the insufferable ethnic wars that at times happened in the small towns that dotted the highway, he petitioned Garnet to bring her out of there. But Garnet and Nan said no—it was impossible to do that—and it was for her own good. The money was paid, and everything was sufficient.

Garnet had the peculiar strain of being implacable in small matters. Nan felt Mary must stay where she was—it was imperative that Mary be taught in French, by the French and for the French. The Englishwoman was a discredited member of the family. And she was gone. Enough of this English nonsense—she was betraying her own culture. As always in Canada, one is not caught between two worlds but between three or four—not between two competing interests but a multitude. That is, the convent was not as bad as Mary would let on, or as life-affirming as Nan often suggested to those who sometimes questioned the wisdom of having sent Mary Cyr there. Not all the Acadians were mean to her— but enough of them were silent when she was being treated meanly. And she would be disgusted by this in her lifetime—the silence that allowed bigotry toward the Catholics when she was in university was the silence that allowed the same thing against her Englishness by these pretty little girls who said she must be a Protestant.

She could have switched sides easily, given up her mother—if she had been less a person. She could have chosen a different side, and be welcomed. But she decided to stand and fight.

And John hoped for her but could do nothing about it.

John now wondered down in Mexico if it would be known. That is, if her final two months at the convent would become known—and if this would become part of the indictment against her. That is, Facebook and the internet would play their parts like those juvenile boys once did. She had become a figure of fun on the internet. But she had been before, in the convent, and after trying to make friends she tried to fight back, but was hopelessly outnumbered. Here she was on the edge of the frozen bay, wherein the Tracadie River flowed—plunked down in the midst of them.

So she wrote home and asked for a small pistol, to protect herself:

"Only if need be—I will use it sparingly."

Of course that did not happen.

4.

PERHAPS IT WAS FATE, FORTITUDE OR DESIGN, BUT MARY CYR had one friend, someone as picked on as she—a girl with blond eyelashes and blond thin hair, weak eyes and a sad comical little grin, who came there by way of Caraquet. A girl who liked and dreamed of a boy named Lucien DeCoussy.

"*Et il est si mignon et spécial*," she would say—many times a day.

But unfortunately no one thought little Denise was.

One might see her picture in a thousand Canadian yearbooks from mid-century on, the girls who walk with bleak-coloured sweaters along rows of grey lockers, carrying books with a kind of hopeful plea, through the storms of our oddly quaint villages and vicious sub-zero winters.

Mary promised her a donkey—or a horse, whatever it was—if she would be her friend—yet Denise Albert would have been her friend anyway. So being outcasts, the two of them were put together in a small back bedroom, away from the others.

This idea that the English wanted to destroy them, and Mary should not only realize this but her soul should respond to it, was a matter of great and subtle concern in those long corridors the nuns walked, silent and determined to wrest out of these children spontaneity and love. (Of course not all of them, and even those who did could be at times kind to those in their care.)

But Mary's soul rebelled against this idea, and she could not join the insults fired at the *maudits anglais*. And Denise would not, because of Mary.

That this has been played out two hundred thousand times in our country on either side of the spectrum, with little leeway for self-blame is something unspoken. And this formed Mary Cyr's philosophy: get back at those who from the vantage of victimization attacked the grand-children of their supposed victimizers without confronting themselves.

And she saw this, in the sweet-smelling Acadian girls and in a western Canadian named Ernest Vanderflutin, who had as far as Mary Cyr was concerned the audacity to speak against her mother.

It became her philosophy—to fight them to the death—but it took some time to develop.

With Denise as her only friend they were put out of the way.

Mary Cyr once said, later on:

"Away from the pure ones—they are after French purity like others cherished certain Germanic qualities. Oh, they won't say that, but their politicians will demonstrate it. Someday I bet they will have laws in Quebec against having English on signs—and call it progress."

(This of course was one of the many things she said that came to haunt her later. And she would say as many things about the English over the years: *You can always tell an Englishman, but you can't tell him much!*)

But their punishment came because Mary refused to learn, or attempt to learn French—the real trouble was Mary had a hard time concentrating on anything the year after her father's death and should have been excused—and Denise could not comprehend why other students disliked Mary. Mary's marks that year ranged from 35 to 65. Most of her marks fell between 50 and 60. In the distilled afternoon light through the great, elongated windows of classrooms they sat side by side—separated from the others.

Sister Alvina had warned them, had strapped them, and then sanctioned them.

They locked the door on them at eight at night. That is, not only Mary and Denise but all the students.

Their window was three storeys up and had double-pane glass, and the window itself was nailed shut. The main dorms were off to their left; the nuns slept on the right—something that Mary Cyr often seemed confused about when speaking with Denise.

They were locked in after evening prayers. And that is where the two planned their escape. In the lingering smells of supper and chapel and Lenten monotony.

And to that end Mary deliberated and plotted. For two weeks at night she sewed rags together while little Denise slept, Mary sitting up until three making arms and feet and fashioning heads, and hiding it all under her mattress.

"*C'est quoi ça?*" Denise asked one evening.

"Dummys."

"*Pour quoi faire? Mettre dans nos lits?*"

"Sure," Mary Cyr answered

"*Nos lits?*" Denise asked again.

"Sure," Mary Cyr conceded without knowing what was being asked—for she had not been able to make much headway with the language of love; and Denise looked up at her in a kind of strange, hopeful awe, with her little chest bones visible under her blue nightgown.

"Okay then, two donkeys," Mary said. And she winked in affection and went back to her sewing.

It was March 26, late, dark in the long hallway, and Mary arose, put her feet on the cold floor and woke her friend. Moonlight came in and she could just sense now how late it had become. The old nun down the end of the hall coughed in her sleep, and the downstairs clock gonged.

The wind blew steadily over the bay, and Mary Cyr had keys in her pocket that she had stolen from Mother Superior's desk while she was on her knees. These keys would open their bedroom door and the front door as well.

"*Maintenant?*"

"Sure, buttercup," Mary said.

The little girl—that is, Denise Albert—had no idea where they were going or what they were exactly running away from. But she sat up, smiled and began to dress. That in fact was what was so sorrowful—her childlike trust.

Under the grey blankets of their beds they put the two dummies Mary had managed to sew—something that would fool no one, especially Sister Alvina, but which Mary Cyr believed was more than pure genius—and left at 1:29 in the morning, Mary carrying a pillowcase filled with crackers and cheese and a lettuce-and-tomato sandwich, and

Denise clutching the rosary she had almost forgotten but had remembered just in time.

Now and again moonlight shone through the large back window on their little bodies as they made their way down the three flights of stairs and out the door, Mary taking Denise by the hand.

"There is only one problem," Mary Cyr whispered. "The river."

"*L'hiver?*" Denise asked.

"No—the river—*rivière*," she whispered.

And they walked along, both alike in size and disposition, their bodies making shadows on the side of the convent walls.

Then they had to slide down a short, steep, snow-covered hill. And then walk through a field of fire-red alders, picking their way through so the branches would not sting or cut their faces.

They got to the river and walked back and forth. Mary looked it over, walked out three metres and walked back.

"It is as solid as a training bra," she said. And little Denise stepped out as well, her eyes filled with hope, and fear.

They were trying to cross the river to get to the village of St. Clair. That would save them a five-kilometre walk to the bridge. Mary Cyr was intending to phone her grandfather to take her home; or to some island where, she told Denise, they could smoke cigarettes and live on a sailboat.

The convent was on the west side, surrounded by a brick wall, with the elongated penitentiary sadness of iced-over, naked trees, branches bent in elongated despair.

And the sound of a late-night plow in the village streets. Mary did not know, nor would she have been expected to, that the river mouth was opened halfway across and you must stay to your right to have a chance at living any longer.

Denise, with her white eyelashes and her ears that poked out under her woollen cap, did not make it to the other side.

But how had it happened? It was one of the many tragedies to happen in Mary Cyr's life. She bravely went first, to mark the way, and made it across the ice; saw little Denise hesitate and start to crawl on her knees. So Mary Cyr yelled:

"Go to your right!"

Or that is what she believed she was yelling.

In actual fact Mary Cyr got two simple French words mixed up: *droite* and *gauche*.

"*Allez gauche*," is what she actually said.

And the girl simply crawled as quickly as she could into the open water, holding her wooden prayer beads. Mary heard the splash, a kind of small cry and then silence. She bravely ran out onto the ice to help, swishing her arm frantically in the water. But she wasn't able to touch her.

Then suddenly it became horrifyingly clear, in the soft sudden luxuriant moonlight.

The little girl had slipped under the crystal-clear ice, and was looking straight up at Mary as Mary looked down at her. In the light of the great spring moon little Denise, holding her breath, staring into Mary's face—and then she simply sank away, with her arms outstretched, as if wanting a hug. The prayer beads sank with her, disappearing into the dark rum-like water.

Denise's body was not discovered until the following spring, the prayer beads still clutched in her hand. Mary was whisked away—that she was even on the river was mentioned only briefly in the papers. The local priest, because of the connection with the convent, was outraged for a while but then said nothing more about it. People said he had been paid off by the Catholic hypocrite, Blair Cyr. No worse kind in the mind of the secular. But in actual fact Mary Cyr went to confession, and the priest could and would not say anything more. He did feel terrible that he could not. For he learned in that confessional that she and Denise had been bullied and tormented, had run away. And in fact he believed her.

It was the second disaster in her life. So what would all this mean—now? You see, Mary Cyr was made controversial by design—she always became the story rather than the story itself. And her enemies took delight in this. And when she fought back, they could and did say:

"She hit her head, you know, when she was young. Terrible, but it left her bonkers. Do you see she walks with a strange little limp and lisps at times? That's her head injury acting up."

This was in fact true; she did lisp over certain words, and she did walk strangely at times. And she did have a head injury, which made her very unpredictable in her anger.

She now told him that she had given Victor twenty dollars and he had bought Florin a toy truck, yellow and orange. She had helped him pick it out. It was called Maxwell the truck.

"Please see if it is at my villa—perhaps Florin was there," she whispered.

She then sat in her hot cell making a list of names, of people who might say something mean against her. The list got so long, she ran out of paper.

5.

MARY CYR MARRIED TWICE AND WAS DIVORCED ONCE, WIDOWED once before she was twenty-seven. Her first husband was the man who took all he could from her, and beat her twice mercilessly, a man who John went looking for with his service revolver when he found out. Her second husband was a man of eighty-five who reminded her of someone. And with her luck she was able to outlive him. So at twenty-seven she was a widow.

Her third and as yet final husband was a boy named Lucien—a fisherman from Neguac who she forgot somewhere in Spain. In fact he too was dead.

There were terrible fights in the family over whom she married and why she was getting married, and what she was to do with her life. Lawyers alternately hounded and protected her.

John had been hired as her bodyguard. The trouble was—he believed that she had married the first man to get back at him. And he felt that though she had said many times that she didn't want to act in any way but virtuous and find love—he felt she would do something very dangerous and she would do it to prove to him that she was free. Whatever freedom she had was to come at a terrible price and be used in curious ways against her. She could be violent too, and John knew from experience how violence worked in the human heart.

"I want you to find out who killed Bobby for me—if you do, I will say nice things about you," she wrote John once, after not being in contact with him for two years. "I will even mention you to Princess Diana—and as you know, she lives in a castle and has a whole hush of boyfriends—"

But he could not tell her who killed Bobby, her son, because she herself had a hand in it. Of course he knew it was an accident—but what would that matter now? It was as if all her life she was making a mad dash toward the horrid jail cell in the withering Mexican heat. And now she had found it.

He sat on a bench inside the roadway leading to the villa, and looked toward the L-shaped pool and some lounge chairs covered in dead leaves in the blazing afternoon.

There was a faint smell of some Mexican flower and farther away a haze, and the smell of diesel and the *thud, thud* of a jackhammer on the roadway, which she too must have been able to hear in her cell.

A Russian couple sat by the one functioning pool. A German man and his wife lay on lounge chairs at their little villa, which overlooked the second pool, filled with a foot-round puddle of dirty water and a small tide of dead leaves. He walked over to talk to the Russians for a moment, and asked if they remembered her and Victor, the boy.

"Oh, the American," the Russian man said.

"Canadian."

"Ah. The Canadian. She seemed happy—why would she do it?"

"Well, who said she did it?"

"Everyone—even in Cancún, we were there two days ago—they say it too. All the papers say the evidence is incontrovertible," the Russian advised. "Though he did errands for other people too." He scratched his stomach and looked about, and yawned. There was the smell of burning leaves somewhere, and a lizard sunned itself on a rock.

The German shaded his eyes when John approached him. He smiled and said to his wife: "*Kanadisch.*"

John spoke to them a moment. It wasn't at all as if he had any authority here, and he knew it. But the German man and his Dutch wife were pleasant to him, and aware of this as a special case.

Yes, the German said he remembered Victor. He came to the resort every day with the little boy—his brother. But he had no idea what had happened. There was another boy, named Ángel Gloton, who seemed to protect them. They were good friends.

"Ángel Gloton?" John said.

"Yes." The German nodded

The woman asked:

"*Haben sie dich den korper sehen lassen?*"

"Have they let you to see the body?" her husband translated.

That was a very strange question, John thought.

"No, not at all," John said.

The woman looked cautiously at her husband.

"*Meine Frau ist Ärztin,*" the man said. "My wife is a doctor—she is interested."

They explained that she was the first to see the body. The manager of the resort ran to her and asked her to come to Mary Cyr's villa because he knew she was a doctor. She saw the body for about five minutes, but then the police came and asked her to leave.

"It is all silly," the German said. He shrugged. "It seems far-fetched, to say the least."

"What does?"

"Well, they say it was arsenic," the wife said, shifting into English, which was a little unnerving.

"He was beaten for some money, perhaps. Or something. But no one gave him arsenic—he had bruises just around his neck—but the room was dark and I wasn't in there long."

"Still, we think that would be easy to prove—and then once we prove it, she can go home," the German said.

"He was grabbed and hit?" John asked.

"You would know in a second—yes—by someone larger than that woman. Anyway, I am sure Miss Cyr couldn't have been able to do that to him."

John nodded.

They both looked at him with wide, knowing eyes.

"I see," John said.

"But," the Dutchwoman said cautiously, "you have to be prepared for what the authorities can do here." Then she looked at him. "*Het is andere wereld.*"

"It's another world," the German translated.

6.

LATER HE WENT TO FEY AND ASKED IF HE COULD GET INTO Mary's rooms—that she wanted something from them.

"What does she want," Fey asked, looking up at him curiously from his desk.

"She wants her childhood comforter," John said. Perhaps he shouldn't have told—but he was only a tourist and this was a murder investigation.

Fey shrugged as if he did not comprehend. But John knew he had. Fey spoke to a police officer, and John was led out and down the street toward the resort again.

John was let into her rooms at 3:34 in the afternoon; a two-bedroom townhouse villa shaded by coconut palms, and an old broken lawn chair on the balcony overlooking the empty back pool and the water in the distance. A lizard scurried along the brick tile and hid; another moved and craned its neck toward him.

A disordered apartment. But it was disordered by a search. Both beds had been slept in. There was a bottle of gin on the cupboard—and the bottle was three-quarters gone—and there was police tape around the dresser. There were two books on this dresser. One was *Introduction to Conversational French*. The second, open and half-read, was *The Royal Twenty-Second Regiment in Action*—a history of the Quebec regiment, the Van Doos, that fought heroically in both world wars.

The comforter was in fact rolled up near the headboard of Mary's bed, and she was right—it looked as if it was part of the pillow. Whoever looked at the bed did not look at it as being particular. Besides, this room was not searched like the other bedroom, where the young boy's body had been found. He took Plu and put it into a plastic bag he had in his pocket. And there was something inside the blanket's pouch. Her diary.

He put it into the plastic bag as well.

Then he went into the other bedroom.

John looked everywhere in that room, in the closet and behind the balcony door curtains. He went to the balcony door. There was a stain on the door pull. What did that mean? Well, it could very likely mean that the boy was bleeding outside, before he ever got to the townhouse.

John realized something else. The youngster was also spitting—perhaps he was trying to get his breath.

Certainly they should know this by now. So if they knew it, they wanted to deny it. He shrugged, went into Mary's bedroom and sat on the side of the bed, trying to catch his breath. He felt a lump in his chest, as if he wouldn't be able to breathe, and then stood and walked unsteadily to the counter and took a drink of bottled water.

He suddenly felt the first cold inkling of the intractableness of the past and how it would play into the charges against her.

"Victor is dead, and little Florin is missing—"

And even though he knew nothing about them, he felt a sudden well of sympathy and despair.

Later that day John went back to the police station and inquired about the toxicology report. That report, no matter in what manner collected or no matter how tepid, did not have to be released until the trial—and the trial might be twelve months away. But the German and his Dutch wife already knew the police were going to say it was arsenic. Now that it was considered arsenic, it would take weeks to say it was not and have anyone believe it.

"Everyone knows it's preposterous," the Dutch doctor said. "But now that she is in jail on that charge they will not or cannot change it." She said she had spent years in Mexico and understood them.

"*Zodra dit een nationale verhaal wordt zal ze niet veranderen,*" she said, quickly.

"It's a national story and they won't change up their minds," the German translated.

Besides, the worst of it was—John had to get back to the cases he was working on in Canada. A case concerning a woman named Velma Cheval.

And the secret was Constable Fey knew this. Perhaps was waiting him out.

John was allowed to see Mary once again. It was now four o'clock.

The sun still burned in the sky over the water as it settled. There was a smell of early supper. He asked her.

"NO. I wasn't his girlfriend—do they think that?"

"Yes."

This seemed to catch her unprepared, and in this a kind of revelation overcame her—her features looked amazed at the "thing" now developing against her.

"But he was just a little boy—he was going to help me. He was young enough to be my son—almost grandson."

"Help you do what?"

"Help people. I came here to help people. What else in my life can go wrong?"

John looked at her frightened, almost hilarious, gaze and said:

"Hopefully nothing else!"

He remembered her as a child. Many times he had to protect her because of the fear the family had that someone would abduct her. Initially that is why he was hired. Although John was never made privy to why this worry had resulted, he was almost sure there must have been a threat. Perhaps it was the idea of her mother coming to claim her? Now he was almost certain of it.

So they made a game of looking out for strangers—though John had thought after meeting Garnet that she had been surrounded by them most of her life. He gave her his number when she was a young girl and told her to phone him whenever she felt uncomfortable about anything.

"Oh—" she now said. "Dear me."

7.

"I MADE A MISTAKE," MARY TOLD JOHN THE FIRST NIGHT SHE phoned, which was the first night he had given her his phone number. She may have been eleven or twelve.

"Yes, I made a terrific mistake, Mr. Constable Captain Delano."

"What mistake is that—it couldn't have been that bad—"

"I—puked."

"You did—"

"Yes, at a dinner party—I got nervous when they started talking about the business and how my cousins were in the know, and Nan said, 'They will steal us blind,' and I said, 'I think I am going blind,' and my eyes got wobbly, and I up and puked on the table in front of the guests."

"You didn't."

"Yes —well, who wants to be stolen blind—and my eyes got blinky."

"I don't think they will do that," John assured her.

After that she phoned whenever she could to tell him something. Perhaps she made many of the crises up, just to be able to phone. But he could usually tell when she did this.

There were episodes of depression, and a sailboat she gave away.

"To some First Nations fellow—from some First Nations reserve—to do some First Nations things with," she explained.

There was an episode where she scratched the face of someone. One where they said they would take Bobby away because they heard her shouting.

"I shout only because I love," she answered. "Only a social worker or a marriage counsellor would not know that."

The theory it was arsenic was revealed to the press the next day, and there was arsenic in the storage locker beside her villa; and the boy had tested for it—that is, it was in his system at his death.

"Arsenic," the paper said.

There had been a hurricane, and people had bought arsenic to take care of rodents at the villa.

Another hurricane will come because the men had died in the mine, they said. And now look what the poison had done!

Mary had been brought into the police interview room twice. Both times they had handcuffed her and put leg shackles on. She walked between two officers: one male, one female. The female officer serious, with a bulletproof vest, and a Glock pistol on her belt.

There in the room was the prosecutor Tallagonga, sitting at one side of a small, dark-oak desk and looking through the files, a heavy-set woman wearing a matronly skirt. Of course she could be great fun when she was not working.

She would ask Mary a series of questions from a printed brief. Why had she come here? What reason did she employ Victor? How long did she know him? Had she slept with him? Et cetera. And with every answer Mary gave, Tallagonga gave a cynical, meaningful shrug—as if to say: *You have not convinced me.*

So therefore the truth would not convince her.

Now Mary heard how she had killed him.

Arsenic.

"Where is Florin?" Mary asked Tallagonga during the second interview.

"You seem to be quite obsessed about Florin," Tallagonga said sternly. "He is a Mexican child, my dear—not a Canadian one. Was there something about Florin?"

"Yes," Mary said. "There was something about him."

"Oh—what was that?"

"He is a child of God," Mary said, defensively.

Tallagonga smiled ruefully a second and then closed one brief and opened another with the snap of an elastic, which she manoeuvred backward to her left wrist, looking at Mary as she did so. "Are you penitent now, my lady?"

"More than you might imagine," Mary said.

Tallagonga, when she was finished her questions, pressed a button and said, "*Estoy por aquí*," stood and gathered her material, and a buzzer opened the door.

ARSENIC.

Mary Cyr looked at John with a prisoner's shocked disbelief, and he could feel the same drafts of hot air that lingered on her skin. She looked at her arms as if inspecting for measles, then up at him, and then looked to the side as she spoke:

"Tell me, where did I get that? Where would I get it—I wouldn't even know how much to give—"

"It is total nonsense. I know it and so do they," he said. "But," he added, "you do have people on your side—a German doctor—or his Dutch wife is a doctor—they are at the villa just down from yours—they both say you are innocent—and they want to prove it. The Dutch doctor saw the boy's body—he was beaten up."

"A German man and a Dutch woman," she said. "Well, there you have it—I always liked them."

He said nothing.

"Can I see a paper?" she asked.

"No—it's better you don't."

"Why—I suppose they have a terrible picture of me—"

"You look fine," he said. "But I think—"

"What?"

"I think you need a shower."

"You mean I smell?"

"A tad," he said.

He had not wanted to tell her that. But he had to.

So he asked. They said no, unless she used the one outside in the back; the one everyone else had to use.

"Not with so many spectators," he said.

"There would be no spectators," Erappo Pole said, astonished at the arrogance of this Canadian.

All this time John was furious, but he knew he couldn't show it. An hour or so later she was allowed to go back to her villa and shower.

A crowd of women and children followed her there. A policewoman escorted her, and put ankle shackles on her, for another picture. The priest and altar boy came out on the front steps of the church to watch her walk by, the priest's garments caught up in the wind in, John thought, the intractable moment of defining himself not as a spectator but as one asserting his approval.

8.

BY MID-AFTERNOON OF THAT SAME DAY THE LAWYER HAD COME. He spoke to Mary Cyr for an hour and then went and saw John; it seemed just to be polite; or perhaps Mary insisted. But John did have some questions for him.

Could bail be set? No.

What the lawyer did do is elaborate on the way the Mexican authorities would not rush this case. So he could not rush the case either, so John's other questions would take time. That is, the case would be carefully researched and could take up to a year before a trial in front of a judge.

"But she won't be sent to the prison?" John asked.

"Certainly not—at any rate not right yet—they will wait and see—in fact, the case might be dropped," he said. "I am trying to see if we can't get the charges dropped so she can go home. We will find that out in a day or so—" He went to say something more about this and then decided not to.

"That would be best," John said. But there was something in Señor Xavier's eyes that made Delano less than completely enthused.

"Or at any rate, Mr. Delano—I might be able to make a deal," Xavier said.

"About what?"

Xavier sat forward on his seat, his face more enthusiastic, his long fingers placed neatly in front of him.

"Well, perhaps she admits to an accident and does three years," he whispered. Then, lifting his fingers off the glass table, he took out a cigarette and lit it, a white cigarette in a very white lounge, in his immaculately cut sharkskin jacket.

"I don't think that is very much of a deal if she has done nothing—and how can it be an accident if they are charging her with giving him poison?"

John said all of this very calmly because he was used to speaking clearly and calmly when he felt he was right.

What John was trying to say was he did not believe Tallagonga had any intention of prosecuting this until she found out who Mary Cyr was. Then they filed the charge, called her guilty and looked for a lifelong prison sentence because she was on the board of Tarsco Mining. Which people were now saying was connected to the mining disaster here.

And John realized something else. Depending on what penalties the family would pay, the case against Mary Cyr might or might not proceed. That is why Xavier had said that the case might be dropped. All of this John felt, but he could not say, because Xavier wasn't quite sure either. And he could not tell John the reason—which was that there was Tallagonga and Judge Gabel here—but in Mexico City there was someone else, and this someone else was preparing a very different case against very important people. Xavier knew something about this but couldn't for the life of him say it.

Xavier did explain Mary had to pay rent on her cell and pay for her extra food—fruit and vegetables. Pay for clothes, water to take a shower, soap and towel—pay for any luxuries like chocolate—and a beer if she wanted. She was free to order here what she wanted as long as she had money to pay for it. They were not draconian in that regard.

For instance, she had just been charged ninety-five dollars for taking a shower at the resort. If she took a shower at the jail, she would be charged two dollars.

And he said the other prisoners for the most part seemed to taunt her one moment but like her the next—already she had given them ciga-rettes and chocolates—and twice she was asked for her autograph. But she had to be kept in her cell because they could not risk someone assaulting her.

"Some of them never had anything—*nada*—if she is kind, they will like her after a while. And it does seem being kind is in her nature."

John then lost his temper—which he had promised himself he wouldn't do.

"But she had nothing to do with anything. She will be framed for a crime she has not committed because she sits on a board of a mining company she knows nothing about. The Cyrs had nothing whatsoever to do with the implosion at this mine."

"Oh, conspiracy? No, that is too ugly a word," Xavier cautioned. "That is highly unlikely." Although Xavier knew this was true, he also knew that in order to negotiate her freedom, he could never say it while the very idea of negotiation meant knowing all of this exactly.

John went and spoke to the porter, and asked him about Victor and Florin.

The old porter, who now turned and tried to run away every time he saw John—sometimes he tried to move as fast as he could on his feeble feet, at other times he tried to remain stationary behind a plant—told John many things. Well, a few of the same things in many ways. John knew he was bothering him, and besides, the old fellow was frightened of getting in trouble. But John could not help it. So the porter told him this: The youngster Victor would hobble about in old torn boots, with his young brother by the hand—his look was of a child searching for someone.

"Perhaps his mother?" John asked.

No, his father and mother were both gone.

"Did he have anyone to look out for him?"

Young Ángel Gloton did. They had grown up together, and like most boys who grow up together there is a bond—Ángel looked out for them. For instance, if they were selling trinkets on the beach to the tourists, Ángel and Victor would be inseparable—if there was one, there would be two—and have Florin with them. Then in the last two weeks Victor was alone.

"Why?"

"Ángel wanted him to do something and he wouldn't. Ángel came and asked me to tell him where he was. I found it strange he wouldn't know."

"Do something or see someone?" John asked.

The porter shrugged.

But he said ironically that no one named Isabella Tallagonga ever gave young Victor a second look as she drove her black Fiat up to the courthouse, or passed him on her way to lunch with the judge, Vincente Gabel. That the boy was alone after the bump at the mine. Sometimes you could see him sitting on a bench all hours of the night. At other times they said he went and slept on a coal heap near the head frame. The look was heart-rending—almost incomprehensible—one child holding his brother's hand, and think of the millions who had this heart-rending incomprehensible look!

What would such a look be? Only one look—John knew it well from the streets in other places. Abandonment. Except for his friend Ángel Gloton, who believed he was helping him when he wasn't. So that meant to John that those who trained Ángel Gloton, the adults in his life, had something to do with the death of Victor, and Ángel, trusting them, did not know this.

"I am sorry I didn't pay attention now—" the old porter said. The porter was almost eighty, shaky and unable to bend. His hands trembled slightly.

"All of us always are sorry," John answered. "I have been sorry over things I did not do or say to my child all my life. But it shouldn't have been left to you."

John went to see Mary and told her this. That is, he told her she had picked the right person to help, no matter what happened. That Victor did what he could do to feed his four-year-old brother; to find someone to listen to him, Victor. And perhaps he would be listened to yet.

"Yes, yes, where is he?" she asked again about Florin.

"Victor was worried about him too—did you know that?"

"Yes—well, no—I mean I don't know anymore!"

"When it rained, he took Florin to the dump at the far edge of the Calle Republica and slept there because they no longer had their father's rooms. They were frightened to go there because someone was watching them or trying to find them."

"Oh my God Jesus Christ," Mary said quietly. "Oh my God Jesus Christ."

"Yes," John said, looking up at Father Ignatius's "¡*Viva Cristo!* on the wall; Oh my God Jesus Christ.

"The flowers of abandonment on the city streets of the Old World," Mary said, looking up at him with a kind of melancholy love.

"Or is this the New World?" Mary Cyr asked, "I sometimes forget what world it is."

She was not allowed to walk back and forth in the hallway as some other prisoners were. At first a couple of them threw shit at her, to show their restrained disapproval. Then they would walk back to their cells gaily laughing and moving their hips with the comfort of women who knew where they stood.

After a time, however, throwing shit on her stopped. Then other prisoners were coming up to the bars of her cell, asking for cigarettes, and hand lotion and things Mary tossed their way without thinking. (Some of them—well, most—were going to save them to sell as souvenirs—some of them already had.)

9.

DEROLFO WAS AN IMPORTANT MAN. IN HIS YOUNGER YEARS HE was a doctor who warned of a flu epidemic in his state; afterwards he was promoted to the department of the secretary of health. Then he ran for governor. He served a term and was defeated when he re-offered. Still, he became quite rich as governor. Then one of his friends got him into business as an important figurehead. Now he was on the board of governors of Amigo, part owner and CEO.

By yesterday afternoon he would have given it all up to be a country doctor, which is what he wanted to be. He had stolen over four million dollars in money allotted for refurbishing the mine, plus hundreds upon hundreds of thousands more in laundered money to keep him quiet. He never thought there would be a bump—a disaster beneath his feet. His colleagues told him his mine was safe. But he himself had never been more than a hundred feet into it.

He had earned, besides all that he embezzled, four hundred thousand a year.

When Tarsco sent the money in order to refurbish the deeper runs where the men had to work, and people began to greedily divvy it up among themselves, he asked if the mine was safe.

It was the day after 9/11. The money had come in, and no one was alive on the other end to let people know that the transaction had even taken place. That was awful, of course—but it was also the beauty of it.

DeRolfo felt bad about this, so he said, after asking if the mine was safe:

"Ahora los chicos me dicen que la mina es segura."

"Too safe," a colleague said brashly. "Yes, it is almost too safe—the men are getting lazy—because it is too safe. If they were a bit more worried, they would work a bit harder."

Gidgit, his wife, looked at them all with a kind of clever insatiability that was almost perversely sexual.

"Besides, we have done the refurbishing," she said, "So all is well."

DeRolfo knew this was a complete lie, but said nothing.

He actually thought the men had perished, when he ordered a halt to the search. Still, he knew what a search would do: it would reveal that all the catalogued improvements he had given to the country's minister of mining were bogus—not one of the major implementations had happened. So he was glad they were all dead and he could stop the search. If they reopened, it would be easy to say such implementations had been destroyed.

Then out of the darkness, a boy, almost as black as pitch, because he had been sitting on coal heaps, brought him a *tape*, and begged him, with tears running down his dirty face, to start the search again.

Confounded by all of this, he had no idea what to do. When the boy turned the tape on, however, he heard the unmistakable tap from three hundred metres beneath his feet. At first he said he couldn't hear the sound. But he could. It had come drifting up from underground through a series of open pipe work that for some reason allowed the faint tap to be distinctly heard at that spot on the surface. The men were calling them, begging them to listen.

So he went and told his wife. His wife was furious.

"Tell him we need the tape—*dile que necesitamos la cinta.*"

So he got a policeman he sometimes paid, Erappo Pole, to go and tell the boy he, Carlos DeRolfo, as head of the mine, needed that tape. That they would be able to tell if the men were still alive. The boy started to go and get it, but suddenly decided something was wrong. A terrible, horrid feeling washed over him at that moment.

So the boy, Victor, said he had lost it.

"But," his wife said, "we cannot believe him—we have to get the tape!"

So they sent Erappo Pole out again.

Victor, now scared to death, took his little brother and went to the back end of the mine, and hid there.

He sat down and looked up at the stars, and every time he heard a sound, he would get up from his hiding place and look for the source of that sound.

Unfortunately a week or so later he was careless and they saw him. DeRolfo had driven there with his wife, who under her gloves had brought a pistol that Hulk Hernández had given them. Ángel had told them earlier that evening:

"He is frightened, he don't trust you—but I think he is up near the old head frame—that's where he started out for."

"We only want to help him—" DeRolfo said. "Before something terrible happens to him."

Ángel smiled, as if to say: *You don't have to tell me.*

So Victor was given up, and they saw him hiding under a piece of tin.

DeRolfo grabbed him about the neck from behind, and the boy gasped for air as DeRolfo lifted him off the ground. His feet dangled, and a sad gasp came from him. Dr. DeRolfo could not stop—he was so frightened of what the boy might say he kept squeezing on the boy's windpipe. The boy began to pee his pants.

There was a sound of air trying to escape, like a whistle, and then he realized the boy's windpipe had been crushed.

But there was no tape on him.

The boy simply lay there. His dreams of helping to find his dad, lost in his tousled brownish hair, his little face bronze.

He and his wife took Victor's body and drove it to the resort. They threw the boy out where some beautiful flower arrangements sat. It was midnight. Or thereabouts. They suddenly decided to blame it all on Ángel Gloton.

"There was a big fight between them—I know for a fact," Gidgit said, and she seemed upset that this fight had occurred. "Ángel is crazy—I know that—he is taking steroids for his punch—I know that for a fact."

None of this was true, but they knew this for a fact.

They left Victor on the ground, and the wind was blowing very hard from the sea, the night's stars were out. Carlos and his wife were driving home.

"We have to go back to the mine and look for the tape," Gidgit said. "*Dios mío.*"

She blessed herself and he blessed himself.

They waited for two hours and drove back carefully.

His wife looking behind her every few seconds.

"*Tengo miedo, miedo, miedo,*" she kept whispering. Then she lit a cigarette. "*Sí, tengo miedo,*" she said. And then in English, "Scared shitless, Carlos—"

"*Sí, sí,*" he kept saying, but she was annoying him.

He pulled the car over and got out. He searched with his flashlight along the perimeter of the old boxcars, all the way to the shaft and back.

Still he couldn't find the tape. He turned around to leave, and a child of four was staring at him, looking at him with large dark eyes, holding a toy truck with the name Maxwell on it. He smiled awkwardly and hopefully.

"*¿Dónde está Victor . . . dónde está mi hermano?*"

As is sometimes with children, he looked to be not totally aware of the question he had just asked, because his eyes were searching the car and the beautiful woman sitting inside it, looking out at him in shock, wearing a necklace of pearls. She rolled the window down and tossed her cigarette out:

"*¿Quién diablos es él?*" she asked. "*Car—los—Car—los ¿quién diablos es él?*" Who the hell is that?

"*¿Dónde está Victor?*" the boy said again slowly.

Carlos quickly looked around and said:

"Oh, I don't know where Victor is—let us find him. *Estarás con él esta noche.*"

You will be with him tonight.

Now both knew exactly how Raskolinkov felt, but perhaps not quite yet. Not yet. They took the boy with them. For two hours they tried to figure some other way as Gidgit spoke to the child. She kept looking at her watch.

Time was going by.

"*¿Dónde está mi hermano?*" the little boy asked. In fact, Florin asked nothing else.

"*Víctor está durmiendo. Ven conmigo,*" he said.

Victor is sleeping. Come with me.

For two hours Carlos and Gidgit argued, accused each other of many things, and worried about what in the name of God they were going to do.

"You set our own trap," is all he said to her, over and over.

Now furious with the miners who survived, furious with how greedy miners were, furious that they expected a handout, she did nothing but explode in curses.

"Do you know what will happen if we are caught? Prison for life or Hernández." This is all she said.

They gave the boy McDonald's french fries—and told him Victor would meet him after he ate them.

Then they stopped the car, and DeRolfo held the gun in his hand. The Beretta they had on them that Hernández had told them to dispose of twelve months before.

But DeRolfo couldn't do anything. He knew where this gun came from, knew what it had done—and sighed.

His wife became more and more impatient. She told him to take the road toward Bruno's Bar. So the lights of the car reflected off the stone walls and the small patios. It was a sweet warm Mexican night, with the heavy smell of trees, and bats skimming in front of them as they drove.

The boy looked out the window. He put his left hand on her knee to straighten up.

He smiled at her and said:

"*¿Donde?*"

And then she simply stabbed him deep into his side. You could even hear a little slice.

"*Cuando no funciona nada más,*" she said.

When nothing else works.

The little boy, half sitting on her lap, was scratching his knee, and when she stabbed him, he continued to scratch his knee, and then in a delayed reaction he looked up at her and said: "Ou-ouch." He dropped Maxwell the truck, went to pick it up and then just closed his eyes. The french fries fell to the floor.

They took the boy to the dump, put him in a garbage bag they found there, doubled it with another garbage bag they had and left him in another pit, far away from the mine. In fact they could hear the rats as they walked back to their sky-blue Mercedes.

"*Mis zapatos están arruinados,*" Carlos said.

My shoes are ruined.

Because both he and Gidget were nervous creatures, they began to giggle.

10.

CARLOS DEROLFO INTENDED TO FIND VICTOR THE NEXT MORNING and do the post-mortem. He would trace the murder back to Ángel Gloton, and that would be it. They would have people at the gym say how much Ángel had changed, how mean he was. That would be the scenario.

But Victor wasn't there! Where was he?

Carlos went along the grand walkway, with its beautiful high-end shops for tourists, and when he arrived at Information, there was already a crowd near one of the townhouse villas. And there was already a doctor on the scene—what bad luck that a Dutch doctor was at the resort.

"No," DeRolfo said when he heard. "How long has she been inside? She has no business in our business—I will look at the child."

He walked into the dark room, and felt a cold, clammy air on his skin. The child was lying across the bed in a pair of jeans and a T-shirt. DeRolfo had no idea Victor had still been alive the night before. Now he was in this room.

"*¿Dios mío qué ha ocurrido?*" he asked.

What in God's name has happened?

People stepped aside when they saw him. The old porter greeted him with a gentle, approving nod of his head, and extended his hand to the boy as if showing a display

"*Hay demasiada gente aquí,*" he said softly. And people were ushered out.

He could not say it was natural causes because of little Florin, who might be found with knife wounds. He still had to say it was murder for anybody to treat it seriously. But he panicked and could not think of saying it was Ángel's crime, because Ángel was standing beside him, looking as horrified as anyone there.

So again as night follows day, things happened.

He patted Ángel gently on the shoulder and asked the porter who was renting this place.

They told him that a woman named Mary Cyr lived there, and she had gone to the airport an hour before.

"So it has to be her," Ángel said.

"*Sí,*" he said quickly. And this set all in motion. Little did Ángel know that if he had not been in the room, he very well might have been blamed.

"Find that woman," DeRolfo said, tears in his eyes.

"*Ella hizo algo a él. No estoy seguro de lo que.*"

She did something to him. I am not sure what.

He knew he could not say she had picked him up off the ground, like he had; he felt he would have to give some other reason. But still he had missed his chance with Ángel. Yes, he still might blame him—but within seconds everyone wanted to suspect the woman. The boy, Victor, was not as strong as Ángel, but he was still a strong young boy—no, it would be hard to say she had strangled him.

As soon as he did the post-mortem—he insisted he do it—he realized it was arsenic. *She poisoned him.* This was ridiculous. Showing the DeRolfos for the bumbling cowards they were. In fact certain of their associates laughed uproariously. But, it seemed plausible for a certain kind of woman to do. And when he saw her, he realized it could be got away with. And so Mary Cyr became that certain kind of woman.

Now, with two little boys dead or missing and the entire town of Oathoa, the entire state, the entire country yelling for her blood, DeRolfo must play the part he had unintentionally created for himself when he decided to allow powerful people to pay him off and launder money at that coal mine.

One of the persons most outraged over Mary Cyr's arrogance was the DeRolfos' own daughter, Sharon. Sharon who was a photographer and had been brought up so privileged she had her pick of eight horses in their stables. She was so liberal he and his wife couldn't do any-thing with her, so certain of her anti-religious self-righteousness they couldn't talk to her more than three minutes without getting into an argument.

His wife was sure with all her daughter's liberal views that "*El mundo se va al infierno.*"

The world is going to hell.

So what would she say if he and Gidgit went around confessing to things? Besides, Carlos thought of what Sharon believed about what she called unwanted pregnancy, so he said:

¿Qué dos niños importa, si muchos son asesinados a través del aborto?

What do two children matter when so many are killed through abortion?

That made him feel a bit better in this day and age. But not much.

When he told his wife, Gidgit, that he missed his chance at blaming Ángel so had called it arsenic, his face beamed at his own supercilious brilliance. However, she looked at him in delayed shock and, holding a peach in her hand, said:

"You are a complete idiot—"

His face darkened, and he started to complain that she never gave him credit for a thing.

Still they continued on.

In a week or so one of the policemen he knew, Erappo Pole, would find little Florin, and he had to set that up as well. But as yet, he did not have the tape. Maybe the boy had lost it—and if he did, all was fine. Mary Cyr would be put in jail. What was more incredible is that the police had discovered that she was *the* Mary Cyr. Had he heard of her?

No, not at all?

"So do you want to know who she is?"

"Sure, you tell me!"

Well then—la te da, da, da . . .

And so the life of Mary Cyr began to be revealed.

"What is that bitch doing down here!" Gidgit asked quietly when he told her. "That's what I'd like to know."

"*Sí, sí,*" said Carlos, shaking his head at the scandal. "*Sí, sí.*"

11.

EVERYONE IN TOWN (BECAUSE MEXICO, LIKE ALL OTHER PLACES, has far more good than bad) was trying to find Florin. The young girls texted each other, and the boys set out to look; the schoolboys joined groups to look, and at school there was talk of the awful woman who was killing children. So this was the story on Facebook—and Carlos S. DeRolfo could do nothing about it now. In the height of luxury, in his brand-new Mercedes with the gold leather interior and his custom-made steering gloves, he couldn't raise his fist against it.

However, if you thought it over, the design he had created, the web, was rather exquisite. Inimitable, really.

The streets near the gated beach estates and walled villas were full of people now, corrugated shops suddenly were opened. There seemed to be a great many lights on. People drank in the tapis bars here and there as John Delano walked farther into the town of Oathoa; the sound of two-stroke scooters racing along—somewhere there was a shout. The tourists oftentimes stayed in the walled and gated communities. It was a lot safer. John did not.

He realized a familiar but more than other times a disquieting feeling, of being known, and being followed. So on his way back to the villa a boy stepped out of a hat shop—sombreros for *turistas*—and looked him square in the eye.

"Where is Florin?" he asked. "If you know where he is, tell me now!"

John knew this boy was Ángel Gloton. He knew he was a boxer just by his stance. "I do not know," John said gently. "I wish I did."

And he passed on, and the boy watched him go.

"Everyone knows that Lady kills people—" he said in his broken English. And then, for effect: "*Todo el mundo conoce a Amigo.*"

"The case will be prolonged—this gives us time," Xavier had said, "to discover a flaw in their case."

"The flaw in their case is that they do not have any case at all," John said. "Someone did something to the boy and he died. The murder might not have been intentional, but there you have it. They were looking for something—evidence."

"Evidence."

"Of course evidence—about the mining disaster. I do not think they have found it. Could he have seen something, maybe?"

"What—what would he have seen?"

"I am not at all sure yet—but I know someone must still be searching for something. Unless he saw something and they killed him for that. Or something about a tape, so maybe he heard someone talking and recorded it?"

"So—"

"So," John said, lighting Xavier's cigarette, "they have no case—"

"The world has no case either. It had no case at all against little Victor, but there you go. It had no case against the miners, but there we are."

"I know," John said.

"And that is why everyone in town is upset—because she is Mary Cyr, and no one can find Florin—the child."

And now people in Oathoa had heard that a book about Mary Cyr's life was about to be published. That she was known in Canada, at least, as a very bad lady.

Everyone spoke about a book. A book was in the air. All the newspapers were full of her. So a book would have to be the next thing.

The book was the thing in which to catch the conscience of the queen, John thought—a rather sad thought about her empty life—a life that could have been so full—or was that a lie—that is, John in some way had come to believe her life was full and joyous and she was innocent and joyous, and they were willing to kill something innocent and joyous too, because she had been born into a family with money. He thought of Sharon DeRolfo walking backward in front of her with a camera, disinterestedly snapping pictures in the warm night air, now and then looking up, moving slightly to get a better angle, yelling to onlookers:

"*Copia de seguridad fuera del camino.*"

Back up out of the way.

And tossing her cigarette down as Mary tried to navigate in her leg shackles, now and again looking up pensively at the camera.

PART THREE

1.

THERE WERE BUILDINGS AND HOUSES MARY CYR HAD LIVED IN and owned, places in the world she had travelled with lovers she no longer knew—there were parties she had given hoping to be liked; and tons of money spent in a thousand ways.

There was the time off Portage Island when they said they were going to kidnap her. Two drunken young Native men she had trusted—that was when she was eighteen, and believed there were no criminals, just the misunderstood. (Oh, she knew very well there were criminals—what she wanted to let on was that she was liberal; she wanted, needed, to prove this to her friends. To the friends who said, "You don't know anyone, really." And to her enemies who said she was a bigot—a charge she would never get rid of. So she went out on a boat to prove them wrong.)

The two young men had gone out on a lark to steal some lobster traps, to reclaim their Indigenous rights, and she had gone with them for moral support.

But then they decided, after drinking hermit wine all afternoon in that treacherously blazing sun off the bay, that instead of lifting lobster traps, they could snatch her. They could hold her, in order to get all of their rights back. So they had a conference, speaking in Miq'maq while Mary sat listening, filing her nails and commenting now and again.

"I can't see you getting away with it, my dears," she said.

All of them were more than a little drunk, and she as drunk as they.

The First Nations boys decided they would reclaim and then resell the land her family's estate was on, and after reclaiming it, they demanded four million dollars. After keeping her for a day and night, Mary finally managed to talk them out of it, by saying it was not really her estate. And if they wanted, she would see to it they did get money if they could get the boat started and take her home.

When they returned from the island in a little outboard motorboat, she was handling the outboard motor, while the two young men sat up front with their hands on the gunnels, staring at the blue-green water.

She did not want to charge them, but the police had already become involved, and Nanesse and Garnet made it a point to. That meant it was brought before the courts with Mary Cyr as a witness. And that also meant that she tried to protect them when she was on the stand—which did make it seem as if she was in some way complicit.

The boys received two years less a day in jail. And then the rumours started—that she had set it all in motion herself, for the money. She wanted to get the money from Garnet and go to Cuba. Garnet actually believed this and asked John to investigate her. John said he would not.

Sixty days after they had returned in that motorboat the youngest Native boy, Charlie Francis, took his life in the Moncton jail. Was she blamed for that as well? In a way, yes. They said he and the other Native man had been forced into complying with her wishes to steal her family's money.

If that supposition was against her when she was eighteen, what would happen to her now?

He lay on the bed in his room, trying to look at his notes, and to think of her when she was little. He lit one damn cigarette after the other.

"I have my diary hidden in the room—please find it and destroy it," she had whispered. "It reminds me too much about too much of my past."

She had travelled to every continent in the world, she told him once.

"Except for Antarctica," he said.

"How do you know—in fact I have gone there too, on some kind of big damn ice-killing machine. And it's not half as nice as the brochure says it is, and all the penguins do is stand around and blink."

"Why do they blink?"

"If you ask me, they're snow-blind."

Was left as an orphan.

The years had flown by on crooked streets, avenues with no name, houses with terraces above cities she did not know, until this moment.

2.

AFTER HE GAVE HER PLU HE WENT BACK TO HIS ROOM. HE TOOK the diary from the garbage bag he had placed it in, and began to flip through it.

He discovered that they were in France when Mary Cyr met the Russian ambassador. It was a big, big plush place, as Mary Cyr noted, with "lots of plushes around—red chairs and things!"

There was a publisher there too, one of the French publishers, and a woman, a patron to the arts named Madame Something-or-other, who coughed right in Mary Cyr's face, and talked about someone's wine empire.

"Empires come and go," Mary Cyr said, because she had heard that on television; Mary Cyr was seven when she said this. Her mother was a British woman, completely out of fashion in the new Canada and thought to be small-minded.

Mary heard it as if by osmosis. The British had destroyed everyone in Canada, didn't you know? And her mother was British. She did not think of it, however—in any particular way—when she was seven or eight or nine, until she was one night invited to sit at the big table, with the adults. It must have been in the early seventies by that time.

That's when she met the man named Ernest Vanderflutin, the son of one of the men her grandfather had helped in the Netherlands. Ernest had come east to discuss selling his shares in the iron ore mine.

Yes, he was young. Yes, he was tall. Yes, he was good-looking. Yes, he had finished his doctoral thesis; yes, he had written a book.

Then at supper there was a sharp disagreement between Vanderflutin and her mother, over British imperialism. (Or this is how she remembered it.) It might not have been anything, but Mary always made a great deal of it. She always hated the idea of how her mother was ostracized that night—ganged up on. And she never forgave any of them.

Whatever happened—whatever it was—it turned her against this man. And it turned her against Nanesse and Garnet for taking his side.

"Why?" John said, when she was seventeen, telling him about it for the first time.

She thought for a moment—a long moment.

"Because," she answered slowly, "whatever Ernest Vanderflutin was in favour of seemed at that moment so easy to be in favour of—it is like those men who continually bash the Catholic Church—at one time they were probably all little towheaded snitches for the Brothers and acted in little plays about Bethlehem. The ones people like myself would never get picked for."

She looked at him and gave a small intense smile, one that disappeared as suddenly as he had seen it. It allowed one to see she had battle scars.

"Vanderflutin struck me as the same. His father owned land, farmland out west, that had been taken at some point from the First Nations—but all of a sudden it wasn't *them*—it had to be a bigger target, a bigger scapegoat: the British—they seem to be the easiest to blame—they were the racists, the imperialists. I found that out, that night long ago. Vanderflutin was white and hid behind First Nations prowess he did not possess in order to scapegoat the Brits. My mom simply became collateral damage. Yes, I am sure some Brits were sons of bitches, just like some Dutchmen. Anyway, I have met enough First Nations sons of bitches to know it is a sham anyway—so being called racist by them is probably a blessing. It is like being called a sexist by some feminists—it is a badge of honour—which you, John, must well know by now. So I care for no opinion. How I wanted him to like my mother and me—but now I care less." She said this as pollen blew in the air about her head, and the smell of sweet flowers mingled with the drafts of heat and paint.

"So I don't give a damn," she said.

But in a way, of course, she did. It hurt her very deeply, as a condemnation always will.

"Sticks and stones may break my bones, but names will never hurt me" was also a lie.

Besides, she said, Ernest was likeable, yet young and quite silent about the Dutch and French participation in the divvying up of the world.

"The diamonds and the rubber trees, and the rest of the fuckin' swag and loot," she said. "So everyone, he said, hated and made fun of the English—and had the table laughing—the Irish hated us, the French, the Americans and the whole bloody lot—so I said, well—let's see if I can't fight back. My best weapon is my counterpunch."

"That night—"

"Well—if not soon after."

That long-ago night when he visited the house to receive the offer for the New Brunswick mine, Ernest said that British Loyalists had destroyed New Brunswick.

"I'm glad the French are still to be found here—they did not manage to get rid of all of you," he said. *"Comment peut-on dire qu'ils ont une joie de vivre?"*

Nanesse being an Acadian girl (though she had lived much of her childhood in Quebec) was very delighted by this turn of events. She had not expected it—and she looked with piety and triumph at her archrival— Mary Cyr's mother, Elaine, that little English *salope*. Of course this was the subtle grasp for power within the family that Elaine, never welcome as a war bride, did not really understand. In fact her little daughter, Mary Cyr, saw it much quicker than she did.

"Les maudits anglais," Nan was capable of saying at least eight times a day.

"So, Mr. Vanderflutin, you are on our side," Nan said. (She pretended she meant on the side of the table, which meant Mrs. Cyr as well, but Mary knew instinctively that nothing could be further from the truth, and it was a way to further ostracize her mother, who had not lost a smidgen of her mild British accent.)

"Oh, of course I am always on the side of the underdog, the Métis and the First Nations." He smiled. "What good person wouldn't be?"

"And you think like we do—finally someone who is progressive. We have to get rid of the mayor of Moncton—a bigot—and the mayor of Campbellton and Saint John—big English French-hating bigots."

"How absurd. In this day and age?" Ernest said.

So he had his opening and began to tell jokes.

At one point he said that he had heard the Natives could smell the English a mile away, and that the English knew nothing about horses, and would continually lose them. Nanesse laughed very gaily at all of this, though she herself could not go into a barn without coming down with hives if a horse was in it. And neither in fact could Ernest.

However, Ernest spoke this in French to the more progressive end of the table.

"*Ils peuvent sentir des kilomètres,*" he said.

"*Mon Dieu! Non, je ne le crois pas.*"

"*Oui,*" Vanderflutin said, his face filled with pork chop and mirth.

All of this had started earlier in the day, when he was talking about soccer and European rivers. That is, at twenty-four he had to tell all he knew, about what he knew, to everyone he knew, believing that before himself no one ever knew.

Garnet had said:

"How do you like the Miramichi?"

And he had answered:

"Oh—yes, well, pretty of course, but I'll be back on the Rhine soon." And smiled as if to say: *Nothing else could or should be said.*

Mary stared at him, as he spoke earlier in the day, with a strange and childlike curiosity, her head suddenly confused about something, and then went and had a bath.

As she lay up to her chin in the water, listening to the voice of the young man elucidating to them all the things he knew, and all the things he had done, and all the things he intended to do, she felt sorry for her mother, who seemed not to be included in any of the talk. She waited desperately to hear her mother's voice, and each time she heard it her mother was soon interrupted, and fell silent. She heard Nanesse tell her mother to bring a chair from the other room. Then tell her to take the cups away. All the while Ernest kept talking. And Mary Cyr all of ten or eleven was furious.

So little Mary Cyr dressed for supper that night, not sure of these thoughts she was having but realizing that she at least had them, and in having them she wanted to protect her mom from everyone else in that room. Her heart at that moment was filled with a protective and sorrowful love.

But it seemed there was no reason to speak of Europe at supper. No one spoke of it for the longest time. Well, Garnet did say that he had gone with his family to visit Beaverbrook's papers when he was a boy.

So Mary tried to cut her pork chop and was very silent. For the longest time no one was speaking about much of anything.

But Mary eyed Nan with her beautifully clever eyes. She knew something was coming. And she was right. Nan was waiting for an opening. And then someone at the far end of the table—a fellow, a former teacher of physics from St. Stephen—mentioned how pretty the Acadian villages were in winter.

Nan looked around the table. She took a drink of water from her crystal glass. She smiled at the compliment, even though she had never been in one of those houses.

"*Des maisons très belles,*" Vanderflutin said. Again there was a pause.

"Oh *oui,*" Mary said, hoping to stop Nan from speaking, "*Très belles— très belles*—a few more *très belles tout le monde—rootie tout le tout tout*—and a few more *très belles.*"

She laughed loudly at this, shaking her head at her own joke, thinking she had made quite the impression, but no one spoke to her. So she rubbed her nose with the inside of her wrist and picked at her pork chop again.

Then suddenly Nan said, in her most subversive and antagonizing way, that the villages would be even prettier if the British paid their enormous debt to good decent people; that their dealings in all the former territories were now being exposed, and they should pay restitution, starting in the provinces with the Acadians. Who suffered just like Mahatma Gandhi in India.

"It would come to billions," she said, putting potatoes on her fork. "Yes—billons upon billions," she said, covering the potatoes with green beans.

"*Mais les anglais ne payeront pas,*" she said, giving a quick frown and shake to her head. "*Mais les anglais ne payeront pas,*" she repeated.

"*Oui, ils le feront!*" Vanderflutin declared, with astonishing compassion. "*Il y a un règlement de comptes à venir.*"

He was looking at Mary Cyr as he said this, thinking that she must be some little radical. But she didn't have a clue what he said, and only said, looking about for dessert:

"*Où est le grand . . .* cupcake?"

But no one paid her any mind at all. They all looked at him. Nan stopped chewing, and then continued chewing slowly.

Vanderflutin nodded. Yes, everyone wanted him to shed light on it. That is what he had done his doctorate on: British imperialism in the colonies. So he took a gulp of water and cleared his throat. Then he smiled at them all. He began to mention stodgy names and poor legislators, factors in land disputes, hidden and secret betrayals by people like Sir John A MacDonald, and very bogus land claims.

"I have come to the astonishing conclusion that the world would have been much better off without the British," he said. "Or I should say better off if the British hadn't left their foggy Isle."

He was quite animated, but he, as a historian and political scientist, did not understand one basic thing: the *Balkanization* of this little household.

In fact Mary Cyr had four nationalities in her—Irish, Scottish, French and English—and very likely Micmac as well. So at this supper, listening to Nan and their guest, she would decide *who she was once and for all.* And she would never waver once she decided.

"The English did nothing in the Second World War either, and wouldn't have lasted without the Americans," Nan said. "Isn't that true, Ernest. Churchill with all his aimless puffing of his cigars—as much of a tyrant as anyone else I would say."

"Quite true," Ernest said, lifting his fork to make his point.

Suddenly Mary thought in her mind's eye of her mother, who, as Mary's father had told her one night, had run up ladders during the Blitz to throw buckets of water on burning roofs; sitting there politely as Mr. Vanderflutin spoke about the decimation and the ruining of culture English people did. Even if it was true—it was truth told to do the devil's work—and she would not forgive him.

Mary was sitting at the farthest end of the table of about fourteen people. It was the very first night she had been allowed to sit at the big table. There were lilies floating in a glass bowl—the bowl was smoky, and she could see her face distorted in it. During the first course of the dinner she made faces at herself, in this bowl, until Nan told her to stop.

Then she picked up her napkin and tucked it under her chin. She yawned and then pretended to smile, so as not to be rude.

But as the meal progressed, and as her father was not at home, she saw how the family had turned on her mom, without having the decency to say they were—who now had no one to shield her. Their family was Scottish and French—but she, because of her mom, was half British. So she had to suddenly make a choice. It happens in very subtle ways in almost every Maritime family sooner or later.

"Oh, my *père* too—old *père*—said the *anglais* knew nothing," Nan said. "We were here hundreds of years before them—yes—let me tell you—we loved the First Nations and they loved us. THEY LOVED US! They hated the British, and all their schemes, but they loved US."

"*C'est la même chose dans l'ouest, je suis* afraid," said young Vanderflutin.

Mary looked at her mom and winked her support. She saw her mother's lips tremble. That wink would be the wink that was her destiny. That tremble would never be forgotten.

For the next half-hour or so, at everything Vanderflutin mentioned about anything, did not matter what, Mary would give a great "Ahh—haaa!" And then put her head down.

"No—I didn't do much farming myself," said Vanderflutin.

"Ahh—haaa."

Or:

"No, I have never fired a rifle—I had one—I didn't fire it."

"Ahh—hhaaa."

Enough to make everyone look at her, and then she would be silent.

Then, during a brief silence, she said to herself:

"I had one once—I didn't fire it. Ha." And started to giggle uncontrollably.

"*Marie—mon Dieu, mon enfant—mon enfant terrible,*" Nan said.

"Shhhh," her mother said, for the fifth time.

3.

SO SHE WAS TRYING TO EAT HER PIE AND LISTEN VERY CAREFULLY while not spilling anything on her red dress. She could still feel water in her ears from the bath she had had before supper, and once in a while she would give her head a shake, or pound one side of it with her hand.

But then at a pivotal moment, just when Garnet and Nan had joined in against the Brits, and the Expulsion, which they said destroyed thousands of lives, and her father was not home to protect her mom, Mary spoke up. Her voice changed. It did not become older; it became, however, purposeful and strangely hypnotic. And her eyes showed flashes of brilliance as they darted here and there.

"Well," Mary said, "that is not very nice of you, Mr. Vanderflutter—even if Aunt Nan thinks so."

"It's Vanderflutin." Ernest smiled. He was still feeling the general giddy emancipation of the table, and did not catch what Mary had said.

Still, she kept her eyes averted, and suddenly spoke most solemnly to her pie plate, but very quietly so it was hard to hear her.

"I am sure it is exactly like something like that. I mean a Flutter or a Flutten," Mary Cyr said, now looking straight ahead, now casting a short bright glance his way. "But still you are at our house, and have just gotten a nice piece of pie—and you should eat it. For my mother is British. And she didn't mean to be British, but she is. So it is very mean of you and my aunt and uncle to say those mean things about her country. She did not mean to kill all the Indians, perhaps just some of them, or expulse all those Frenchies, but I guess—well, maybe they had it coming. Who knows what they would have done to the British in their place. Maybe boiled them up or something—ha ha ha— off with their heads, because well, there was a big revolution in France and they went about doing that to everyone—even killing their own queen, who had a nice wig, which I saw in a picture—and was wondering so much if she wore her nice wig when her head was lopped off— and I wondered too if the French ever really forgave themselves for being so—mean!"

"Mary," her mother said. "You are being rude—very rude, dear."

"Mean, to their queen," Mary finished. Then she took a big gulp of milk, which gave her a moustache. "Yes, a bit mean to their queen!" And then she sang:

"Riding in a cart up to the head off chop!"

Vanderflutin up until that moment did not know Mrs. Elaine Cyr was British. He had simply assumed she was so quiet because he himself was so brilliant.

Now he did not want to backtrack, just explain.

"I am talking about imperialism, which was a disaster for many a country, dear. It is what kept the class system here. Someday you will understand what it is I am saying. I am seeking a new awareness for women and men."

"The class system, that's it exactly—that's it exactly!!" Nanesse agree with a certain triumph.

Mary was silent. The whole table was silent. Everything seemed silent. For a while. Then suddenly Mary spoke; said in a strange almost altered voice:

"But you are saying bad, bad things about—my mommy in a way—I mean—my ear here is all plugged up a bit—but in a way, so if you do, I will not like you And from eight this morning I waited to meet you and like you because my mother wanted to meet you and like you, because she said, what is that word—big word, hmm—no, no—the word—made her excited last night to tell me you were coming—the word—*INTELLECTUAL*—and she wanted to talk to you, because you had your degree or what it was called—and now—look what it has become."

She gave her head another pound or two while she said this.

"*Elle a été touchée à la tête et elle est souvent confondue,*" Nan said, with a severe look toward Mary's mother.

"Ah." Vanderflutin nodded and smiled. Of course that had to be it! He smiled as if he had finally caught on. That's why she was pounding her head. That's why she laughed about his rifle. She was an idiot.

"Well, I certainly want you and your mom to like me," Ernest said, and looked at Nanesse and winked.

"We are not making fun of your mom," Nanesse said. "And Mary, dear, you are part French." Then she looked at her husband. "*Mon Dieu, elle est partie française.*" And she gave a look of slight mortification.

"Well, we are not making fun of the French, are we—are we? And what may I ask—just to ask—is Mr. Vanderflutter?"

"I am Dutch, dear."

"Ah. I see," Mary said mysteriously. "Well I suppose being Dutch is fine!"

Then she was silent and the meal continued. And Ernest reached over and patted Mary's head and smiled at Nanesse again, to show he knew she was something of an invalid, a "special person," as he was taught to call them.

"And what do you do?" Mary asked after a certain amount of time.

"I am a writer."

"A good one?"

"I hope so."

Everyone laughed at this, and Mary laughed as well, became giddy and got the hiccups, took a drink of milk to calm herself.

"There there there," Ernest said, patting her gently on the back.

But he would envy little Mary Cyr from this moment on—and be determined to both destroy her and impress her. And he would never manage to do either.

"Tell us about yourself, Mr. Vanderflutin," Nan said, and she reached over and squeezed his hand a moment.

He began to speak about his doctorate and his supervisor and how he wanted to have his book about a criminal English raid on a First Nations tribe published by "*the* Canadian publisher."

Nan nodded, and then said she proposed a toast to Vanderflutin and his *caring and concern.*

"It is so good to have a man who bravely tells the truth at our table, who will stand up for what must be said and say it. I am delighted that you have come here tonight!" Nanesse said, adding as she stood, "Let us toast Mr. Vanderflutin!"

So they all did this. Elaine picked up her gin and drank, and then had the maid get her another gin. Mary watched her mom carefully, and then studied Nan and Vanderflutin closely. She knew something was desperately wrong with the evening. Later she was to see it in university, among academics and civil servants. She would never find an answer to them. She would also at times fall for it herself.

Now, however, she began to question whatever it was he said. Rarely had a mother so defenceless been defended so well by a little girl. And Elaine was by turns mortified and honoured by her.

Mary seemed to be in a certain state where she couldn't stop herself. Her face looked red and hot, and her eyes looked from one person to the other in complete defiance. It was the defiance of a person who would always find her best courage when backed into a corner. People did become concerned about her. But she realized now, she did not have a friend at the table. Most just thought she was being a saucy child, very ordinary at dinner parties with the spoiled. They tried to ignore her.

"Mary," Nanesse said, snapping her fingers in front of her face.

Twice they said the discussion was over, but twice Mary continued on. That is, she would be silent—everyone would hear the embarassed clink of forks or spoons, and then she would say:

"But—just a minute—wait a minute—so I am thinking it couldn't be like that—I mean making her feel bad, why should you, you see, Mommy wasn't even born yet—and besides why was the raid just by the English—the man you mentioned sounds Irish to me—or Scottish—and you said the fort was called Macleod, so perhaps you really do not know the difference between one country and another—you yourself have a house out there—was that on Native land, I wonder, at any time in the past maybe three hundred years—then if you think the English took land, you should up and give yours back too? Sorry, I got a bunch of hiccups. Forgive me while I begin to hiccup."

Hic

"Mary."

"I am only thinking of something."

A long pause.

A hiccup.

"Wall Street—" Mary shouted, suddenly, and looked from one to the other. "Yes, I heard it at school—just last month—Mrs. Fletcher—Fletcher the Wretcher because she has morning sickness someone said, which whatever that is—anyway, she says one day—the *Dutch*—and you say you are—" (here she pointed one little finger at him) "put up Wall Street in New Amsterdam to keep the dirty natives out—that's how much they loved their good ole Indian pals."

"Mary, stop."

"I am done—"

Silence.

"Done like this dinner."

Silence.

The polite scrapping of forks and a small mention of the weather.

Hic

Silence

Then—yelling:

"What is that word—word—that word everyone is always looking for—oh, just a minute, I dropped my fork here—there—ha—got it. No—that word—word—oh yes—well, I was hit in the head, you know, which is what everyone always tells me—you can't be right about Nazi uniforms because you had one hell of a wack in the noggin—oh—yes—FRAUD."

"*Elle est hors de son esprit*," Nan said, and then in English to Mrs. Cyr, "She is out of her mind."

"Mary. Stop this instant!"

But Mary had gone into a trance, lolling her head back and forth.

"*The* Canadian publisher—yes, yes, how great that must be! I bet you if they ever did have a truly great writer there, they would scorn him, and ridicule his greatest books. And lie about him. So I guess you will have no fear of being ridiculed by them."

"Mary."

"Okay—I will."

Silence.

"Become a writer too—and show you all—maybe do up some poems:

" 'There was a wobbly Dutch boy

Who had a great big plan

To blame the good old English

While living on Indian land.' "

"Mary that is enough."

The scraping of forks and knives.

Then silence. Then once again, suddenly furiously:

"I don't think you have a clue about the woods or the rivers, like my father or my friends' fathers —oh, I have a rifle, but I never fired it—like the French in the war!"

"Mary, leave the table."

She took off her napkin, left the table, walked all the way around it, and came back to her seat, picked up her napkin and tucked it under her chin again.

Nanesse spoke while looking at Mary and then slowly looking down the table toward Mary's mother: "She is a confused young girl and a very saucy one—she has learned things from *someone* about the Second World war –and certain things that are incorrect, but she has yet to learn about her Acadian culture, unfortunately."

The former teacher from St. Stephen, the one who had inadvertently started this debacle but mentioning the charm of Acadian houses, looked far down the table at this little girl and was overcome by her, realizing that all her splendid fury, her bright eyes and the expressive movements of her hands, were because she was Acadian, and that she was valiantly protected her mother, who was not. He felt he was seeing the traits of a very brave child. He knew something of her father, also an Acadian, who had gallantly flown a spitfire with 292 Squadron in Britain, and thought of that man's genes now conducting the fury in Mary Cyr. He would remember her forever, having met her this once. He would remember her as an Acadian child protecting her British mother, and taking on all comers.

There was a long silence. Nan began to converse in French—which was a clue about what the rest of the night should involve. It should not involve the deranged young daughter of the frivolous Englishwoman, who had married the son who was in competition with her own husband over the business.

"*J'adore les orchidées, mais ma peau est pâle,*" she said out of the blue, looking across at the orchids on the table.

"Oh, *mais votre peau est belle,*" said Ernest Vanderflutin.

"*Auparavant, il y a longtemps,*" Nan said, smiling. She looked at Mary's mother to join in, knowing she could not speak French. It was a way she had of maintaining an upper hand while pretending to offer help.

Mary listened to this quite politely and then, with her head down, looking at her pie, spoke:

"Daddy said to me just the other week or so that my mother was in England watching the battles over her head between Spitfires and those damn Messerschmitts—how many of us here were doing so?"

"Mary!"

And then she said more petulantly:

"Running with buckets to put out fires—up on ladders—while Nan was somewhere snoozing in Quebec—keeping her skin on. I don't know what the Dutch were doing, but I can bet it wasn't that much."

And then as she chewed her pie like you would bubble gum, and sat back as if suddenly exhausted; and full, she continued as she pushed her plate aside and gave a small belch:

"I am going to tell the table this—all of you!! You should realize you should be nice—to British people—and even to the French people, like Aunt Nan, who is certainly hard to be nice to."

"Mary," her mother said. "I am not at all upset—so dear, don't you be."

Then her mother said, as if to mollify the tension:

"Yes, well, some of the British were real bastards!" Everyone laughed and agreed with her that they were.

Vanderflutin smiled and suddenly lighted a cigarette, patting Mary on the back and looking up at exhaled smoke as he did so. There was again a painful silence. Except the man from St. Stephen asked quite politely for another butter roll. Vanderflutin drawing on his smoke, holding it in long nervous fingers was content to now discuss his love of libraries. His trips to the Sorbonne and his time spent in Italy. He mentioned his genuine love of François Villon.

So Mary paused, bent forward and tried to pick up the last piece of her pie with her fork. It fell to her plate and she looked up quickly, hoping Vanderflutin did not see it fall. Then she tried to fix the bow in her hair. Then she suddenly whispered while looking at her plate:

"Some of the British were real bastards. And I am sure some of the Dutch were not."

"Mary!" her mother cautioned. And she stood up to take her away from the table.

Suddenly her father came into the room. He stood at the door, smiling at her. He had come back from a five-night visit to camps in the woods. She felt her heart lift—she looked at Vanderflutin, who nodded, looked grave and ashen-faced and said nothing for the rest of the meal. Nor did Nan, who was intimidated by her younger brother-in-law. If Mary or her mother had just once mentioned what Nan and Ernest Vanderflutin were saying, her father would have been enraged. He had flown a Spitfire in the war, and later brought his bride home from England—he loved her like he loved no one except Mary, and he hated two things: demeaning a person because of nationality or because of religion. In fact he would never do so to the Dutch, who he knew had suffered much during the war. But Mary—Mary Cyr could not bring herself to speak.

Her mother was a beauty then, with wonderful brown eyes, and Mary was quite right—she had seen much terror in the skies. She had tried to save her own father, who had been trapped in a burning building. She held his hand while he died. Her right hand had been scarred by the fire. It was "whittled down," as Mary sometimes said. She covered it with a glove most times, and at other times left it under her shawl when she sat by the evening fire.

Sadly it is what caused little Mary Cyr to begin a life of nightmares. It is what caused her mother to be an alcoholic.

An old woman a distant member of the family—one of Nan's aunts, who lived in some part of one of their houses—shouted at Mary Cyr one day because she was making too much noise, pointing at her as if she was frightened:

"You will burn up just like your English granddaddy—" and laughed loudly and spit.

Mary could never get that out of her mind.

However, this particular dinner party was written about in her diary only years after it had occurred—so had she really said all this? Or had she made it up? Had she really recited that poem, or, more likely, had she just included it as an afterthought? Much of it may have been imagined.

John did not know. He, however, did know this: she would always take on whom she had to, no matter what the cost to herself.

4.

AFTER SUPPER, IN THE BIG SQUARE MAHOGANY WOOD STUDY where Garnet and the foreman of the woodlot operations—and her father—met, Mr. Vanderflutin sat there expecting their rather handsome offer to be made with appeals to him to accept.

Mary sat outside the room, and watched his shadow. It was a very tall shadow, for he was very tall, and a thin shadow, for he was thin, and it was, as Mary once said, a very thoughtful shadow, for Vanderflutin was thoughtful.

He was thinking of three million dollars. What he got was accounts overdrawn, the amount of ore brought out, the need to sink a new shaft, make a new rail line out to town; bank notices that the Cyr family had overseen to keep the mine going. He got to see his father's intemperate spending, his fly-by-night schemes to become a great Dutch merchant. What Blair Cyr thought at this time was that Dug Vanderflutin had been a hero in the Dutch resistance—he had certainly invented himself as one—and at this moment no one had any idea that this was not the case. And so there was a good deal of sympathy for his son.

What Ernest Vanderflutin got was an offer of $201,000 in a certified cheque, and as Mary's father said:

"Take it or leave it, Ernie—but it is the best we can do at the moment. Really there is nothing more."

He sat there fidgeting with his hat, and Mary felt sorry for him. In fact, she ran to him suddenly and handed him a stick of Doublemint gum.

He took the gum, and smiled wanly. And he took the offer.

This would give them controlling shares of a mine they did not really want, and because of what they had already invested from 1959 on, controlling foreign shares of a coal mine in Mexico. But the New Brunswick iron ore mine needed upgrades.

"We must go to see if number three shaft will be flooded," Garnet said to her father later.

It was a day's drive by car, an hour by plane.

"Sure, we can fly over tomorrow morning, because I promised Mary I would be home tomorrow night," her father said, while he held Mary in his left arm.

Just off the cuff—like that. Nary a thought that it would cost him his life.

Just before her father put her to bed that night, she made him promise that when he came back, they would look for the picture of Dug Vanderflutin that she had seen in a book.

"Well, when I come back, we will look for it—you and I," he said.

But he did not come home.

As for Nan, she would tell her elderly aunt a week later that:

"*Elle va étudier dans un couvent afin de maintenir son français.*"

Mary Cyr was to go to a convent and study French. She would become French.

As she was supposed to be. And those terrible outbursts had something to do with it.

So everything was set in motion at that crucial moment in Mary Cyr's life. All because of a Dutch boy who hid behind a Native prowess he himself could never share, and Mary was too stubborn to let him pretend he could.

Later she would be proposed to by another western boy of the same stamp. She kept running into them wherever she went, so there must have been many of them around.

Later Mary Cyr told John in dribs and drabs many of these stories. And after her mother died, she hated—or pretended to—those "neutral bastards," who did not take a stand in the Second World War. Especially the

Dutch and the Irish. And most especially Quebec. Ernest was Dutch; Nanesse spent her childhood in Quebec; she threw the Irish in for good measure after she had, she said, "Read up on the pricks" like De Valera and Stephen Hayes.

"Irish. Who could ever kick who was down in the teeth with more glee than the fuckin' Irish?" she asked him once. "For all their St. Paddy's Day bull."

"I am partly Irish and so are you."

"I got so many people packed into me I don't even notice them squirming around in there," she said.

She had a list. A list, she said, "As long as your arm."

That started, she said, with brave men basking in Harvard while Canadian boys in Spitfires roared up to the clouds to tip the wings of VI rockets so they would fall into the sea. One youngster who did that was her father.

"But you know how much the Dutch suffered," he said once.

"Yes," she said quickly. "I know. And so did Anne Frank, having to climb those stairs, up and up to the last attic in the fuckin' world she would ever see."

In fact he had just found out that for years Mary had a Dutch pen pal she called "My dear, dear little Dutch friend."

He also learned over time that she called the English to task over those very Acadians she had rebelled against and those Irish too. That was later, when she was in England with the very rich and important.

In the end she didn't even have a cross thing to say about Mr. Vanderflutin. In fact her last three entries about him were full of guilt and love.

Once she showed John a big glossy picture book called *The German Soldier as Paris Tourist from 1940–44.*

She looked at him very politely and said:

"One must ask why they were able to be tourists."

Yes, she was a good hater, even if she too was partly French, and even if in her compassion she could hate no one at all. No one at all! (Which in John's mind is what the liberal progressive thinkers, like the First Nations actor who called her a white racist, never understood.)

Once years ago she told him that secretly she had always felt sorry for President Nixon. Because a man her uncle knew, and whom she did not like at all, once said:

"We got him!"

He had come into the room saying, "We got him!" before he had even said hello. He was a tall professor named Flowers.

"You see," Mary Cyr said to John with a wise little whisper, "that gave it all away. So I couldn't be mean to Mr. Nixon after that."

She told John she had tried not to tell people she had felt even the least sorry for Mr. Nixon. No one else would.

"We'll get all the bastards," this man said.

Mary Cyr thought for a while and then said to this man:

"He visited China."

"What does that matter?"

"Well, have you?"

No one answered her, so she put her head down and studied her soup. Then she brightened a little and said:

"And he took his girlfriend—which was nice."

"What girlfriend?" her mom asked.

"That one—the one they say every time he leaves to go somewhere— he is kissin' her."

"Oh, Mr. Kissinger."

"Yes, that's the one," she answered.

It was shortly after her father had died, so surely that was why she had compassion, and people forgave her.

5.

JOHN REMEMBERED MUCH OF THIS, THIS BRILLIANT ORIGINAL love of good-heartedness—even if by now she herself had forgotten. And *brilliant* was the word, and *love* was too, even though no one took her as being brilliant or loving.

"She was hit in the head—it caused some kind of hemorrhage or something; she is as dumb as a turnip," John was informed when he inquired about her, when she was about twelve or thirteen. That was because she would stare at the wall for days after her father died, not speaking to a soul. She at times slurred her words.

One doctor said she was suffering from a kind of epilepsy, another that she had had a trauma to the brain, and maybe even adding it up, some swelling to the brain, which caused her to imagine a past that did not exist—and one could not believe what she said.

"So do you know anything about this?" he asked.

"No—not a great deal," John said.

"People, you see," the doctor continued, smiling, "are probably very kind to her—but in her state she doesn't think so, and she will never forget an injury—mark my words—she will remember the slightest injury ever since she hit her head when she was little."

He said this both as if there was nothing that could be done for her and that he was actually happy this was so.

Her father, she once told John, had always tried to be fair.

And then she asked:

"Didn't he?"

"Yes—I am sure of it," John answered.

"Even with all his money? Like his two hundred dollars in his pocket or what it was?"

"Yes."

"Well, then I will be determined to be fair."

Then later, when she was twenty-two, and an absolutely beautiful woman, she said:

"You know I will give the world away—but I won't if people ask me for it."

She had begged John to marry her—why in God's name hadn't he?

———

Her mother came to Canada wooed by her dad, with love letters two a day; came to a great family, and found herself in some way dwarfed by it—or at least out of place here. Her downfall was her Britishness at a time when the British were the easy target being pilloried in books and plays, shown in American movies to be treacherous; when the monarchy was looked upon as a farcical, silly thing that disregarded Quebec. And Mrs. Elaine Cyr listened to this year after year without comment; in fact, without even being allowed to agree.

But Mary would never be so accommodating.

"I will never betray you, Mom," she said. "No matter if the world does— I will see to it that you are respected. I will take on anyone who says because you are English, you are bad."

Still, Mary worried about the money.

"Don't worry," her mother said. "You're rich enough."

"A quarter of a million or what?" Mary Cyr asked when she was twelve. "Enough to buy a sports car or what? Because honest to God that's all I ever want."

She was born the day President Kennedy died. As she was slapped on the bum (perhaps she didn't even have to be slapped) so came the word drifting up from Dallas, along the network her father and grandfather had mastered. It was a grey, cold day in New Brunswick when she was born, with little tiny pickaxes of snow falling from the blind sky. Here and there school buses were being loaded with children—and none of those children would be nearly as well to do as she was. Even naked at birth she had much more influence. Her mother cried, and cried, thinking of those women in Europe having to give birth during the Blitz or the bombing of Dresden. She cried for them, in her soul, because she heard:

"President Kennedy has died."

Later Mary said, very seriously, that she didn't quite get all the fuss.

"Why all the hubbub?" she said when she was nine. She told John that they were having dinner in a restaurant in Boston with an American her father knew. A senator or some such.

She tried to think of something to say about Americans.

"All the what, Mary?" her father said.

"All the hub—bbb—bub," she answered, staring at her ice cream and moving it about with a spoon; with a red ribbon in her black hair, she lifted her eyes quickly and then lowered them. "Jackie O. Why all the fuss?" she said. She stopped moving the spoon.

"I don't know," the American answered. "I have never been sure myself."

"Hubbbb-BBuuuub," Mary said once again, and then, "you take a hub bub and I'll take a huber bub—and I'll be in SCOOT LUND before ya!"

"Shhh," her mother said.

So she began to move the spoon again.

Then she said:

"Peace—that's really the big thing, isn't it, Mr. American Senator." Then she shyly put her head down and, moving her head to the right just a tad, said as if to herself: "I mean speak of hubbub—"

Nothing better.

PART FOUR

1.

IN THE FALL, IN THAT HOUSE THEY LIVED IN THEN ON A SPLENDID bit of land overlooking the great Miramichi Bay, there was some crimson flush of sun on a leather-backed chair, and the smell of gin. Mary would always think of night when she smelled gin. Or when she drank it—and she drank "tons." She learned to drink to take away the terrors after a certain time. That is, after her father died, and her mother was more and more excluded—until she ran away, then tried to get Mary back. But she had been away too long, and her chance had come and gone, and she was still a British citizen and Mary Cyr was a Canadian.

The driveway was long and lonely. Yet they only lived in one small part of the estate—that stretched to the grand house far beyond them. Blair's House, it was called—after her grandfather. But he was almost never there. There was a helicopter pad but rarely a helicopter.

After a while she was invited to spend holidays at relatives' places. Mary would wait alone, in the giant foyer of some house outside Saint John, where her cousins lived, with a suitcase and a small book bag, and people would open and close doors beyond her; hearing this she would stand up and wait, and then realize no one was coming to welcome her. Then she would hear another door open and she would stand up once again and unbutton her beautiful grey winter coat, thinking she was going to be taken in to see someone. All the presents she had saved for, spent her own money on, wrapped by her own hands, would be sitting beside her on the bench. But another side door would close, not the door to get her, and she would patiently button up her coat and sit down again with her suitcase at her feet. "All my cousins I love," she wrote. "I do hope they love me!"

They would remember her sooner or later, and she would be put at the very end of the table (sometimes they would have to clear a place for her) and then she would try to reach the glass of water that was hers, for the Christmas toast!

"Hurrah."

Then she would be put on the train, and travel home after the holidays, holding some small, significant present she was given, as night formed against the telephone wires and the shadows lengthened on the trees. It did not mean that they did not love her. It did mean they were all interested in themselves, in the business, in the future—the train would rock against the icy tracks, the window covered in ice, and she would lie with her head against the leather-backed seat, dreaming of when her mother would come home.

Her grandfather lived most of the time in the Bahamas. On the stairs wall in her grandparents' house in Saint John there was a picture of her mother speaking with Senator Jack Kennedy and Lord Beaverbrook, and another of her grandfather shaking hands with Winston Churchill. After a while her mother's picture with Kennedy was taken down—and Mary spent the entire spring of 1976 looking for it. The idea of her mother being an outcast made Mary an outcast. Like her mom she would someday travel the world. Trying to find peace.

The evening just before dinnertime the shadows spread out from the trees, and the cement water shed looked homeless and sometimes came the cry of a frightened bird. Sometimes two frightened birds.

The pinewood was red and the setting sun came down on it, on the shale of the driveway, on the old flag, on the bitter mud that was almost frozen, and yet still perfunctory under the waning light.

"I guess we own—houses of many kinds," Mary wrote when she was eleven.

They owned an oil refinery; they owned hundreds of thousands of hectares of land; they owned service stations, iron ore mines, docks, wharves, papers, steel, fishing camps; and yes, houses of many kinds.

2.

JOHN HAD BEEN CALLED TO HELP LOCATE HER FATHER'S BODY, because they did not want his death publicized before they were very sure. It was because of the markets, and what might or might not occur.

The Cessna was a speck far out on the ice, burning like a beacon. The snow was still numb and falling down. You started out walking toward the plane, and realized it was still miles away. The body unfortunately was never found.

Garnet had not taken the flight back. People had always said he wanted to get away because there was an old girlfriend he wanted to see that night.

"The luckiest piece of tail he ever had," some foreman of his said.

Still, Garnet had asked her father to go and inspect the shafts, so she blamed him for Murder.

"Murder most fowl," she wrote in her diary, and drew a little bird with an arrow through it. This diary was in John's possession—he had found it, luckily enough, before the Mexican police.

Worse, the diary showed all of her childlikeness. That is, it still had a little lock on it. John, whether or not he was supposed to, snapped the lock and began to read. He was hoping it might be about recent events and give him a name to go by. But it was a vastly different diary.

It had almost every day of her life in it—year after year after year—not a day missed—not anything left out, although sometimes only a line or two explained the day:

April 5, 1971
Mommy made me crakkers and chese

July 17, 1972
Got to go to the beech with my big white towell

October 29, 1975
Carved a pumpkin—I put it at the end of my bed to scare the hell out of me when I wake up.

Nov 1
The boys I met out trick or treating told me that my dad is alive. Then they ran. I followed them all night—all the way to the big highway.

"Where—" I said. I said, "Where is my dad?"

June 7, 1976
They won't let me have a dog, so I've captured 5 ants, and will train them to be my pets. However, I think I broke one's leg—it's kind of hobbling about, looking worried that the other ants will now begin to eat him.

August 1976
Mommy has gone away again—I am trying to sit in one place with a book on my head to balance myself—

April 29, 1978
Mr. Cruise told me, well, he just said any time you want to talk to me about your dad or mom, you come to my office and just knock.

May 4, 1978
I kind of talked a blue streak about my dad—how he was the best in the world, you wait and see!!!

September 28, 1978

I was there, so I told Mr. Cruise about my dad—and he said:

"My dear girl—my dear, dear girl" and I just went gulp—like 5 times.

November 19, 1978

Mr. Cruise took my virginity—should I tell Uncle Garnet?

November 21, 1978

Mother died today—sometime in the early morning—

Ker plunk.

3.

SO JOHN FOUND OUT MUCH, THAT HE WAS SUPPOSED OR NOT supposed to see. But much of it he knew.

For instance, she went to The Hague—but this was only mentioned by a line: "I am in The Hague—there are so many names!"

She was looking for something about Mr. Vanderflutin, who had made light of her mother at that dinner party—the first dinner party where she was allowed to sit at the big table. What she did find was something about Ernie Vanderflutin's father, his time during the war—and a picture from 1946 of a baby being carried through the jeering crowd by its mother, whose head had just been shaved, making her look like a lonely little bird. That child was Ernest Vanderflutin. From that moment on she could not help but feel terrible sorrow for him—even a touch of love.

She found all of this out before Vanderflutin did and said nothing about it. Even when she read things he had written against her own family. Things about her adoption by Nan, which she only discovered when she was fifteen. How he laughed at them for adopting her. No matter how she thought of them, she could never partake in his hatred. To laugh at a couple who adopted a child. But then, it was not her world, the world of menopausal men. Strange how it hurt her to have him out-raged at this; remembering Nan's blessing, her present and party and yes, her attempt at love.

John saw a small ticket saved from Den Haag Moerwijk. A train station.

And rain in Amsterdam. She discovered the Dutch were so fussy that if you crossed the street against the light, which she did by mistake, they would hiss at her. That's purity for you, ho, ho.

The ticket was unused and worth six guilders. There was some kind of trip to the forest where the palace sat. She visited Anne Frank's house, the place she hid. Then Mary left and travelled to Paris. She had dinner somewhere near the Eiffel Tower, went to Le Select, even though by that time she deplored Jean Paul Sarte and believed he once drank a bottle of wine there. (Or this is what she said in her diary.) Like John said, she was a very good hater.

Then she drifted over to Berlin, reversing the same route the German Panzers took in 1940. She went to the Neues Museum in all her delight-ful innocence to see one thing.

The bust of Nefertiti.

She stared at it for two solid hours. And then, as she wrote in her diary:

"I turned and left her to herself. To herself forever, goodbye."

4.

AT ANY RATE, THREE YEARS AFTER HER FATHER'S DEATH MARY'S life was in upheaval. Her mother had a boyfriend named Doc—some "long-dicked youngster," or "*La grande épée*," Mary overheard Garnet's wife say one night. (Mary was not supposed to hear this.)

Still, her mother wanted to destroy herself quickly, and that was not Nan's fault. Not Garnet's either. Her alcoholism was full-blown now.

Why did she hook up with Doc? This was to become part of Mary's obsession. Her note in the diary was:

"He tried to sell her Mercedes—the fight wasn't her fault!"

Her mother and Doc had gone to Europe—to Dénia, Spain. Her mother sent her a list of Spanish words to learn, and told her that someday they would live together in Alicante, near the warm Mediterranean Sea. And won't that be fun and lovely, her mother wrote.

"*Pescado*" Mary wrote in her diary a number of times, fish; and *jumo naranja*, orange juice.

So Mary was alone. She sat in the garden, against the evening breeze—once, she tried to kill herself by holding her breath.

John flitted through the pages of the diary—hoping to not see anything that might incriminate. But it was all a blasted incrimination of a sad life.

Then he realized this about Dénia:

Years later she would take her third husband there—the one who had chest hair. The one who was surprised that she actually had use of a Lear jet. The one John felt sorry for—

She sat in the front seat of the Lear, and he sat behind her—his whole body looking uneasy. He was actually shaking.

"Can I ask—well—who you are?" he asked. He wore his brother's suit, and his tie was too large, and his white shirt had a stiff collar. His shoes were big, brown and seven years old—and he had worn them only two times before.

"I am your wife."

"I know, but—is this—is this—well, is this your plane?"

"One of them—I think—yes."

"One of them?" he asked, gulping slightly.

The one whose name she kept forgetting. The one she brought to the villa and entered the patio, the interior palm trees under the moonlight, and sat in a wicker chair, with her hands on the arms and her feet flat on the marble floor, with a sudden smile on her face at how bewildered he was that she, Mary Cyr, could simply do this. The smile, however, was not guile or triumph—it was a smile almost of resignation. As if to say:

Yes, now you know—I have a bit of money—not too much—somewhere in the vicinity of a hundred or so million. My family has about nine billion. I think—not really that sure.

She placed her feet flat on the floor. And wiggled her two big toes.

What was *toe* in Spanish—she hadn't the foggiest. *Puntera,* was that it?

There was the sound of the Mediterranean against the night's black shore. And some people were making too much noise on the beach, with a patio light shining. There was a loud Spanish curse, and a slovenly inebriated woman walked by.

"Hell—where's Franco when you need him," Mary said.

"Pardon?" he asked.

"*Infierno—¿dónde es Franco cuando lo necesitas?*" she said.

She looked at him and gave a plaintive little smile—a little whimsical dash of teeth, her hair falling over her bright face. And then she went and got herself a glass of wine. Would this marriage last? She was praying it would last the night.

He could not say anything—he had lost his voice. He was petrified. She opened the bottle, with her back to him. It made a glorious pop. Then silence.

"When it is silent in a villa, you can sense the cold on your feet," she whispered.

The night was filled with the scent of glory and wine, and deep darkness down on the stone steps that led to the shore.

Oh God, if this could only last, she thought.

In her diary she wrote that she wasn't talking about her marriage.

Only about the night.

Her first husband was different. John drove down the highway, in his own car, with his .38 on the seat. Walked into the house, grabbed him by the neck, put the gun in his mouth and pulled the trigger.

It wasn't loaded.

It was, as far as he could think, perhaps the worst thing he would ever do. He told no one about it—not even himself.

"I'll sue—I'll sue—I'll sue the whole family for every cent they have—" the man said.

John went back to his house, and sat in the corner shaking.

"I did not do that," he told himself.

That is, if you asked him tomorrow to swear on a Bible that he had not done this, he would. Sometimes you just cannot admit to what you turned into, even if it was only for a second.

That's why Mary ended up forgiving them all. Perhaps even herself.

5.

THERE WAS THE SON OF A PAINTER SHE MET ONCE, ONE OF THOSE painter's sons—the type of man who was invited to a party only because he was the son of an artist, and made a point of being a radical because it was in vogue to act like Jesus (though he dismissed Jesus for more revolutionary principles) and save the world; who after his usual amount of rum bragged about how well he knew the poor, so began to needle her about who she was, and how much damage her family did with their monopoly on so much. You know, how much money and ruin and trees they had cut down—how many lives they had ruined. (Not the twenty thousand families they put to work.)

"We will expose your family sooner or later," he said. "You will be exposed."

She sat there, at fifteen years old, politely listening to him. She had dressed up for the party and had begged to be allowed to go—and there were grown-ups there, she pleaded with Nan. And she would come home by eleven. It was two nights after she had been officially adopted, and Nan did love her. So did Garnet. So did Perley. Though she would be reticent to take the adoption seriously, she loved them for trying.

And finally, our painter's son said, sneering:

"You and your bloody family with your Lear jet."

There was so much of that, defending herself against boys she did not know, boys who would be boys all their lives, and who did not know her.

Mary Cyr held up her hands, timidly showing four fingers.

"Four—Lear jets—at last count," she said.

Later, after everything else failed, he was studying to be a social worker, in a building her father had donated to the university.

When she was fourteen, her family sent her to boarding school. She packed her Plu, some cookies to share, a transistor radio to listen to the be bop a loo bop of the day, and eye liner.

In boarding school they talked about dropping acid and who might do it, and about a certain Mr. Cruise, who had nice buns. He spoke to them about marijuana, how it was easy to grow. He was subversive in a very noncommittal, intelligently theoretical and comfortable way. He was a man from the United States who had moved to Newfoundland because he had protested the Vietnam War; a man who had his degree from Memorial University and now taught English. He said the people there were very backward. He could imitate the premier of New Brunswick or Newfoundland and did it so successfully that everyone, even Mary, whose godfather was her father's friend Premier Hatfield, also laughed. He knew how to fix the problems of unemployment and poverty, and said he had devoted his life to doing so. He said he was going to change the system.

"I am subversive in all my tendencies and I want my children to be as well." (He called the students his "children," although he had none and would never have any of his own.) "But being subversive in this place is very trying on my nerves."

"Well, you be subversive and I'll be subversiver," Mary told him one day. She was intrigued by the idea of subversion, at least for a little while. Until she saw what it was.

That autumn she was fourteen she stood beside Cruise in the warm gummy gymnasium when he was speaking and the back of his jacket was covered in chalk dust, and he was saying something. He was so brilliant. As brilliant as a scientist. Some even whispered that he was a Chaucer Scholar, who shouldn't be here—he was wasting his talent in this boarding school for young heifers. He was a Chaucer Scholar from Newfoundland, which made it all the more romantic—romantically serious.

So after she met Cruise, she was going to be a rebel, and rebel against the system—and in fact, John knew, she did do this, in a way Cruise could never manage.

The idea was, especially for people like Cruise, that if you were any good, you shouldn't be here. But he was writing a long epic poem—about the poor:

> On the draught of land the poor come out
> And in their misery look about
> And looking about do they spy
> Grey, grim, grim grey assaults their eye.

Of couse it wasn't quite like that, but it was unfortunately something like that. Mary Cyr had memorized it. It stuck in her head so that even years later she could recite whole lines of it—seven or eight lines. This is what she started to recite to her third husband, Lucien, in Spain, after she poured the wine, and there was wind in the palm trees, and a German man was walking his dog, and there was a long lonely song playing, and someone clicking castanets and then things went silent.

"A man quite a bit like Chaucer wrote that," she said, looking at her poor befuddled bridegroom. And then shrugging, she said:

"Well, what do you want to do—let's see—I bet you a thousand I can pee standing up!"

She got no reaction from either declaration.

6.

MANY OF THE GIRLS SAID MR. CRUISE WAS DEVOTED TO THE underprivileged, and even fed them at a soup kitchen. This made her angry at herself and her own family's wealth. She told Mr. Cruise, about how sorry she was that her family had money.

"You are the only one to understand!" she said, blushing and hoping he not dislike her.

That is, her family had millions; owned papers, oil, shipping—all those things that ended with *et cetera*.

Especially when she heard of how many millions. Like, it wasn't a million—her mother had along with her brother-in-law the Cyr fortune—and their part—not the greatest part by any means (that was owned by the other, more stable, side of the family, mind you) but still a nice healthy wad of it—was somewhere near the vicinity of 380 million.

But Cruise was here to teach them—to:

"Teach these rich young ladybugs what the world is all about."

And the silly man had actually read enough required literature to think he knew about the very world his job had allowed him to hide from. He had joined enough protests, he had caused his parents enough grief. Yet Mary knew at fourteen, or at least suspected, something was wrong with certain planks on his socialist platform. She did not quite know what—but something. She was, you see, that smart. But she was in awe of him, and how he could say:

Whan that Aprill with his shoures soote
The droghte of March hath perced to the roote,
And bathed every veyne in swich licour.

Yes, it was true—she was in awe of him. She knew that. She needed someone to like her and she wanted it so much to be him. To be liked by this fresh-faced tow-headed radical to young ladies (and it seemed young ladies only), with his blond hair a tad longer than most, and parted to one side, wearing owlish glasses and smoking a pipe. And on occasion wearing leather cowboy boots. And speaking of the problems that faced in the world, which it seemed only certain liberated people could solve. He did not know that he, too, was a product of his time.

Sometimes she followed him and him not knowing she was there—and she was thinking, that she wanted to prove to him something, and she thought often of him, in the long melancholy days when she was alone:

A knyght ther was, and that a worthy man,
That fro the tyme that he first bigan
To riden out, he loved chivalrie.

Chivalry, he told her—all along any watchtower that was the required thing for men. If men did not have *chivalry* toward women—God help them!

And this is what he had taped to the front of his office desk:

"O scathful harm, condition of poverte"—Chaucer!

And she said to him sitting on a bench beside the gymnasium when all the world was covered in an inch of snow and her right knee was itchy:

"I cannot find my father."

And she looked up at him, almost terrified.

"I dream, you see—like Daddy is there—and I well, go there, and then he has his back turned and is walking away—" she paused and gulped a tiny tad "—you see?"

But then quite as out of the blue as her father's death, she suddenly heard one night when she was following him:

"Mary Cyr—perky little ass on her," Mr. Cruise say. "In her little school uniform with those gorgeous, beautifully pointed little titties— my my. That's the girl who should be taught with her white panties slowly taken down."

He laughed a guffaw and guffawed again, once or twice all the way up the street. She assumed she was not supposed to hear this; she had been walking on the other side of the long, interconnected rows of hedges and it was close to ten in the evening, and he was talking to someone from the tavern down the street.

The very next day he lit a cigarette and gave her a puff in secret; he said he would show her a marijuana plant—but *not to tell*. He moved his blond hair out of his eyes as he spoke, and sunlight came through the large rectangular window.

"Oh no," she said, blushing. "I wouldn't tell."

"You promise you won't—for the secrets are just between us?" And he touched her back. She flushed and he guffawed and later they walked down the wonderful road.

"You take the high road and I'll take the low road, and I'll have a guffaw before ya!" she said like the child she was. So he spoke to her about going to Edinburgh on sabbatical.

"Maybe if you want and it all goes well, we can go together?"

"Oh wow," she said, and again she blushed and smiled.

Scottish too—yes, learning Gallic—that was a big thing for Mary. She knew eight words. But Cruise was for the poor. *Poor little driblets. Little Celtic driblets.* So she was for the poor too—and asked John when she was home to take her to some poor people. (In fact John knew this was a façade—because she knew poor people—she always had—.)

To her Cruise was sensitive. That's what Mary and so many other girls thought. Sensitive—a beacon of light to young ladies. She was like a moth. That's what she thought one night—a splendid little moth-like creature flitting toward him. And she knew if she could impress him, perhaps others would be impressed as well.

For this is what Mary hoped to convince people of, even though she had like, about, around, somewhere, the fact was, 380 million in her arse pocket. She needed to prove once and for all that she too was *understanding*. It was a very great thing back then, and as time passed, to be understanding. So many loud obnoxious and overbearing men and women told her she must be. And so for a little while she tried.

Cruise's first name started with an *N*—Nigel—so she called him

NC, and they sang when they walked down to the beach to see the marijuana plant. He slapped her little bum—like that, a tiny slap—just a momentary blush on her white buttock. It made her feel strangely wonderful—as if—well she couldn't describe it really—even now she couldn't describe how that first touch made her feel—that blush.

"Oh my dear me."

It was done so quickly he pretended he never had done so—he was like that.

Years and years later, she saw a young woman run down the road naked in a protest against some fur-bearing millionaires, and she said, "Oh my dear me," almost with the same intonation, the same self-depreciating plea to the world. She could see the small triangle of dark hair between her legs before the policeman wrestled her to the ground.

"Oh my dear me!"

They were protesting against her, against her money and some new frigate her family was building.

It was a plea that always came when people laughed about her lisp or staggered walk, or adoption into the family she already belonged to. Or when she herself filed papers to adopt a child in 1994 and was refused *because of Bobby*. And the papers got wind of it—and wrote about her the way they did.

At night in the gloom of her room she would wrestle with all of this. All of this old sorrow, like small stones in a broken bottle. She knew quite well of the fathers or mothers who refused to claim children so other imperfect, deeply flawed but willing men and women willingly would. Would care for them when they were ill, carry them through the streets of foreign countries to find them medicine in a world whose language they didn't know. Love them, be willing to die for them in a second. How could someone ever put their noses to the pain of that? She found out after a dreadful time, that Nigel Cruise and his wife, both childless, both committed to the betterment of the awful world always did. And when she found out, once and for all that this is how they thought, she could only say:

"Oh my—dear me."

She was like that. But that was later—it was in some distant time.

7.

CRUISE TOLD HER HE HAD A BOOK—A GREAT BOOK HE WAS WRITING.

So for a while as a young girl she was enthralled by this book. People around the school spoke about it. Because it was the first time many of them had ever met a real writer. This book had wizards and goblins—and he told her that the wizards were women, and the goblins were men—usually people in politics or the church who tried to dominate and subjugate women. She read twenty pages of it. He told her it was very *risqué*. The bishops would certainly be against it.

"Very *risqué*," he said when he gave her a few chapters. She held the pages close to her heart and ran down the hall.

That night under the glow of lamplight she read how the goblins impregnated young women—and the wizards always used their great powers to terminate the pregnancy. Once that happened women gained power over the goblins in the legislature and banished them. Then freedom reigned. That's about all she could make out. The words were far too big, words like *"perpetuate gendered violence in a heteronormative, patriarchal, goblinized society."*

Or something as brilliant and special.

"*Risqué*," she said when she handed the pages back. "*Pure genius.*"

"Yes—but what does it remind you of?"

"I am not sure."

He frowned just slightly then moved back toward his desk. And she felt scared that she wasn't grown-up enough. So she quickly added:

"I got the pages mixed up—here let me—unscramble the pages!!" And she took the Manuscript and tried to make it as neat as she could. Her hands were shaking and she felt her eyes water.

He smiled, came back, bent down and kissed her on the forehead. And then suddenly gave her a tiny little peck on the lips—just a tiny brush. At this moment was the moment of deep moral crisis in his life. But it almost always happened, and later she would discover through certain channels that it happened at private schools, in Cape Breton, Ontario and Connecticut, and it always concerned a young student— it almost always included private instruction and lectures in his office about his attempts to free the young female. It almost always promised something—willingness to publish an essay or a story. It almost always happened just before he resigned and went somewhere else. In fact, he already had put feelers out to go somewhere else. He snubbed and ignored girls who had boyfriends, snubbed and ignored girls who had happy homes. That was a secret. He had not much use for young children, toddlers or babies. In fact he had never looked a young child's way. He would never be seen put out by one. He would always find a way to gain sympathy for his deep selfishness. But all of this was somehow special to her then.

She would discover all of this, of course—discover over time by the detectives she hired to find out where he had gone, that she was neither the first nor the last. Somewhere in-between. She would keep it to herself. She discovered over time that he was not from Newfoundland, he only preyed off their dreams, he was not a Chaucer Scholar he only wished he was, and he did not have a PHD. She would keep it all to herself. Partly because she was ashamed. But wherever he went later on, she used whatever influence she had (and she did have much) to have him dismissed *before he could do it again.*

Before he could so it again became a big phrase for her.

But that was later. Now was now.

"Now, what I want you to realize is my book deals with political freedom for backward women, women who must be taught by progressive people—when I publish it, it will be looked upon as quite subversive—do you understand?"

"Oh yes—of course," she said. "Sub-ver-sive—yes I think I understand."

"Good—I want my brightest and favourite student to understand. My brightest and prettiest student. My prettiest and most grown up student. Now, get out of here. I have work to do. But I will see you later—I will meet you—"

"Where?"

"By the big tree."

And she smiled gaily and ran back to her dorm.

Then that very night in the corner by the big tree, wearing his three-quarter-length leather jacket with his big tan cowboy boots crossed at the ankles, he said:

"No, you have to hold it in—take it into your lungs and hold it—let me show you—like—thi-sss."

She held the smoke in until her head got very dizzy. She leaned her head for a moment on his arm and closed her eyes.

"Pure genius—" she whispered, feeling faint and then giddy. She smelled hash and tabacco and the waxy smell of his leather coat. He helped her back to the room, his arm around her back so she wouldn't stumble.

"Imagine my dear we are arm-in-arm on a pilgrimage to rescue young women from the snares of orthodoxy—can you imagine it?"

"Yes," she whispered, "snares of Orthodoxy—gotcha."

He turned and hugged her, and said:

"My sweet girl."

Her diary entry had these words:

"I'm as high as the sky. It is like I am floating with no clothes. Shhhh—don't tell Captain Constable Delano—he would never understand a man as smart as Mr. Cruise, saving us all from Orthodoxy—so he'll be mad."

And then:

"Oh—look. Snow."

Her diary said that Mr. Cruise was all for the poor, and imbibed only on the better class of wine, that he held up in his wineglass to the light in his office and then would look at her and wink. They would be there together after English class at four o'clock. His tie would be loosened, his jacket opened. And he would pour a little.

"I take this easy—almost twenty dollars a bottle," he would say. Then he would take a drink, look at it and say, "Nineteen ninety-five."

Garnet did not drink. Nan drank only sherry—but her mom, when she drank wine—Mary was certain it cost more—but of course she was far too polite to say so. That was something else about the rich Cruise didn't know: they could be so politely silent when the middle class thought they knew.

But she took a drink too out of the same glass, and he spoke to her about Mary Shelley, Mary Wollstonecraft, and *the vindication of the rights of women*. Here she felt safe away from all the torment, and he showed her his books, taking some of them off the shelf. Little did he know that she, Mary Cyr, would read much of Ms. Wollstonecraft in the coming years, in order to attempt to rid herself of a memory of him.

"If my little Denise had not died, I do not think this would have happened," she wrote sometime later in her life.

He was her first—that is, the first one she chose to hold up to John as an example of what a working-class hero should be. (There were tons of them after.) John, however, did not fight her views at that time. He simply met the man at a basketball game, and shook his hand.

"Isn't he great?" she said. Her face flushed. The smell of basketball and sweat. The November snowflakes falling outside the black window.

John drove back home thinking of her; of her exuberance over this teacher, a crush like so many schoolgirls had—and feeling sorry for her, and perhaps beginning to love her. He looked into Cruise at that time, discovered there was an incident with a girl in another school somewhere. But John, if he remembered it, did not find anything when he followed it up.

She wrote in her diary:

"I'm in love."

She loved Cruise. He was her protector. Nothing bad would happen to her now. She walked along the cold corridors of the penitentiary like stillness of mid-afternoon with the snow falling, waiting for a letter from her mother, who was visiting Spain with her man named Doc. The family had a large villa there—she had been to it once. Her mother's letters had become more—how did you say that word—more—more what—*like a hippie—no—like a what was it—she was more*:

"Out of her damn mind. A complete loon. Saying I had done her in. I was in cahoots," Mary wrote in her diary.

She showed John those letters she had received. She did not dare show them to her uncle or aunt—or to anyone else.

"I think she is hopped up on some regular grade A pills—more highfalutin' than regular aspirin," Mary told John.

Her mother wrote letters about the Germans in the villa above them—who were all Nazi sympathizers who looked like Mengele—and how many bottles of wine were missing. Letters that young Mary Cyr struggled to decipher. She would sit at the desk in her room and open the envelope—with a characteristic blush of happiness that the letter had come along into the mailbox, with a big stamp of Franco on it—and the stamp stamped over with black ribbon-like official ink—and here it was, in front of her little face. But then sometimes *Dear Mary* would be right in the middle of the page—and paragraphs would be driven across the pages every which way.

"I am preparing to buy a farmhouse outside Dénia—called *¡Dios mío!*" She said she would move there—it had an olive tree or two, some oranges in the piteous sun.

Mary would soon have tears running down her cheeks.

Elaine Cyr had lost a fight with her brother-in-law; and was now looked upon as an upstart in the family circle—a wanton renegade of some sort. That is what they told Mary—Nanesse told her that her mother was something of a renegade.

"The British have lost their empire—and are now floundering about—your mother is one of the flounderers—she'll be crossing the sea in a bathtub next."

She went up to her room late that night with big sock slippers on her feet.

She wanted to run away and be a renegade too. Just like Mary Shelley.

"You be a renegade and I'll be renegadier than you. Just you wait and see!" she wrote her mother, and then put "with love." Yes, the British have lost their empire—well, at least they had one.

She put the note not into a bathtub—she couldn't find one. She put it into a bottle and later that month on a trip to St. Andrews threw it into the sea.

8.

HER MOTHER WROTE:

"Wait by the gate with your suitcase—the big overblown white one—fill it to the brim—and bring your black shoes. I am coming to get you."

But before Elaine could, there was this lousy fight with Doc that made all the papers, over a 1975 sky-blue Mercedes. She was locked in jail in Spain. Later it was all hushed up. But after that Nan maintained she could not come back and claim Mary.

Mary went back to Rothesay and went to school. That moment—the short ride to Netherwood—was done on a dark November evening. She remembered a leaf falling down against the windshield of the chauffeur-driven car.

Two weeks later her mother came to Saint John.

"I want to take my child back to Spain," she begged them. "I have enrolled her in the American school there."

"You can see her, you can hold her—you can live with her here—but, my dear, you cannot take her," Nanesse said.

Poor Elaine began to break some small things—a porclain vase with the filmy shadow of a dancing girl from Egypt on it.

"My vase," Nanesse said.

Nanesse sat in the front room—not the living room, or even close to it—but in the front room, wearing a silver dress, with a pale oyster necklace, and her very soft white, white hair covered in a simple silk scarf, and gave the order for her mother to be evicted from the house, ten minutes before Mary was supposed to arrive.

She spoke in her most matronly French:

"Nous n'avons ni envie ni besoin de vous ici."

We neither want nor need you here.

And in English:

"Go back to Spain and no one will stop you from breaking vases."

Her mother was forced from the property. She stood at the gate, and looked like a derelict in her high boots and fur, a cigarette in her gob. A little sideshow among many sideshows, so, so long ago.

Mary shivered sitting alone in her room. It was true that Nanesse and her mother had been in a power struggle. It was true too that her mother lost. The lawyers had taken care of it. It had to be.

After this Nan showered Mary with presents, made a point of calling her a daughter—tried as best she could to be a mother. She had always wanted a little girl. It is not that she didn't try, and it is not that Mary secretly did not love her. She knew in fact she couldn't be with her mother. But her mother left her in empty anguish, and Nan couldn't fill it.

Mary saved this anguish up until some years later on Nan's behalf she was speaking to a group of Acadians on August 15. She sat most of the day in silence and heat. And then a memory jarred her and she thought of her mom's faint smile. So she got into an argument with one of the organizers.

"How delightful," she said to the organizers, "that you New Brunswick Acadians were invited to visit France by Charles de Gaulle when he visited you here in 1967—and how much better it might have been if more of your fathers had gone there to support him in the spring of 1940. Well, my father was Acadian, and he did go! So, shame on you!"

———

She spent eighty-five thousand looking for her father the summer of 1990. It was kind of like looking for gold. In fact, she once followed a rainbow across the bay, in her sailboat to look.

Didn't pan out.

9.

SO THEN SHE WAS ALONE AND HAD A PENSIVE WORRIED FACE, kept written notes about her plans to go away; and other girls did not seem to like her and someone talked about her mother, said she read that Mary's mommie was a big fat drunk and someone said Mary had stolen her hat. (She had not stolen it; she had, however, hidden it—very well.) You see the secret was, for some of these girls, Mary Cyr was just a Frenchie from the other side of the province, no matter who her family was. And they delighted in telling themselves so. It proved to these sweet English-speaking children they could still be superior after all.

Mr. Cruise then spoke about Chaucer, and he was saying:

"There is considerable inconsistency in the spelling of vowels and diphthongs. Vowels are commonly but not regularly doubled to indicate length."

If you missed that, he said with an intoxicating grimace, why, you missed Chaucer himself.

He lit his pipe and looked at them through his big owl-like eyes.

"Chaucer's language then, my girls—my dear little pickannnies—is Late Middle English of the southeast Midland type—"

And he smiled, showing yellow, straight and well-established teeth.

Yes, and he had them all scared to death of vowels, and of other Chaucer practices, about which he said:

"Oh, if only the language had remained—so the Wife of Bath could now today feel at home, in some amenable, understandable dialect."

Then he said to her, in one of those silly motions of his right hand:

"Follow me, my little protege—"

That's what he called her, his *little protege. He liked her more than he liked anyone else!*

And she walked back to his study, thinking these Noble thoughts. Reclining before her, he spoke of suffering. He spoke of many people in history who tried to do the right thing, like Mary Wollstonecraft. And what he was taking on was something that was always insidious and power hungry.

And then he said:

"Why here, let me show you."

And the snow fell and made them feel tweedy and warm, and comfortable with the soft fire burning in the fireplace, and the butt end of wood turning to ash, glowing out in the late day. Little by little burning like a soft smell of smoke and a sweet heartache.

She stood there in his study. She was the first to arrive, but the rest of the girls came too, and gathered round him there.

" 'O scathful harm, condition of poverte!' "

It was growing dark. But Mr. Cruise's voice was soothing. It made her feel like he was a superior person to everyone there—who knew so much. He now told them about Ho Chi Ming, and the Ho Chi Ming Trail. He talked about suffering. He showed them a horrible picture of the child in Vietnam running with her clothes off. He frowned, against the embers of coming dark the soft table lamp.

"People like me were trying to stop this. I went and protested—" he said. His voice was now guttural and far away.

All of them by now had gathered around the desk. She stood as close to Mr. Cruise as she could. She manoeuvred to stand beside him as he spoke. She was his favourite in the whole wide world, and she was now so alone. She felt her stomach go like jelly when he stood and his hand somehow touched her right breast. He left it there. His hand hidden from the others, from the sound of a whistle, hidden from the lights of the hall, hidden under his tweed jacket with the expensive patches, lingered just there. There was a smell of facial hair, and suddenly a dead crispy laugh.

"Oh oh," she said, and blushed. It was the first time she had been that close to a boy—and it was a man over forty, who was married to the most wholesome woman, an activist too who fought for abortion rights (ho de ho ho ho)—but his hand remained, silent and still. No one else could see where it was. He was Cruise, who knew how to say all the right things about people in distress. He was now looking over her shoulder, talking to a girl they had nicknamed Beeswax, a girl who walked clumsily and had huge legs, a sad girl who Mary liked, and as he left his hand where it was, he closed it slightly—just slightly over her breast. But his eyes were distant and he was now speaking so passionately about America not standing up, damn it, for human rights of any kind—*and I mean any kind*. He said this as his hand dropped slightly and moved down her stomach and then just before the secret spot was taken away. No one else saw this hand move. She became as weak as a kitten.

He would now begin to write his great novel he told them about brave women who were the real oracles. Only the best women became them. That is what he wished them to become!

And everyone was silent and sad—and he said they must become the new force for change. That change must come, damn it all, and it must come now.

"What's an oracle?" Mary asked.

She went back to her room. It was dark and cold, and Beeswax came and sat beside her. But Mary was in a daze. She was in a daze because of what had happened, and how she still felt his hand upon her—his fingers touching through the fabric of her blouse and bra the nipple of her right breast. Beeswax whispered that she knew Mary had taken the hat, and they might get a ransom for it—perhaps extra chocolate pudding at supper. And Mary nodded. The window was iced over, and Beeswax said:

"People think you stole the athletic fund—did you?"

"Why in the world would I do so?" Mary asked.

"They just think because your family is so important you think you can take it."

"I would never do so!"

"Mary, I have some cheese and crackers." And opened up her secret stash and smiled. Mary had few friends, but those she had, smiled.

Afterwards, after Beeswax had left, and the day was drowsy and slipping into night, with now and again the sound of laughter from far down the corridor, Mary lay down in the dark on the top of the bed, with her clothes on, her legs tucked up, and she closed her eyes, remembering that Mr. Cruise had slapped her behind on the way to the beach, when they were alone and the earth tasted of decay. She remembered how he had touched her right breast. For the first time she suddenly felt damp and hot between her legs.

At eleven that night she went to the window, wearing her pyjamas, and looked across the cement common, looking out almost in pensive distress, and saw his light on, on the third floor, glowing softly, like a Chaucer Scholar, way up there.

10.

LATER, AFTER HER MOTHER WAS REMOVED FROM THE HOUSE, and she had rushed home to see the mother who was no longer there— she imagined Mr. Cruise coming to her deathbed, and reading her a poem. She would be lying there, in her pyjamas, the top would be unbuttoned just enough, and he would sit beside her. Nan would enter, crying, and NC would stand and say:

"Abdicate!" Or some word that was just as special.

The next time she went to the office, there were only two or three other girls. He spoke to them about Vladimir Lenin—he had a picture of Lenin and Che on his office door, with the smoked glass so you couldn't see in. All his walls were lined with seditious books. He took down a book called *Chaucer's Rebellious Certainty in the Pardoner's Tale.*

Chaucer, he said, was a literary hero of a traditional radical disposition. Then he said:

"He was murdered by the pope—you think that strange?"

Then he added, in an even more angered voice:

"'Damn it all it does frustrate to know that at this present time, in this province, children are willy-nilly going hungry to bed." The excruitiating passion he displayed was of course false, but she did not catch it then. And she felt sorrow.

"Willy-nilly? Hungry to bed?" Mary said sadly. Suddenly tears came to her eyes. Tears seemed to bless her at this moment. And he smiled tenderly and wiped her tears away with his thumb. As if that is all he would ever have to do to stop those tears from falling down, or to erase the memory of poor little Denise Albert.

"Oh dear me," Mary said.

She had written him a poem, and hoped he would read it, and see her love for him:

I said goodbye to thee at night
O my angel desperate bright,
You fight for the poor with all your might;
If you leave me I might die of fright—

Something like that. She practised it in front of the mirror—she even touched her right breast with her left hand to remember. She snuck out along the masterful hallways and left the poem in his essay box. When she turned away from his door, to sneak back quietly along the hall, her beautiful young face was filled with fear and terror and joy.

She wore her school uniform, her little plaid top; and skirt, and high white socks, and sat on a bench on one side of the common, under a hazel tree, and watched his window.

Girls passed by in the dusk, and where would she be in seven years, she thought—and startlingly enough she thought: Where will I be in thirty whole years from now.

Then she took out a small penknife she had brought from her room, just to carve her name in the bench.

"I like Mr. C.— Mary Cyr."

It is still there, faded, and painted green, against the sky. Many people who come to the school will sit on that bench just to say they sat on the bench where Mary Cyr signed her name. The name acquired over those thirty years, the whimsical and even olfactory sense of charm and grace, dabbed every school generation with new warm green paint, but never covering the name that was written—being that name was Mary Cyr.

That is what John had gleaned from her life before she was fifteen— and then she was just short of fifteen, and her mother died.

11.

MARY CYR ALSO KNEW THIS:

The attacks on her family were fairly constant; especially when the New World of the baby boomers became vocal, against cutting of wood and shipping of oil, and pumping of gas. To say the attacks started at any one place is to miss the analogue of its source. The Cyrs were moneyed so they were attacked. By professors for the most part—one visiting professor from Ohio who couldn't comprehend how one family made so much money, and therefore believed that he was sent, as Mary Cyr once said, goateed and bucktoothed, as a saviour to the province. Yes, he in his combed beard was going to show us, on his tenured salary and his mean disposition, where we had all gone wrong. The only time Mary met him, he was carrying books back to the library and had chalk on his arm.

John read these attacks on them from the time he himself was nineteen, so Mary Cyr must have been well aware of them. For the most part the Cyrs could not, and did not, answer back.

The family was attacked gleefully, because of what wasn't spoken about. You see, the Cyrs were moneyed but from the Maritimes, and this supposed anomaly caused a great deal of consternation among people who had never had money or were not from the Maritimes and had never been able to think for themselves; that is, their money was not

Upper Canadian so it must be coarse or vulgar or exploitive—it dealt in gas and oil and lumber and papers. It had a monopoly on things that the moneyed from Ottawa or Toronto never seemed to grasp, but things that were absolutely essential to keep everyone alive, which were of course not looked upon by the art crowd as needed. There was something so lacking refinement in it. Supposedly. And there was a good deal of gloating about who they were. This was really the reason for the harangue against them. And John had discovered this, and that is why he went to work as Mary Cyr's sometime bodyguard. He felt he would protect her. Why? What was the secret?

It was simply this: Mary Cyr's father had given John Delano a job in his woodlot when the mill refused to hire him. One day, as John walked the logging road back to the truck that would take him to town, Mr. Cyr picked him up. They talked about what John might want to do.

"I want to be in the police—I want to be an RCMP—but with how I was as a kid, I doubt if they will look my way."

Mr. Cyr said nothing. Ten days later John was called for an interview. Seven months later he was in Regina. Nothing was said, but he knew Mary's father had enabled him to be accepted.

John knew from the time Mary was six or seven her family was a completely easy target. Of course he knew too some of it they richly deserved.

Some of it, however, they did not. Although they were noted as one of the richest families in the country, they were the epitome of what one shouldn't do with money. Although if you asked anyone what they did with their money, nine of ten people would never be able to say. The professor from Ohio did not know that he sat in a building donated by the family, to level his attack upon them with curious professorial fair-mindedness.

What was unforgivable was that Mary herself was attacked from the time she was thirteen.

Early on Mary Cyr developed a sixth sense about all of this. She knew what magazines to avoid, what books not to pick up. She could tell by a headline in a rival paper if her family was about to be pilloried. Sometimes she was told not to read certain things: about oil spills or satirical jibes against them. It became a joke that her family was oily, gassy and greasy.

But so much of her life was spent in discovering things that they had tried to hide. So over time she picked out what was happening.

Over time she discovered that someone who was attacking them most from the time her mother left to the time Mary Cyr travelled to The Hague was Ernest Vanderflutin. He had become a well-known commentator in Europe. In the late seventies they had dealings in Europe, and people were interested in who these Cyrs might be.

So he had been hired to do an article on them for *Der Spiegel*. He was called in Europe, for a time, an authority on Canada—so his articles often appeared about Trudeau, or NATO, or Canadian economic policy, or on a few occasions Canadian commitment to peacekeeping roles.

He called his article on the Cyr dynasty "Masters of the Fiefdom."

Some said these articles, when they were republished in English by Canadian or British magazines (the British, Mary realizing, not giving a damn about them, the mongrels that they were), helped drive Mary's mother to her death.

Whether that was true was really impossible to tell. Mary knew what store in Saint John sold copies, and read most of them, as she sat alone on a bench in the corner of an upstairs room. The magazine would be opened on her lap, her face was pensive, her eyes would blink slowly reading:

> The grossness of what they call Canadian culture and money is now
> in Argentina with her boyfriend. Sometimes she turns up at a benefit
> drunk. Her family, which exclude her, has no idea what to do with
> her—she is a British woman, of course, with all the baggage that
> entails. Her husband, the brightest of a not-too-bright lot, is dead;
> her daughter lives somewhere within the family enclave and goes to
> a private school. They want to adopt her as their own. Of course one

must not mistake this adoption as love. The family is really quite incapable of that. As for the daughter, to say she is a 'spoiled child' is to lessen the very term. A little girl named Denise died in her presence—no mention of that was made in their so-called papers—I guess it is a Maritime thing. MC, as she is sometimes called, is both privileged and spoiled, but of course has no family left to speak of. As for her grandfather Blair Cyr himself, he is a man with ultra-conservative—even militarist—views, who has made an empire on the backs of the New Brunswick Acadian worker and now lives out his days in the Bahamas, much like his mentor, another ghastly New Brunswicker, Lord Beaverbrook, once did. New Brunswick is a place about as minimally in the scope of world affairs as a backward place can be. It is amazing that such ruthless newspaper barons grow from its soil. Or is it? Still, the grossness of this Canadian money and supposed culture wants to buy into German property, industrial sites, mining operations, and Swiss papers now—I am simply saying don't be deceived—everyone sooner or later gets what they pay for. Ask the average New Brunswicker who toils in the woods and mines, or on the docks for this empire.

It was so gleefully dismissive it revealed all the artifice it pretended to expose. As Mary read, she would try to breathe slowly. She would set the apple down and turn the page, and pick the apple back up, and take a nibble without closing her eyes. Far away on another continent her nemesis sat down to supper amused at his own glandular verbosity, with his wife, who for the moment cherished him, and made a long-distance call home to her family in Canada to read parts of his essay. In fact, Mary could see them at this moment in her mind's eye. And she suddenly understood that everything she was—British, Catholic, rich, even now adopted—came under the umbrella of available target to those who shunned kindness. And she realized this by the time she was fourteen. She was quite a bit on the outside of any side there was. She could suc-cumb and be like the Kennedy children—take on the world in the predictable way the privileged left often have—but she had far too much integrity to do that.

So she picked up her apple again and continued to read:

The British, as false as this is to thinking people, still believe in empire—sometimes simply for the sake of it. Yes, they have meddled themselves out of Europe finally, but still have small pockets of the Queen's Devoted Subjects at various rocky corners of the world. You might as a thinking man or woman find that difficult to believe. Still, I have seen it. Speak to the French in that province and you will know. One would think living in Loyalist New Brunswick you were travelling back in time, where British soldiers of foot still marched in the streets keeping the proud noble savage, the only good thing Canada has created, down. This family will not be stopped any time soon. They have created a bubble of respectability around their odious doings and have at their disposal billions of dollars while filling the air with deposits of dirty oil, dirty pulp and paper and dirty coal! They own a coal mine in Mexico—the workers there toil in unbelievable horror—the horror, ladies and gentleman, like all horror, is real.

She scanned the article five times to find out. He had neglected to mention his father had once owned the same coal mine. And he had neglected to mention that Mary Cyr's family was Acadian as well as British. But that must have been a mistake.

Ernest Vanderflutin was written large; *PHD* was written large as well. And that was the flaw—

In fact this article would start her quest—and it would not end until The Hague and three European private detectives who would discover for her who his father, Dug Vanderflutin, had really been. That he had run away from the rubber plantation and left people who had been loyal to him all his life to die under the Japanese.

Sin—yes, we all do it; she wondered if he knew it.

Still and all, the terrible things said about her mother and even her aunt and uncle were about to leave a very permanent scar on Mary Cyr; and someday in the future—when you looked closely—it was as if this scar was visible, even though not a mark showed on her beautiful and tortured face. That, and how people were later to say that she destroyed her own son.

She would finish reading the article and then burn the pages. Then she would lie in bed trying to think of what to do with her own life.

Hence her trip eight years later to The Hague to find out about Vanderflutin's father, which she knew about from the time she was ten. The strange thing was, Ernest Vanderflutin did not. That is where the little Dutch girl, her friend came in. She lived in the same town Mr. Vanderflutin came from. She knew about Jewish boys and girls being sent somewhere because their fathers couldn't pay enough to a man named Vanderflutin. This pen pal's aunt, Linda van Haut, ran to one of them, handing him a pear, and said:

"*Plooi dit in uw zak.*"

Tuck this in your pocket.

And then the truck clattered away.

That was the only good thing that had happened during her stay at the convent. They were allowed to have a Catholic pen pal from a foreign town. She picked Norma van Haut. So over time she discovered— well, there were others who discovered it as well—what Ernest himself would come to know one bleak day sitting in a restaurant in Geneva.

12.

SHE DECIDED AT THE AGE OF FOURTEEN TO GET HER MOTHER'S fortune for her. So she tried to have meetings with Garnet about the business. She would stand in his upstairs office, looking at the far corner of the rug, as she spoke. Still, she was only a little girl, uncertain of what she was saying exactly—but trying to direct the great business in a way that her father might have wanted it, with a scribbler or a notepad in her hand, some scrawl written down that she was sure would solve things, if only she could manage to make Garnet listen. She got nowhere.

So she tried to take it out on Garnet's son, Perley, who had done nothing in his life except to try to be accepted by her.

"Nanesse wanted a girl, Perley—and she got you—you play croquet like a little fairy. That's why Nan wants me. How can you blame her?"

And: "You were all in it together," she would whisper to Perley at night when they were at the cottage at Burnt Church. You could hardly hear her voice—it came and went like the wind drifting through the trees. "Spending my money on an iron ore mine—I don't even know what iron ore is, but I know one thing—it's not something I would wear—unless in a pinch. And you don't like my mother, well then, I don't like you—if you liked my mother, I would make a concerted—is it concerted? I think its 'concerted'; Perley, is it 'concerted'—effort to like you—but fair is fair, so beware! I hate you and the Vanderflutin and the Irish, and the Frenchies and the—who are those people who live in that country—you know—"

Silence.

"Who are those people who live in that country way over somewhere, you know—you know—they gave Ernest Vanderflutin a job?"

Silence.

"The SWISS—that's it—I hate the SWISS."

So after a time Perley would strain to hear what it was someone was saying, and he would hear the almost melancholy, yet sharp and forceful whisper, coming to him through the naked summer wind, the trees outside waving in the sweet darkness and lights far away down the shore road.

"You were all in it together," her voice would be suddenly heard saying amid the storm blowing across the yard.

"In what?"

Again silence.

Silence and sadness and hurt and silence.

"You all had a hand in killing my father and sending my mother back to England," came the voice, peppered through the wind, like the pellets from a shotgun.

"We did?" Perley would ask, shocked and confused, as he lay in his bed, and she lay in hers in the room across the hall.

"Yes—you all had a hand in killing him, and driving my mother insane, and making her go out with someone named Doc, and now I am certain you want to kill me."

"I don't think that is true, Mary."

"Something has gone on, and I am about to find out what, and then the heads will roll. And—"

"And what?"

"And I want my money—it's my money—and the whole lot of you have it stuffed in your big fat pockets!"

Perley would get out of bed, in his pyjamas, would walk across the hall in his large woolly slippers, and standing at the door of her room, he would try to explain:

"But you get your allowance just like I do."

"I bet you have thousands wadded away in your pockets—"

"I have fifty-five cents in my drawer—"

"Well, thirty-five cents of it is mine!"

He would stare at her. The blankets pulled up to her neck, her head quite still, her dark hair ribboned out against the white pillow. Her beautiful full eyes would be staring straight at him, emotionless. The wind would whisper and moan over the bay.

"I want my money because it is my mom and daddy's—besides that, I need it to travel with the only person who cares about me—and he said he is going to publish my poem—so wait and see!"

"What poem—what person?"

"Never you mind—never you mind—traitor!"

The large cottage had a long upstairs hallway that led to the balcony, and Mary Cyr most often sat in the small room off of it, painting her nails, and watching the boats out in the water or staring with brooding intensity at something unspecific, a First Nations boy walking along the beach, and then go back to her bedroom. Sometimes she would bring binoculars to the window, and people would notice this young girl staring out at them with a pair of binoculars, disquieting their walk.

"Is that the Cyr girl—"

"Yes—people say she's not right in the head. She is dangerous, so they try to keep her inside. That's the curse of being rich—there is always one or two of them that are completely insane. They screw themselves, you see—since they trust no one else to screw."

"Is she the one—you know, who pushed that young French girl into the water? You know who held the little French girl's head under the water until she drowned?"

"That's what they say. Ever since she decided to be English."

She heard them, and said nothing. She sat at the dinner table and was silent.

She began to read all she could about the Second World War. After a time she began to slip notes under Perley's door. Handwritten notes that said:

"The reason you have no friends is that you are not friendly. In the Second World War you would be the first one shot."

"I would be your friend, but what's the use—you're not a fighting man."

And: "You will never be kissed—and if you are, it will never be with a tongue."

Still at fourteen she was already a wonderful hater. She knew very much about the war, and her grandfather's part in it. Except, she did exaggerate how many people he had saved.

Still by the time she was nineteen she could argue very convincingly why she thought Hitler lost the war in the east—sending Army Group Centre to Kiev to support Army Group South, when the road to Moscow lay open, and then deciding to attack the non-strategic city of Stalingrad:

Just, she said, *because it had a nice name.*

She spoke of these things to people who would visit—when she got the chance to speak. But often if she didn't care or approve of them, she would talk about astrology and the alignment of the stars, things that Nan was interested in. She could be self-interested, and frivolous, and turn against someone for no apparent reason. Some days she loved Nan; some days she didn't. There was all of that too that John knew about her.

But interjected into this, almost out of the blue, was:

"What Aunt Nan will never admit, going on like a soothsayer about the cosmos, is one relevant fact: none in her family picked up a gun against the Germans. But in my family it was almost second nature. Even Garnet—yes, even he—was stationed in Britain during the Blitz. So now you know. But give it to the Germans they fought all the way, now the Soviet T-34 had a problem—it had to lower its gun to reload— so that was the only chance the Tigers had against it—but then— well, the Canadian boys in Italy had to fight against those Tigers with Shermans—still, they found out they could take them out by firing not at the armour-plated front—but at the tracks. Slow them down with smoke missiles and then fire at them when they appeared in the mist. The Canadians fought like bastards all the way to Rome, and then the Americans got the trip through the Eternal City first—not really fair, is it?"

She told this to the former governor of Vermont. She just stood up and recited it. Then she left the room.

"*Elle est très perturbée,*" Nan would explain, because French seemed always able to say it better, looking after her as she walked up the stairs dragging a beach towel. "*Maladie d'esprit—maladie d'esprit.*"

"Ah," the former governor said, confused at it all.

But that was in a future time.

Now she was just a girl who tormented Perley with notes, most of them untrue. And many things about the Dutch, Garnet, Nan and the business that were also untrue.

When Perley approached her about these notes, Mary said she did not write them and knew nothing much about them. But they were written in pink ink and she had three pink-ink pens on her desk.

PP, as she called him, tried to help her in family matters. He tried to include her. In fact, that day she was left in the outside room at Christmas, buttoning and unbuttoning her coat buttons, Perley was the one who said:

"We have forgotten Mary," and ran to open the door. There she was, sitting on the bench with her suitcase beside her and Plu folded on top of it.

PART FIVE

1.

SHE HAD STUDIED ON HER OWN THE BATTLE FOR HONG KONG.

After the fall of Hong Kong the Canadians were marched off to concentration camps. They witnessed beheadings on the side of the road.

Men drank their own piss, ate their own shit. Thirteen million Chinese were slaughtered by the Japanese between 1937 and 1939. It was something never mentioned in a book she read called *The English Patient.*

She read Vanderflutin's book as well. Vanderflutin's book, in the style of the day, in this post-colonial world, often mentioned the sins of the English against the First Nations—but, she discovered, didn't much mention his Dutch, or how they left the Natives, which they themselves tyrannized in the Far East, to the Japanese when they fled en masse to Rotterdam.

And of course in those two books racism was prevalent but prescribed as a condition of only certain English-speaking peoples. And certainly could not be prescribed to any Dutchman, or man of colour.

Yes, bravery, that's the ticket.

In the little enclave that supported Pedro and the others, they passed around a jar of warm salty piss as well. Some of the men prayed; others swore at them for praying. Fights broke out in the blackness over whether to smash the Virgin against the wall. And sad as it was, on day six a boy of seventeen was killed because someone said he had tucked a pear away.

He had a girlfriend named Gabriella. They were supposed to have gone to a dance that Saturday night—in fact, that is all he had talked about. He lay on the ground between them with his thin neck broken. They searched for five grim hours, accusing each other.

No pear was found.

2.

BY THE TIME JOHN WAS ASKED TO CHAPERONE MARY CYR THE summer after her father died she had a very good knowledge of her uncle's hold on the papers, her grandfather's increasing departure from the reins of the day-to-day affairs and her other cousins becoming more and more important in the empire. By the time she was fourteen she continually inquired about things, and had whole lists of numbers and monies written down in scribblers and hidden in the closet of her room upstairs. She was doing it only for her mother and father—in a real way, in a truthful way, she never considered herself to be rich.

Though to look at her, you would think she did not know any of this. She was fascinated by it all in a kind of eclectic way; she was a kind of person who has spontaneous inquiries about something, presses everyone about some issue, and then would let it go as if it wasn't important. Then a year later she might say: "Well, what about the dredging—it was supposed to create three hundred new jobs. Or at least 297—that is what you maintained—but no one dared ask my opinion, so then what about that?"

They did not know for the life of them what to do with her. They asked her what she wanted to do with her life. She told them she was a poet—and a good one, as opposed to being a poet and a bad one, and that she would soon have a poem published by Mr. Cruise himself, who was, she said, "A regular genius—of the Newfoundland variety."

That is, genus *Newfoundlanous*.

"He told me it would be published in *Tickle Lace* as soon as they have space. He just has to tickle a few things here and there to make room."

For a month or more she did nothing but look distressed and read poetry. And quote it to them at the table.

Then one day the Newfoundland captain of their ship, the *Eeekum Seekum* visited, and sat down to brunch with them.

"No no, dear, he and she are not Newfoundlanders at all—not even close; they come from Oregon."

"I don't even know what that is—sounds like a spice. He is a great activist—everyone says."

"Mr.Cruise is an activist, and so is she. That may be true. But they only slay the dragons already mortally wounded, those dragons the hired beaters have already chased from the cover of the woods—at least from what I know about them, my girl. "

But she didn't believe that—never believed it, and did not listen. In fact she plugged both her ears with her fingers, and the captain gave a laugh.

Garnet and Nan worried about her—for no matter what the world thought, no matter if they could show it or not, they did love her. But she felt she had no love.

So she went back to Rothesay.

She was at Rothesay Collegiate that November when someone arrived to speak to her.

It was her cousin. He came one afternoon to tell her something—he was tall, fair-haired, with a smile. He took her hand and spoke to her. His name was Greg, and she had never seen him before—or she had, but she did not remember. He was twenty-four or twenty-five—much of the corporation was being handled by his father, the uncle she did not know—and Blair Cyr was leaning more toward them. They spent much of their time in Nova Scotia. But she did not talk to him about money—it seemed the mention of money would be shallow, even shameful. He spoke to her about duty—about doing something with her life, about how her father would want that, and insist upon it. He smiled and took a leaf from her windblown hair. It was November and all the lights were on in the great stone building with the tower. Did she know, he asked, that the stone building, the edifice towering over them, in the cold brilliant evening, was donated by the family? She felt small compared to that donation, to that building, and to him. He told her that it was important that the family remain together. That important tasks were there for her.

"Will you do that for me?" he asked.

She nodded without speaking she was so amazed to have him standing beside her.

She realized she inhabited a place on the wrong side of the family—like a small star at the tail end of a galaxy, just hanging on, and he, Greg, was part of the giant nebula in the centre, directing with his smile the unquestionable antics of the firmament and the music of the spheres. She looked at his long dark winter coat, with the collar turned upward against his strong Celtic jaw, his handsome face just exposed at twilight, his black tight-fitting gloves, his immaculate shoes and foot rubbers—and she smiled hopefully. This was the man who along with his older brother had been compared to the young Kennedys. She did not know that he had been sent down to Rothesay to give her a talking-to by the family—that he did so as a representative and not as a cousin. He spoke to her about why they needed woodlots, why they had dealings in steel and oil—why they had gas stations and papers. They had been a family on the fringe, and they simply refused to let that define them. She asked only one question. It was about the iron ore mine.

Oh well, they had bought it just as they had bought a potash mine. It was a family decision. No one knew a tragic event would unfold. But they had to think of sinking another shaft, and flooding and closing off an old, unproductive, one. They had to see it up front and close, so an inspection was needed. Did she now understand why her father was on that trip?

"Yes, I see," she said. "But was it a mistake?"

"No—I am sure it wasn't," he said. "But as you know I was still in university then."

Then he kissed her on the left cheek, close to her ear, got into his black sports car and drove away.

But he forgot to tell her what he had been asked to tell. Of course he did not forget. He felt she would learn of it from someone else—her uncle Garnet later that evening. But she did not. That is, the terrible fact that her mother was dying. She had overdosed late the night before; people found her lying in the street. They wanted to keep it as quiet as possible, even from her—or more to the point, especially from her. Nan suddenly felt it might be their fault—guilt often follows the living through the quiet corridors where the dying are. And Nan loved this little girl, this *enfant terrible*, even if she could not say it. Nan could actually be filled with love, as long as you obeyed her.

When she was pregnant, Nan had been promised a girl by a priest who took her aside, and his eyes fluttering in his sad, emasculated face declared:

"Yes, you will have a girl—send her to the convent. She will have many trials, but she will be known as a saint."

But Nan's sister-in-law got the girl, Nan had Perley and Nan was heart-broken.

That night, the night her sister-in-law, the *maudite anglaise*, was dying, she said a decade of the beads, and suddenly thinking of that little English girl who had first come to the door on November 3, in a new grey hat, big scarf and big winter boots so that everyone laughed, saying, "Yes, everything is wonderful, don't worry about me. I'll get used to the cold." Remembering that she looked just like the actress Vivien Leigh, she burst into tears.

That same night as her mother lay dying, now and then opening her eyes and asking for her, Mary thought how nice it was for Greg Cyr to see her. How nice it was for him to say anything at all to her. She would follow his career for the rest of her life, vainly hoping in some childlike way that he would send her a greeting, mail her a card.

She went to bed happy and sleepy. *Someone from the family had actually come to see her!*

The next day she woke early. She took a shower and dressed, in her clean green plaid skirt with the pin at the front clasping it together, and looking like a little Scottish lass, ran to see Mr. C., who wanted to speak to her about her "tremendously powerful poem." She hadn't seen him in over a week. And in that week, unknown to her he was filled with deep anxiety, wondering what to do about her— Mary Cyr.

He walked toward her, his cowboy boots making a distinct clicking sound. He clumsily swept his blond hair back as he walked. His strides were confident and lengthy. They were alone, just the two of them in the long dark hallway. He smiled and stepped too close, so she felt his knee against the inside of her legs, parting them where the pin kept her skirt together. Her legs started to buckle and she felt weak. He held her up by gently placing his arm under her elbow and kept his knee where it was.

She closed her eyes shyly, and then opened them.

Try that on for size.

When she went back to Rothesay after Christmas that year, Mr. Cruise, her favourite teacher in the whole wide world, had given his resignation and gone away with money from the athletic fund. He had left at night, after dark in a storm by train with one suitcase. She wrote him letters, letters addressed to *Nigel Cruise Newfoundland*, but could not get in touch with him. So she addressed another letter, *Nigel Cruise somewhere in Newfoundland*.

He had gone back to his home. Sometimes she would look to see if her poem had actually been published like he promised in the dozen or so journals he promised he would send it to. But it never was.

So she wrote in her diary:

"Mr. Cruise took my virginity—should I tell Uncle Garnet?"

In the end she did not tell anyone who it actually was. John would be the first one to know. The family could have easily discovered whom, but they needed to forgo a scandal, and in the end created one worse. In the end she was a child alone with her child. In the end, without Mr. Cruise knowing it she hired detectives from Halifax to watch him on her behalf.

So he wouldn't do it again.

3.

THEY WERE DANCING, OUT IN BACK OF THE JAIL—EIGHT OR TEN
women and a few children. John watched them. They wanted her to hear
and see them. Her cell, no more than three metres away. What were they
singing? Whatever it was there was more of them arriving and believing her a demon of some kind. One of the women was Lucretia. Lucretia
egged the men on—wanted them to drag the American bitch from her
cell. But she was always stopped by her sister, Principia—who begged
her to contain herself. Once, Lucretia peed herself she was so excited.
In the many scenarios and more than a thousand press reports about
what happened the last day, this would not be mentioned immediately.
It would of course when the real book came out.

Did they know the real book would someday come out? The real
book that would never blame her for being British, being Catholic,
having money, caring for a child she couldn't cope with, being adopted,
making mistakes she regretted with both lovers and friends? The book
that would say in whispers that she was a great woman—ho de ho, ho,
ho, a saint?

That book?

Perhaps, perhaps not.

But you see, this was a time when people like Lucretia felt absolutely
free in the ability to not contain themselves. So she laughed gaily, saun-
tered up to the bars and looked in, proclaiming:

"¿Qué es una mujer como usted haciendo aquí?"

What's a woman like you doing here?

And shaking her head sorrowfully.

One night the German he had spoken to came and stood beside him.
John asked what those women were saying.

"Über einen Mord, oder Mörder, in Oathoa," he said.

About a murder, or a murderer, in Oathoa.

The German handed him a litre of wine, and he took a drink. *"Gut,"* he said.

Then the German said:

"Things will turn about—it will just take time."

"Okay," John said. "Thank you."

They were secretive, this German-Dutch couple—they looked like two conspirators. John wasn't sure why. Some of the things John asked they shrugged at. At times they spoke together quietly. And discreetly.

The Russians were pleasant but a little inscrutable. Two American women simply assumed, when John did speak to them, that she was guilty of something—anything at all. And that people like her should leave those poor Mexicans alone.

One other thing the German mentioned. It was a long time ago, but this Mary Cyr was his wife's pen pal years ago—this Dutchwoman was once a Dutch girl named Norma van Haut.

"So she will fight to the death for her," he said, "and if she will, so will I."

Just like that, off the cuff. The German seemed happy and expansive, just like a vacationer should. But with his bull neck, heavy frame and delighted, fearless eyes, dangerous.

"Does Mary know?"

"No—and neither did my wife until late last night. Then she put two and two."

Here he smiled and stretched a bit, and they watched the setting sun. Then he said:

"My grandfather unfortunately was quite a good SS officer who fought against the Canadian First Army. He was friends with Dug Vanderflutin."

4.

MARY CALLED HIM IN HER VERY PLEASANT VOICE; SHE WANTED him to go home.

"There is no use you being here—they want to fry me—well, at least the ones who throw shit in my face—the others are fairly nice—I keep giving them hand lotion—you know for when they carry shit around— *o scathful harm, condition of poverte.*"

"Shakespeare?"

"No, Chaucer."

"Well, I am staying for a while. And by the way, they have done away with the death penalty here."

"That's nice of them—not just because of me, I hope."

But she wanted him to go home, because he was being threatened and followed each day. Though the last thing she would do is tell him she knew. There was also something else—which she was frightened he might discover:

One of the things they had to fight was the fact that she had brought so much money with her.

John did find it out.

There was already all kinds of speculation in the papers about why she brought this money with her. John wanted to know how the papers got wind of this. But no one would tell him that.

When her lawyer Xavier came to see him again, John inquired about the money because he wasn't sure how much she had on her.

"How much did she bring down—fifty thousand?"

"One point nine million."

"One point nine," John repeated, his face suddenly becoming ashen. "Dollars?"

"*Sí*, dollars."

This changed everything—that is, it was in the prosecution's favour, and something they did not tell the defence until after the papers had reported it. Now Xavier had to not only admit that she had brought this money but make excuses as to why she did.

Why had she brought so much money down on a private plane if she did not want to do something underhanded? Xavier asked. Not that he believed, ever, that she intended to, but the justice system would make certain that the public thought this. The prosecutor made it clear she believed Mary Cyr came down to bribe some mining official. Xavier said he knew she didn't, but it made everything more complicated now.

"People have known it since the beginning," he said. "They kept it from me until they could make something of it—they know the public is becoming more and more incensed. Whenever I try to counteract that, they have another tidbit—now it is the money, she brought, as a bribe from Tarsco. Your picture is also in the paper, as having been sent down by the family to try to get the charges dropped. It puts you in a dangerous position."

"Well, I am more interested in the position she is in," John said.

But the money allowed certain people at Amigo the opportunity to put this tragedy behind them and blame her.

"You and I both know that is insane. What happened at the mine was criminal—the search was suspended because something criminal was happening," John said.

Xavier looked at him, with a peculiar gaze, as if to say: *How did you hear that?*

John then said:

"Why did she say she brought the money? Not to shop, I hope."

"No—not to shop—but to start an orphanage. To help people."

"I see," John said. "Of course."

"But the prosecution tells us that that is impossible to believe. She was here to bribe someone at Amigo, so they would not reveal things."

"Except," John said, "I believe her, and so do you, And I do not think Amigo wants anything revealed—because if anything has been criminal, we will find out that they are the ones at fault."

"The fact is not that they are at fault but that this will now be used to establish her guilt," Xavier said.

"You know and I know, and Señorita Tallagonga knows—she is innocent," John said. "Everyone knows she is innocent—"

"*¿Por qué no habló del dinero?*" said Xavier.

Then he repeated it in English: "Why wasn't I told about the money? It makes my job very difficult."

He seemed hurt. His face had the look a person has after a certain kind of infidelity, one by a tradesman who broke a promise or took you for too much money.

5.

TALLAGONGA WAS NOW FOCUSED ON THE MINE, SINCE EVERYONE else was as well. If she could get Mary Cyr convicted of being criminally responsible, as a representative of Tarsco, it would make Tallagonga a national figure. Blaming an English-speaking international would show the prejudiced predilections of certain kinds of people. None of this, however, could be said in this way, but it could be understood, in the way all things were understood these days. And the campaign to promote Mary Cyr as an example of the last vestiges of colonial thought was pronounced within the very jurisdiction Tallagonga worked. Of course it was the French and the Spanish who had dominated them before, but one colonial power was as good as another. This is what John was beginning to sense. It was in the drafts of air from the sea, and from the roadway dust. The charge of murder had got her into jail, but now this was even bigger, much more international. And indeed bigger was better for the world audience.

But then something slightly more favourable happened. The German-Dutch couple spoke to him again. At first they were not going to get involved. However, given his wife's connection with "the woman in the cell"—as the tabloids in Mexico called her—the Dutch doctor, Norma van Haut, decided she must help. So they did something clandestine, to prove to themselves that Mary Cyr was innocent.

After people were declaring Mary had poisoned a child, Norma van Haut took samples of children's hair, indiscriminately—those kids who hung around selling them lotto tickets, or worked setting up umbrellas on the beach. Each child whose hair they snipped they gave five euros to. They sent the hair to a friend who worked in Phoenix.

Yesterday he phoned them. The doctor told John that all of these children—just as she suspected—had traces of arsenic, because of the poor ground water—which meant that so many of the people here would have had the same amount as Victor. That alone would be a cause to discredit the charge of poison. And they would make sure the findings were presented at the trial. The Dutch doctor said she would testify that she had seen bruising on the body around and about the neck, which Señor DeRolfo for some reason overlooked. That along with the disproving of the arsenic theory might help.

She was also sure that Ángel Gloton had seen these marks as well—for he stood beside her for a moment.

The German then told John he had sent these findings to Constable Fey, who seemed to be heading the investigation.

But they did not get an answer back. They did not know what Fey might be up to, or if he had any preconceived notions. That was the trouble with the world, the Dutch doctor affirmed.

"*So wie wir vermuteten*," the German said.

Just as we suspected.

The Dutch doctor, tall and blond and beautiful, believed nothing was farther from the truth than the charges escalating against this Canadian woman. And it was years ago, and people certainly transform or change—and Mary Cyr was nothing like the young girl who wrote to her in all her innocence—but when she went to visit her, she still felt they were connected in some remarkable way.

"*Die ganze Welt will sie schuldig machen*," the German said.

"The whole world wants her guilty," the doctor translated.

"It seems that way now," John Delano said.

"We will see to it the world hears another story!" the Dutch doctor said. And she smiled. "We have to, don't we."

"But you see they will make her an offer—and it's an offer she can't refuse."

They asked what that would be.

"They will offer her a deal—admit either to the murder, or to criminal responsibility in Amigo," John said. "I feel it in my bones. They will tell her that if she admits to Amigo, then they will blame her family, and she can go free—if she admits to the murder of the boy, then she will do hard time."

6.

MARY READ DOZENS, IF NOT SCORES, OF BOOKS, STARTING FROM when she was fifteen. That is, parts of books, a line here, a paragraph there. History and philosophy, mainly. Caesar's conquest of Gaul, the works of Plutarch—the rise and fall of Hitler. The rise and fall of American gangsters.

She wanted to learn about America, she wanted to learn all she might about England (which she could criticize every bit as easily as she did France or the Netherlands); the rise of facism in Italy, Japan in the Second World War, the plight of colonial India, the Indian wars in the USA, the plight of Jews in Hungary, the plight of Anne Frank.

She picked them out of the large library in her grandfather's cottage at random (a library that needed a ladder to climb to the top row of shelves) and would sit on the beach with them, like giant props, her sunglasses hiding her eyes.

She might carry to the beach Kant, Schiller, Descartes, Jung, and raise her sunglasses as people walked by, as if to say: *Pretty impressive stuff, ain't it!*

She read *The Rise and Fall of the Third Reich*, and two books on Churchill. She read a book on the secret life of insects published in 1895.

But then she forgot a text on the beach, and it was washed away. Her footprints leading back to the cottage lighter by the weight of one copy of the *Epistemology of Phycology* than they had been when walking down to the shore.

Two days later a First Nations boy came by with it, it weighing much more because of the water and twice as large, the pages wrinkled and thickened by salt.

"Here is your book, miss," he said.

"Thank God," Mary said. "I couldn't sleep without finding out what was going to happen."

Then she ran about, trying to find him some money—woke Perley and asked him to empty his pockets.

"Can't you do anything right," she screeched when she discovered his pants pockets empty. "Where is all your cash?"

She ran back downstairs and opened the oak cupboard, and found a marshmallow and handed it to him.

"I don't need anything, Miss Cyr—"

"I know, but I insist—and there's a lot more where that came from."

The youngster was the unfortunate Charlie Francis, who like everyone else had a secret crush on her.

However, in August that same year, on a particular windy warm night, just after dark, she was seen carrying a huge bear trap toward her enemies' house.

They came to her cottage—the RCMP.

She had three girls, who she did not get along with, and planned her attack to maim them—but really it was not an attack—at its very sharp point it might be called a *warning*. She had only warned them. When the RCMP came to the door, Mary had devised to look busy by grabbing a book off the bookshelf and sitting with it—poring over its contents, glancing up at them as they came in. It was a book on the life of Sir Ulrich von Liechtenstein, the German poet of the Middle Ages. She seemed to be immersed in it—and did not seem to notice them. They asked her if she had been out.

She looked up at them, wearing brand-new pleated white shorts, a crisp yellow blouse, tied at her stomach, new white sneakers—and told them that:

"I have been here all night reading about—" here she paused to look at the cover of the book "—poor Sir Ulrich—the love poet of the Middle Ages, who passed away quite suddenly January 26, 1275."

"*Elle est très perturbée*," Nan said to them. "*Elle est très perturbée—elle prend des médicaments.*"

She is very disturbed—she is on medication.

The RCMP said they understood. But they needed to speak to her nonetheless. Did she put down the tome on Sir Ulrich long enough to devise an attack?

As far as the RCMP report went, and John Delano had read it, she was planning to set this bear trap and leave it on the steps two cottages away, in order to get the "rich" girls who'd made fun of her friend Debby Dormey's stutter—a little girl who lived on the upper road, near the highway; lived her life in three rooms with a small bathroom in the hall; a girl Mary Cyr had suddenly befriended, and treasured. (Did she befriend her because her mother was an English war bride like her mom? And both of their moms were dead? Very likely that is where the impetus came from. Yes, John knew it had to be that.)

7.

"DEBBY DORMEY" WAS IN MARY CYR'S GREAT DIARY— one-eighth of the way in—on a page that contained a house, and snow-flakes falling down: a Christmas scene without a Christmas tree, drawn quite well in Mary's hand.

"My friend Debby Dormey lives here—someday we are going to travel," was written under it. "The only one I need in my life is Debby Dormey and that's a fact. We will go somewhere—maybe Istanbul— then we can both sing that great old song 'Istanbul'—'Now it's Istanbul, not Constantinople'—ta da da."

But John knew that did not happen. Debby was a youngster who would die before the age of nineteen. She would simply get sick and die, and Mary would be sitting at her bedside holding a pineapple that she had picked up at the market in order to make her feel better. It was a terrible and tragic little house, and Mary Cyr's brand-new Jaguar would be pulled up outside of it, near the half cord of hard rock maple in the muddy yard. Some trees would wave, some crow would call. Mary Cyr would be clutching the girl's hand and saying:

"Hang on now—we are transporting you to Toronto—I have a plane flying in—please hang on. Look, I got you a pineapple—"

Debby would whisper:

"Oh boy—you are so kind—I've never been in a plane."

Mary Cyr of course did not know any of this when she took the time to draw and shade in that lonely picture on a blank page of an almost forgotten diary, with the words *we will be happier in Constantinople*. But John realized it told something about her. Not only about her tragic closeness to death but something about her boundless life.

Each Sunday afternoon that summer, she and Debby went and placed flowers on Mrs. Dormey's grave.

FROM MANCHESTER was engraved on it. She had wanted to be buried back in Manchester—that did not happen. Her husband had no money for that. He gave her a small plot near the woods she hated. She had been a war bride just like Mary's mother—and she never got to see England again. For the last four years of her life she simply stared out at the great fields of snow beyond her house. Her husband had promised her a grand life in Canada—and he perhaps thought he had given her one. He worked as a fisherman in the summer and a pulp cutter in the winter. He bought an old second-hand truck, which his wife hated to be seen in but did not say so. She embraced everything he tried to do, made the best of it as much as she could. She was in the Irish downriver community, many who still carried wounds left over from the time of the potato famine. She tried to fit in, but she was as solitary as Mrs. Cyr.

Everything Debby's father tried to do did not turn out. Debby's mother spent the last of her money helping him open a garage up on the corner, and a spark ignited a fire there. Mary remembered passing by that garage on an evening in August and seeing the sign that advertised a free Coke with each fill up. Then passing it the next morning and seeing its blackened timbers after it had burned down. To a crisp. Only the sign advertising free Coke remained prestine. Mary did not know Debby Dormey at all then.

However that was the last of Mrs. Dormey's money. Afterwards Mrs. Dormey wrote letters home, lying, and sending pictures of her daughter standing on the steps of the Old Manse Library when she was five, pretending the library was their house. (It was once the childhood home of Lord Beaverbrook.)

When her husband found out one night, he laughed loudly, and told all his friends at the community centre.

She learned to laugh at it herself, and then laugh at herself. And then she pretended she had never taken the picture.

One day, when Debby was nine or ten, her mother stopped eating—but she did not tell anyone. Her husband was working in a camp some miles away, and she was alone. Each day when Debby came home from school, her mom would be in the same chair. The television would be turned on, but the only station would be blurred and extremely snowy.

Sometimes Mrs. Dormey would stare at it all night.

Debby became the mother—began to cook and clean. She would put supper in front of her mom.

"Oh, Debby—I've already eaten too much today!"

When she began to lose weight, she stuffed her clothes with old copies of the Cyrs' *Morning Telegraph* and cardboard from the back shed. She lived like that, in a state of slow starvation for over three months.

She died longing for an England she would never again see. And perhaps it did not exist anymore.

Debby was finally sent to her aunt to live. And that brought her closer to Mary Cyr. They became for a while inseparable. Mary told her she would never leave her.

8.

MARY BECAME AWARE OVER THAT PARTICULAR SUMMER THAT rich girls from Oshawa thought they were much more sophisticated than the girls and boys here. They had made fun of Debby's stutter. So that is why Mary had the bear trap—the details of which were filed away in an RCMP office.

Mary, John knew, could be overwhelmingly kind, and there were times when she would not be.

The day Mary Cyr heard about someone making fun of her friend's stutter she walked down to the shore to see these three rich girls whose families were renting a cottage near hers. The cottage was much like theirs, yet with extra asphalt shingles near the chimney instead of flash—which is how it was picked out when you were out on the bay in a sailboat. Poor Debby's stutter had come when she realized her mother had tricked her—that when they took her clothes away, she weighed less than seventy pounds. Suddenly all those months overwhelmed her and she could not speak without an impediment again. And it seemed that in that impediment all her love, hobbled out against the air, against the warm sunlight or a winter scowl—but always it was love, tormented and crippled.

"What's up?" Mary Cyr asked those girls.

"What's up?" one of them imitated.

"They are three rich girls," Debby whispered. "So we have to be careful."

For some reason Debby did not consider that their wealth and the wealth of everyone they knew, would not compare to a stipend of what Mary Cyr's own family was worth. Actually, at that moment neither did Mary Cyr. To her they were rich girls as well.

That is, she was as open to strangers as most New Brunswickers are, and therefore just as open to insult.

After this Mary became silent in their presence and watched them carefully for about a week. She would get up early and wait for Debby at her house, with a pail to pick blueberries carried in her arm. Debby wanted to pick enough quarts to sell, so she could get new clothes for school in the fall—they made $21.95 one day.

"My god—I never thought we could earn so much," Mary said. "Now let's go buy something special."

Debby pondered, counted on her fingers and said:

"But I am saving for my new clothes."

"Ah. You know what—you save for them—because I have a few extra pennies on me—so I will treat you."

"Really?"

"Yes—I think I can manage it."

That evening walking back from the store, the Oshawa girls came up beside her on their bicycles, asking her who she was. She did not answer.

"You work picking berries?" they asked.

She did not answer.

"How many can you pick in a day?"

She did not answer.

Then they asked who Perley was; however, they did not know his name.

"You know the ugly fat boy—who goes down to that boathouse to swim," they said. "Is he your boyfriend?"

"Do you go out with him? He has such a big fat belly," one said.

"And such a small dick," the second said. "We saw him change."

They all began to laugh hilariously, mimicking to make her cousin the scapegoat they could all transgress; drove ahead on their bikes and then came back. She watched as they pedalled in slow circles around her.

"He's her boyfriend!" one shouted, and then all shouted in gregarious unison.

"He is. With his small pecker."

Mary studied them for a long moment as they surrounded her. Then she smiled.

"Whatever he has—I guarantee it is more than any of you three deserve," she said quite politely.

"Pardon?" the one Mary disliked the most said; the one who was middle class enough to forever contrive to lead a group of girls just like this, the other two wickedly devoted to her, as sycophantic as beavers.

And Mary continued:

"I said he has much more than the likes of you will ever deserve—besides which not one of you is as good as you're CRACKED up to be, something that your poor husbands will someday find out. In fact—"

"In fact what?"

"In fact in ten years all of you will be at each other's throats—nawing at each other like beavers on birch, can't you just feel it."

"No, we can't," Rhonda said. And she drawled out, "Not ever."

"I saw you down at the beach picking up crabs—I would never pick up a stinking crab." The second girl grinned.

"Oh, I am sure you will pick up crabs sooner or later," Mary said.

9.

FROM NOW ON THESE WERE THE THREE GIRLS WHO WOULD always be the three girls she compared herself to—the ones who needed a book club or a group to join; the kind who required a leader, and a leader weak enough to need followers, and to follow the trends, who would never be able to deal with life without compatriots or discussions. Mary would in private call them the three tight-assed, well-oiled twats.

They drove away on their bikes ringing their bells, like jubilant halle-lujahs. Then the night became silent. And Mary Cyr at that moment rejoiced in the fact that her own life, such as it was, would somehow be disastrous. She saw it in the distant star now appearing in the white sky. She looked up and breathed the life-giving salty air.

The girls from Oshawa did not know who she was—or who Perley was—but they had made a lifelong enemy in her. They had made fun of her orphaned friend, who carried her lunch to school in a paper bag, who thought she could make a fortune picking blueberries to buy a new outfit for school, and her poor hopeless cousin, who would be hopelessly devoted to her his entire life.

She did not know much—or people thought she did not know much—but she knew it was shameful to torment the poor, or those outside the world looking in, like Perley was.

Then for a while they did not bother her. They played golf and croquet and snap on the porch of their generous cottage and didn't think of her at all. They wore bright summer clothes and had reasonably well-groomed dispositions.

But the night that she found her name in the RCMP files for the first time, she and little Debby Dormey were caught with a bear trap. Or at least leaving a bear trap. She explained she was not going to set it—she did not know how. It was there simply as a warning:

Be-W-ar was written and taped to its giant legs. And then they ran away when a cottage porch light came on. So she was reading a book about Sir Ulrich when the RCMP came to the door, the heat pulsing off her body, her bare brown stomach heaving with the weight of exertion and, as John Delano knew, little Debby Dormey hiding in the beach towel closet off the inside porch.

It was the first time she was in the RCMP register, as she would describe it—and it would be the first of twenty-seven times.

"In the register—and not once did one of them ask me to dance—not even John Delano—too chicken, I suppose."

And the misdemeanours would culminate—culminate in many things, John supposed, until her son, Bobby.

10.

IT WAS THE BEGINNING OF HER WAR AGAINST CONFORMITY— but of a very specialized sort of war—a kind of clandestine one. One where she was the silent observer of the disastrous world. That is, from then on, she distrusted women as much as men—she disliked their easy

acceptance of role-playing, of bogus sisterhood and victimhood that
university courses not only taught but encouraged—found them just
as shameful in their pettiness and malevolence toward those who were
cast aside. And worse they had tormented Perley, a woebegone who
believed he could never measure up, and only wanted to befriend them.
Who still in this modern, progressive day went to church and believed
in someone called God. So she defended him, and therefore she would
be alone. But she knew too how men used women like these, pandered
to them in politics and literature in the way the middle class had to
always coddle their own. And she hated the men for their lies every bit
as much. She hated those who used the First Nations as well, for they
formed the same kind of manufactured pieties. She realized listening to
First Nations leaders speak that too many of them expected this and
needed it, so both they and whites could use the tragedy of the past to
embellish their pretenses—and if you stared them in the face and told
them so, told them that their victimhood was now obscenely corporate,
they would counter with the plight of those reserves they themselves
had never been to, and declare you a racist. It was on the tip of their
tongues to call her a racist, and she finally said:

"So what. If they call me one, it cannot be true, because so little in
their life is."

Even in her tragedy she would give more than she received and find
herself solitary. Even in her rages against others she would be kinder.
And the men, many of them boasting, and ignorant of her greatness—or
at least her potential for greatness—would come and go from her life. As
John read her diary, her past became like a crystal stone, a golden
moment in the sun. Yes, he thought, in spite of it all, there were golden
moments in the sun.

Then there were these entries in the diary, which placed it about
1994:

September 28

I took off to go around the world—I was going to visit John Delano, who is attached to the UN (he doesn't know, but I got him the job), but I didn't have the nerve. That is, I didn't want him to see me all lonesome as a Buck Owens song, looking like a complete ghost—and bemoaning my fate. All my plans are broken apart—like a shattered mirror that you walk across by accident in a dark room—I must take stock of myself before something bad happens—and I will— yes, I know I will! First things first—I have to get my past straightened out. I saw him one time, you know—at an airport—I had taken a flight into Montreal. I was trying to find the pilot I had fired, to hire back—to tell him I was sorry. As I walked into the terminal, my first love was sitting there alone—in a hard-back plastic seat, reading a book, I'm sure it was some very smart avant-garde thing—and I was too frightened to go near him, and I went into the washroom, shaking all to bits, and I wept.

October 5

I've decided to take the plane to Newfoundland and visit Nigel Cruise. I am not sure why.

Oct 6

I took a car and drove along some potholed highway and then three back roads. Lots of big moose loading themselves up on munchies. And there he was in the place he owns. The place I had never forgotten and never been to, called Harbor Shore. I came up to this gaunt man sitting in a wicker chair. He shaded his eyes to get a better look at me—and then the years bled away, and he recognized whom I was. He must have been startled that I had come here.

He stood and came forward, gave me a slight fatherly hug—you know the kind that most men use to imply modesty with still the faint hope of getting you in bed, done with pretty sister-in-laws or favourite co-workers. So I sat with him. And looked at him, and his face, which had become cynical from playing the cynic. Boyish from always being just a boy. You know fighting the system and up the revolution.

Nigel Cruise didn't publish my poem in *Tickle Lace* or anywhere else in the entire world (I checked up on it, even in Sinapore when I was there; thinking perhaps he had sent it to Singapore) and I had believed—maybe hoped—that he was always wanting to ask my pardon. That is all it would have taken. He could have said, "Sorry I didn't publish your rather magnificent poem, had a devil of a time—tried to convince the editor of its worth—but well, there you have it!"

I would have said, "Sure," like that.

But when I sat there, I realized his mind was such that maybe he did not think of me too much. Or the athletic fund. He escaped at night to Annapolis Royal, where another school wanted his services. I was forgotten. That is, until the day I arrived in a rented car at his door. I remembered how much my hero he once was with his talk of literature, and brave Mary Wollstonecraft and all that jazz. How true that all must still be for certain fashionable people. He had not published his book. I had it rejected at my grandfather's publishing house.

So I said to his wife:

"Mr. Cruise did not get his book publishd, but maybe his strength lay elsewhere. You see, he taught me about the metrical purposes of Chaucer, the world of meter and rhyme—positively goose bumps, *when april with its shouers soote*. And then of course—the forceful ideas he stressed too in modern film—*cinéma politique*, I believe he called it. Before that (*ha ha ha*) I had only watched movies—Mr. Cruise spoke only of films. We digested them like vitamins."

Dear diary, I have discovered this horrible truth: it is against my nature to turn people in or out. Don't get me wrong—I suppose I do think certain people should be turned in—but I could not do it to he who in a way had become so like the priests he mocked and hated, childless, frustrated and menopausal, willing to blame everyone he once loved.

Besides, who isn't charged with ill treatment these days? I was with cruelty to Bobby by people exactly like Mr. Cruise's wife. She too a writer of some estimantion. So I said to her:

"I have just read your book on abuse within the halls walls and stalls of the Catholic Church." And I got her to sign a copy.

Of course I hadn't read a fucking word of it—but Rory maintained that women were free to lie. It fact it was a duty, to confound men. Men were so gullible.

Then to be polite I spoke about his book, that he was still labouring over.

"Are you still?" I asked.

He nodded a little, but didn't seem to want to speak about it anymore. He was jealous of her book the detectives had told me. Hers had seemed to hit the mark.

"It is on our Newfoundland politics too," he said.

"Well, you can't ply me with enough of that," I answered.

"Yes," he said. "Now movie talk is definitely in the works—but I am thinking, does it destroy the product—"

"That is so admirable." I said.

"What?" he asked.

"To use a word like *product*."

For a while we were silent. I felt sorry for it all. All of it. For her much more than she ever knew.

Rory pointed out a bird of some kind, on some bush of some kind, and I smiled in some way and said:

"Oh dear me."

She knew all kinds of birds—different types of pluffers, I suppose. It's a part of the new language of social advocacy now. To speak of flavouring vegan dishes and pointing hummingbirds out. To forgo God and church for a yoga mat.

She told me she had published her book with an Ottawa publisher. I looked very surprised.

"Ottawa—I thought it was published here."

"Oh no—Ottawa, my dear." She smiled.

So she had published her book on child abuse among us Catholics. That's almost like every second book from the Atlantic provinces these days. Didn't know, however, that it was my family's publishing house. Didn't know I advised the board on it without reading it. She who had put up with him and his dreams. I realized looking at her, at her wrinkled hands and saddened unenlightened face, I would never reach her age. I had deep sympathy for the betrayals she had suffered.

We then had lemonade that tasted far too much like lemonade. We had dried bananas, and sliced apple and cheese. Then she put down a plate of orange slices and chocolate and said:

"These are really to die for." In that middle-class way I find that always exalts too much over the mundane, that proves she is part of a sorority somewhere, has girlfriends—lifelong and all that jazz. If only I could have something—one true friend, lifelong and all that jazz.

I asked him if he had ever heard of a man named Vanderflutin.

"Oh," he said, "heard of him. But you see, the problem with Vanderflutin," he said, "was—well, for a while he was all the rage because of the Cree—was it the Cree?—yes, did good work—admirable to take up for them, the First Nations—yes, well—we need more of that—go against the Brits, and all of that."

"But do we need much more?" I asked. "Or do we have enough people trying to gain instant virtue and coin off the past—using today's wiles to draw and quarter those poor sons of bitches who lived in another time and bourn us?"

He was startled. He looked at me in apprehension—my beau who I wanted to dance with that time there—against some great shrubbery of love. Now they had no transpassing signs out so they wouldn't be bothered by the local children, the snotty ragamuffins—those children advocates that they were.

Little by little I had him excluded from one job and then another.

I had no choice. I couldn't allow him to do it again. Every place he applied to I would contact:

'Its all in the letter' I told them. 'But it's all quite confidential.' I would say. I never had to send the letter. I never even wrote it.

They both of them had nowhere left to go. He had left her twice the daring man and come back home. But it was her I felt desperately sorry for, for it was her I had betrayed. No matter how much I said I played no part, I had.

"Now, the book on child abuse," I said to Rory. "It is a real eye-popper. Abortion saves the child from pain and protects the woman. Yes, I can see it all now. Sometimes I half wish I too hadn't been born. That they in their Catholic charity had ridded me of my desperate self. Of course, who among the poor or unwanted would give up a moment of their life for your inestimable opinion of its worth!"

They stared at me in amazement, and I shrugged and played with my fingers.

Trying to think, I closed my eyes tightly. Remembering little Denise Albert and her prayer beads, so happy she had had them blessed. And how there was something so sacred in her smile when she took the Host at church, and how she tried to defend me by picking up a snowball against all the boys and girls chasing me one day, and how they knocked her down. She was one of thirteen children, given thirteen years of life.

But then we were all embarrassed, for no one knew why the fuck I was there, and neither did I. All of a sudden, after almost twenty years, I come traipsing along in a rented car. There was a pause that lasted about a minute or more—which seemed like an hour.

"You are strikingly beautiful," she suddenly said.

Mr. Cruise nodded slightly, knowing that was a truth unbearable to him now. So I looked at him, and he gave a start and put his head back a tad, but I was probably as terrified as he was. My hands shook, and I rapidly tried to light a cigarette with my silver lighter—and then blew smoke in a daze and then dropped the cigarette at my feet. They both looked at me then looked at each other, realizing now I was in an awful state.

Still and all, he did not know he had knocked me the fuck up— and I had come to ask—well, not for child support—but for some kind of acknowledgement. You know of it all. Just a brief handshake at the end of the drive and a whisper to say, "I am sorry."

They did have a young man named Ned they called a nephew, who lived in Toronto and worked at a homeless shelter, handing out sheets.

I began to laugh gaily when they told me this, laugh sweetly like a meadowlark, so frightened of them both that I was. So terrified now I was here. So worried I would spill the beans. I scratched my knee and looked up at them as if guilty of some monsterous knee-scratching crime.

Finally I got up to go, but Rory held me back, asked me if I had something revealing to tell. She smiled as if she wanted me to confide.

"I do have something important to say," I said.

I felt him go ridged—right ridged, as they say, right before me fuggin' eyes—as was want to be in the papers for the poetry meself—but I did something very strange—you know what it were that I done—I done what me fadder bred inta me.

I opened me purse, took out my embroidered chequebook, my gold ballpoint pen, and wrote dem up a cheque for twenty-five hundred dollars, to be used to help some fuggin' child or other, maybe grab up a bortion with all that Protestant middle-class sincerity, or buddy like that there—money Christ boy—no problem—

In fact I did it because I wanted to. I wanted them to have the money because I knew how much they needed it. There is something uneering about how the progressives seem to fail. But I gave the money strangely because the last time I went to confession (which was five years ago, before midnight Mass in Bartibog New Brunswick), the priest said: "Maybe you could do something for someone you dislike, begin to put your ghosts to rest."

Well, dear diary, I might not have believed him, but I was all for putting my ghosts to rest. Nor did I dislike them—not really at all.

"Here ya r," I said, handing the cheque over, right across his lap, to his wife sitting on her sensible Adirondack. Then I snapped the top of my pen and smiled. The snap of the pen registered almost like a Supreme Court decision; the kind that echoes slightly at midday and is sad.

I didn't look at him. I had on a pleated skirt and wore a simple ochre blouse, with just the top button undone, and a silver cross on my neck; you know, to ward off vampires.

"That is an awful lot of money," my love said, and he laughed uncomfortably, looking about.

"Give it to the homeless shelter, please—the one where your nephew hands out sheets."

The wind came up, again, and the bushes in his little grey yard seemed to whisper and cry out like sprites from a century before. I thought of Denise Albert and tears came to my eyes. It was suddenly so gloomy and cold I wanted; well, I am unsure— perhaps to die.

Rory gave us space to get reacquainted; went out and tried to fix a tree branch in the weakened sun.

Then I looked back at him, kept my eyes on him. I was thinking of the athletic fund. Of the escape by night on a train covered in golden slivers of ice. I thought of how he ran away from me— and how I denied he had. How I would never tell on him, because I thought he would never tell on me.

But the worst of all—worse than anything else—he never published my fuckin' poem in *Tickle Lace*. Not a goddamn line of it.

Finally his wife came back. I was silently staring in front of me. He sat off to the side. Neither of us was looking at the other.

"It is so kind of you—but why did you give so much money?" she asked. "Why did you want to come here?"

"Well, because of your book. I need to tell someone. You see there was a man who abused me too," I said almost in a trance, "but I think I got over it."

"You got—over it—my good heavens," Rory said. "Yes, we had heard something—both of us were tormented by what happened to you—so that is why you've come to us—you read about us in the *Globe and Mail*—you want us to see you through this?"

My hands were shaking, terribly. Because you see, I am one of those very few country-bumpkin Canadians who never read the *Globe and Mail*, and I thought they had caught me.

So anyway, I wore an orchid in my hair. My hair fell in front of my face, but he could see my hint of a smile. It must have looked like a shark's smile to him, especially when the sun burst from the clouds and caught it through the wisps of sad dark tresses.

"And why didn't you report it—if you had just reported it," Rory said. "Someone like us could have done something. But your family stopped you— I heard that may have happened to you," she said with sympathy.

She went inside and came out with her tape recorder, tested a microphone with a little whistle, and holding it up to my face and turning the tape on to Play said with such proficient intensity:

"I was a counsellor, dear—you can trust me. Now, tell me, was it in your family?"

I did not answer.

"Who was it in your family—your grandfather?"

Said nothing.

"If you don't tell us who it was we cannot help."

I realized how big a catch I was to be for her.

Perhaps the biggest. I realized I would be known as that always—the biggest catch. I would never be one of Nigel Cruise's great wizards after all. The ones who take over from the men. I would never be allowed to be that kind of woman who could take on sin and change the world. I would never be Mary Wollstonecraft.

I was suddenly desperate. I listened to her tape recorder. I looked at her and realized I had seen her all my life. She was the rapacious sophomore coming out of class on a late November afternoon, having had all her prejudices recently justified by the prof.

I tried to think of something to say. I went over all the NHL trades and thought of various Canada Cups. In fact at that moment I wanted to fall to my knees and beg forgiveness from them both. Don't please ever think that strange.

I had a distinct foreboding that I would be blamed unto death. I had a sudden vision, that someone, I never saw his face, would cut my hair to the bone before I was killed. Perhaps it was just the way the wind now blew in the trees.

I was terrified I would tell on him. I didn't want to so I bit my lip until it bled, brought forth an embroidered silk handkerchief that until that moment I didn't even know I carried and put it to my mouth.

Then, looking at the blood, I finally spoke, quietly:

"I was alone, my father had just died, my mother was ostracized from the family circle—and I wanted someone to like me—a man to like me—so I always thought it was my fault—I was just a little girl and he was well over forty years old. I was in love with him he was so special—I wanted to impress him. I even wrote a poem to him once." (I laughed gaily at this, like a meadowlark.) "You see man oh man, maybe he could have known better, and just kissed me on the cheek or something. I know now it was all my fault."

"YOUR FAULT—" Rory said, with what she assumed was love and compassion in her words. "Who was he—a neighbour, a friend, a relative most likely. Just give me his name. We will see he never has another peaceful moment as long as he lives—I will rent a car, drive to his house and knock on his door—confront him in front of his wife—I will—you see I am that brave!"

"I don't know if I could ever be as brave as you." I smiled shyly, which seemed to make me even more beautiful.

"Well, you do not have to be, dear. That's why I'm here. I have been a social advocate all of my days. So has my husband. You are in

the right place to get this done," she said. "I will support and protect you. (Here she reached out and took my hand. She saw I was
crying and began to cry as well.) "So just tell us his name. We will
both of us protect you. Forever. You will never have to fear again."

"Tell us his name," Cruise said softly, his eyes wide and pleading.
"Why don't you, dear, dear Ms. Cyr, just tell us his name?"

She went dancing at a new bar in Tracadie. You could still smell the
pinewood from the stage. Her left hand waved high in the air, her right
was placed against her bare stomach as she whirled. She wore no panties.
Her jeans were so tight men imagined her wearing nothing, and her
breasts were full, her eyes were strangely wondrous. She herself looked
at no one, drank tequila in a shot. It was September 1997. She wore no
brassiere. Not a man could take his eyes off of her. Not a man in the
whole goddamn fucking place.

But no one there knew who she was.

No one at all.

PART SIX

1.

HERE WAS THE TIMELINE AS FAR AS JOHN COULD DISCOVER:
When Mary was found to be in Mexico, in the same villa as the dead
child, she was brought into custody. They boarded the plane just before
it began to taxi, and she was led out in handcuffs. They were told to
search the plane and they did so.

They brought her back to Oathoa. They took her to her villa and
spoke to her. Later in the day they brought her to jail, took her blue
Canadian passport, and two officers looked at it. Then they telephoned
someone. A man came in, looked at her a long moment. Looked at the
passport. Then a woman came in. This was Isabella Tallagonga.

She spoke to three police officers, looked Mary Cyr's way and left.
Mary stared at her full hips, which seemed to denounce Mary as she
walked. This would be the woman who accused her.

Mary sat alone in the room for an hour or more. She asked to see a
lawyer, but no one paid attention. Finally she asked to see the Canadian
ambassador. But the police officer she spoke to just shrugged as if he
didn't understand.

Then the door opened. A policeman came in. She was told to stand,
put her hands up on the painted hands on the wall, and was searched by
a policewoman. A cavity search was performed, with sanitized gloves.
Everything in that room looked green and dowdy.

There was a lot of shuffling and boisterousness inside the small outer
office. Two police officers stared at her through the window glass of the
door while she was being searched. First one huge officer with a bull neck
would peek in, and then a much shorter officer. Her bra had been pushed

up and her skirt had been taken off. When they looked in the window, at her beautiful full breasts, she simply stared at them.

Then the man in the suit came in again after she had dressed. He was Señor Gabel, the judge. He looked at her, nodded, said:

"Señorita Mary Fatima Cyr."

And left.

Doors opened and closed and she was told to sit on the hard green wooden bench again. An hour passed.

The short police officer came in, and started searching through the clothes in her suitcase. She stared at his hands when he did this, the angry red hairs that sprouted above the latex gloves.

"When did the boy die?" he asked her, as he looked at a pair of her shoes and then her brassiere. He looked at her with superciliousness, a noncommittal arrogance that was highly practised.

She thought for a second they were speaking about her son, Bobby, and started to turn white and tremble. This was noticed. But the question was asked again, this time with the boy's name. It was asked very politely.

"When did Victor die—did you intend to just leave him?"

And that was when she found out Victor was dead.

She looked up, trembling, and her picture was taken by Ms. DeRolfo, who was standing in the open doorway, chewing gum. That evening Ms. DeRolfo wore a white pantsuit, and a pair of gold earrings—and Mary noticed for a moment a pair of expensive patent-leather shoes.

Then two other officers dressed in white suits came into the building—with a huge suitcase. They put it on the table, snapped the lock and opened it.

"How much is there?" they asked.

"Almost two million," Mary Cyr said.

They put her in the cell. The big officer with the bull neck, Erappo Pole. By the third evening she was charged with murder, corruption of a minor and degradation to a body

How could she get her Plu and her diary? And suddenly John was there.

2.

A DAY OR SO WAS MISSING FROM THIS SCENARIO—THAT IS, JOHN did not know when they actually did charge her with the murder of the boy. Nor was he sure if it mattered now that she was charged.

It was murky, but the timing could not have been worse for her. Her arrival in Oathoa had happened just at the crucial moment, when the court was under pressure to investigate the mining disaster and ruled that the miners' families had legitimate claims for compensation.

They needed to recover the bodies they said, very sternly to her— something that did not seem to matter four days before.

The paper *Gringo* reported that Mary Cyr, who had sat on Tarsco's board of governors, might well be charged with additional counts of manslaughter. Now all of Mexico wanted her blood.

"Of course," Fey said. "Her family owned the mine. She wanted to pay off Amigo and get away with giving only two million—we have that under good authority." (He did not say this until he was told to say it.)

"You have it under good authority," John said, not even as a question, but more as an indictment against the statement. "Why would you think a woman like Mary Cyr came down here to do anything like that? I am sure she knew nothing of the coal mine. And in every document, you will find it was Amigo's responsibility."

Fey looked at him, as one does someone terribly naive.

"Oh, I see—" Fey said, "we have never seen *Americanos* coming here to influence us? To trifle with us?"

"She is Canadian," John corrected. Mildly. "*Canadiense.*"

"Ah, well," Fry said, as if to sympathize.

"Where is the money now?" John asked.

"It is safe—in a bank, it is hers, it will not be touched," Fey said. "She came down to meet with the head of Amigo and give him the offer. But she had to try to seduce a child. She is a sick woman," Fey said. "That is, there is something wrong with her. Her family tried to hide it from us, and the world" (he said this to personalize the struggle) "—so I do feel sorry for her—she never got the help she might have needed. Do you know, for instance," he said, smiling now, quite handsomely, "about the bear trap?"

"What bear trap?"

"The bear trap used to mangle young girls' legs when she was a child? And the young convent girl who roomed with her, who drowned—the Mother Superior could do nothing with her—tried to keep her on her knees and keep her out of mischief—it's all here. It is published on the internet and will be out in a book. It will be published in New York and then we will see."

And he tossed John the first instalment of those speculative things about to be placed in front of the public with photos by photographer Sharon DeRolfo. It was going to be done by one of her former friends in Toronto—a man he met just once.

John looked over the article, comments from all over Canada, most unflattering toward the Cyrs, and a picture of a young girl. It wasn't Mary.

Who is that? John thought, looking at a faded picture of the child, standing in small white boots in the snow, her hands in a rabbit muff.

But after a time he realized it was the 1974 Easter Day picture of the tiny, extremely hopeful-looking Denise Albert.

But there was one good thing Fey told him. Tallagonga had relatives in Mexico City who wanted her to keep this high-profile case in order to secure her reputation. And a prosecutor in Mexico City named Alfonso Bara, who was her rival, wanted the case there, but Tallagonga won out. So the case would proceed here.

"What about what the German gave you?" John asked. "Doesn't that rule out the toxicology report?"

"That can't be discussed now," Fey said.

3.

WHY THE TIMELINE WAS MURKY FOR JOHN WAS THAT THERE WAS stagnation once she was brought into custody. Things did stop and people did communicate with each other over what should be done. Mexico City was consulted, and so too was the Supreme Court.

Why? Because as much as they thought she was a big fish—bigger than a flounder—the idea of the autopsy saying arsenic was immediately thought to be ridiculous. They identified other causes, and did not know if she could be held.

"That's the most asinine thing I have ever heard," Tallagonga said. "He has to come up with something else or we will not hold her." She was so furious she threw the autopsy report across the dark-oak desk, and ground her teeth and then, held one tooth with her thumb and forefinger that the grinding had made sore.

Yet saying "We have to come up with something else" did mean she would be held.

And that was when Erappo Pole came into the room, and said in a heartbreaking voice that he was certain the littler boy, and this is what he said: "*El niño mas pequeño se ha ido.*"

The littlest boy is gone—or the littler boy is gone.

And his chest heaved sorrowfully.

So the idea of arsenic no longer obsessed them. The idea of the children's deaths did—and it did not matter how they had died or went missing— she, Mary Cyr, was involved with both.

For Tallagonga, who had like Judge Gabel often talked herself into and out of judicial procedures against certain people, this was the result of four years of flawed legal actions against DeRolfo and others. They just simply did not see it as being such.

Others, however, in other places, did.

So the idea that they as law officials did not know this method involving arsenic was suspect was foolish. But they had to keep going with it, as long as they had it.

What it did do, however, is allow people in certain places in Mexico City to begin to speculate about the guilt of Mary Cyr or the innocence of someone like Carlos DeRolfo.

"He has turned into the crookedist bastard in the world," one of his former friends said. "A real cocksucker. And he is scared shitless of everyone, especially Hulk Hernández."

So to say that none of this was known was untrue. In fact all the untruth associated with the case was in a way known. Yet things were allowed to continue. Erappo Pole. who was paid some four hundred dollars a month extra for saying what Carlos DeRolfo asked him to say, did not think that he himself had done anything wrong in this case. The case was up to other people. He might know Mary Cyr was innocent, but it was not up to him to decide. Still, even Erappo Pole knew that to charge Mary Cyr was taking a big chance. And it might over time be a disaster for him. That is, once you are doing things that morally make you slide, you do slide, and the slide reaches speeds that make it hard to find traction. So you give up trying to find traction. You may have started out as a youngster thinking traction was possible. But after a while it is no longer feasible. Traction only limits the possibilities. Once this is realized the free fall is guaranteed. And this is what happened to Erappo Pole in the past twenty years. And it had all started with a wink from a man, at a fiesta, which said:

I know you, you are a good guy—you'll look the other way.

And Erappo Pole had. And from that moment on, he was relied upon not only to look the other way but to make sure no one else looked either. So then, that is why things were at a stalemate initially. What Xavier had hoped and prayed for two weeks ago was that a penalty would be paid out from Canada through his office in Cancún to Amigo, and once the penalty was paid to Amigo casualties, the court would allow Ms. Cyr to receive a suspended sentence.

This is what Xavier had worked on tirelessly, but it carried within its marrow a fatal flaw.

4.

SO THEN TO GO BACK A FEW WEEKS:

Xavier had painstakingly worked something out privately the second night she was in jail. He had had the help of the Canadian ambassador, and he had phoned the one Cyr he could reach, Perley, and had spoken privately. The deal worked out was so secretive no one else knew the details. Pressure was brought to bear on both Tallagonga and the judge, Señor Gabal.

The murder charges were ambivalent. The reports coming in said they were speculative at best, because even before John had arrived, Fey had determined the child had been outside when a struggle had occurred, something that John Delano himself had figured out within a day.

Xavier offered a tentative deal to pay the families of the bereaved and the Town of Oathoa twenty million. This incidentally did not sit well with Tallagonga, who was placing all her hopes of her future on this case of murder. But she was overruled.

If the deal had been accepted, Mary Cyr was to board a waiting plane that night. Her name was not to be mentioned. She was to be whisked away as so many rich seem to be.

This was signed off on. She had until that moment not been charged with anything more than carrying money into Mexico. She was in protective custody.

All was well; all was certain.

Here is what the deal was: To get Amigo off the hook for suspending the rescue search, Tarsco would pay out twenty million dollars and admit they had been responsible for the disaster. This was the secret deal, which would have allowed Mary Cyr to go home. A plane would be sent, and she would be flown out of Mexico. Perley agreed and called his older, worldlier, cousin, for he had no ability to release the funds.

Greg listened to the conditions and said:

"It's impossible. Never. We simply cannot take the blame for something that was not in our power to stop. There are negotiations ongoing with both Canada and the States—if we admit to this, how will those negotiations go?"

This very deal would be an admission by Greg Cyr that the mining sector of his empire was careless and dangerous, and did not care for its workers. He would not do it. He could not. To admit to negligence on this scale was political suicide.

When Greg said he couldn't pay because it would ruin them politically,

Perley said:

"But what will happen to Mary?"

Greg said Tarsco would not pay out twenty million. And he immediately got his lawyers involved. And this immediately looked like he was hiding behind this legal facade. And this did smell very bad. But even if he had not called on the law firm he retained in Mexico, it would still have looked every bit as bad. Somehow not admitting to responsibility made Tarsco look responsible.

"The Cyr Corporation will not pay that amount."

This made Amigo look very good in the eyes of Mexicans, who now emphatically believed multinationals like Tarsco had devastated their country. So they turned their eyes to the one in the cell. *The one they had.* And it did look like she was the sacrificial lamb.

However, her cousin Greg had no idea that Mary Cyr would be charged with the murder of a child. But as soon as he said he would not pay, she was—charged with murder.

This confounded him, and Greg then did something worse. He said that he would pay nine million—that is, almost half of what was asked— if Amigo paid the rest, and the charges dropped against his cousin. All talk ceased at that moment.

Xavier had worked very hard and long for nothing. There were moments, John saw, when Xavier's homosexuality was evident, and though Mary Cyr believed that gays were too self-righteous in their belief that they were the only ones victimized, she certainly relied upon him now. She relied upon him very much indeed.

And he had worked day and night for her for well over a month.

Mary Cyr knew with the Cyr Corporation coming under suspicion over this money that the situation was tenuous at best.

"My good dear friend," she wrote Xavier, after she realized all he had been doing for her. "Don't despair, things always have a way of working out—I will be either dead or alive, but the truth will be discovered."

But of course the police were completely irresponsible. They had no idea how to stop a billion dollars' worth of drugs flowing across the border, but they could stop a single foreign woman who they suddenly claimed had an ounce of marijuana on her; could look outraged for the sanctity of their country, keep her in jail for days, browbeat her, say it was an insult to their national sovereignty, then finding out it was all a mistake, let her go without an explanation. This is what had happened a year before to an American woman.

In a way this is exactly how things now happened to Mary Cyr.

There was one other thing that might be mentioned, that John would discover without the help of the Mexican authorities. A woman named Little Boots Baron had encouraged whom she could influence to let Mary Cyr go for two good reasons. One, she would inevitably receive some of that money paid out by Tarsco. (She might get as much as half of the nine million that Greg had finally offered.) Second, she was well aware of the international media storm this would create, and was very aware that her own safety might be in jeopardy if people began to seriously look into Amigo accounts. When John heard this name, the sixth day he was in Oathoa, he knew immediately it was the name of a powerful person—clandestine, and perhaps the power behind people like Carlos DeRolfo and Hulk Hernández.

Later he was to find out that he was right.

Little Boots was Hulk Hernández's employer. She was the overseer of everything that had happened at Amigo Mining concerning the funnelling of money. She was one of the principal overseers of everything that happened in their state. Very few people spoke her name aloud.

5.

ALL THIS TIME SHARON DEROLFO CAME AND WENT, FRIENDLY, positive and hoping for pictures. With a ring in her nose, her short hair and dark eyes, she reminded Mary Cyr of those young women who had disliked her in university for being wealthy—who could in the end burn her at some stake. This is what she thought as she nervously lit a cigarette.

"Those who burn bras will sooner or later burn people," she had once written in her diary. "And why burn them—just take them off and put them in your third drawer. One might need them when their boobs begin to sag. Burning bras really is an affectation of the young—who want to exploit their sexuality by pretending they will not be sex objects—if that confuses me, imagine how it confuses men."

"Cyr company Tarsco will appeal Amigo claim, while Cyr doyenne trapped in Mexican jail," a headline in one of the British newspapers read.

"Charged with murder—the ongoing saga of Mary Fatima Cyr," read another.

"Vixen with her fixin's," read a third, superimposing a bottle of arsenic in her hands.

In the *News of the World* her face was turned toward the flash in the hot night air. Her eyes were large and beautiful.

All papers carried the same picture of the little waif Denise Albert—the child of the convent, lost long ago, who had once helped Mary Cyr escape.

ESCAPAR A UNA MUERTE SEGURA

Because she had trusted Mary Cyr, little Ms. Albert only:

Escaped to certain death.

"A black widow never had a more enticing web."

Suddenly on March 15—people marched against Tarsco on Parliament Hill. It was led by Ms. Rory Cruise's protege Ned Filmore. Snow fell down on him. He wore a large parka, with the hood up, his face covered, and you could see his breath on the cold air. He was carrying a sign—and there were about sixty people, but she couldn't be sure. She kept trying to understand what it was they were shouting:

"The oil flow has got to go."

And:

"It's not who Cyr employed. It's what their industry has destroyed."

That was it. She suddenly looked pleased with herself that she had figured it out.

Yes, yes, she thought, that's it!

Mary saw it on Mexican TV. Black bean soup and bread were in front of her, but she had not touched a meal in days. At first she had wanted to eat and couldn't, and now she couldn't eat.

She was in fact slowly drifting away from every one of them.

She looked up at this Ned, saw some ice on his beard, and his wide, accusing eyes. He was very good at accusing.

"I knew you when you were young," she said to the slouched dark figure far to the north of her. She could have been Cato three thousand years before. Perhaps she did not know this.

She was exhausted, hot and tired. Nor had her nausea or diarrhea stopped. She found it difficult to breathe and she asked for a puffer. But as yet they had not given her one.

"It's snowing there—look, we're having a late-winter storm. *¡Nieve!*" she exclaimed like a child, looking around, beaming in pride at how inexhaustible Canadian snow seemed to be. Wanting to share it with the whole world and realizing she was alone in her delight. Just like the time she was in Morocco and tried to get the Stanley Cup final on TV.

But she was sick and one of the other women said she smelled. She did not complain at all to Mary Cyr; she complained to the guards, and taunted Mary when she could—though Mary did not know what this taunting was about. But a couple of the guards smiled at the naughty things this woman said.

Mary was not faring well. So something had to be done. And a ruling came from Tallagonga that she should have a bigger cell with a larger cot—for they did not want any recriminations. There was one cell that was indeed larger. It was the cell people had been put into years ago, before they were hanged. It was larger because they usually hanged more than one person at a time.

They could place a small fridge in it, which she had said she could pay for. Then she would be allowed to shower across at the villa, which in fact she was still paying for.

So at five the next morning she was woken by two guards. One was Erappo Pole.

"Yes," she said, "what is it—am I going to go home?"

She had been dreaming of snow, on a little lake, just beyond the cottage, and all was white and pure, and snow fell on her white hat.

But she was woken from this dream. They did not speak. Both of them wore gloves and white plastic bibs. They grabbed her, one under each arm, and dragged her along the hallway, with the other prisoners still asleep, and then out beyond the room where she had last met John Delano. (Her heart was glad.)

She was taken to another cell—it was slightly larger and more solitary. It had its own table, a bigger cot. And looking out into the hallway, she could see the television easier.

That afternoon she was once again taken out and allowed to shower in private at the villa.

Then she was brought back, her hands cuffed before her, shackles on her feet.

"It's strange—I often think of Bob Dylan," she wrote. "He could make a pretty good song out of all this, I bet."

6.

ONE LIFE TO LIVE, HER FAVOURITE SOAP, WAS ON IN SPANISH, SO she watched it every day if she could. She never knew if she liked John Zak or Danielle Faraldo as directors. But she liked Tanya Clarke and

Nurse Betty, and Chris Cardona as Carlo's thug—and all the main actors and actresses.

The bed here was larger. And there was a window. She could still see the blind donkey that had become her only friend. Though her view of it and the paddock had altered so much it was almost as if she was looking at a brand-new donkey. However, within five or ten minutes she realized it was the same one.

One wall of this cell was painted green, one was painted red. And there on the red wall, halfway up, was ¡*Viva Cristo!* painted in green, as if the damn thing was following her about.

The little woman guard told her that she had heard that this was the cell Father Ignatius had been taken to an hour before his execution, to be fed his last meal.

"Ah," Mary said, "they killed him bit by bit—the world is very good at doing that."

"*Muy malo,*" the guard said, and she blessed herself. The guard did like Mary Cyr.

Looking through the bars, Mary could see the *blessed* women loitering around her former cell, yelling insults to her—looking perplexed, then speaking to each other—then looking into the cell again. She found this very funny and began to laugh. Soon one of them heard her, and they all rushed over and across a little patch of grass. They all gathered about the cell window. Looking in. They all took turns patting her still-damp hair.

Lucretia said:

"*Mi amiga ¿puede consigo mi foto contigo?*"

My friend, can I get my photo taken with you?

It seemed for one moment all of them were thanking God she had been found. Lucretia had staked her life on Mary Cyr paying a huge price. The idea, of course, was that everyone, no matter who they were, now believed they had the right to interfere with Mary, to say something to her, to exploit her fame for their own satisfaction—and Lucretia Rapone did just that.

"Devil," she would say. Lucretia said it with such a lively tone one never knew if she was joking or not—but behind it there was a hidden thought—devil was what Mary might be or might not be depending on what Lucretia could achieve herself—and that was the idea. Your victim is the devil if you benefit by your victim being one. So she would say *diablo* and shake her head as if she was joking one moment, and then look balefully about the next depending on who was around. Then she would ask Constable Fey what the charges were going to be, and what were they coming to in this day and age, for a woman like that to be able to just come down to Oathoa and do whatever she wanted with children.

Constable Fey would look at her with a particular moral disgust and tell her to go home. Tell her she should be careful not to become too, too involved. Tell her that she did not know what was actually happening and it was wrong for her to think that she did. But Lucretia would only snap gum and look with brooding eyes at him, and then with complete disrespect spit when John Delano walked by.

"They have sent ruthless people down to protect her," she would say. "Mark my words."

But she still wanted her picture taken with Mary; and so she got one with both of them standing side by side.

Sometimes Lucretia would get tired of all this protesting and would sit on the sidewalk with her feet splayed out; smoking cigarettes, and waving to certain men as they drove by.

"Are you taking care of things, Lucretia?" they would yell.

She would stare at them closely to see if they were making fun of her or not. If they were making fun of her, she would throw her finger out at them; if she decided they were not being too rude, she would sigh and nod and say:

"*Todo en la ciudad queda a mí.*"

Everything in town is left up to me.

Then they would all laugh and catcall, and Lucretia would stand and move away, along the street to some more favourable spot.

One day Lucretia was interviewed by a television couple—who did investigative reports for Mexican daytime programs. This was a married couple, whose three years of investigative reports never strayed into anything too dangerous. And psychologically this particularly gruesome case was a bonanza for them, for the entire world was now furious with this *unwholesome* woman, and this woman was no Little Boots Baron (who these investigative reporters refused to believe existed, yet who they knew watched their program daily), but she was a childlike woman, spoiled and naive. And a Canadian, to boot—that is, from a country that never exercised too much power.

So they came south with a camera crew to find out about her, and interviewed a woman who was said by the locals to know very much about the case.

Lucretia Rapone.

And suddenly halfway through the interview a feeling overcame her. She blurted:

"They were my children—both of them."

"*¿Fueron sus hijos?*"

"*Sí, sí—mis hijos—oh mis, mis hijos.*"

Her life was changed from that moment. Her bold face, with her wide earrings and dyed-blond hair, was seen everywhere; in all corners of the world. In fact, if a week after that statement was made you were walking through a street in Nairobi and suddenly looked to your left—to a news kiosk—you would see a picture of Lucretia Rapone, the mother of the murdered child.

The woman who had waited for her husband at the mine. The woman who searched for little Florin every day. The woman who knew what it was like to lose a son already, and who was in agony. Who went to the jail to see her tormentor, to beg her tormentor to tell her where her little child Florin was. This is why she went there—poor Lucretia! Poor Lucretia had no idea that she went there to find out about her child until it was mentioned in the newspapers.

But Mary Cyr was too cold-hearted. Mary Cyr said nothing.

7.

GREG KNEW WHERE THE COMPANY'S ASSETS WERE—THAT IS, HE knew what ports those ships that flew under Tarsco's banner were near to—one was off the coast of Newfoundland—another was entering the Panama Canal—and one was heading toward Mexico, off the coast of California, and it was that ship, the *Eeekum Seekum*, that he felt should change course to its home port of Vancouver. He was right to do so—for as soon as it entered Mexican water, there was a plan by Mexican authorities to board it, and force it to port. His caution, however, was only looked upon not as concern for crew but only for the oil cargo. This was not at all fair, but fairness was not a premium when it came to Mary Cyr.

Which was to say that everything done exacerbated the idea of her guilt, even that which was intended to mitigate it. That is, people might have seen the seizing of a vessel as a condition of her discharge. This only reinforced the idea of Greg Cyr's heartlessness. And it seemed the captain's order, hard to starboard, made in simplistic Newfoundland brogue, set the tone for that. Perley, knowing this was to come, was like the man who does not want to witness a combat in the ring, or a tightrope walker. That is, he continued to peek through closed eyes, at the television stories parading her as a monster.

When Greg ordered the turning of his ship, Perley was at a loss over what to do. He simply left his office and sat in the park. Some days he went to the museum and walked by rows of yesteryear's relics—many artifacts donated by his own family.

And certain people—some who went to our local school with him, and now were down on their luck—knew he was at a loss. And they watched his every move.

Perley went for a drive along the highway, all the way to the cottage on the Miramichi. He stopped into the tavern and ordered a glass of draft beer and a pickled egg. He sat alone and no one there knew who he was.

But everyone was talking about his cousin.

"Ole Blair himself popped her cherry—what I heard."

"Ya, an I myself had a chance to bang her one night at a bar, down-river—she even offered me money, but I said no."

"I woulda taken it."

"Na, not worth it."

Perley went outside. He stared at his new boots; his new fifteen-hundred-dollar coat; his thick heavy-rimmed glasses; his big-buckled belt, which he liked. Yes, he thought, he was wearing four thousand dollars on his body and all his life he had been a fool.

He went home shaking and cold. He sat in the sauna for a while with his heavy coat and boots still on.

"I must go down," he told a reporter—and he was interviewed on television saying so.

"You—what could you ever do?" the reporter asked.

"I could trade places with her," he said.

Two more weeks would pass, where Perley would threaten to come down, to trade places—two weeks of agony for Mary where she seemed powerless to make him understand. He nor John, nor her former lovers, could ever help her anymore.

And then suddenly a Mexican man came to him, Perley, when he was on his daily walk.

"I can get your wife out of jail," he said.

"She is not my wife—she is my cousin."

"Well, I have come here with her blessing—but it is up to you—it is entirely up to you."

Her blessing.

One payment—cash—American money—and she will be home—I will give you my cell phone number—you let me know—but if you tell anyone, the deal is off—*amigo*.

Perley did not tell anyone. He forgot about it. For a number of days. He said nothing. Then he realized he couldn't sleep. He hadn't eaten a meal in days. Oh, it was not true. It could not be. He was not sure the man was even Mexican. But what would most of us do?

He dialed the number.

PART SEVEN

1.

THE GIRLS THAT SUMMER—RHONDA, BONNIE AND GAIL—SHE called them "Tootsie one," "Tootsie two" and "Tootsie three"—of course she called them "the little foxes" as well—retaliated. They bided their time but then struck out at the most unfortunate and vulnerable of the Cyrs one windy August day when the east wind blew down along the flattened grasses, and the swings were empty, and the sky too blue.

On that day, so long ago, the three girls accused Perley of "exposing himself" in front of them down at the boathouse. They declared he had yelled at them to look at him at the exact moment he held his towel open. They all ran up the beach traumatized to beat the snot out of Moses, as Mary Cyr later exclaimed, screaming and crying. Their theatrics is what caught the attention of a man mowing his lawn, and a woman lying on her lawn chair just down the beach.

"Those poor dears," the woman said. "Certainly looked completely distraught!"

"Did you know what they were distraught over?"

"No, but I was clever enough to guess."

One does not know how well people have been trained all their lives to say just those proper things, to emulate one another's outrage in a pinch. In fact it was what the girls so unconsciously relied upon; it represented the mimicry of those who have lost their way and wish to scapegoat those they can put on display.

So the police for a second time in a month had to come to the door of the large cottage. For the second time one of the Cyr children had been caught up in scandal. For the second time the family was bruised and subject to ruinous gossip. And what was becoming clear is the Cyr children felt so entitled they simply assumed they could torment other children.

Perley stood on the veranda with his head down, ashamed and unable to look up, even when Garnet told him to. He was told to go to the Rhonda Cottage (this was the name the kids had given it) and apologize, and he was driven in a police car, with kids following behind, shouting and laughing, until the police car stopped and the officer told them to go home.

So the word got around that he had exposed himself in front of girls.

He couldn't look at the girls when he apologized. (Or in fact any other girls for years.)

He stared at his flat white running shoes and the dust that filtered upward when he moved them. He had not done so, he whispered; he had not even known the girls were there. No one believed him.

Mary Cyr stood up for him. She stood up for him immediately and ferociously, like a queen with a dagger pitched against a thousand men.

"It's a lie—those girls—Tootsie one especially is a liar—they spied on him to see him in the buff—and then ran to tell—yes, all of them are spies—I know a family of Vanderfluffer people and they are spies—chronic English-hating spies just the kind that we have in Canada—maybe one of the girls—I suspect Tootsie two is a Vanderfluffer—she has all the wiles to be one—insincere, middle-class values—schoolgirl, needs to be attached to people, mouth packed full of braces—has friends, sometimes smells nice—just the type."

And then she walked away, and spoke of it no more. But it was the middle of summer—days were listless and the shades of trees where hammocks were strung left their shadows across well-manicured lawns and multitudinous flower arrangements in the sun.

Behind those doors of the great cottage, larger than most houses in the province, beyond the smell of oak and wood polish and blinds pulled down to exclude the sun, behind all of this was someone else. He was there when Mary Cyr was peering out the window with her binoculars—he was there when she watched the girls walk up the lane.

Now and then she would turn to him, binoculars still in her hand, and say:

"Do you want to see them, Bobby—all of them will go on diets, and be concerned about equality, enough to make you itch, and will have pleasant-looking faces—rely on CBC news stories about First Nations, have some cause like pro choice, be well known as advocates—they would put someone like you to death, Bobby—do you understand, Bobby, poor Bobby—poor little Bobby, perhaps you don't."

Then she would hurriedly look through her binoculars again.

"Ah yes—there they go—look—sand in their shoes, smell of the sea, wind in their hair, their little freckled, blushed faces—pathetic—they will turn on each other—wait and see! And when they do, when that time comes, I hope I am there to witness it all."

Bobby Cyr was not supposed to be Mary Cyr's child. He was supposed to be a child of one of the relatives who actually never really existed, a relative who could not take care of him and had given him to Nan and Garnet. (This was Greg's idea—and Greg's side of the family was *the* side of the family.) Bobby was in fact not supposed to live. But he did live. And he was born in a stable, a manger of sorts—the barn out back, near a beautiful 1948 teakwood motorboat that hadn't been in the water in years. Mary went to the barn because she had successfully hidden her pregnancy. (This was the disgrace Greg was sure had happened at his wedding after she had drunk too much champagne, and acted, as Nan said, "like her mother." But no one knew for certain. They only knew it had to be her fault.)

Nonetheless Bobby was a child suffering from many "debilitating illnesses," as was later revealed. The idea that Bobby was a *child of incest* had started somehow at the moment of his birth, and it did not matter where the rumour came from, or exactly why it came. The rumour manifested itself and became more and more pervasive: Blair Cyr, a horrid

Catholic mogul, had impregnated his favourite grandchild; and that is why Bobby was the way he was.

After the RCMP came to the house, people followed Perley calling him many names: pervert, rich pervert, dickless pervert.

Finally, he took to his bed. He lay in the semi-dark room of midday—his eyes half opened to the grey air and the stream of light from the closed window blinds, his huge gut half impaled by a pale light, and the sound of wind now and again just rustling those blinds, and the pervasive scent of sea and dust that filtered through the vents and walls, with shells that he had collected on trips to the small islands and beaches of the bay lying dormant in the corners of bookshelves, painted colours that he thought were special when he was five and six years of age.

"Poor Perley," she said to Bobby. "He has no one to help him—he is surrounded by traitors—"

He called Mary to him and said—all of nineteen years of age:

"They make so much fun of me—I can't stand it anymore—I am so unfit, so useless I want to die—if anything else happens, if one more thing happens, I will kill myself. I will drink poison or something—or shoot myself or something."

She was sitting on the edge of his bed listening to him, her eyes wide and compassionate, and then suddenly she jumped up:

"Shape up—shape the hell up—die—for those people—those giddy girls—with names like Rhonda and Bonnie and Gail, and their wholesome Protestant complexions—what do you think they think of Bobby and me—my Catholic name—Mary Fatima Cyr—they have been taught to hate Catholics, and they always do what they are taught."

"But they don't know about Bobby!"

"Of course those people know about Bobby—and they stare at me as if I am some tramp. They are the ones who started the story about my granddad. How dare you say you will kill yourself! Die over a woman named Rhonda who will curl up her nose at any one who does not fit in, tattle on anyone who is down-and-out, be irreverent at only those things she is taught are safe to demean—Christ, Perley, snap out of it—what will happen to me if you go around killing yourself!"

Then she ran downstairs, ordered Mildred, the cook, out of the kitchen, and took to the stove and made him vegetable soup—even though it was thirty degrees Celsius outdoors—and brought it up to him on a plate with crackers and a big glass of milk.

"I hear you have an issue," Rhonda said to her the very next day. "I hear your issue is a boy, a deformed boy, and you keep him hidden in the house."

"I have more than one issue," Mary Cyr said. "And all of them are much greater and less deformed than yours. And will be much greater than yours in times to come."

But from now on, she would be alone.

Garnet and Nan had tried their best not to expose her to scandal to hide the child everyone knew about, and this was the result. In fact the result would be much worse. It would with time be the harshest result in the world.

2.

JOHN KNEW MARY WAS AND WAS NOT THE ARCHITECTURAL genius of her own demise—as was so often stated after she turned thirty. She had too much genius for that, though it was not genius acknowledged. But John's was a consummate intelligence too, factored into everything by an X. If Mary Cyr does this, what then is the end result? The end result is either A or B—but it may very well be C, predicated on if X becomes involved or not. X was John Delano. X was involved with her since she was twelve years of age, was the deliverer of warning cries she, and her family, often received and too many times frivolously ignored.

Too drunk, too careless, too flippant.

3.

ANOTHER WEEK PASSED. THE HARSHNESS OF SUNLIGHT increased; the sound of the sea took on a difference, a kind of languid unsettled quality. The old porter said with a smile that he knew there would be a grave storm that would come before Easter Sunday.

John went back to his room with a bottle of water, and took his pills and looked in the mirror at his worn face and haggard eyes. He tried to think. Someone had just tried to run him over—while he was crossing the street. But of course, how could he be completely sure? Perhaps it meant nothing. He drank a beer and paced back and forth. Then he went out.

The sun had disappeared and a breeze blew in from the sea. Now and again clouds formed on the horizon, and moved quickly over the town. He went to the back of Mary's villa and climbed the stairs. The stairs led up to the patio and back entrance. A deck chair, with Mary's book on the Sistine Chapel still sitting on it. John noticed a splotch of blood on the tiled roof—almost impossible to see because of the tiles' rusty colouring. Then, following it back down the stairs, there were small drops of blood. When he crossed the road, he could tell in a second that the boy was thrown here or had fallen. He walked another ten paces and saw where a car had turned and driven off. Then he noticed small sprays of blood on the cement wall. This was where little Victor had been after suffering an injury.

So he walked back across the road and up the stairs again, inspecting the blood. The way the blood had dropped John believed it was from the boy's nose.

He tried the handle on the door and it opened.

He went inside, went to the bed, and then turned and walked over to the window and looked out on the street.

That night he went back and had a beer with his friends.

The Dutch doctor and her German husband.

They told him they were taking their findings to Mexico City—they would see someone there if they could. They had already spoken to the Dutch ambassador, who knew a lawyer there—perhaps he could help. They were very upset. But frustrated at all the obstacles now in place.

Unknown to John, Fey had conducted the same investigation he had— he had walked the same path to the wall, and he was certain the boy had been almost killed and then thrown from a car. He must have tried to make it to the room, and collapsed. Fey also was certain he knew whose car it was. When he mentioned this to Erappo Pole, he got no response, just a baleful look out the window, as if he, Fey, had turned against his own.

"He was thrown from a car," Fey said in a slightly singsong voice that seemed to tease Erappo into nodding.

Mary Cyr would not have been able to do that. That and the Dutch doctor's findings that a small amount of arsenic was in the children she tested made Fey rethink the case. But of course, he did not have to rethink it. He was playing both sides—one for his commanding officer, a devotee of Tallagonga, and one for the greater investigation being conducted in Mexico City.

Victor and Florin had come to him, after their dad was trapped underground. That look of a child, the hope he had of being believed, the fear he had of Mr. DeRolfo, who came up as Fey was speaking to them—all of this concerned him. Then a week or so later Victor was found dead. It was very convenient for certain people.

Fey could not convince Tallagonga of this—she did not want to hear it. Her future depended on her not hearing it. So she had to counter it. And Fey knew she would. And if this went on, this lie would give Mary Cyr twenty years in prison. It would mean the end of her life. There was also the callow glee at giving a foreign woman this much time. It was terrible, but he knew that came into it. But what did Erappo Pole say when Fey said he was concerned?

"Think of the execution in Texas of Raoul Lorta."

This was a criminal who the Mexican Government had recently unsuccessfully petitioned to have his death sentence commuted.

"But she is a Canadian," Fey said.

"*Uno es el mismo que el otro*," the man answered brashly.

One is the same as the other.

If Lorta could be executed for murder, when he was only a drug dealer and was never proven to have committed murder, Mary Cyr could be convicted of murder if she was a board member of Tarsco. And that was Tallagonga's reasoning to a T.

All of this would be known by the world, after the fact. And the worst of it was, as a demonstration of the frailty of human nature, those who would be compromised by it all secretly knew this and for the life of them could not stop. They were being pushed along by the very force of these events and the terrible rage it caused. Even DeRolfo sensed he was doomed the longer this went on, the longer Mary Cyr was held, and even his daughter, who had been interviewed by the BBC, CBC and ABC, knew halfway through the ABC interview—halfway through the interviewer asking her a question about police investigation of other suspects, when a chill came over her as she remembered Mary Cyr's smile—she knew if Mary Cyr was the least innocent, they were doomed. But she too, with a book deal, could not stop.

They have moved my room. I have my own fridge, Mary Cyr texted John that afternoon.

Do you want to come for my birthday—
I can drink and dance here alone in my cell.

Then she texted:
It is not my birthday, really.
So there will not be many guests.

Then she texted:

Unless we count those outside my window.

Mary at times would dance by herself. She had learned to do that quite well long ago.

4.

IN TORONTO SOME YEARS BEFORE, MARY OWNED AN APARTMENT building near the Annex. She retreated there after her son, Bobby, died. She wanted to be alone—and yet she had always been. And here too, she was alone, surrounded by people.

There were many fine buildings and many tweed-wearing professors and many ideas, and much talk about equality, and many high-end civil servants to run along the pathways with. She joined many causes, and her name was in the paper. She was seen in the company of certain slightly famous men. They were all politic in the right way, hoping for environmental laws, "No Smoking" legislation, and determined to curb military spending. They grew up in the age of those who hated the military. For a time—a small amount of time—she thought this was radical, and they, the people she knew now, were brilliant.

They were in an understated and mostly unspoken way all against her family, its hold on papers and oil, and its great mining company Tarsco. They never said this directly, but they implied it in many ways. And so she knew she was being used.

She went here and there, had dinner with the leader of the provincial New Democratic Party, gave money to charities supported by people she had just been introduced to. She joined Greenpeace, wrote an op-ed article against Greg's proposed pipeline. She appeared on talk shows. She had met Winnie Mandela. She looked bright and cheerful, wore white shoes buckled at the ankles. She was seen in the company of a man with grey hair. Once in a picture she was standing behind—

just over the right shoulder of—Princess Diana, somewhere in England.

She spent spring in France. She said she was going to open up a daycare, but for some reason didn't get a licence.

She came back to Canada. Certain of her acquaintances in Toronto met her at the airport. They were all fraught with worry over her and her family's repressive tentacles. Some were draft dodgers from the Vietnam War, living out their lives in obscurity in Canada. The men often wore brown leather jackets, and had soft, greying beards that emancipated them from sexuality and embraced class struggle without ever being in a poor man's house; causes like Palestine and Hamas filled their days. They spoke about the RCMP and the tyranny of the army. John used a contact in Toronto's 51 Division to find out what she was up to. Her new friends collected around her. They drank in small bars, glasses of pale red wine, and stared out at traffic and spoke of transformation and change—and could she help them.

"Sounds about right," John said when he heard about her newfound commitments. These were Canadian men doing Canadian things, John supposed, because there was nothing left for them to do.

She later wrote:

"Their democracy came at the pleasure of the United States and most of them were too blind to see their own part in this. They all believed they were under desperate control, when they were freer than 90 percent of humanity, and on their own wouldn't have lasted as long as a three-minute egg."

Most of them were just affluent enough to pretend to hate the wealthy, knew enough First Nations celebrities to be concerned about Aboriginal rights. Yes, all of them in some way or the other—those at any rate who found out who she was—wanted to influence her against her own family for their own benefit. That was where the lie really was. They needed her to insinuate themselves into her family and become advocates against it to hold her up as the one they protected. She would stop oil exploration in the North Atlantic; oil tankers from docking in Saint John; freight trains with oil containers, going east. She could be used as a prop not for her life but for their advocacies. Still, they turned up the heat when the wind blew, and had their furnaces checked in the fall.

"Do you understand any of this?" the source asked John.

"Unfortunately yes," John said.

"Can I ask you one question?"

"Sure."

"Do you still feel in any way part of the country you were sworn to protect?"

She took some cocaine. She was arrested.

One of the men she hung around with was Ned, the protege of her former friends Mr. and Ms. Cruise.

Ned was an important man now. He had long ago left the shelter. He was being paid a good salary to promote eco-management and be an environmental crisis watchdog and a member in good standing of a certain pro-Palestinian organization.

"I have been there," he told her.

"You have—where?"

"That's apocryphal," he intoned.

"Oh—I see—I have been there too," she said.

"Apocryphal?"

"No—actually."

"Environmental crisis watchdog—"

She liked the sound of it, she said—it rolled off her tongue. It was worth, she said, her honourary doctorate.

5.

THAT WAS THE TIME WHEN PERLEY PHONED JOHN, WORRIED about her again, after he and Greg had gone to Toronto and she refused to see them. This was a month or so after John had gone to her cottage demanding to know where she was, and had run slapdab into former prime minister Brian Mulroney and the glass of freshly squeezed orange juice.

"Your family told me not to bother with her," John said.

"Sorry, John—it wasn't me. I just want someone to talk some sense into her. *Please*."

So John flew up on a beautiful afternoon in summer, took a taxi into downtown, and found her apartment building (that is, the building she not only stayed at but owned) and waited for her in the lobby, with the security guard watching him out of the corner of his eye and pacing with his hands behind his back.

Mary came in late that night. She had two friends with her, one was Ned and one was Ted—those kinds of men who will always want to be called males. Ned carried keys in his hand, his ponytail and partly baldhead oddly complementing his stark blue denims and his thousand-dollar leather jacket.

He looked at John with mildly ironic eyes—the kind that never seem to go out of fashion but never know the truth. Her second friend, Ted, somewhat broader-shouldered, somewhat more exuberant, was a robust leftist of the western Canadian stamp. Which John felt always had a bit of the pedestrian goofball in it. He was in town on a visit, to give a lecture on oil drilling in the western Artic, and Mary Cyr was a name and he had lucked in. Ned and he had met her for a late lunch and it had gone on for hours. How could her family be involved in any of this—did she not understand how they were ruining the habitats of millions of *viable entities?* (That is what they chose to call animals and plants.)

They ate well, dined well, drank long.

She of course had paid.

When the two men found out that John was the RCMP officer, they looked knowingly at each other.

"He's the one who loves you?" one of them said.

"Yes—he is the creepy old man who loves me," Mary said. "And now he has come up here once again to ruin my fun. My family sent him to spy. He most likely has bullets on him."

John had heard her speak like this before—once every three or four years she had to be wise, in some way that lessened her.

He told her that was not at all true. She was too drunk to care. She spoke of the occult—she spoke of New Orleans—of being in Haiti. Then she was silent. She slumped against the wall as she lit a cigarette. The security guard said there was a No Smoking policy. She ignored him.

John asked her if she would like to come home, said that everyone was worried about her.

"Never again," she said. "Back to thieves and ruthless cousins—I want nothing to do with them—or with you."

"Then I am no longer obligated to be your bodyguard—" he said.

"Then you are fired—" she said, "and you won't get paid."

He let her in on a little-known secret. He had not been paid in years. He had taken it upon himself, travelled here and there, without being paid a dime. The two men with her thought this entertaining, the idea that John had travelled at his own expense for seven years. In a way John did too. Then Ned said:

"Maybe you better go?"

And John stared at him, this pale forty-year-old boy, with his schooled morality almost deafening, and smiled.

The robust leftist from Edmonton or Saskatoon, one of those places that have by intellectual standards become somewhat burdened by their universities, asked her to marry him. He was that in love with her, that much smitten. He had divorced, remarried and divorced again—always seeking love but never loving enough to be granted it.

He had been in town a week. She knew he would—propose; she had waited for it, to let him down as gently as possible.

They went on this way, she and her friends, always being outraged at the world that held people like them back. They were part of the central casting of a new stratagem of unease. They were forever adopting the correct posture. They in the end never freed anyone, simply themselves from any deep obligation.

She noticed this about them after John had gone. She noticed the sun on their thin wire glasses, their smooth beards and unimpeachable ponytails, all signifying a certain uninvolved academic status. She waited for John to return so she could tell him that she hadn't meant anything by her slur that she loved him, in fact the only thing she ever did was love—but he did not come back. She remembered too that for the first time Perley had gone to her great apartment in her grand building, had walked in, saw her lying across the bed naked in the middle of the afternoon, and had dragged her to the bathroom, where he threw her into a tubful of cold water. It was the first time he had been furious with her—he too had gone home. Sometimes in the middle of the afternoon she would look around, hoping they would come back. But they did not. She found herself looking at the phone, hoping it would ring, and when it did, she would pick it up saying:

"John, Perley?"

Yet it was neither.

But then came 9/11. They watched the buildings fall, at the great heady blame cast on the men jumping to their deaths out of those tower windows. Neddy spoke about the attack against the US being a good thing, justified—or perhaps engineered by the CIA. (Which if it was she supposed might have been a bad thing.) One has to know the intellectualized Canadian to know this—which means that on the face of it they never have one position.

"So that is how you think of it all, Ned?" she asked on September 13 of that year.

"It should be how all people think—all people who want a better world."

"Oh dear me."

6.

NED BEGAN TO BE NOTICED AND APPEARED ON A TALK SHOW called *New Wave,* which employed people who had drifted away from the CBC or TVOntario.

"America has no one to blame but America, I am afraid. It's what I've been saying for years."

He came back to the apartment, telling her of speaking engagements and an op-ed piece. She stared at him quietly, wearing a black dress, sitting on a white sofa in the middle of the September afternoon, drinking a glass of sparkling water. He was somewhat startled at the blackness of that dress, and her quiet features. She simply nodded as he spoke. She wore another black dress the next afternoon. Then she went and bought another one.

The way he spoke of it being his time, the way he announced himself, she felt, looking at his rather Anglican face, might be as bad as the wars now happening.

"Don't you see—this is my opening—MY TIME," he said, drinking red wine one evening as dark approached, "It's my time—my time to tell the world who I am."

"Oh yes of course—I see," she said. "It is your time. How fortunate you are. That's the way it is. I mean it was so many other people's time as well."

He did not understand her—Neddy Fillmore.

But she did understand him.

She waited for John to come back. She had it planned; that is, how she would approach him—how she would allow him to talk her into leaving. But he did not come back.

She wore black for some months. Then one day she telephoned John Delano and left a message:

"I've figured it out," she said.

A week or so passed where no one saw her.

Then out of the blue she phoned her Toronto friends.

She was going to have a great, grand party at her two-storey, four-bedroom apartment on the eighth and ninth floors of her apartment building, she told them. She invited them all—even the robust leftist of the western Canadian stamp—to come.

She told them the key to the private elevator would be with the doorman.

They came, almost a hundred of them—to drink and party at the Cyrs' expense. But the hostess did not show.

Only a picture of her cousin Warren, the Cyr who had died in one of the 9/11 towers, sitting on the big marble table in the foyer. His smile seemed to give him away—a kind of restive yet tender smile, the first-born son of the important side of the family, the one who was the most secretive and influential. The one who gave over three million dollars a year to charity without ever announcing it to anyone.

She had left bottles and bottles of wine; goat's cheese and liver pâté.

They waited, and they drank, and then they became aware of something, and almost ashamed. It was simply the weight of this picture with the date of his birth, and the date of his death, September 11, 2001, etched on a silver sleeve below his name, and their hostess not showing up. But the new black dress she had bought hanging alone in the corner. They became aware, silently, all of them. Then they remembered her dressing in black all those days while they preened over those barbican deaths. Her black dress finally seemed to unnerve them all. And they drifted out one at a time, to the private elevator, and all of them stole away, in their fashionable all-weather coats, well after dark.

Ned left her a note:

"Where are you, love—hope your family has not influenced you again unduly—I have worked quite hard to free you of all of that."

Yes, and free her of the 1.9 million he had asked for to help with his concerns. Grave concerns about the deforestation in Malaysia, the new territorial demands by Israel—the 1.9 million she in fact had taken from her bank to give to him—to spite everyone—just hand it on over, a chuckle-headed thing to do, ho de ho ho ho.

But she did not hand it over after all. If one looked at the phone records, he phoned her more than a dozen times a day:

"Please get it touch. I am desperately concerned about you—we all are—everyone—"

And his note remained on the table in the foyer for three months. For three months she wore black. The apartment was left silent and empty. Silent as a tomb, and as empty as those 9/11 tombs would always be.

7.

SO THEN SHE LEFT, AND NONE COULD FIND HER, OR KNEW WHERE she was. But people surmised. Her family asked John to find her once again. But he could not do so. Not for a long time.

There was a lake the family owned. There was a boat she lived on— or a cottage laid out in the wilds of Quebec. She had taken a helicopter somewhere—her friends said her family had muzzled her because she was too vocal. Something was going on. Months went by—who knew where she was? She sold her apartment in Toronto at a loss within a week for 21.4 million, and came home to New Brunswick, to hide from all the terror of the world. She had enough money to last 230 lifetimes.

Sometimes deep in her lair she would watch television. And once, sitting in the gloom of a giant room, facing the TV with her head in her hands, she watched a BNN interview with her cousin Greg. Every now and again she would reach over and pick up a grape. She waited, even hoped, but he did not ever once mention her.

She rowed out to sea. She took walks in the dark. She once handed five hundred dollars to a boy who was walking alone, along the highway in the cold.

"Bobby?" she said. "Bobby?" But she must have been drunk.

She visited the First Nations reserve, went to a band meeting and apologized. The band council was silent; she had her head down, playing with her fingers. She was trying to apologize for Charlie Francis—if they knew this, she wasn't sure. Tears came down her cheeks. She was trying to explain she had nothing more than a marshmallow to offer him one day.

"Please, Miss Cyr," Mrs. Francis said. "Come, dear, and sit with us and have a cup of tea."

She went into the Oyster River area with her quarter horse, Jaberoo. She spent two days alone near Aggens Pool.

She rode her Harley 883 along the Acadian coast wearing a sleeveless leather vest, moving through the gears as gracefully as anyone in her high leather boots, her hair braided and her arms bronzed. A small tattoo of Bobby above her left breast. She spoke to no one when she paid for gas.

Then she was gone again. Someone said they had seen her in Brussels, looking up documents. Some said she visited Vimy Ridge. Then Sister Alvina received a picture of a very beautiful woman standing near the shrine at Lourdes:

"For old times' sake," it said, "I had to visit this blessed place." Mary Fatima Cyr.

She came home. Lived in Halifax for a while. She had a sense of impending doom; she was quite sure someone would try to destroy her.

She had no idea that Warren had gone to a secret meeting that September morning to start an investigation about Amigo's dealings.

"My golly," Warren, who never swore, said. He was looking at what his lawyer had secretly collected about Señor DeRolfo's partners, and how the mine had remained open all during the time Tarsco had asked that it be shut, and had sold the coal without revealing it to them. Millions in extra profit, from a decrepit grave. And he had just arranged and sent them fourteen million dollars for upgrades to reopen a mine that had never closed but that was used as a legitimate front for other things.

He discovered that morning that DeRolfo did not control this mine— other people did.

"My golly," he said.

Ten seconds before the plane hit one floor beneath him. So the money was received and he was gone. All of this would come to light because of Alfonso Bara and the people he had in place in Oathoa, including his biggest asset, Constable Fey.

If it was in time to save Mary Cyr or not, no one knew.

8.

ONE NIGHT AT THE GRAND COTTAGE ON THE MIRAMICHI ALMOST six years after Warren died she woke in a sweat, sweating so badly she had to strip off all of her clothes.

"Yes," she said, "yes."

She looked out at the stars—one so far distant it was just a tiny speck in the vastness of space. Beyond the North Star, well it must have been a home to many, many things.

The moonlight came down on her—and two boys drinking in a scow could see her naked in the moonlight.

"That's the crazy one," one whispered.

"My god, look—I can see her beautiful breasts."

She continued to look out at the star.

"Maybe I will go there," she said.

So she did. That is, she was continually worried that her father's money had been wasted—why she felt this she did not know. But there was something about money going out near September 11 that always troubled her. Where had that money gone?

So she went to Saint John the next evening.

She walked into the small, utterly nondescript office in Saint John. There was no one there. The pale moon shone down over the harbour, the lights from the bridge glittered. There was not a sound on the street until a bar closed, and then she heard some melancholy singing;

" 'Where have all the flowers gone,' " And then it was quiet once more.

She worked only by the light from the computer. She believed any money going into or out of Tarsco belonged to her father. And in her mind, that was in fact like a computer when dealing with all of this, she believed some $14,267,918 were missing that should have been part of her father's estate. Warren had been mentored by her father, and they had both operated Tarsco—that is why Mary was on the board. So where this money had gone and why no one had tracked it after all of these years, she did not know. But she did have a report from Amigo, that came to Tarsco, by a man named Pedro Senora, who said the mine had never done upgrades. This was the report that made her aware of what Warren might have been doing.

She sat in Warren's office, which had not changed since the day he had left for New York. He had planned to be back in the office the next day. His favourite jacket hung at the back of the door. One of his favourite fishing rods was leaning against the corner. He had planned to fish the Cains River that late September.

She noticed all of this with a kind of whimsical sadness.

She went through the Tarsco files. The old Tarsco files, which were in an older, desk-model, computer covered in dust. But as slow as it was to come to life, it did show much about Warren's last days.

A sad note to his wife, Jackie, where he apologized for something unspecific. A note to his oldest boy—eleven years younger than Mary, about the fishing trip they were going to take. Then she found a file called Restoration Accounts.

What she found in this file was both sad and strange—the official transcript and the transaction of the monies sent to Amigo for a complete upgrading of the coal mine in the town of Oathoa in September 2001, on a small banking email sent out from New York and copied to his office that same moment, and then forgotten altogether. Money sent to Amigo that had never been recognized as sent. Forgotten and drifting in cyberspace, and yet received without confirmation that it had been received on the other side. That is, in that turbulent time where everything in the world had stopped, a simple transaction had been missed.

She looked for five hours for some reply from Mexico, from Amigo, some measure of assurance that the money was received and the Code of

Conduct, as Warren had written for the mine, was implemented before it was reopened.

But there was nothing at all to indicate that anyone had answered or would answer. The money seemed to have drifted somewhere and disappeared. It was a major amount of money—but if you were part of a company worth billions, it was not impossible to overlook during those terrible weeks. The mine had been operating ever since—closing only for holidays and certain union disputes.

Yet one small banking matter buried in an old address in a defunct computer confirmed the transaction had taken place, and that the Amigo mine had received the money—and the money, she was sure, was now gone from Amigo. It was nowhere.

So as a precaution she sent these transcripts along to the corporate lawyers in Mexico that Warren had retained, asking them if they knew about it, and could they verify not only that the transactions had taken place but that the safety measures were implemented. Frustratingly it took some more months to be acted upon. But finally the lawyers did act.

One of those lawyers was Mr. Xavier Santez. Long before Mary Cyr was on his radar, he had sent all of these questions that he received "from some busybody at Tarsco" to a young prosecutor from Mexico City named Alfonso Bara, asking him to:

"*Seguimiento a esta solicitud.*"

Follow up on this.

Bara sat on these transcripts for a good long time. But it was:

"*Tan claro como la nariz en la cara.*"

As plain as the nose on your face.

That people on Amigo's board had funnelled this money into a shell company run by Hulk Hernández and had divided it up among them. When questioned, they said the upgrades had all been done with their own monies but that monies promised by Tarsco had not come. So it was, as Bara knew, a lie in both directions.

The trouble was Bara did not act when he should have acted, and Mary Cyr was frustrated by the long delay.

Mary finally decided to travel to Oathoa. And she knew she would be putting herself in danger—but she was furious that her family had been cheated.

She arrived actually over a week before the catastrophe. But she carried 1.9 million on her to do something for the people of Oathoa who she suspected Amigo of misusing—the same amount of money Neddy Fillmore had asked for, being as he was concerned for the welfare of the world.

Then came the implosion and then came Victor with his improbable tape.

And then things in the small resort town of Oathoa became very strange.

And just as she was about to fly to the Canadian ambassador, to tell him what she suspected, that she was trying to get Victor Sonora to trust her, she was arrested for the murder of her little friend.

All of this John would come to know, later on.

That is, after it was all over.

PART EIGHT

1.

ONE DAY, A WEEK OR SO AFTER PERLEY SUDDENLY APPEARED ON TV, condemning people saying cruel things about his cousin, Principia took Gabriella to the DeRolfos' to help her do the work. It was Lent and Gidgit asked them to come early, for there was a lot of work to do to get ready for Easter. Easter was Gidgit's most important festival, and everyone in town knew this.

For Principia and her daughter, Carlos and Gidgit DeRolfo were the most important people they could ever possibly know. They tiptoed about the house when they cleaned it. They walked by family members with their heads down. They spoke softly when they spoke. They did not in any way betray a confidence about anyone there. They were ghosts that came and went, and had small and simple lives, and treasured the kindnesses of these important people.

On the list of things to do that day was an order to clean the inside of the Mercedes. It was ordered by the impatient Sharon DeRolfo, who wanted to use the car for the weekend.

Gabriella said she would do this. For her it was very special to be in a Mercedes, no matter what the reason.

So Sharon backed it out and left the doors open for her.

"¿*Puedes hacerlo? Necesito impecable.*"

Can you do it? I need it to be spotless.

"I don't even want a french fry left under a seat," Sharon said in English.

She said this warily but did not wait for any answer.

So little Gabriella took wood polish and a damp cloth and a small hand vacuum and went to work, thinking that someday she too might drive a Mercedes. And then she thought that yes, she knew a girl named Mercedes. And then she thought of her father, who had left Principia to go to Los Angeles. And then she thought of the tape. And she thought that yes, she might give it to Sharon DeRolfo, and that would be good because Sharon DeRolfo was a firebrand.

Sometimes young people are so in awe of older, more worldly people that it seems a shame not to live up to their expectation. But very few are able to. And certainly Sharon DeRolfo fit this peculiarity herself.

As Gabriella vacuumed, she was thinking of her father and the tape, when her hand touched something lodged under the seat. She didn't want to leave anything in the car—it had to be spotless—but the item was caught up under the seat and it did take her a while to get it free.

Then she tossed it behind her into the grass. Then she stopped, turned around and looked at it. Astonished.

It was very strange—Maxwell the truck, the toy she had helped Victor pick out for Florin. It had been under the seat of the Mercedes.

She finished polishing the wood, and the stick shift, and the steering wheel. Then she went back inside. She had Maxwell the truck in her dress's big front pocket. She was about to show the toy to her mother, when she heard someone come up behind her.

"Who told you to clean the Mercedes?" Mrs. DeRolfo asked.

"Sharon," she said, turning quickly, the vacuum still in her hand.

Mrs. DeRolfo looked at her, quietly, intently, and then said:

"Okay," and shrugged.

Gabriella was driven home by Mrs. DeRolfo, who gave her twenty-five dollars for her work.

But she could not even say thank you. She had the toy truck in her big pocket. When she examined it, it had blood on the side, near the back wheel.

Gabriella told her mother that night. Showed her the truck, and asked, "What will we do?"

"*No podemos hacer nada. Nada en absoluto,*" her mother said, frightened.

We can do nothing. *Nothing at all.*

"Think of Ángel," her mother said. "And his future."

For a few days no one at the DeRolfos' thought anything wrong. Mrs. DeRolfo thought nothing of it—and then one afternoon it hit her, like a hammer in the stomach. She suddenly remembered Florin sitting on her lap holding a toy truck. Where had that toy truck gone?

And suddenly Señora Gidgit said:

"*Hijo de puta.*"

Son of a bitch.

Too late Mrs. DeRolfo realized the little girl might have found it. So no matter what happened in Oathoa—the truth would come out, and the DeRolfos were doomed.

Unless they themselves did something about it.

2.

IT WAS ALL OVER THE TEXTS AND THE EMAILS AMONG THE KIDS at school that Florin had been thrown into the dump for the rats. That this had been done by the policeman from Canada, and that Ángel Gloton—the young boxer—was going to take care of it all. This was a rumour all over town, so that Ángel Gloton heard it as well.

Young—still filled with childlike hopes and dreams—he did not know how he was supposed to do so.

Ángel went home thinking of his friends DeRolfo and Erappo Pole, the great man and the policeman—both of them were training him for the Golden Gloves. Erappo had taught him to hit with his whole body, his legs moving in time with his right hand. The power in both hands came from his forearms, and he had an unbelievable heavy punch like his father had. He also could move his head, and feint very well.

Both said he had a great career ahead of him—as great as the great Salvador Sánchez—but was that true? Ángel did not know. He could move well—and he could bang; but he had a hard time backing away when pressed. But right now he believed them—and in order to keep this belief in himself, he had to believe them when they spoke about what had happened to Victor and Florin, his friends. DeRolfo said it was that woman Mary Cyr's fault and Erappo Pole said so too. They told him she had killed her own child, and a little convent girl years ago.

"*Una niña en el convent*," they had told him.

He was so sick to his stomach over Victor he had actually vomited. So when DeRolfo asked him to report on John Delano, to follow him, he had been doing it for days. He would report as well as he could. The idea was that John had come down here to free her—and so would use tricks and lies in order to do so. But tonight something bad happened. Ángel was not only kind he was honourable. But tonight Mr. DeRolfo's wife, Gidgit, asked him if he wanted the gold-plated Beretta. He asked why and she looked at him seriously, studying him for a moment. Then she laughed as if they both knew why—and that he was pretending he didn't know why. It was obvious in her laugh that they both knew why. Wasn't there some unspoken trouble between Ángel and the policeman from Canada?

"Between me and the policeman from Canada?"

But Mrs. DeRolfo only shrugged and laughed once more.

"*Deberíamos matarlo*," she said, her dark eyes, with false eyelashes, widening as she said it. And she said it again: "*Deberíamos matarlo.*"

We should kill him.

Then she put the gun in his hand.

"*La arma es hermosa*," she said.

The gun is beautiful.

That was her fatal flaw. She was supposed to have destroyed this handgun—but it was just too beautiful to destroy.

3.

HE WENT HOME WITH THE GUN HIDDEN UNDER HIS SHIRT. HIS hands were shaking. His mind was mixed up. In fact he knew he wasn't even angry at the policeman from Canada. If one wants to know if Catholicism does any good, it did the world of good for Ángel. He could not kill anyone. Yet now he was supposed to.

His apartment stank of dry, dead air and his aunt's hairspray. His aunt Lucretia was playing casino with two friends, and she was losing and unhappy. There was a poster of Jimi Hendrix on the far wall and a picture of Carlos Santana. There were dirty dishes in the sink, and the night before they had had to kill a scorpion sitting up on the counter.

Lucretia collected money from those boys who sold lotto tickets—it was, as John figured out on the first day he was there—a scam. The tickets were used, and of no value, but the tourists did not know this. Lucretia ran this for Hulk Hernández—but this is not what she ran— that is, the selling of lotto tickets was a way to get to know certain children, and she had transported female children for prostitution into the States. And this is what Principia suspected. That is why Principia's husband travelled with them across the boarder—and now he had disappeared. Principia did not want to blame her sister, but could not overcome the feeling that something had happened to her husband. Nor did she know that all these elaborate schemes, frauds, cons and thieveries were the domain of those the DeRolfos relied upon.

This was information Constable Fey had but as yet couldn't use.

So John Delano was in a very strange, dark world—as dark as a coal pitch. He was very bright, but it would take him months to fathom it all—why charges were laid and why they were not. It was all because of a strange coalition of loyalty, which he did not understand as yet.

Ángel brought in money from working digging ditches for the new sewer pipes, and then he would go to night school. His boxing took up most days of the week. He was now training for the Golden Gloves, which were going to happen on Cinco de Mayo.

His mother, Principia, worked for Mr. DeRolfo housecleaning three times a week. So Principia would say nothing about that family. *Nada.* Lucretia often asked her sister to put in a good word for her—saying that she could be faithful to them too.

Ángel disliked his aunt very much. He disliked the way she bullied her family—gave orders, and teased him. He remembered how she had teased Florin, to distraction, making the little boy cry, and then would walk away, her hips swaying in her tight jeans, a smile on her face. She had done that so often that once he had thrown a jab into the wall beside her head, trying to warn her to be kinder. But it did not work.

He came home one night last weekend and she was passed out on a kitchen chair, naked from the waist down. In fact that was the only time he felt truly sorry for her, for he had heard Hulk Hernández had beaten her.

He covered her gently and went to bed.

She was often drunk.

The only thing good that had happened to Lucretia lately was the fact that Mary Cyr was in jail—every day there was more salacious gossip about her, and every day Lucretia went to the jail to try to get a glimpse of her, and to speak to people about what should be done with her.

"*Ella debe ser sacada y batida.*"

She should be taken out and whipped.

She said this shaking her head profoundly.

"*Asesina,*" she would say, and bless herself. She would bless herself and light a cigarette and flick the match into the air. Sometimes out of spite— or some kind of prevocational tendency deep inside her, she went and teased the old donkey that Victor had taken care of. Because the donkey was almost blind, she would poke at it with a stick, and when it tried to run away on its small feet, she would look as if disgusted with it.

Her friends thought Lucretia was out of her mind thinking Mary Cyr would somehow make her famous—but Lucretia did think that.

"*Mary Cyr me hará famosa,*" is what she said.

Whenever she finished with the donkey her face would be pleased and sweating.

"*Asesina,*" she would say to Mary. "Prisión del Rayo—" and she would step right up to the bars of the cell. But then she would see Mary Cyr's face, and she would say:

"*Mary Cyr es hermosa,*" and smile.

"*Todo el mundo tiene una tía loca,*" Gabriella would tell her brother when he got upset with how disgustingly she spoke.

Everyone has a crazy aunt.

"*Sí, sí.*"

4.

TONIGHT GABRIELLA CAME IN JUST AFTER ÁNGEL. HIS SISTER looked at him and went into her room. A moment later she looked out from the blanket that separated her room from the hallway, and said:

"*Ángel, ven aqui un momento.*"

So he got up and went in. There was a poster on her wall of Los Angeles, where she still believed their father lived and was almost ready to send for them. There was a poster of Britney Spears and one of Selena. An old crucifix hung near a picture of her grandmother—their grandmother. And beside that picture on the dresser, a statue of Our Lady of Guadalupe.

Ángel sat down and lit a cigarette. (He knew he promised Hernández, who owned his contract with Dr. DeRolfo, not to smoke.)

His body looked as tough as the young boxer he was. His eyes were large yet narrowed like a cat's. He was a boxer who was considered very unusual—he was completely generous and compassionate. But there were many boxers like that. And there was something that went along with this compassion—he was very vulnerable because he was gullible.

Gabriella's boyfriend had died in the bump. Everyone was killed instantly, and she had run to the mine. She had only started dating him a week or so before. And all of a sudden she was in mourning for someone she didn't know very well. So she wore a black skirt to school—and she had to admit it was thrilling to have so many girls surround her and hug her, and keep others away from her.

Then one day early on when she went to the mine (which she had promised to do as long as she lived—but of course she had stopped going there by now), she saw Victor and his little brother. And that is where it happened—that is, he very quickly handed her something and said:

"Give this to Señorita Cyr."

But before she could do so, Mary Cyr was arrested.

She now wanted to show Ángel what Victor had left her—she herself had listened to the tape. But she wasn't sure what she should do, or what it was she was hearing. The idea of who she now was, was of course very strange—once her boyfriend died underground she suddenly was a hero, all the girls loved her. Now that Mary Cyr was arrested, they all clamoured about, asking what she would do—asking if she was going to the jail to protest the death of her true love.

Yet now she realized that if she really wanted to be a hero—if she really wanted to protest—she would have to do something that seemed to be against every fibre of her being. She would have to reveal what Victor had given her before he was killed. And she herself was only fifteen years old.

"Victor wanted me to give this to Mary Cyr," she said, haltingly.

"*¿María Cyr?*" Ángel said, startled. "*¿No no, María Cyr?*"

"*Sí—sí*, Mary Cyr," she said.

And with that she turned the recorder on. She told him there was something coming from underground, and she wanted him to listen and tell her what it was.

"*Nada*—I hear nothing," he said before it even started.

Esperar, she said.

Wait.

They could hear Aunt Lucretia curse out in the kitchen and say:

"*Hijo de puta.*"

"*Esperar*," Gabriella said.

Wait.

Ángel waited, bothered by his aunt's loud cursing. Now and again he would look to his right and listen to her curse, and then he would look back toward his sister.

Gabriella's eyes were pleading. He glanced away toward the statue of the Lady of Guadalupe. For some reason he had his eyes riveted on that. And then he heard something terrible.

Tink Tink Tink Tink—sounding like a spoon hitting tin.

It was, and Ángel knew this, someone's unmistakable calling—*TINK TINK TINK*.

And it was terrible because Ángel knew instantly where it had come from.

He stared at the statue and felt a brief pang in his chest. As if it came from the Mother of God.

"*Sí*," he said.

He looked at her and looked away once more.

"*Si sabía el señor DeRolfo—si sabía—¿qué vamos a hacer?*" she asked.

If Mr. DeRolfo knew—if he knew—what are we to do?

Then she took Maxwell the truck out of her dresser drawer and placed it before him. He stared at it, unfazed, and then looked up at her. Then back at it.

He did what he always did when he was confused. He got angry and blamed his sister for being lazy, and silly, and superstitious, and too Mexican.

He went to his room. There was nothing in it except a poster of Juan Manuel Márquez and some old weights. He lay down on the small bed, so that it creaked.

"No," he said.

But he had to do something—because important people had told him he was angry, and everyone now said that because he had been Victor's best friend, he would do something; and if he didn't do something, he would be a coward.

5.

ÁNGEL GLOTON TOOK THE BERETTA—AND WENT OUT THAT night. The trees were waving, slightly at their tops. The buildings were dark. The idea was to kill John Delano, who had helped Mary Cyr with the most terrible crime, killing Florin. He was going to do this now to prove to Gabriella that he knew who were the real criminals. Even if he was caught, they wouldn't really blame him. With men dying in the mine, and with one boy missing and one dead—they would look at him in awe. This is what he was thinking. He would go to Delano's villa, knock on the door and have the gun ready.

But things did not turn out that way.

Constable Fey pulled his police car right up on the sidewalk in front of him. He stopped and started to go around the car, when Fey opened the passenger door and told him to get in.

When Ángel did, he didn't look at Fey. All the exaltation and feelings of grandeur had gone, and now he suddenly felt ashamed.

"What are you trying to pretend?" Fey said. "You have no idea what is going on. If you are thinking of confronting that Canadian policeman, think again."

Ángel didn't speak. Fey reached over, took the gun from Angel's belt and put it in the glove compartment.

He shrugged. Fey said he would tell Ángel one thing.

"What?"

"No sabes lo que está pasando."

You don't know what is going on.

But Constable Fey did—much more than John thought. Constable Fey had just in the most unlikely way he could have imagined retrieved the Beretta that was used in the murder of Ángel's father. He had been trying to find it for eight months. It had gone from Hernández to a woman named Little Boots, who gave it back to Hernández—who had given it to Carlos to get rid of. Carlos gave it to his wife, Gidgit, just after the disaster. She was supposed to dispose of it, but it was so beautiful she did not. Fey had lost sight of this gun, which had come from Erappo Pole's locker at the police station. Suddenly he found it in Ángel's posses-sion. He also knew Ángel's father was dead, but would not tell him that yet. Ángel's father had known about Hulk Hernández and Carlos DeRolfo, and was trying to expose them, to save children like Gabriella.

So Fey told Ángel, who seemed at this moment filled with an indig-nant self-righteousness, to go home.

6.

AS FOR AMIGO MINING, XAVIER HAD RECEIVED REQUESTS FROM Tarsco about accountability some eleven months before. He had sent them on to his friend in Mexico City, Alfonso Bara—who as yet was silently watching the rather extraordinary machinations in Oathoa and the great case being driven forward by his arch-enemy, Isabella Tallagonga.

At first he was envious of her landing what seemed to be such a grand international case—but now he saw flaws everywhere. He knew because of the documents Xavier had sent him that the international company Tarsco had asked for an inspection of the refitting that had never hap-pened. Bara also knew from these documents sent by Mary Cyr from the office when she went there that long-ago night that someone at Tarsco had most likely sent fourteen million dollars for upgrades to the mine's infrastructure—and he suspected that none of this money found a home beneath the surface. Now DeRolfo was lying on two fronts. First, that the upgrades were done, which was a lie; and second, that Amigo had paid for them because Tarsco was negligent. Another lie. The first lie told because they had kept the mine open, the second because they needed Tarsco as a scapegoat because of the implosion. Yet one lie effectively cancelled out the other. That is when Bara knew Mary Cyr was innocent.

Usually Bara wouldn't care about someone else's jurisdiction. But he had his own career to think of, and Tallagonga believed in her heart this case would trump Alfonso Bara's career. That she would get what they both wanted: under attorney general. Actually, both wanted to be part of the under attorney general office—both wanted the same, soon to be newly open, position. So he waited, and said to his wife, who was born near Oathoa and hated the DeRolfo family:

"No seas impaciente—¡no seas impaciente!"

Do not be impatient—do not be impatient!

So Bara said this also, in private to his allies in Mexico City:

"I think we should excavate, maybe bit by bit, and see what upgrades Amigo did do, now that we know millions were supposedly given them—then we will know who to charge with a crime."

So no matter what happened in Oathoa—the truth would come out over time, and the DeRolfos were doomed.

And Dr. DeRolfo had other things to worry about. Terribly ruthless people now knew he had lost the Beretta and it was with the police. DeRolfo had not known his wife had given this gun to Ángel, but by now Erappo Pole did, and had told Hulk Hernández this. That is, that this would implicate them both sooner or later. Hernández visited Carlos DeRolfo and told him that people expected certain things from him— that is, they wanted the investigation into everything to go away. That it was attention none of them wanted or needed. That the longer it went on the more attention it would create. But Carlos explained, *I am doing my best.*

"Yes—you are doing your best, making it an international incident— there should be no incident over this at all—there should have been no press whatsoever—people here are very angry—" Hernández laughed when he said this, as if DeRolfo's mistakes wouldn't result in a bullet to the head. But both knew very well that they would.

And worse than that, Carlos was asked to go see Constable Fey. He went into the office, sat in a chair and looked at the bulletins on the board. Fey saw him looking at the forms for deep-sea fishing, and asked him if he had ever done such. Carlos shook his head.

"No, no."

"Well, you should go—it's a very good time," Fey said.

Fey opened the desk drawer, took out some pictures and tossed them his way.

"What do you see there?"

"A male child of fourteen in rigor mortis," Carlos said. Sounding very official.

"The male child you found in the villa of the Canadian?"

"Yes—that would be him."

"And what did he die from?"

"My deeply held opinion is that it was arsenic."

"Your deeply held opinion is that it was arsenic—yes—well—you are the doctor, Doctor—but my deeply held opinion is that he was choked, his throat was constricted—by someone picking him up off the ground—and then dropping him. My deeply held opinion is that he lived an hour or two longer than that person thought, and suffered greatly —but managed to struggle to Ms. Cyr's villa."

Carlos looked at the pictures, perplexed, as if he was studying something he was unaware of.

"No—" he said finally, and looking up at Fey gave a weak astonished smile.

"*Sí,*" Fey said, nonchalantly picking the pictures back up, "*sí, sí.*" He nodded to no one in particular. "It was a chokehold by a man—that's how he died—and—" he continued nonchalantly as well "—it happened outside—*sí*—outside—in the wild blue yonder (this he said in English)— out there—near the coal pit—that's where it must have happened— arsenic—no—there is coal on his feet—and on the bedsheet too—it is quite amazing your friend, the policeman Erappo Pole, did not notice this, when that Canadian police officer John Delano noticed this in five minutes. And we both know the Canadian officer is *stupido*. But maybe he is not." Then Fey went around to the doctor and put his left arm across his throat and held that arm with his right hand, until Carlos felt himself beginning to choke.

"Like this, *amigo,*" Fey said.

"Well, perhaps it is that Canadian police officer then—think of it—perhaps it was he?" DeRolfo said, still with Fey's arm across his throat, and the memory of the sad little boy gasping for air.

"No—I do not think so," Fey said.

Carlos tried to protest, but Fey said nothing more. In fact, he busied himself with other things in the office and began to speak to someone else—as if Carlos DeRolfo wasn't even there. Fey then went back to his desk, where he put the pictures away, took the Beretta out of the same drawer and handed it gently to a female officer.

"*¿Es la pistola que desea probar?*"

Is that the pistol you want tested?

7.

ALL OF THIS MADE CARLOS AND HIS WIFE MORE UNPREDICTABLE, more terrified, more hysterical. And caused them to plan terrible things one moment (like shooting five or six more people, including Hulk Hernández) and give money to charities the next. Their daughter, Sharon, came back from a morning ride, and was astonished to see them huddling together near the stables behind some bales of hay as she rode up, as if they were in hiding.

Once, she had to grab her mother by the arm and say:

"Momma—it's me, Sharon—it's me. What is the matter with you?"

Hulk Hernández now realized they had to be taken care of, or else he would be in trouble. He also realized that Gidgit was not above killing him. He also knew that they would be blabbing their mouths off at the slightest sign of trouble.

So as he drove around in his big SUV, he realized things were coming to a head, and something had to be done. He hated the Canadian police officer. But he hated the attention Mary Cyr had brought to them. It was almost as if he and Erappo Pole were in a cell with her.

"Why can't you get the gun back?" he asked Pole, in a sly, accusing manner.

"I tried. I tried. They have taken it out of his office, and locked it away—*con el ejército.*"

With the army.

"Well—we pay you for that not to happen," Hernández said.

So then soon after Carlos had visited Constable Fey, far away in another state the phone rang, and after the caller asked for someone, saying they needed to speak *mujer a mujer* (woman to woman), a voice hardly ever heard came to the phone:

"*¿Sí? ¿Qué pasa ahora?*"

Yes? What is it now?

This was the voice of Little Boots Baron. And it was not at all a happy voice anymore. And who was impertinently calling her was Gidgit DeRolfo.

The worst of it was, Little Boots hadn't even wanted to be involved. The plan was put to her one September day a few years before by Hulk Hernández—money sitting there probably unable to be traced—and he a good friend of hers, willing to do her bidding, working right there— did she know DeRolfo and his wife, no; would she like to, no! But she could be persuaded to take some of that money—she could also, Hernández said, launder much more of her own money through the mine, and it would be held in an account for her. Hernández was already laundering some. But Little Boots would be treated much better.

"How do you know this?"

"Mrs. DeRolfo approached us. She needs help with the money."

"Well then—let us not disappoint them."

From that day forward no matter how dangerous it was, the mine could not stop production, for she, Little Boots Baron, said it could not because much of her money was laundered through it.

No matter what they told her about methane, or damage to the structures after three-hundred metres, or water seeping in the walls, she always said the same thing:

"*No—tienes que siga funcionando.*"

No—you have to keep it running.

So the DeRolfos did just that.

Little Boots had no interest in them at all. Or in those miners who toiled underground. However, she now was a little bit interested in Mary Cyr. Now that there was press, now that there were pictures, now that there was too much attention, Baron was adamant the attention must remain where it was: on Mary Cyr herself.

"*Es importante que las estacas para ella convertirse en muy altas,*" she said to this annoying caller.

It is important that the stakes for her become very high.

"They will, *señorita,*" Gidgit DeRolfo assured her, in a weak, terrified voice. "Just you wait and see." For Gidgit had phoned begging for reassurance in a terrified voice.

It was that weak terrified voice that signed her and her husband's death warrant.

"And what about Sharon?" Hernández asked later when she told him that the DeRolfos must be silenced.

"Ah," Baron said, hanging up. She had made too many decisions already.

What Little Boots Baron realized that same night looking at those same pictures, taken in the past few weeks by Sharon DeRolfo (a woman whose life Little Boots had just decided to spare), was how much she and Mary Cyr looked like sisters.

"*¡Mi alma, podríamos ser gemelos!* My soul, we could be twins!" she declared.

It made her quite happy to look like someone so well known at the moment. But when she turned toward the mirror, unlike Mary Cyr's deep and compassionate loveliness, her almost holiness, Little Boots's own face was dead, like stone. This is what she realized: that she would never ever get any compassion back.

8.

"*MEA CULPA—MEA CULPA—MEA MAXIMA CULPA*" WAS A caption in one of the more sensational papers in Mexico City. *Der Spiegel* published it as well.

Mary Cyr did look to be praying. Which of course was completely outrageous, that a woman like her would pray. It was joked about in the common room of the English department at the University of New Brunswick by a woman she had once insulted. And the men, of course—those who believed in equality, and gender parity—all those things they were always taught to agree to and accept—being as they were in school from grade one on, and never having left the classroom, did not think that their glee at her demise was anything more than appropriate. For all of them most of their lives existed to do what they had been taught, to create and destroy scapegoats.

So then was this line:

"She fired her pilot, Mr. Claude Devereaux, because he didn't manage to land a plane at the exact time she wanted—"

There were also quotes from her past:

"The French are racist."

"The Dutch are even racister."

OR:

"Who in hell could like the Swedes—especially their hockey coaches—they hate the Canadians, it's our patriotic duty to hate them back!"

"How dare she say that about Swedish hockey coaches," one well-known *Globe and Mail* hockey reporter said.

Then there were these two short summations by former friends:

"By the age of seventeen she had already been criminally responsible for drowning her little Acadian friend Denise Albert, and well known as a bigot. Then there was Bobby. She would never ever admit it, but Bobby had been fathered by her grandfather—and was abused." WJ

And:

"It is also suggested that she seduced her own cousin—when she was seventeen." WJ

Sometimes the reporters would say their information came from other sources—BB or DC or LE.

"Who the hell is LE?" Mary would say. "It's not fair—I don't even know any LEs and he said I slept with him—I don't remember sleeping with any LEs—"

9.

THAT SAME NIGHT, RORY TOLD HER HUSBAND WHAT WAS happening with his former student. It was on the front page of the *Globe*. It was now all a disaster.

"Good god," Cruise said, astonished, looking over her shoulder at the picture in the centre of the front page.

"I feel responsible I didn't help. I mean, I should have seen the signs— yes, seen the signs."

Rory looked at him and nodded, just at the dining-room table, just at dark. Cruise left the room, walked up the stairs toward his study.

But Cruise was fortunate. He was extremely fortunate that the instincts of his wife, of his sister-in-law, of their protege Ned, as well as everyone he spoke to and most who were interviewed on the many CBC programs that worried over this case, that their instincts were entirely misguided. The great fortune for Nigel was that people who had very well-known CBC Radio talk shows never looked beyond the fashionable way to take the moral higher ground by pretending concern over the Cyr dynasty. In fact Nigel's whole life and the lives of his colleagues had been filled with misguided ambition and misplaced admiration. And this is what allowed them to protest their tenure, to go on strike while their students at the university, who had paid their money, were hostage to their demands; to look miffed when people did not see their worth, to become parasites on First Nations causes that would gain them attention, and to prey on the naïveté and idealism of the young.

Professor Nigel Cruise often thought back to those days at Rothesay and that night—or was it two nights? Yes, he thought he took her good and hard the last of those two nights. Then he began to realize what he had done, became frightened and ran away. That is, he realized (and there was no other way to say this) when he screwed her good the second night (because it was too difficult to enter her the first so he made sure she was very drunk the second) that he was violating a little girl who wanted to talk to him about her mom and dad. A beautiful child. He became aware of it after he came inside her—

"Ouuooo— Ohhh—it hurts," she said as a terrible plea, and she looked up at him in pain—looking just like who she was, a tiny little girl and nothing more. If he had been brighter and nobler, he would have said:

Please, please, Mary, I beg you and God to forgive me!

But he had never been that bright.

At any rate, tonight he went into his study. The wind whined and whaled. He was still trying to quit smoking, but he snuck one later. He walked to his desk to find where he had hidden the matches, and pulled things out of the drawer, while putting his head down trying to see where they might be.

They were stuffed at the very back, but when he pulled them forward, something else came out: an old, yellowed sheet. He turned it over to look at what was written on it. Surprised, he dropped it. The wind blew and the light dimmed in his study. He picked it up again as the light returned, and he read it, his lips moving:

" 'I said goodbye to thee at night.' "

It was the poem little Mary Cyr had written to him—the one he told her he would publish someday in *Tickle Lace*. He had never done that. In fact he had never done anything for any woman, except use them whenever he could to promote himself, as the rather enervated feminist he chose to be. Not once in his life did he ever have to deal with people John Delano dealt with to keep people like him safe. And that was fine for him.

He looked at the clock on the shelf, wondering what time it was in Mexico.

PART NINE

1.

MARY CYR WOULD STAND AT HER CELL WINDOW SOME NIGHTS
and she would remember bits and pieces of poems—trademarks on the
road of life she had once thought was a destiny. She was unsure now of
any destiny. Even Shakespeare's soliloquys did seem to leave her now.
But whenever she remembered a poem, she would yell it out the window
at the donkey:

> "I wander thro' each charter'd street
> Near where the charter'd Thames doth flow
> A mark in every face I meet
> Marks of weakness, marks of woe.

> "In every cry of every man
> In every Infants cry of fear
> In every voice, in every ban
> The mind-forg'd manacles I hear!"

Not many knew what it was she was shouting. But she shouted to the
donkey anyway, and was content. The poems made her raise in the air,
above all the town, above all the people, almost to the stars she saw the
night she realized she would always be alone.

Mary and everyone she had known were in all the papers now. Some
in one paper or some in another but all of them somewhere. More and
more gossip, from her life in Canada, was coming in to confirm her guilt.
And this pleased everyone. Especially the stories of her and her abuse of

children and how because of this she was refused permission to adopt.

"Yes, they are right—they are all right—I am a disaster waiting to happen to the world," she once remarked, after being turned down, hoping against hope to adopt a child she would call Denise, a child she would love.

Mary stared at the opaque picture of Denise Albert published just that day. The snow must have been really falling when it was taken—it must have been the week before the big escape. Oh yes, the aluminum shovel, the faint lights shining through the window, the sky turning toward night—there Denise was standing on a small patch of desolate earth.

Mary herself had been too busy making little dummies to pay much attention to all Denise's sad lively talk about her grandmother and how she missed her house, and Denise had the sniffles—yes, she remembered that. They had become very close because of their planned escape. Because of the hatred of those teenaged boys who had signalled them both out.

"They put smmow down my underpants," Denise said.

"Smmow? Oh yes, *neige*—" Mary said. "The snowy kind. They called me an English twat—ho hum to all that." She remembered one, with his little toothpick-like beard, rushing after her, trying to run her down with a block of white snow.

Mary Cyr had fought back. If people were going to call her *anglaise* and bigoted, she would return the favour without batting an eye. She did this all her life, with the French, the First Nations, the Irish—and when in Europe, the Dutch and Swedes—not to mention the French again, and the Swiss, the Scots, the Poles, some Chinese, and of course the English too, after a while.

Perhaps it started at the convent. You take a person and put her where she does not belong because you believe she must acquiesce to your will, as Nanesse did, and you will start a rebellion. And no one could rebel like Mary Cyr.

"I am supposed to write about victims? My god, the Acadians are always victims—especially down around Dieppe," Mary wrote in an essay. "But they are no less bigots than the English—"

That essay allowed her to fail her Canadian history course (she was supposed to write upon the Expulsion of the Acadians)—but it also allowed her a last trip to Mother Superior's office, where she was able to lift the keys. Mary in her sweet Machiavellian way knew as much. And of course as John maintained, a hater as fine as Mary Cyr never in her life actually hated anyone. In fact at the end, she could not hate a soul. Not even Nigel and Rory, or those dozen men and women who wrote against her. Not one.

"*Merci de m'enseigner à danser,*" Denise had said, rubbing her nose.

Thank you for teaching me to dance.

The little lights were dim and the little room was warm, and the corkboard had that very picture of Denise that was now famous—and also a picture of her small dog looking up at the camera.

Sometimes Denise would smile. Sometimes she would simply start weeping.

Mary Cyr kept working.

"I tell you, Denise—two donkeys and we will live in Bermuda." Mary was almost sure of it. All she had to do, she said, was telephone the international number for her grandfather and he would send a ship to get them. She was sure of it as she led Denise by the hand down the cold stairway under that moonlight so long ago. It wasn't until she was outside and the great door closed with a gentle *thud*, and she felt the night cold on her face, that she remembered: the river. They had left the keys on the inside, and the door was locked.

"Perhaps if I had told her to dress warmer," she had said to the priest. "Or fit her with water wings, blew up a tire with some air. But she must have sunk like a stone anyway—a poor little Acadian stone. *a coulé comme une pierre*—or some such.

I only heard one cry, then not another peep. Maybe I should have jumped in after her. What's *gurglup* in Acadian?"

She now stared at the picture and the caption under it:

"*Un grito que debe ser escuchado.*"

A cry that must be heard!

Then the line "*Los ricos confunden privilegio y ética.*"

The rich confuse privilege and ethics.

"Poor little Denise—your picture that you had kept in that small little room of ours now gone all around the world. I made you famous and you didn't even thank me."

Then she thought of other things.

Other things in her life just as traumatic that were now being used against her.

She thought of Sharon DeRolfo, as Sharon walked backward snapping pictures. Her eyes were dark and steady, the stud in her nose gleamed in the light from the street, her short spiked hair gleamed as well. She possessed in her beauty a universe filled with zealotry and determination; and she strode backward in front of Mary as if she knew her. She was, however, insecure, and hoped Mary would not have read what they had written. Even for Sharon DeRolfo, who took all those pictures now floating here and there about the world—one of which would appear on the cover of the book—it was a little too cruel.

But Mary read—Mary insisted she be allowed to read whatever was said. Her lawyer Xavier secured this for her from English papers. But she collected all the others. Even from Latvia.

"I wonder what the Latvians are saying. Surely to god I'd get a reprieve from the Latvians—Grampie was very nice to a majority of Latvians."

Day upon day upon day. She ate alone at her little table—with a candle—and a big napkin tucked under her chin. Writing down nations she could trust on one side—three—and nations she could not trust on the other—thirty-seven. Then rubbing out the three, and making it two, and then adding that one to the other pile, making it thirty-eight. Then she spoke to herself about the problem of roving reporters:

"The trouble is, if a country has roving reporters—that's what's so good about the Balkans, so few of their reporters could be called roving reporters. They are much better at staying home."

And:

"At some point you have to realize the United Nations is just not for you."

And:

"It's always worse when the reporter is a sissy."

She put down an article and lay back on her bunk.

"Well, I didn't batter or kill anybody—it must be a poor translation," she decided. "And who in hell is EL?"

That afternoon the little female guard came to the cell and said, in a happy cheerful voice:

"*María ¿tienes un cigarillo?*"

Mary threw her the pack.

"No, no—keep them, *mucho gusto*," Mary said when the woman tried to hand them back.

She put her hands behind her head, sniffed and tried to think. What was in her bones, in her blood, in her very brain, was an absolute revulsion for the world. Nothing they were saying about her was true, and yet she had manoeuvred herself into this horrid position. And now those who existed on scandal and insult, on harm and hate, were making the most of it for themselves.

2.

DEBBY DORMEY TOOK SICK, SOMETHING IN HER DELICATE LITTLE bones. Much too much picking blueberries in the hot August sun, probably.

Mary heard she was ill so she drove up from Halifax and went to see her.

When she visited her, she initially thought they would have a grand old time talking and reminiscing. She saw a frail little girl in bed, with some orange juice beside her, the blind closed but the sun still able to come through its torn fabric, with the noise of giant trucks on the highway. She telephoned Montreal, and sat beside her friend.

"Wait, the plane is coming," she remembered saying as she held Debby's hand. "I am taking you to Toronto's Hospital for Sick Children—"

What happened? Yes, Debby could not wait—she promised Mary she would—but she could not.

"I will just close my eyes," she said. "I will open them when the plane gets here—okay?"

She drove her pink Jaguar along the third-rate road toward the airport, and after swerving into the chain link fence, jumped out, and ran to the plane, and fired the captain—who had been in the family's employ for nineteen years—who had never failed them before.

As she slapped him across the face, he stared above her head, hat high on his forehead and his tie flapping in the wind.

Then she sat down on the cold asphalt and wept, her skirt covering her like the petals of a flower and snow wisping across her face.

Tried later without success to hire him back.

3.

THE WOMEN OUTSIDE HAD BEEN THERE ALL AFTERNOON, SOME of them eating watermelon and trying to spit the seeds at her bare feet. They had made a game out of trying to hit her toes with the seeds. The big toe got them a hundred pesos.

"*Golpeé el dedo gordo del pie*," one would shout.

I got her big toe.

"*No, no hizo*," Mary would stand up at the bars and yell out.

No, you didn't.

She realized—yes, just like the girls at the Rhonda Cottage so long ago—she was in a fight with three women.

She had never bribed anyone—well, bribed them with a donkey here or there—but if she was to get out of Mexico, she knew she must bribe the right person now. And she had not thought of the prosecutor or the police—or Señor Gabel, the judge—all of them justifiably outraged, or pretending to be justifiably outraged, at her—because that did bring themselves a great deal of attention—no, she thought of the three women who taunted her—and turned her sights toward them. After watching them for weeks, Mary knew a lot more than people might think. She knew Principia knew the truth about Victor but was frightened. She felt this because of the way Principia did not want to look at her when the others called her a murderess. Did not join in the exultation. Why was this? Mary had watched her for weeks now and knew her well. She saw, a crack in the armour of sisterhood. That is, she knew too she would sooner or later have to play them one against the other.

Then there was Lucretia—yes. She was the one who above anything and anyone wanted to be Mary. And Mary knew this—so she gave her things—but she distrusted her, and would never ask her for help. For Mary, honour was implicit, and her character was such that she would go hungry rather than ask for help from those who tried to undermine her.

Who, as she said:

"Pissed in my face and called it rain."

Nor did it matter at this time if she lived. But in her fury, she wanted the truth. She wanted Principia to finally admit something. That is, she wanted to get back at Lucretia Rapone, for her sneering. If it was revenge—well, Mary was human too.

"*Ver que ella no salirse,*" Lucretia yelled whenever she took a break.

The guard, always helpful, smiled and translated:

See that she doesn't get away.

"How kind everyone has been," Mary said.

She had lost weight, had diarrhea and was worried about a sore on her hand. But not overly—that is, Mary did not worry so much anymore.

Mary Cyr at moments of tension or fear had learned to do one unnerving thing: smile. She smiled now at the old scratch on the wall:

"*¡Viva Cristo!*"

Did she even believe in that anymore? Oddly enough she did not know. Maybe Christ lived, maybe his great grace still lit the world; but where was it? Not for her—but where was it for those Mexican miners buried alive?

She stood and looked out at the stars, so far away in the purple sky— and the moon over the sad little donkey in the old field beyond her. The donkey for the past three weeks had been left alone. Now no one came to see it anymore except little Gabriella.

"Maybe they will eat you," she said to the donkey.

Yesterday Sharon came, to ask for another picture. Mary complied. She stood, in a simple white smock and a pair of shorts, and Sharon started to snap her photos.

"*Una mujer muy bonita*," she whispered. Then she looked up over the camera and then focused once more and snapped the shutter again. Yes, and Mary saw in those nervous, temperamental artistic movements money and privilege—private lessons and schooled leftism, concern about the world taught by unworldly professors. Suddenly Sharon stopped snapping, and lowered the camera, and stared at her, pensively, her own face white. And she knew that Mary Cyr suddenly understood that her own family had money and power, that she was the daughter of Carlos DeRolfo, former governor of the state, and what she was doing was probably inexcusable, deplorable and a lie.

That is, her photography, like Ned's activism, was nothing much more than a fashion statement in a world where fashion statements mattered more and more, and more.

And quite suddenly Sharon's arms began to shake. Mary smiled, the very same way she had at Ned Filmore once long ago.

4.

THIS EVENING MARY STARED OUT AT THE SKY, STILL SMELLING the night air and the warm breeze, with some money in her hand, wondering what to do—wondering what John was doing—wondering if anyone back home even cared for her anymore. So Mary watched the women for over two hours—two long hours she did not move a muscle. Finally, she saw Lucretia. Mary got the wooden crate that she had been sitting on, and stood on it. She wanted to talk to Principia, so she had to get rid of Lucretia.

"*Lucretia, cigarillo, por favor,*" she said, holding the money out. "*Cigarillo— Voy a compartirlos.*" She was calling trying to look as pathetic as she could possibly be.

We will share them.

The woman looked over at her.

"*Aquí,*" Mary said, "*aquí—cigarillo, por favor.*"

"Here—cigarettes, please," and she handed over five dollars in American money. "*Cigarillo, por favor,*" she said. "*¿Algunos de ustedes mis amigos?*"

Some of you are my friends?

Lucretia looked at her a moment, frowned at the murderess, then shrugged and took the money. It was the greatest of victories for Lucretia to be able to come to the jail and get the crowd worked up. She often talked of dragging Mary out and killing her. Almost, as if she was joking. But Mary knew she was not. That some fate somehow awaited her in the shadows of the trees and the head frame of the desperate mine. She realized it when she yelled out, in solitude:

" 'I wander through each charter'd street—' "

And sometimes at night she was terrified.

But whenever Mary asked for something, she usually gave half of it away. So Lucretia put the five into her skirt pocket—and looking back over her shoulder said:

"*Mi pequeña señorita encerrado en su celda,*" and she laughed. Mary laughed as well.

My little miss locked up in her cell.

Now when Lucretia left, and walked toward the confectionary shop across the road, Principia was alone.

"Psssp-ppsssp," Mary said. You could only see her hands, and her eyes. Principia looked her way, stunned and almost shamefaced.

"You know what is going on," Mary whispered, standing on the crate and on her tiptoes, her dirty fingers around the bars, her fingernails chewed down. "You know I have done nothing—*yo nada, no melesto, nada mi*—help me prove it, and I will give you two million— *dos millones dólares*—*nuestro secreto*—*por favor*—between you and me— you know I am telling the truth. What is it— *Verdad, mi verdad.* Someone else did something—something terrible, and you know it. You know who it was— Do you know who it was?" she asked, and nodded her head.

Principia walked over to her, looked at her with a glum, frozen look. The frozen look came because of how close Mary seemed to be to the truth. She stared into the darkening cell, with its smell of moisture and cement. She started to speak; she was going to be angry.

Then a look of intelligent sadness came to Principia's black, shining eyes that to Mary spoke of circuses somewhere long ago. She smelled of night air and a kind of Mexican domesticity that tried in spite of poverty and crime to be kind and decent.

She suddenly touched Mary's cheek with her right hand, saying, "*Mi poco, poco femenino*," and turned and ran up the broken hill. There were tears in her eyes.

"Two million" Mary called, snapping her fingers as if it was nothing. *Nada toto bien*—nothing at all.

Then she went and sat on the little milk crate and watched a spider climb up the wall.

She felt that sooner or later they were going to kill her in some gruesome way, and she was terrified. Yes, at this moment she would almost trade places with anyone—anyone, to let the cup pass by.

She realized she had just peed herself.

5.

THE DAY ENDED. NIGHT CAME. TONIGHT THERE WERE LOTS OF parties down the street. Lent was ending. People in the other cells were yelling out to her.

"*Asesina*, do you fast at Lent?"

"*Sí*," she would yell. "I always give up my freedom."

She turned her light off and stood on the crate to look out. She smiled in a kind of whimsical delight at all the happenings without knowing what the happenings were. It was music and she was like a child whenever she heard music—like a child whenever she saw fireworks.

There was the smell of gas, and a great fire above the crowd, and everyone was laughing and talking. It was, someone said, Lucretia Rapone's idea.

She called out to people from her cell:

"Hey, what's going on—what is it that is happening now?"

After a while the crowd broke away from the square—a dog ran by her, and the old donkey walked toward the near fence with its head down.

But then, people came back to the jail, carrying drinks and food. They gave her a tortilla and a drink of wine. Someone said she was beautiful.

"A beautiful devil," they said.

They told her they had burned an effigy of her, to save the town from calamity.

"Thank god for that," Mary said, turning her head away while handing the tortilla to a sad-faced youngster who had an old crinkled face, and reminded her of her son.

"There you go, my child," she said.

Lucretia seemed to be hoping she would be more upset.

"Like Joan of Arc," Lucretia said, in English, handing half of the cigarettes over, smiling in the darkness, her face covered in soot. She helped light Mary's cigarette through the bars with a Zippo lighter. Then she lit herself one and stood for a moment in silence, looking at the little woman. Lucretia's face was glassy with heat and sweat. All the other women were one with her, obedient, it seemed.

"*Muy hermosa*," she said, and she moved her hand up and down at the wrist to show her approval.

Then she handed over something else—one of the effigy's glass eyes that had not burned.

"Maybe you can see what we will do to you." Lucretia smiled.

Mary said:

"Thank you," and handed her, her pair of six-hundred-dollar designer sunglasses. It was her favourite pair. Lucretia smiled, and even though it was eleven at night put them on.

"*Tú también eres famosa*," Mary said; though her Spanish was not good, she knew more Spanish than French. You are famous.

"*Sí*," Lucretia said. "*Sí*."

"You will be very famous—when I die," Mary said. "My death will make sure of it," and though she was terrified before, she did not feel one bit afraid now.

The next day Gabriella began to visit and feed the donkey—and Mary waited for her visits across the street with great, almost feverish, emotion. Every time she saw her she stood on the small orange crate and lifted herself to the bars. Some days she would wait looking out at the street for the young girl to come.

"*Mi amiga*," she would say. "*Mi amiga*—" It took a while for Gabriella to trust her, to come close enough so Mary could say, "I know I know you were a friend of Victor—I know he wanted to give me something— do you know what it was?"

She did not know how long things would take, but someday—in some way she would be free.

6.

THEN THERE WERE THOSE OTHER GIRLS, FROM LONG AGO. SHE waited for them, for over ten years, to have a falling-out. Rhonda was the ringleader, the one who accepted her role, who dined out on each new trend, forever seeking a sky-blue life. And they doted on Rhonda, on her beauty and grace. They fell out over the ski chalet business they and their husbands had all entered into.

After three poor seasons they were in debt and all were blaming one another. All wanted funds from one another. All sued one another.

And when they did, when they were fighting over property taxes and ski lifts, when one husband would not speak to another, when each was trying to sabotage everyone else, when Rhonda tried to take $170,000 out of the joint account before an audit came and froze the account, Mary appeared one day out of the blue, in a pink scarf and new spring hat. It was April and the air felt still fresh and cool along the streets of the resort in the Laurentians. She had driven from Ottawa in a purple Jaguar.

She brought the creditors into the room, with a lawyer. She sat with them, looking across the table at Rhonda, seeing how miserably they tried to use each other, and she let it be known that she knew. Then she bought them all out, paid off their credit for twenty cents on the dollar. So with their bankruptcy she was in the end able to make a good deal of money.

As she looked over their files and statements, it was clear that Gail had been treated the worst—the girl who had believed most in friendship, who had invested her entire livelihood, losing almost everything.

"Ah. Every day the fairy tale is proven true," Mary said.

"What fairy tale?" Rhonda asked.

"Why—Cinderella, of course."

Mary then cautiously showed Rhonda four pages of expenses that proved she was having an affair with Bonnie's husband. But only to her, and silently—that is, she was not like that—she could not destroy those who had tried to destroy her—at least completely.

Mary left the meeting, coat over her arm. One of the husbands called to her:

"Please, we'd like to negotiate."

She did not look back.

The group called Lite Snow Enterprises lost $2,467,000. Or thereabouts. She paid less then three hundred thousand.

So Mary Cyr could do what she wanted with it. She studied it. She shrugged. She had no use for it.

She went to a charity for the Toronto General Hospital board and had her picture taken with Kiefer Sutherland and Randy Bachman. It was in all the newspapers, so those ladies would see it the next day.

For three years those women were broke. They knew what it was like to be poor. They knew what it must be like for a child to pick blueberries in order to buy clothes for school. They knew too, when their affairs with each other's spouses became known, what it was like to be ridiculed for sex, to have their bodies talked about and mocked. As poor Perley had been long ago.

They fought and cursed. They sued and counter-sued one another. They had to sell homes and move residences.

And then one afternoon—it was in April 1996—she simply sent the deeds to the property back, gave them title to what they once owned, with the stipulation that they must remain in partnership even if they hated one another until she, Mary Cyr, was paid back every cent, not twenty cents on the dollar but every dollar, or her largesse would be rescinded; and a charity tourney had to be opened and trophies given up in Debby Dormey's name.

"You are being awful—what did we ever do to you—"

"Nothing—nothing at all."

After that phone call, she sat in a corner, tears in her eyes. She knew it was a terrible thing to do—in fact she wrote in her diary it was the worst victory she had ever had.

PART TEN

1.

MARY CYR DROVE DOWN TO MACHIAS, MAINE, THAT SUMMER OF Rhonda, with Bobby in the back seat wearing an Expos baseball cap over his bald, vulnerable head. John had discovered after all this time that it was to find Perley, who had gone to Maine to join the Marines. Except, being a Canadian, he couldn't, and being terribly out of shape he couldn't either. So he got drunk and tried to drive home, and found himself in the Washington County Jail in Machias, terrified and alone. He wasn't allowed to make an international call, so he telephoned a business associate of his father, and asked him to contact Mary—Mary alone, no one else.

It was Mary Cyr who drove down that evening and posted his five-hundred-dollar bail. He was led out through the back by a sheriff's deputy, who undid his cuffs and handed him back his wallet and sunglasses, and car keys in a plastic bag. Mary had to find a mechanic to get his car out of impound and drive it north for them, and that cost another two hundred and fifty dollars.

Once across the border Perley could drive his own car. He had not lost his licence in Canada, and Mary Cyr had managed to keep it out of the papers in New England.

"I will never forget this," he said.

"What're cousins for—" Mary asked, holding Bobby in her arms, looking at him through her designer sunglasses.

She laughed. It was a lighthearted, sudden laugh that captivated him, and that now, after all of these years, made him attempt to help her—to organize a payoff or an escape.

He in fact had planned it meticulously—he had been planning it for a long time. In fact he too would bring money with him, to Mexico City—he would see one man he had been in contact with: Alfonso Bara. There he would offer payment to allow himself to trade places with her. That is, if it was Tarsco they were so concerned about, he had more shares in Tarsco than she ever did. If they wanted someone to take the blame for the Amigo Mining disaster, they could have him, as long as they left her alone. He had sat alone at home thinking of this for days— and it seemed to him the only way in the world to help her. At first he had thought of an escape, and he had paid two men twenty thousand dollars to set this up. That was the cell phone number he was given. Hare-brained and farcical, it summarized his own unfortunate misunderstanding of the dreadful world. But the men had become very elusive in getting back to him. So now he was planning to take matters into his own hands.

Yes, he had it all planned, and the plan seemed entirely workable, as long as he did not actually think about it. Once he began to think it over, it became more and more foolhardy and undoable. The two Mexican men he had hired, who said they knew people in Oathoa who would help him, no longer returned his calls.

The problem was, he could not say no to their proposal and not think it might be her only chance. So he paid them the money. And in truth, if the truth be told—did he once think they were Mexican?

He had placed the money in an envelope and met them in downtown Saint John near Harbour Station.

"We will phone you by Friday," they said.

He waited two days for a call on his cell phone. At first every day— no, every moment of every day—he was filled with exuberance, thinking every time his cell phone rang he would hear her voice.

Then, little by little he began to look at his cell phone suspiciously and then annoyingly— At the last he couldn't look at it.

On the tenth day the phone did ring. He picked it up. It was John Delano's friend Constable Markus Paul.

They had picked these two men up—they were in a tavern bragging. People were so angry they had done this to him they had phoned the police.

They had been in jail since last night.

"The two skinny little runts," Markus said.

Did he want to identify them and press charges? They were not Mexican. They were First Nations men, and they had two whites with them, who had helped them set it up.

"They had been planning this for weeks, looking both you and Mary Cyr up on the internet. I am sorry for your trouble."

The money would be returned.

Worse, Mary would remain where she was.

"I am gullible and stupid," Perley said. "I am stupid and naive."

"No," Markus said, "you are not silly, or naive—you are just an average person trying his best. You would give anyone money to help her—and you know—I remember her when I was a youngster—and so would I. Don't despair."

2.

NOR COULD PERLEY KEEP IT OUT OF THE FAMILY'S OWN PAPERS—though he had tried. He wrung his hands, his face became red, he sweated. But he could not keep it out. The story had first appeared on the back inside page—not the picture but the story without her name. It had moved in the last week to International on page four. That is where it was until yesterday—a heavily edited version, to be sure—but because of this, people were ignoring his papers and going online, where everything that was published in the New York tabloids was more salacious. He looked in the mirror at his great big ears, his huge stomach, and sighed.

The sun came through on his large body and his large head, and he looked at his cell phone, and then at his feet, pondering what to do. He was waiting for a call from Greg, who was in a meeting. Now he had to wait, because Greg had an empire to run—shipping and lumber, et cetera, were all his province now.

"I love Mary," Perley said. "She is the only one who ever loved me—"

But his father said something that he sometimes said without thinking—something that callously defined his own self-interest—without realizing how it sounded.

"Well—she is to receive the seventy-eight million—but if she gets into trouble—well, then the money reverts back to the family—the family pays off Amigo Mining, and everyone is happy once again. They might even let her out of jail sooner. You know, let her do fewer years. Or maybe to a woman's prison here—and you could visit her at Christmas."

Perley looked at him in childlike wonder and disbelief, and Garnet managed a timid smile.

"Just saying, son," Garnet said

The next morning Perley was rushed to the hospital. He'd had a slight heart attack. He was only forty-six.

But as soon as they put a stent in one of his arteries and placed him on medication, he was out of the hospital and making plans to go and rescue her. The trouble was, of course, she had heard about it.

3.

AFTER PERLEY CAME BACK FROM MAINE THAT TIME, HE TOLD her he was useless; he didn't even manage to join the marines. He stayed in his room and would not even read the notes she put under his door. Finally she used her own key (the doors of the old cottage had skeleton keys) and came in, when he was sitting bare-chested in his underwear. He had one of his grandfather's machetes in his hand, thinking he could kill himself with it. The machete they were going to use to go to Oak Island and discover the treasure, a long time ago when their hearts were young and glad.

"We'll be more rootin-tootin than that good old Dug Vanderflutin," Mary had said to him. They were seven and eight. They had found those old India-issued British imperial helmets up in the attic and had walked about with them on their heads, sat at the table with them on, winking at each other—collecting rope. Making a potato salad. Sneaking quarters to buy chocolate bars. Then they had found the machete, and a map—which they themselves had picked up at a service station, and were heading to the door, with a picnic basket, when Nanesse and her old aunt stopped them.

"*Tu ne pouvez pas imaginer ce qu'elle est sur lui—une mauvaise influence,*" Nan said later that day to her husband.

You can't imagine what a bad influence she is.

It seemed only a moment from then until this moment when he held the machete and looked at her.

She told him he didn't need to.

"Need to what?"

"Need to join the marines to be a man—"

He stared down at his feet. She took the machete from him and tossed it on the bed. But she did not leave.

She stood back and undid her skirt and slowly tossed it aside. He looked up at her. Her blouse came down over her creamy thighs, but she unbuttoned it slowly. She looked at him, stared at him a long moment. Then took her blouse off. She was now naked except for a small pair of black panties. His mouth opened and his eyes blinked. He began to breathe heavier, and his eyes watered. So, giving a sigh, she took her panties off.

"Oh my good god, you are absolutely gorgeous," he said.

"See," she said, quite matter of fact, as she stared at him. "You've just proven it, haven't you! You have all the equipment to be a man—and I can see it reacts just like a man's should—so please understand you don't have to try to prove it anymore."

"You are my cousin," he said, softly.

"At this moment—and this is the only moment—that does not matter."

And then she picked up her blouse, skirt and panties, and left the room naked.

4.

GIRLS AND WOMEN IN OTHER CELLS RELIED UPON MARY CYR TO hand them things—to ask for things, to get them beer, and Mary would dole out—chocolate bars, toothpaste, Tampax—and once or twice a week she sent out for McDonald's for the whole block, even the guards if they wanted. And Principia would collect the money, and write the orders down, saying:

"A Big a Mac—two a Macs—fren fries—" and run to do this for her new friend Mary Cyr.

The cells were above the dirt floor that ran between them. Cinder blocks were placed along the fringe of this floor every few feet. There were two or three chairs, some plants that grew. Now and then a lizard crawled into the cell window and sunned itself between the bars. Mary quite liked them.

Once in a while the other prisoners would take a walk along that dirt corridor, and all of them would end up standing at her cell, talking to her, smoking cigarettes and asking questions.

"Did you do it?"

"No—I have done *nada*."

"Do you like to have—sex?"

"Not as much as people believe, and not with children."

"*Sabemos quién lo hizo*," one young woman said one day. That is, she said she knew who had done it. She said everyone knew.

She was in jail for three months for shoplifting. It was on the tip of her tongue to tell Mary that certain people said it was the wife of Carlos DeRolfo—a woman no one liked at all.

"Who?" Mary asked. She felt sick, became dizzy, began to shake.

But the woman knew better. She shrugged and moved her lips, in an aloof pout, and looked away. She watched other women, to see if they would say anything, and then moved to the back of the crowd. She was only eighteen years old and was just learning to keep her mouth shut.

She didn't look at Mary Cyr for the rest of the day, didn't eat her Big Mac with them but took it back to her cell.

"Ah," Mary said. "*Dinero es dinero*—and truth is truth."

"*Es peligroso hablar*," one of the other women told her. "*Señorita, por favor.*"

It is dangerous to talk. Please, miss—

Mary knew nothing would be said about this, to anyone at all.

So she said nothing either.

She once wrote in her diary about Le Select—yes, she was with some French colleagues. Very nice people—they decided that they would finally call each other the intimate *tu* instead of the formal *vous*—yes, how symbolic, how kind. Until they got in an argument over who should pay for the extra bottle of wine. Soon they were back to the more formal *vous*, and Mary Cyr paid for the wine.

"Le Select is exactly as it should be—full of rather select arses—" she wrote. Now that she thought of it, she liked many of the women here better.

5.

UNFORTUNATELY FOR LUCRETIA RAPONE, SHE POKED HER NOSE into everything in Oathoa. And she did not know that within twenty-four days her life would be irrevocably changed.

Her life was a constant inquiry—it was as if she was a source of persistent curiosity. As if it was her right to find out everything that was going on. She had dozens of theories and suppositions on why the water was turned off on Santa Anna Street, or why a public washroom was shut down. Or why there was a gas leak, or why Bruno's Tea Room was sold. She laughed loudly, talked loudly, and said what she should not. In fact the most distinct feature on her was her rather large mouth that turned upward at both ends as if she was constantly grinning. There was another character trait she had—mean-spiritedness. She always laughed when others were hurt, or when youngsters were teased. She would sway from side to side as she walked, so men called her the pendulum. But no man was able to insult her more than she could insult him. There was a darker side of her too—a side that brought her into contact with people like Hulk Hernández in 1998. And she knew certain things that put her own life in danger.

So over a month before she had walked down the street to see about the new social assistance cheque—having received a tip from Hulk Hernández that she could get two different cheques a month if she saw a certain person who was a friend of theirs, and filled out another form. So then that was the only thing on her mind that day. But just when she started to go to the office—just at that moment, she turned and saw a beautiful lady in chains—and just at that moment as she stepped forward, the young woman she had known of for a long while, Sharon DeRolfo, began to snap pictures. So she followed along at a distance, and heard what this beautiful woman had done. She had murdered a boy, and his younger brother was missing.

It was terrible. So she followed the others to the jail. Then seeing no one else brave enough to inquire what was happening, she put her makeup on, made sure her hair was combed, adjusted the little bracelet on her wrist and went into the office, asking.

"Oh," Erappo Pole said. "We have a murder—you knew them—that boy Victor."

"Victor?" she said. "Of course—*sí*."

So she went back home. Victor—wasn't that the boy she teased, who had the little brother Florin—one dead one missing, well, she couldn't do much about that.

But that evening they said everyone was going up to the church to pray. Then one of her friends phoned and said the women were going to go, to show support for the Sonora family.

So she put on a black kerchief and went along.

There were seven women, all preparing to go to the church, and she simply barged through to the front to see what was happening. Then the women followed her up the steps, and that was the first time she was fortunate enough to have her picture taken. She, at the front, with a large hat, and a veil over her face.

"Who organized the prayer group?" the reporter asked.

"I did," she said, and she looked around quickly and nodded. "*Sí*—it was I."

And so therefore it was.

Four days passed where she became the head of the prayer group at the church. She organized marches to the jail—she taunted the prisoner. She had laminated little pictures of Victor that she wore. One night, after Lucretia was interviewed by that husband and wife on TV, her friend Bianca came to her, nervously, and said:

"Did you tell the TV you were the mother? Well, the reporter from *El Mundo* wants to talk to the mother—he thinks one of us is the mother—so, Lucretia, you go tell him she is dead, that you made a mistake."

Lucretia looked at her and frowned deeply. Then she looked at the other women.

"Those children need a mother," she said. She wiped tears from her eyes. "I will do my duty and be the mother. I already said I was, so I will be."

The other women looked at her. Then they nodded as she pushed through them. And she went out to meet the reporter, with the women following her. But since Bianca and those other women pretended once that Lucretia Rapone was the mother, now it was paramount that they continue to pretend. So now all of them said she was the mother. And all of them began to believe it.

And so Lucretia, who admitted she hated children—often in fact was disgusted by Principia's affection for her children, and had two abortions, and was making a secret deal to help Hernández smuggle certain children north—was now a mother as well.

It was all very strange how it happened, but in this world, nothing in fact was more natural. It seemed all very devious, but in this world, nothing was devious. It seemed very unbecoming, but in this world what was unbecoming? One knows that in this world, from the Peloponnesian Wars on, no deviousness was left unused.

And every time you saw Lucretia she was at church blessing herself, wearing a laminated picture of Victor on her breast.

She, however, knew nothing of the tape recorder, or of the *TINK TINK TINK* that had once emanated from the bowels of the earth.

Gabriella would not dare tell her that.

6.

IT WAS NOW SEVEN WEEKS SINCE THE OWNER AND CEO OF THE mine, in a panic, declared the search over and closed off the opening.

For four or five days after that the men three-hundred metres down banded together. They shared what they had—a few even formed a prayer group.

But then slowly the fact became clear that all was soundless, and the search for them was over. They were buried alive in a five- by eight-metre grave. They could not believe it—and tried to remain calm. But little by little they became aware that their families might still be above them praying, but that the rescuers themselves had left and gone away.

Pedro had a carrot in his pocket for his donkey and he attempted to cut it up.

But something happened, as he was doing this. Seeing one by one the lamps on the top of the men's hats fade and die, seeing the carrot, three of the men started to go mad.

He had shared what he had for his donkey, the carrot and the corn he had in his big front pocket that went halfway down his leg. And then he went back to work. Suddenly it would grow dimmer, and he would look over his shoulder and see that another lamp was about to go out.

Then a man whose lamp had just gone out on his head would say that he had been marked for death, and begin to laugh.

"Someone will hear me," he told them. "I know someone must hear me sooner or later."

Now there were only three lamps left, dimmer and dimmer as the hours passed.

Exhausted, his legs aching, he sat back for one moment. Then once more:

TINK TINK TINK, he sounded.

And those *TINK*s were the very sounds on his son's tape.

The tape was now in Gabriella's possession along with Maxwell the truck.

But all of this—all of this affected Principia as well. She had not seen or heard from her husband in eighteen months, and yet she continued on, needing to believe that everything was fine with him, because people like Mr. Hernández, inspector of the mine, told her he was fine, and poohed any concern. But then once or twice when he saw her along the street, he looked the other way as he drove by.

So she too had hidden much of the truth from herself.

The idea Principia had was if she prayed enough to the Virgin of Guadalupe, the truth would go away—or at least she would look at it differently—or barring that she would be able to forget all about it. But the pressing need to go to the jail every day and to look outraged, to pray again in the afternoon in front of the cell window where that little girl (strangely, this is how Principia thought of Mary Cyr) was—made her realize her lie more and more. Of course she knew Mary Cyr had nothing to do with the murder—*nada*—and she knew also who did, or who must have. But this too, if she believed it, would implicate those she had trusted, and perhaps even implicate her own sister, Lucretia, and could she do so? Then there was the other stranger part of all of this that she wrestled with: even though she knew all, was she self-deceiving enough to pretend not to know? That was the question. And so she tried not to think about it.

Mr. and Mrs. DeRolfo were helping her, helping her son and putting her daughter through school. So as DeRolfo said, Gabriella was like his daughter—he loved her, and the university in Mexico City was waiting for her.

For Principia all she had to do was be quiet, and their lives would be fine. In fact, the very resort Mary had stayed at would hire her in the summer if she could get a good recommendation from Señora DeRolfo. And Señora DeRolfo had told her she would write her the best recommendation in all of Mexico. So what was there to worry about, or concern herself over?

Still, the truth was always present, and the praying did not take it away but exposed it—with each decade of the beads, said in a monotone with the priest who was the most pious of them all, parading his sincere sorrow.

Principia was not at all dumb. What played into all of this outrage was the fate of the thirteen. The thirteen from the town of Oathoa who died in the coal mine—which was supposedly, all of a sudden, the Cyrs' responsibility. It was so much believed to be the Cyrs' fault that even if a survivor came back to life and said they were in error, no one would believe him. Why was this? Because believing it was the fault of a foreigner relieved everyone in town of the burden of the truth. And Principia knew this in her heart.

"*El destino de los trece*" was written on the coal bins' battered walls.

"*El destino de los trece es la muerte*" was held up on placards and signs when they burned the effigy.

Was inside the church foyer.

Was put up in the window of houses.

Was on the walls of two restaurants.

She walked behind those signs, the smell of diesel in the hot afternoons, shouting with the others. She did this because the blame had now been shifted to the little girl in the cell, the *puta*, and because Lucretia demanded she go along with her.

"You have to show support in my grief."

Of course she did not know that of the fourteen million given to implement safety upgrades by Tarsco, thirteen and a half million went into the pockets of the Mexican owners.

Hernández—or "the Hulk," as he was called—saw to it. The upgrades would only go so deep—the great water leaks, the lack of supports, all of it would be rendered unimportant because they were unseen.

When they worried about a mine inspector investigating, Hernández arrived at the mine two days later with a sign that read *Inspector de operaciones mineras* on his front window. He got out with a clipboard and looked very officious.

But though everyone concerned believed this would never be discovered, all of it was in the hands of the young prosecutor Alfonso Bara from Mexico City.

"What do you want to become?" Principia had asked Lucretia one night, in the little apartment they shared with her daughter, Gabriella, and son, Ángel. It was the very night Lucretia was given the designer glasses, which she wouldn't take off even when they sat at home.

"I want to become as famous as Mary Cyr," Lucretia had laughed. Her picture she had heard—that is, Lucretia's picture—was published in the *New York Post*—she had been mistaken for Victor's mother. "Not mistaken," she said. "No mistake—it is who I am."

Then Principia asked who would feed the sorry, mean old donkey.

"I will feed it," Gabriella said. "Okay, Ángel?" she asked, as if that would take care of everything for good.

"I don't care," Ángel said. And he got up and left.

7.

THE NEXT DAY WHEN CONSTABLE FEY SAW HER, PRINCIPIA WAS ON her way to meet Ms. Tallagonga. Why, she did not know. She was called so she went, scared and worried. Mrs. DeRolfo had told her she was wanted, when she was in the living room dusting.

Señora DeRolfo had looked at her, when she was at the house—and said:

"Go home and change and be your best. Be very good—be very wise," and put her hands on either shoulder and looked into her eyes.

And so she walked down the roadway, passed the open beach, passed the umbrellas in the sun, passed the jail and the old, blind donkey.

"*Somos hermanas en esto juntos.*"

We are sisters in this together.

The prosecutor said this holding out her hand.

The world of law never wants to be uncertain. It is dramatic and shifting, but it is reactionary in its stance against perceived delinquency—diligent in upholding what it takes to be an affront against the sovereignty of the nation. Or that is what is supposed by many people, even by Principia and Tallagonga at this meeting on the second floor of the law building in the main square of Oathoa, just across the street from where Delano was having coffee. But in reality it can also be unprincipled and self-serving—hidden in its vales are enough measures of conceit to stop battleships. Tallagonga could no more wrestle her way away from this case than she could fly. She'd taken it up with grave enthusiasm a month ago and was now caught in its hidden files, caught in the media, caught in the international interest and international interests, surrounding it. She was caught in the lie, which for the honour of Oathoa she must believe. So everything that came against her, she would deflect, and then plow onward.

In the glare of international attention she could not now say that it was all a horrible mistake, a lie, and then be certain of her future advancing toward Mexico City. Not if people in Mexico City viewed this as a pivotal case. Still, in her private moments she had asked herself: Should the case go forward?

Little by little she felt Mary Cyr was innocent—there were too many small things that pointed to it. First of all there was evidence that Victor had not been poisoned, he had been beaten and choked by a larger person. It was very strange that Señor DeRolfo said he was poisoned, a doctor who had tried to save them from a flu epidemic years before. So poisoned he was.

Now that Mary was in jail she was constitutionally considered guilty. Besides, if Tallagonga let it go, her main adversary who used to be her friend at one time, Alfonso Bara, would gain the position both of them were seeking, an under attorney general of Mexico dealing in the criminal division. (That is also why Mary Cyr was kept in the jail here, and not in some safer place. Tallagonga needed her to stay here.)

So this was the case that was to prove she was sharper and tougher, smarter and in effect more ruthlessly determined to bring criminals to justice. The woman being innocent was somehow beside the point.

She had Mary Cyr picked up, questioned ruthlessly for hours and put into jail. Despite misgivings she could not now let her go. There were too many things against Isabella Tallagonga if she did so—being a woman was one. She would be looked upon as being weak. It was in a way a blessing that a woman (Mary Cyr) whose nature was revealed every day in scandalous detail was being chastised by a woman (Tallagonga) who had committed herself to truth and the law.

Still, there were a multitude of little problems. She knew that the arsenic table in drinking water for people who lived in the lower end of Calle Republica came because of a chemical spill at the coal mine five years ago. And the Dutch doctor was becoming more and more insistent that this woman, this brazen woman, Mary Cyr, be let go. Van Haut actually had connections in Oathoa, had worked with abandoned children during an earthquake. So she was no one's fool. And neither was her German husband, who had sent those snippings of hair away. Nor did they go back to Germany—Van Haut went home for a week but came back again, and there was the rumour of an international law expert arriving soon.

That was a tricky thing for Tallagonga to live down. But she was tough enough to live it down. Like a strong stream meandering its way through and over pebbles and windfalls, each obstacle she must go over or around, yet she must keep going.

Besides, reading the files she came to believe Mary Cyr was a very bad woman. Her pleas for adoption were continually refused on grounds of instability. That is, she could not love or care for children.

However, this is what Tallagonga did not know:

Alfonso Bara had files given to him through Xavier's office. DeRolfo was guilty of gross negligence and embezzlement. And the money trail Bara now had senior administrative accountants following proved it. Señora DeRolfo was in fact the brains behind her husband. Both were immoral transgressors of things more hideous in nature than Isabella Tallagonga could possibly imagine.

Tallagonga was walking into a web with Mary Cyr as the bait. And no one knew this in Oathoa, except perhaps Constable Fey.

But, something had just come to her attention, which is why she had Principia here. Principia had been offered a bribe—that is what she was told by that young female officer standing just outside Mary's cell. The officer liked Mary Cyr very much, and was engaged to Constable Fey, but she was duty bound to report it. If she did not report it, she would not be doing her duty. And she had to do what her office called upon her to do.

For what reason this bribe was offered did not matter. It was one more bit of evidence. The meeting Principia had dressed for and put on high heels for and was frightened over (1) lest she do or say anything to anger her sister, Lucretia; or (2) lest she do or say anything to implicate herself; or (3) lest she further harm Mary Cyr, who she liked, sat in the chair in front of the desk, her dark hair high on her head, her lips terribly thin and kindly, which gave her the expression, since she was only five feet tall, of a cute gnome, and looked terrified.

"The evidence is overwhelming," Tallagonga said. "So if she is trying to bribe you to concoct some story, beware of it—okay, *señora*? There is no story in the world that will save her this time—not one story about why she brought the money down; not one story about why she hired little boys; not one more story about why she was on the plane the morning her victim lay dead. So if she wants you to invent stories, you will only get into trouble—in some way—and you have gone back to church. I am not a great believer myself," Tallagonga added (to show what state her own remarkably progressive status was and where her support given also ended), "but all this good will toward you could or might be swept away if you lie about something in order to alibi an atrocity. We have one Canadian police officer in town who says it wasn't arsenic, it was a beating—well, yes, she gave him arsenic and she may have beaten him to hurry the process—so what the method? I will go along with it when we get to court. If Canadians are so backward they think that being beaten is less a crime than arsenic, they are barbaric—murder is murder."

The words "alibi an atrocity" left Principia so shaken that she put her head down, and tears rushed to her eyes, and she did not hear much else. Then Tallagonga said that Principia's sister, Lucretia, was known to the police—remember? (Lucretia had been caught impersonating a representative of a chain of jewellery stores in order to get diamond and gold rings.)

Tallagonga then said: "Maybe you and her want to spend ten years in the same jail cell as Mary Cyr.

"Well," Tallagonga then stated. "Never mind blubbering, *llorar mucho*. We both know where we stand."

So Tallagonga excused her, and Principia left and walked back down the cement stairs out into the hot March day. The sky was deep, deep blue. A van with new tourists was pulling up to the gated villas; the fish market, with its signs, was open just down the back street. More reporters had come like wise schoolboys doing a paper. Everything else was the same. Principia turned toward the fish market—you could smell its acrid stench, the flushing water on the floor with its innumerable hoses, just three-hundred metres away.

Coartada—alibi—yes, she was offering one, but not for Mary Cyr. That was the pickle she was in. The picture she had in her mind was not of Mary Cyr in the back of a police car but of a small toy truck Gabriella found under the seat of Mr. DeRolfo's Mercedes when she cleaned it; a little toy truck with the name Maxwell. First Principia had told her to throw it away, but Gabriella kept it.

And now they had it. And worse, they knew whose toy it was, though even now when they sat together watching soap operas on TV, they pretended they did not know. And the sorriest thing was, on one of those soap operas the plot had a situation where the heroine was charged with murder and a female character they all detested, who Principia and Gabriella loved to hate on this soap—had proof that the good woman was innocent. And they were always shouting at the TV:

"*Haz lo correcto—dile a la gente lo que sabes.*"

Do the right thing—tell people what you know.

But yesterday Gabriella did not want to watch. Principia insisted. Yet when they watched, they were suddenly ashamed—and it felt like a thousand tonnes of coal sitting between them in the room.

8.

FOR DAYS AFTER THE DISASTER VICTOR WOULD CARRY FLORIN on his back along the street at seven in the morning, heading to the mine to help find his dad, his eyes searching the faces of the adults, like one of the hundreds of thousands of millions of homeless desperate children in the world.

"Tell the truth and shame the devil," Tallagonga had said.

Victor had tried to tell the truth and the devil had shamed Oathoa.

But not many knew it yet. Soon, however, the world would.

They would know, this unconscionable world, of every step he took in his worn boots, with his tiny brother on his back. That he bought his brother the toy truck because Florin was frightened, and he told him, still with all his innocent faith:

"Tomorrow I am giving the tape to Mary Cyr and then they will start the search again—and Papá will come home—then he will take a job at the garage—*hermanito*—here—are you cold—don't be scared— no one will hurt a little boy like you—adults would never do so."

Administratively Tallagonga was doing only what she was given to do. The file built up so far against Mary Cyr was fat and noble, tied with a big blue ribbon and weighing at least ten pounds. When she looked through this file, she was outraged. Most of these lurid clippings would be compiled in a book, due to come out in the next few months. Sharon DeRolfo had staked her claim to it, but so too did a man—a Canadian who lived now in Milwaukee. He had come down last week, saying he was writing a book. He had the soft hands and the ingratiating look of a pudgy, toupee-wearing gambler. He said he knew her, loved her once and his name was EL.

But he was the fourth man so far who said he was writing a book. They had come into town, looking suspiciously at each other— pretending they all knew her, and that they alone could do justice to the truth.

Still, what people had gleaned so far was in Tallagonga's big, fat, blue-ribboned file, which was supposedly top secret. The tossing of a hundred-thousand-dollar bracelet into Niagara Falls was the thing that made Tallagonga sit up and take notice the first night Mary Cyr was under arrest. That was the very first thing she had time to read before she came into the room to look at her.

"*Fijó el tono*," she said, to anyone who would listen.

Yes, it set the tone.

The decision to formally charge Mary Cyr with first-degree murder was not only not hard it was required. It was not only required but she was compelled by some strange alignment to do so. The idea of church might not be in her philosophy, but luck and premonitions were.

This great case came on the fourth anniversary of her being made a prosecutor. It came on the eighth anniversary of her graduation from law school, and the exact day she was notified that she was in the running to become one of the five or six under attorney generals of Mexico. She would have an immense office, staff and power. Then a lonely-looking little waif was sitting in the interview room at the jail, and she went to see the chief of police and spoke to him about her. He lifted up her passport and showed her the name, with an intense, knowledgeable smile.

"Oh," Isabella said. "Mary Fatima Cyr—*sí*—oh—*SÍ*," and she too smiled.

That smile was to become not only Mary Cyr's downfall; it would in time become Tallagonga's as well.

Besides, over the past eight years all of these great things happened on her birthday, which was a leap year, February 29. It was designed by some great magnetic confluence—however, on two of these occasions it wasn't the twenty-ninth, twenty-eighth or first—once, it was March 3. However, it seemed like it was very much preordained.

All of a sudden it was like grabbing on to a carriage and taking the reins and pushing the horses forward along a road toward some great charmed life. In that carriage Mary Cyr sat in chains, and behind them the roadway burned.

Still, Tallagonga said, it was a terrible decision to have to make.

9.

PRINCIPIA TOO HAD A TERRIBLE DECISION.

She must give the toy and the tape to the authorities. Why had she been offered a reward—because in a strange way that made it all much worse. Now it was as if she was doing everything by design.

She might face jail herself, Tallagonga said, if she took a bribe from that woman, "*puta*," to try to find an alibi. It would be very destructive to the Mexican people. She would be considered a traitor—and for Tallagonga this is exactly what it came down to. Betrayal of the Mexican people.

Principia nodded, too scared to say anything.

"It is up to women to change the world," Tallagonga told her. Principia knew, even in her despair, that this was true.

That afternoon Principia went back to the church, just as every one of the women who were keeping a vigil at the cell did.

How strange it was that they bought little Florin french fries when he was in the car, and then Señorita DeRolfo said she wanted the car so clean she did not even want a french fry to be found—so Gabriella, in trying to extract any leftover french Fries, saw the toy truck. How strange that a french fry pointed to a murder.

And how strange that Principia now hated the sight of a french fry.

Principia knelt and looked at the gaudy altar that looked, with its Christ on the cross and its tribute to martyrs, to be too bloody as well. Candles burned and burned. She blessed herself and kissed her dark-pink beads. Her little lips pressed down as she rubbed her nose, her narrow eyes blinked cautiously, as if she was listening, and she moved her head slightly right and left, looking here and there, noticing the little shrine to Father Ignatius, the priest who had been martyred in 1922 and whose last hours were spent in the cell now occupied by Mary Cyr.

Then as she was staring at the shrine, with its black candle holders and wicks, this answer, which was entirely revolutionary, and went against everything Lucretia had been telling her to do her entire life, came to her:

"Accept no money—take the truck and the tape to Constable Fey. Let that little girl whose life has been filled with mistakes go home. Do it for the Mexican people and for Collette—do it for the memory of what happened to Collette."

She quickly looked away, put her head down, and then looked back at the shrine of Father Ignatius with some peevish suspicion.

Though she was four years younger than Mary Cyr, she nonetheless thought of her at this moment as a little girl, standing on her tiptoes on an old orange crate, happy to share her cigarettes, smiling in spite of everything, saying that someday she would be free.

Collette was the name of the Spanish woman. She knew, like almost everyone in town, that Erappo Pole, the police officer, and the man named Hulk Hernández, who said he was an inspector of mines, had something to do with her gang rape—and that no one had done a thing. One more thing that Ángel tried to ignore.

Nonsense, a voice is a voice and is nothing at all. Besides, even if she felt it was something otherworldly, she lived in this world, with her half-mad sister, Lucretia.

"Tell them I am his mother," Lucretia whispered to her one day as some reporters walked toward them. "Tell them I am his mother. I am Victor and Florin's mother—tell them that."

10.

ANOTHER PROBLEM WAS THAT TALLAGONGA SUDDENLY HAD A star witness to the crime. Mr. DeRolfo told her to talk to Ángel Gloton— that he knew something.

So she drove to find him.

There was wind and noise as if an early hurricane was coming. When they spoke, it was as if both of them were in a whirlwind. And as if—and this was more telling—Ángel could accuse anyone, and Tallagonga would believe it. Not that he wanted to—he was only doing what his friend DeRolfo told him. DeRolfo must know about the tape; he must know about what really happened, Ángel thought. The idea of fighting in the Golden Gloves in May—Cinco de Mayo—and the idea of turning pro pitched and tossed in his mind as he tried to sleep.

So late last night as he was leaving the gym with his hands still half taped, he was told what to say by Señor DeRolfo:

"You have to see the prosecutor—I know what has happened."

He went home and asked his mother what he should do.

Principia said she did not know what he should do.

"*Decir la verdad y el diablo de la vergüenza,*" Lucretia said, piping up as he looked in from her side of their apartment.

Using the exact words Tallagonga had used to Principia.

So Ángel Gloton went to the great building in the square and made his way up the flights of stairs a week after his mom walked down. There he fidgeted and even prayed that what DeRolfo told him to say was the truth.

Meeting Isabella Tallagonga, he told her what it was Victor had said. (Which was what DeRolfo told him Victor had said.) DeRolfo told Ángel he had met Victor twice, but when he asked him to go to the police, the boy was too frightened. He asked Ángel:

"Did he appear frightened of the police to you?"

"Yes," Ángel said excitedly. "He did—he was frightened of the police."

"Well," DeRolfo said, "that's probably because of that Canadian officer. So we will have to tell the prosecutor what he wanted to tell. We will do it for Victor."

He said he would go to the prosecutor himself but he was too involved in the case as the examining physician. So he asked Ángel to do this favour.

So Ángel told Ms. Tallagonga what Victor had supposedly told DeRolfo: that he had been pushed and beaten when he went to the crystal cave because he wouldn't do what Mary Cyr had asked. She choked him and pushed him—that was why he had those bruises on his neck.

"What did she want him to do?"

"She wanted him—to give her Florin—"

"She wanted Florin—"

"That is what he said. He said he wouldn't give her Florin—I think she had some money on her," Ángel said, trying to remember what he had been supposed to say. "She wanted to adopt Florin and take him back—because no one will allow her to adopt in Canada because she is *muy mala*."

This is what Gidgit had heard—had told Carlos—and now Ángel had repeated it.

She made Ángel write a statement, and sign it, and let him go.

Tallagonga warned him not to mention this to anyone else. And Ángel went back outside. At first he was happy that he had done his duty and then he became miserable.

After she read the statement over, Isabella went to Señor Gabel, who was in the office just down the hall.

"So," Tallagonga said to the judge. She feigned the outrage she would have if this were true. "That is what she meant by orphans—she wanted to buy one for herself—she beat Victor because he would not give up Florin, tried to poison him and steal the child. She had at her disposal her own plane. She sees Florin, invites Victor to be her guide, then navigates him into a position of indentured servant—and makes demands because she wants to steal a child. Then she chokes him, pushes him down at the cave. She was the one who beat him. She doesn't think we are human. She was planning to take Florin away in the plane. God knows where she put that child."

"Why would she want to steal a child?"

"Bobby," Tallagonga said, pronouncing the name *Booby*.

"Ahhh." Gabel nodded.

"But Victor, poor little soul, tried to defend his brother—we should have done more to help him—sometimes we are all at fault!"

He too was suddenly outraged.

"*¡Ella vino a México para hacer eso!*"

She came to Mexico to do that!

"It looks it."

He was relieved that this came out. For in so many other ways he had not done his job with the moral certainty he was supposed to exhibit. And he knew as a judge that for seven years now he was a moral coward. He kept buying himself expensive shirts and ties to quell the disaster underneath. Yet, he often thought, who could blame him for that! In fact hardly a man here would have done his job in the same position. A man named Hernández, who was called "the Hulk" by kids, brought in expensive stolen motor parts and stolen cars for the influential men in town— selling Mercedes and Porsches at one-fifth the price. He was also, they said, inspector of mines, which everyone knew was ludicrous. But one day Judge Gabel came to the office and saw a beautiful black Saab sitting in his parking spot. No one told him who had left it there or who left the keys to it for him. He was not a bad man. Never. But there it was.

So this case, this case of Mary Cyr, was the one where Gabel could look authoritative and firm—going against, as he was, such an important family, and have the blessing of everyone.

"This puts a whole new perspective on the evil of money," Judge Gabel said.

"Cyr to be sued for one billion."

That same day in the great sprawling metropolis of Mexico City, on one of the dozens upon dozens of squares, in an office of justice department on the third floor, Alfonso Bara read this. He decided it was time to begin to act. But not to really act—not yet. That is, Mary Fatima Cyr had to go to trial. Tallagonga must try for a conviction—and then Bara would come out with the fact that her department was withholding evidence. He would then start an investigation, would do a recovery at the mine.

Carlos DeRolfo would be charged, his wife would be charged, Hulk would be arrested.

Mary Cyr would go free.

That was the scenario Bara wanted. Tallagonga for all her brilliance would be no longer a threat to his own career.

He was one of those people, so rare, who could wait things out, and seem to watch from the sidelines. But *seem* was the word. All of this was fine. But his friend—an important judge in Mexico City—told him he should start the excavation of the mine now—now—so things could begin. It would be harsh if they found out he waited.

"*Sí*," he said.

So he got a court order and was going to start the process now.

PART ELEVEN

1.

SHE FLED IN THE NIGHT TO SWITZERLAND SOMETIME IN 1984. The year she was waiting to read George Orwell.

She was still young—very young. She had the child by herself in the barn—so when she realized she might even by proxy in some remote way be called Lady Mary, Mary Cyr took it. For wasn't Churchill born in a washroom—in 1874—in Blenheim Palace, of course—so "Lady Mary" sounded like some positive reinforcement.

Of course it was years later. That is, going to Switzerland, being known as Lady Cyr, was many years after she sank her fists into the earth and pushed out as much as her body allowed. Years after she covered up the placenta with rocks and drifted into the house in bare feet, her nightgown covered in blood with the baby wrapped in her Plu.

It took them a week to find it—that is, that she had it. They kept looking for the source of the sound. When Nan found it, she screamed and ran out of the room, waving her arms on either side of her body and screeching. By that time Mary had been up at night with it feeding it, sneaking to the store to buy Pampers.

"There is something in her room," Nan said, screeching and running about the large living room, her eyes wide in a kind of terror, her white nightgown on and a boa around her throat, the small dog called Mugs looking up at her and yapping playfully. Joyous it was to everyone.

Garnet climbed the stairs with the 1900 double-barrelled shotgun given to his father as a present by Clement Atlee after the election in 1945. The shotgun Clement had used on a hunt with Neville Chamberlain in 1935 when they conspired to keep Churchill quiet.

"Quite," Lord Halifax had said.

And as Mary Cyr would say later:

"Quite the arseholes."

So Garnet carried that same shotgun to dispatch with a merciless blast whatever animal she had hidden in her room.

Perley walked behind him with a broom.

Still, it was not a weasel, as Nan said it must be.

It was Mary Cyr's child. Bobby Blair Cyr. They tried to take it from her, but she refused. She refused help, nannies, day nurses—she refused it all. She knew they wouldn't take her to court over it. They knew she would take them. And they had to keep it as quiet as possible.

"It's a monster," Nan said, and Mary overheard.

From the age of six months Mary Cyr's child was getting old, his body was frail, his bones were weak and small. There was at first no sign— but that was because the sign was always there—then a kind of strange pallor to the skin, which suggested something not quite right. She would hold him in front of her, looking at him, trying to understand what it was that was at odds, what was wrong. No one could see him without Mary being present, without her shielding him. The room smelled of antiseptic and a kind of soft mist and medicine, which she had read about in a book.

You see, they tried to sneak the child away from her. That was late in her sixteenth year—so she turned against them—hated the idea of abortion all her life because this marred life was so precious to her. Even in this Catholic household she was alone in that regard—except for Perley, who simply thought that people did not have that right.

Mary screened Bobby's visitors and visitors to the house.

"I think you should leave," she said to more than one person just entering the house.

"Pardon?"

"You heard me—you are a spy for Shell Oil."

"I am not."

"Well—you are still a spy—you look Swiss."

"I'm Irish."

"So you sided with the Nazis—you had the devilish notion that you could make a deal with Hitler—so drink your Irish pint and pretend innocence."

"Mary, be quiet. Father Dolan will stay here if he wants."

Upstairs along the hallway and in those great back rooms no one saw she made a fairyland—which is what she called it—a childhood land with swings and rocking ponies and a small merry-go-round; a giant train set, in which he could sit on the engine and ring a bell, wearing an engineer's hat. His body turning older as the days rolled away. They went together out onto the bay in the small sailboat, laughing and singing. She wrapped him in a blanket when they came in. Then he began to falter when he tried to walk—and then at times it was hard for him to crawl. The trouble was he was very bright—and knew his condition before she did—knew something in his blood was wrong.

And then as all of this was happening, oh yes, Debby Dormey took sick.

One night some months after little Debby Dormey died she came home to find Bobby alone in his room, looking into the mirror as if for the first time understanding that he had been for some godawful reason hunchbacked into the world. He looked up at her when she walked toward him, startled, profound and silent, his eyes large, his nose hooking and his head bald. She tried to touch him and he moved away as if he did not want her to have to care for him anymore.

"Mom," he said.

His lips trembled as if he wanted to speak some great profound thought, but he could not find the words. He looked like a troll hidden under some particular bridge.

"I love you, Bobby Blair Cyr," she whispered, hugging him. "I will never let you go."

2.

SHE BUNDLED THE CHILD UP AND FLEW HIM TO SWITZERLAND. She stayed in a five-star star hotel near the Brunswick Monument, and visited palaces and museums to the Red Cross, and a Dr. Leath, who spoke English with his slight French and German accent, had a wise small face, a moustache that did not go to the end of his lips, grey and white, which made him look pedestrian; like she thought, a bus driver, or a man on European holiday riding a bicycle.

Progeria was what it was called, he told her. There were experimental drugs, and one must realize it was fatal—but that prolongation of life was what they were after. There was some protein that damaged the arteries—that was all. It was, he said, in the blood. The child was simply a child after all.

In her diary at this time she mentioned Lake Geneva, a visit to some shops and restaurants. She had thought her twenty-first birthday would be spent differently, she wrote.

She spent it at the Hôpital des enfants, on the Avenue de la Roseraie, wearing a blue skirt and simple white blouse, and a small gold charm bracelet on her wrist. That only had three charms—one for her son, one for Debby Dormey, one for little Denise Albert. There was one aside to this. A woman from Belgium came in, certain of her privilege, and barged ahead of Mary Fatima Cyr. That is, she still looked something like a girl—and the woman's husband was a magistrate and they had a small chateau in the Swiss Alps.

The receptionist, however, whispered to this impetuous woman in French, and told her to stand aside.

"*Qui est-elle? Qu'est-ce qu'elle fait ici?*" the woman said, looking behind her at Mary in annoyance.

"*Non, vous êtes le premier,*" Mary said. And she went back to the corner and sat down, completely unfazed by the insult.

For unlike that woman from Belgium, she had always been exactly sure of where she stood.

———

Then, strangely enough the other world—the world of other concerns—came back. She did not want them to. But it was as if it was somehow preordained. She had almost forgotten about this world or one might assume she had. But really it had never left her, and in some way it never would.

She had a meeting. It was just mentioned in her diary as a meeting, at two at Les Armures with a man for lunch. "He kept bugging me," she wrote. Was that true? John did not know. She wore grey pants, with a button-up white jacket with black pearl buttons. Her soft hair was short; her eyes were dark, under dark sunglasses. She wrote too that she wore silver high-heeled felt boots—much like, she said, Cinderella.

In 2002 John discovered it was Vanderflutin. The money he had made in Canada—or his father had made—was reclaimed by his family's victims in the late seventies. His father had blackmailed certain Jewish families, took paintings and jewellery from them. It was simply the time—he got caught up in the excitement of it all dealing with important Germans in Rotterdam. Certain of those Jewish families were transported into concentration camps and Dug Vanderflutin had campaigned to join the Waffen-SS. There were Dutch who had done so, who had made that leap, and he was one of them. He stole away after the war, and was mistaken for the other Dug Vanderflutin, who had been lost and forgotten.

His son, Ernest, knew not about it, as Mary was wont to say.

She wrote in her diary that Ernest was:

"A sad man, as much an accident of history as I am. Perhaps his father fought bravely for the other side, until there was no other side left. Then he simply fudged who he was—and got away with it for a long time. I am almost sorry I saw his picture. I wonder if he would be as sorry if it was me."

After his book was published in Europe, Ernest was at the height of his power. Yes, she had followed his career carefully for a number of years.

He went on speaking tours with this book. For a while he travelled far and wide. He spoke about the Cree of the North. He did certain First Nations chants. He had never fished or hunted. He had never lived in a wigwam. He never had a First Nations friend in his life. But the people of Europe never knew this.

Still, a year or two before she went to Switzerland something happened at the university during a talk. A Canadian man was there. He *had* lived most of his life in the rural area of northern New Brunswick alongside First Nations people. He had come over on a grant to talk about development in rural areas. So he went to this talk about Canada. And then, he went back again, to the little auditorium at the university. So he stood and asked if Ernest himself had once done anything he wrote about—it didn't seem that he had. But Ernest wouldn't answer.

He asked him had he been on a trapline, did he know how to hunt moose—take the hide off a deer, had he once fished a stream.

No answer.

Some said this man was in fact Packet Terri and Mary Cyr had asked him to go, and he had done so as a favour. And over the years John Delano felt this a more likely scenario.

The man then introduced his wife, who was a Micmac woman, to the audience. It was as if they were being introduced to a splendid mythical creature. They asked for her autograph—a few asked for a piece of her hair.

Then they simply filed out, and Ernest was left alone.

Three months later Ernest discovered something about his own family while visiting an art gallery. It was strange. He almost did not visit—had no real reason to. But at the last moment he thought of one of his dad's paintings that he discovered was now housed there.

A longing came over him, to remember his childhood, his father's kindness to him. So he went inside.

There, looking at the painting, a Monet, he became very nostalgic for his father, and tears came to his eyes. But suddenly he looked closely at the work, and got a terrible surprise:

CONFISCATED FROM THE DUTCH NAZI OFFICER
DUG VANDERFLUTIN, RETURNED TO THE FAMILY EIDER
BY MARY CYR AND DONATED TO
NUSSBAUM ART GALLERY IN 1982.

He stared at the inscription in utter amazement.

Anxious, almost stricken with fear, he started to leave quickly, but before he could get to the door, he was pulled aside by the Jewish curator.

Again Ernest tried to leave, but the curator held him back.

"You are his son—Ernest?" he said gently. "Then you perhaps did not know this."

But what was more startling to him was that Mary Cyr had known this from the time she had befriended the little Van Haut child, and had said nothing.

She simply was silent, waiting for him to find out about it.

She was, you see, that bright—that excruciatingly bright. In fact no one in Mary's own family had believed her, and she had remained steadfast in her belief that one day the truth would come out.

That is why she had the little Dutch girl as a pen pal and that is the reason she went to The Hague.

Ernest's wife left him. It was not just because of his father. There were other problems, but it all did come crashing down.

Now grey and in his forties, he owned a senior citizens facility, called Holunder Mannich. It was an austere place, where people lived in antiseptic rooms, and watched TV mid-afternoon, ate dinner at quarter to five at night.

After a while, after the curator revealed it all, they began to recognize who he was, those *Altlich*—those Swiss and some Dutch seniors with their lacklustre eyes staring at him as he entered the room, and whispering to one another.

"*Was sagst du?*" he would yell at them, and they would look over at him and turn away.

They were saying:

"*Er ist der Sohn.*"

He is the son.

He would stand in the hallway in the waning light of afternoon, begging them to stay.

He drove a small Volvo, and had a two-bedroom townhouse outside Geneva, with one and a half baths.

"But you see," he said now to Mary Cyr, "we Dutch really wanted no part in the blasted war." And he smiled as if it was his last moral victory.

"Yes—of course no part in the war."

"It was not our choice to fight," Vanderflutin said.

In a letter sent to Mary Cyr at her hotel in Geneva he wrote:

"I have over these past few years discovered things about my father. It is pretty hard for a conscientious person to swallow."

"Yes," Mary Cyr wrote back. "It must be at that. For a conscientious person."

So she went to the meeting. She was sorry for him. His suit was wrinkled, his eyes haggard, his face grey. Most of his business was now falling away, and he had the pedestrian habit of keeping his wallet snapped and looking through it before he ordered anything.

She smiled. Then point-blank she asked him why had he written such things against them? Saying that her mother was a frivolous British woman. For that was the only person Mary Cyr was trying to protect—she never really gave a damn about herself.

"Oh," he said, diplomatically. "Sorry you felt that way, Mary dear. I thought I was being quite fair. And you know as well as me—Acadians are still suffering from British neglect."

She nodded.

"Oh yes of course," she said. That was something, almost admirable. Like his father he was in some way still fighting the British.

There was a picture of Ernest's mother carrying him through a jeering crowd after they had shaved her head for collaborating with the Germans.

She looked something like a lonely little bird. In fact, Mary had that very picture on her when she met Ernest that day. She did not show it to him. Later she destroyed it—

All trace of the mother, the boy, the father, was lost for a long time. Until a young woman began to make inquiries when she was fourteen to a young girl named Norma van Haut, both of them treating it like a kind of Nancy Drew mystery. So now Ernest was caught too, as much as anyone.

Yet she felt empty and full of sorrow for him.

Forever.

He needed money. And he smiled at her with that old mirthful look he had had long ago when she had waited all day to meet him because she believed he was going to be her new friend. That he would see her not as other people, like Nan and Garnet did, but as she was, precocious and brilliant and full of love. But all that was long ago, and gone away. And for the life of her, she had never been able to figure out why.

Mary simply did what she did so well. She wrote a cheque. Perhaps it was as much as twenty-five thousand dollars.

She had it hand-delivered by her driver to the hotel the next afternoon. The driver walked up to him, and handed him the envelope. She had written on it:

"To the Dutchman's boy."

But she never ever mentioned his name again.

3.

SHE TOOK TIME PLAYING THE PIANO. IT WAS HER AUNT'S SIXTEETH birthday. She remembered it now in Mexico, in somewhat of a daze. Yes, it was long ago. And so many people were there. The lieutenant governor of New Brunswick, the wife of the local United Church minister, Bishop Fronlu from the Catholic diocese. Two other sneaky-looking, pleasant-enough priests. Two Maritime senators and their troubled alcoholic wives. The all-inclusive obsequious president of Saint Michaels

University. Many people they had known and loved over the years—but most were people her aunt liked, and who Mary Cyr disdained. Some of them—most of them—had been at the dinner party that night—*the night of the knives*, as Mary Cyr called it. They had sat there silently while her mother's culture and history were being defamed—and Mary Cyr remembered their silence.

Nan wanted her to play. Perhaps Chopin or Mozart—who knew.

"Some little classical ditty, I suppose," Mary had written in her diary.

She was upstairs with Bobby, sitting far in the corner, near the rocking horse. It had been, this party, supposedly arranged for months, but she had been away in Switzerland.

"D. H. Lawrence wrote a macabre story about a rocking horse—and then he went to Mexico—maybe someday we will go to Mexico, Bobby—and just live as recluses—I don't want to go downstairs and play—why should I need to do so if they do not want or need you there?"

Because Nan wanted her to.

"The Anglican minister is coming," Nan had said.

(She'd said this because of Mary Cyr's Englishness.) But Nan, yesterday in her most diplomatic way, told her she did not want Bobby present. Mary had shown her the boy's new jumpsuit she had bought in Switzerland, with the blue hat and shorts she wanted to show him off in. But after Nan held it and smiled, Nan said:

"Maybe he will get tired or cranky."

And then:

"Maybe he wouldn't want to be around all those grown-up people."

And then:

"We have to think of his condition."

And then:

Mary interjected.

"Why, Nan, maybe you are ashamed of us?"

"Ashamed? How can you say that—" But then she said, in French, as she turned away in a huff: "I just thought if he is a boy who is ill, maybe he is better off with those who can take care of him, and not a temperamentally unstable young girl who got pregnant when she was fifteen—*Quelle honte, une honte.*"

What a disgrace—a disgrace.

And added: "I have tried my best to hire the best people—"

"There is no one better to take care of him than me," Mary said, getting enough of the French to understand enough to answer, and secretly reeling from the word *honte*—disgrace.

Then Nan said:

"Well, Bobby is certainly welcome—and you can be certain you have all our support."

Then she closed the door to the side room, and began to sing.

So the day progressed as Mary sat upstairs, in the room beyond his bedroom where his rocking horse and model train set were. She held his jumpsuit. She looked about at all the expensive clothes she had bought him in Switzerland and Paris. And she too had duped him—trying to get him to look ordinary—so she could present him.

"Forgive me, Bobby," she said. "But look how pretty this is—let's get it on so we can go downstairs."

All his diagnoses, all the results of his tests about bone density, were on charts in her adjoining room. All the plans for him made in secret between him and her, both giggling like children during a bedtime story.

"No, Mommy," he said. "No, Mommy. I don't want to go."

He smiled at her as if to ask forgiveness for something he could not help.

She kissed him, held him, put his jumpsuit away.

The baby grand piano had a key that sounded tinny, as far as Mary was concerned. Which is perhaps the only thing she had written about the event in her diary.

She wore a little black skirt, a white blouse with long sleeves. The day was hot, and the piano sat in front of the large window, where the sun beat down. The blouse she wore was complemented by a small black bow tie. She wore her charm bracelet. John realized that this was the bracelet she tossed over Niagara Falls—there was no gold on it. It was simply a charm bracelet of sad memories—

She played Mozart's piano concerto no. 23. It was too long and involved, she said, didn't they think? But they told her she played wonderfully. She looked over at Nan and smiled. She drank down her champagne.

She said:

"Then you must know this one."

She played Chopin's Nocturne op. 9, no. 2. It was in a way—at least in part, even with that tinny key—spellbinding. People clapped. She had drunk a little too much beforehand and she knew it. She wanted to go back to Mozart but did not know which one she should go to. So she said, after her third glass of champagne:

"How about old Scott?"

"Scott who?" Nan asked.

Mary jumped up, and became almost, as people said, another Mary. She played Scott Joplin's "Maple Leaf Rag." She stood up as she played it, looking up at everyone and smiling.

"Here I am, doing the old Jerry Lee," she said.

People began to tap their feet when she played it. They clapped loudly and said, "Let's have the Beatles."

This request came from the sides of the great room, toward the end where the piano was.

"Okay, here's one," she said. " 'Love, love me do—You know I love you—' " She still stood at the piano.

"My soul," Nan said, looking at the United Church minister.

Mary unbuttoned the sleeves of her blouse, and two top buttons. She tossed her bow tie aside. She was hot. It was the gin she had drunk upstairs before she came down. (She had given Bobby a little slurp of gin as well.)

The top of her white breasts were glistening with sweat. The sun had made her dizzy.

"Give me some more champagne," she said.

The maid in her white dress came over with another glass.

Perley, who had kept his eye on her, running to check on Bobby every ten minutes and then walking down the stairs hearing the piano becoming more and more loud, and her speech more and more erratic, asked her if she would like to stop and go upstairs.

"No," she said, glaring at him, downing the glass in a swig and wiping her mouth. "I'm just getting started—Perl."

She still stood. She knocked the piano bench away from her, so she could move to the music.

She yelled at the maid to make sure everyone's glass was full.

"Yes—*fill them glasses to the brim and pace them old cards around*," she said. Nan and Garnet smiled tensely.

Mary put her hands down on the keys with a climatic tone. Then she lifted her head and smiled ruefully, and said:

"One more—it's about a girl and a guy—just one more—come on now, we can all sing along—you must know this one—he is a fisherman and shy—she is a young girl who loves him—maybe someday I will marry a fisherman."

Everyone laughed.

"Okay, here we go—Nan must know this one growing up in Tracadie—I am certain of it!"

Then she sang:

" 'My shy young boy, you fish da peer.'

"Come on now," she encouraged.

So some of them sang:

" 'My shy young boy, you fish da peer.' "

"Yes," Mary said.

" 'On lonely nights I'm real lonely here.' "

" 'On lonely nights I'm real lonely here—' " they shouted.

" 'You know me good.' "

" 'You know me good,' " they laughed.

" 'I wish not to be blunt.' "

" 'I wish not to be blunt,' " everyone sang.

Mary came down on the keys brazenly, suspending time for a moment.

" 'I do not wish to be so blunt,' " she repeated,

" 'I do not wish to be so blunt,' " they rejoined.

She paused, then put her head down and crashed the keys.

" 'But I'd love your finger up my cunt.' "

" 'Ta da!' " she said. "Sing it, Nan!" she said.

" 'Don't want to be blunt— But I'd love your finger up my cunt— Ta da,' " she said. She waited. "Sing it, Nan—'Ta—da'?"

She fell back, slid off the piano chair and onto her bum.

4.

AND THEN QUITE, QUITE SUDDENLY, SHE SAID SHE WAS GETTING married.

They had a wedding of two hundred guests, under a tent in the backyard. She walked about with pieces of cake.

His name was Doc. He was her mother's former boyfriend. John always felt she had done this to get back at him. But perhaps he was giving himself too much credit. All of a sudden Doc was a link to her past, and her mother. That is what she really wanted, her mother. So they got married.

All that gauze and all that giddy celebration for six and a half months. For that skinny little yob. He begged her, so she put him up in a business in Chatham, and he ran it into the ground, stealing from it. Later he was seen with another woman at the Low Tide. It seemed that she didn't care, only wanted one thing from him. He promised to tell her about her mother in Spain—and she waited at night for him, compiling a list of questions. The questions were so innocent, and so full of hope—and she sat on the edge of the couch waiting for him to come home, so she could ask him these—and each day she changed them—tried to think of something more to ask:

"Was she sorrowful?"

"Did they hurt her?"

"Did she ask for me?"

"Did she miss me?"

"Do you know why—you know she wanted to die?"

That is, she knew from the first that it must have been a kind of coercion of some kind, a sad and whimsical, set-in-the-sunlight kind, that made a dalliance out of shame—the kind her mother did not want but that was, perhaps, with her luckless life and her artificial gaiety, the only kind she could arrive at.

The question then that was asked, which made him stop in his tracks, and turn beet red, was:

"Why in God's name did she ever have anything to do with you?"

Questions he always put off answering, until such time as she would sleep with him. But she continually put it off—as if it would be a disgrace to sleep with him. But John wondered now if she ever had.

"Tell me about her days in Spain. What was she doing there—twice she gave you money to go away."

"How do you know that?"

"Because of her letters written to me—because I know what so many think I do not know—so you blackmailed her, that is why she took pills—that is why—you put her on those pills—she was so pilled up— such a pill popper she had no chance to escape you—so do not lie, do not lie, tell me tell me true!"

"It was nothing like that."

"Then tell me—" Holding on to him, "Then tell me—" And again and again, and again, "Then tell me tell me tell me—true—tell me true and I will—I will do a strip act for you—a kind of hoochie hoochie coo."

"Someday I will tell you about her—about a man named Paco who ruined her. Because unlike me he was a gigolo. He took money off of her— and talked her into buying that farmhouse. That's when she betrayed me—so—anyways—that was why I took a hammer to her car—well, someday I will tell you."

"What farmhouse—which one."

"I don't know which one—some farmhouse in Dénia, Spain."

("Paco," she wrote in her diary. "I have to go to Spain and find a man named Paco—there can't be too many of those.")

But the days passed into spring and rain, and dreary hours waiting for him. He knew he wasn't welcome, and he could no longer stomach her insatiable questions, so he went out with friends who were involved in schemes. One was to rob Perley of a fifteen-thousand-dollar watch. These two men he was with would later—with Doc's involvement—get involved in a scheme to take Perley for money over the rescue attempt that Markus Paul discovered.

But that as we know was far away.

5.

"SCHEMES," SHE WROTE. "HE HAS A WHOLE BUCKETFUL OF schemes. He destroyed my mother, in some petty way he had some kind of pettiness on her—I know, I can see by the way he looks."

Doc would sit at the large table at supper—she and Doc, and the boy, and Perley. There the clinking of forks and knives, there the white wine, there the sad smell of flowers outside. There the taste of salt in whispers from the bay. There the portrait of her grandfather. Doc loved to tease Perley, question him. Because there was a secret girl Perley knew, the girl of his dreams. So one night in a buoyant mood Doc convinced Perley to show them a picture of his girl, Caroline. Finally Perley said, "Okay, I will"—and he ran upstairs and got the picture, and brought it to them. He was holding it against his chest as he walked into the room.

"This isn't the best picture of her—she is prettier in person, I will tell you that. The glasses make her look like she has buck teeth, but she doesn't," he said, shyly. And he finally handed it to his cousin's husband.

Doc looked at it, sniffed, rubbed his nose and shrugged.

"The one who teaches grade school?"

"Yes—"

"The one with the red hair?"

"Yes—Caroline—yes."

"Hell yes, Bucky Four Eyes." Doc smiled. "I know her too."

"Oh—you do not know her—not that Caroline—" Perley looked at Mary for some explanation, and then he smiled timidly and said: "It must be another Caroline."

Doc picked the picture up again and looked closely at it. He took the glasses out of his pocket and put them on. Then he picked at a tooth. Then he sniffed and shook his head quickly. Then he tapped the picture and handed it back.

"No—that's Caroline, the one who teaches grade school—yes, I know her—" He took a long drink of white wine and kept his eyes on Perley as he drank.

"You do not."

"Don't get angry—don't get angry, Perley—why, is she your girl?"

"Yes—she is nice—she is my girl—she is my first girlfriend."

"Well, she was many people's last girlfriend," Doc said. "Why, she's had more pricks in her than a second-hand dartboard, Perley—"

"No—you are saying a LIE—I know—it's a lie—I've never even kissed her."

"That must be refreshing for her—her lips are worn thin with kisses— why, the boys in grade nine history class are lining up to do her one at a time. She just wants money, Perley—get over it. Mark my words."

Doc laughed at this, and Perley began to shake. He was shaking so bad that Mary went over to hold him, but he upset the table. He roared at the top of his lungs, and left the room. He went out and walked along the beach. You could hear him crying for some time.

Doc began to laugh, with the three of them still sitting there and the table upside down. What was funnier was the tiny dog was sitting in a chair by himself. So they were all sitting there and the table was turned completely over, with Caroline's picture lying there, and Doc found this hilarious.

So then he stood and yawned, looked at the busted plates and glasses and walked into the far room. He took the keys from the cup on the desk and started toward the door.

He was about to take the Jag, and Mary ran in to the room and said no. Until he went to Perley and apologized to him.

"Apologize—no goddamn way."

"Then you can't have the car."

One must realize that Mary was frightened to challenge him because she might not then discover what had happened to her mother in Spain. And Doc was arrogant enough to think he owned the family.

But still he must apologize.

"No no no no no."

"Then you won't have the Jag," she said.

"I'll take it if I want," he said.

Then he made fun of her child.

The little boy who was told to call him Father.

Doc smiled at her—as if this was the weapon he was waiting to use, and told her the child should have been an abortion, she being too young to take care of it—

She went to grab the keys, but he slapped her. She looked at him. Her nose was bloody. She wiped it with her hand. There were tears in her eyes. She smiled.

"Oh look," she said, "you bruised your hand hitting my face, I am sorry."

He was trembling, and grabbed his jacket to go out.

"You are not going out to see her—whoever she is."

"I'll go where I damn well want. I can't stand all the questions you ask, I can't stand it anymore—not one more question."

"Then here's the answer—you murdered my MOMMY."

That is when she jumped on his back and bit his ear. That is when he threw her down, right over his shoulder.

And then he saw the child looking at him, a look of sad horror on his face, yet a look a child has that everything is fine and he doesn't quite understand. What the look said was *I trusted you, you are my father.* The look in fact was that innocent.

"Go," Mary screamed. "Get out and never come back!"

"Okay, I will!" he said.

Yet something came over him—this sudden idea—one might not even call it an idea but a feeling—an impulsive sensation—and he said:

"Okay—if that's what you want—calling me a murderer—we will just see about that!"

And he walked across the hall, through the large kitchen and into the back shed. When he came out, he had his lighter, and some gas. He picked the small dog up in one hand, the dog looking around the room in befuddled confusion, as he poured gasoline over it. When the dog wagged its tail, some small little driblets of gas flew in the air, much like water from a water sprinkler. Then Doc took his hand and massaged the gas into its fur.

Doc lit the Zippo lighter in his right hand, as if he was performing a sacred ritual.

He even mumbled words as if they were sacred, as if he was a deacon at some ceremony in the church.

"Hear ye, hear ye" was what he actually said. "Hear ye, hear ye now on this day, July 21, 1986."

Mary made a lunge to stop him, but he tripped her and she fell forward.

Then he lit little, joyous, waggy-tailed Muggy Muffs on fire, and dropped it to the floor. Doc's own hand caught on fire as well, and he had to rub at it to put it out, and then lick it.

At first it did not move at all. But the fire started to blossom, from bluish to orange flame, from its tail to its head. Then suddenly the dog, making howling horrified sounds, ran all around the house in a blaze. You could not help but stare at its bulging, perplexed eyes. "Muggy," Mary called to it.

Bobby screamed, and screamed and said:

"Stop it! Stop it!"

And he hid his terrified face under the edge of the rug, so you could still see half of his body, trembling.

The dog ran to its chair, the favourite one it slept on. It tried to hide there—and then fell through an open window. Mary ran to the window and called its name.

Suddenly she saw the yard light up in various places. You could see a maple branch begin to burn, and then the roses, and then sparks fell on the walk that the little thing crossed. So like a demon it ran about the yard, blazing and yelling. Finally it stopped screeching in horror, ran all ablaze into a bush, kicked twice more and the night was still.

"Snow," Mary said. "I want it to snow."

6.

OF COURSE SHE KNEW WRITERS OF ALL SORTS, POLITICIANS, opera singers. She knew most of the living prime ministers—some said she had an affair with one. She sat in her room with Bobby. They lay about playing checkers, singing and making up stories. Bobby had his own Ferris wheel. Albeit a small one. Some days he just sat in it, at the top.

Doc left. The marriage was annulled.

She and Bobby would walk the road at night—just like vampires did. They would wait until the children his age went inside, after their games, their cries of confusion and delight, their yelling and laughter had subsided. Then a child would emerge just as the sun was going down over the bay, and his mother, looking not much bigger than he, both wearing ball caps. They would emerge and turn right, away from the great cottage, and go though the path that she had covered with soft pine nettles gone red in the setting sun. They would visit Jabaroo the horse; they would visit his "pile of goats." They would sit in the barn's hayloft and she would tell him a story about Denise Albert or Debby

Dormey—her two *bestest* friends. She would laugh—laugh and laugh, like a little girl. They would play hide and seek among the soft worn timbers 120 years old—or if lucky see just at dawn the phantom *Man O War* riding the waves on its way to Quebec in 1763.

Then she would quote her favourite Nowlan poem. She would tell him the poem was better than Chaucer. But that someday she would read him Chaucer too.

He would listen to her, his mouth open in wonder at his mother—this very great lady. One night they did actually meet a she-bear roaming out near the cove. It came out on their little path, and without a second's hesitation Mary Cyr stood in front of her son, and stared the she-bear down.

Near dawn they would come back, to this great home, and when the sun was rising Mary would tuck her son into bed, and lie beside him and sing him to sleep, and he would sleep until afternoon.

Perhaps she didn't handle it right at all. Both the Catholic Church and social workers said she hadn't, after Bobby died. Perhaps there never was a good way to handle it.

This was the year that Mrs. Cruise was publishing her great book.

It chronicled her advocacy for change. *A feminist in the age of feminism. No one could be braver*, Mary once said.

Perhaps Ms. Cruise did not know it was Mary Cyr's family's publishing house. Perhaps Mary Cyr who knew much about her by the detectives she hired, knew enough to care about her. Knew enough of her own betrayal.

Mary discovered that it was there, one day when she and Bobby were making a great castle with Lego. The castle was going to be big enough to sleep in—have a moat filled with crocodiles and snakes—some man-eating tigers too.

She had to protect him, and Lego was the best retardant against all things wrong.

But she left the Lego where it was.

She went to the publisher. It was a cold November afternoon and she arrived unannounced in Ottawa—on the date she had lost her virginity long ago, to a man she once worshipped in a childish way.

The editor had refused the book, but since her grandfather had major interest in the company, she asked them to please reconsider. The book was meticulously bound and ribboned. It was such an innocent affair in the end. And Rory assumed it was groundbreaking, assumed there was actually something new in it.

She picked it up, flipped through the pages—made a mark in the middle with her pen, and said: "Reconsider."

"Reconsider—Ms. Cyr," the editor said. "It is not the kind of book we consider here—we do mostly political books—this is a sociological study—And—" here he whispered gravely "—it calls for the government to have a policy of national euthanasia. The poor woman believes in that way she will help the world."

"Well, so what?" Mary said flippantly.

"Well, people like your son—not in so many words but surely in the implication."

"I am almost certain that it would. You see it's all the rage now."

"What is?"

"Liberal Lunacy."

"Well—what is your relationship with her?"

"I knew *him* once when I was young." Mary said, and here her voice faltered.

"But he is much older than you are."

"By centuries, it seems."

"I had planned to send it back with a rejection slip."

"Publish her, please. Do it for me—I will pay the publishing costs."

"And who will I say gave the acquisition go-ahead?"

She simply wrote on the top page of Ms. Cruise's grand opus: "Stet, Mary Fatima Cyr."

Then turning away, she said:

"Euthanasia of Bobby—why, of course. Why didn't I think of that."

So she secretly helped to save Mrs. Cruise's book with the Ottawa publisher. It was published that year. It made a splash among certain advocates. She did this for revenge against her beau. It was something she kept secret.

"I never read the fuckin book. She strikes me as a sad creature—"

She felt guilty. This started her wild excessive binge drinking, her solitary parties with *Vogue* magazine, and a forty of gin. In fact she ended up in detox on a summer night. Poor little Bobby watched the ambulance take her away. And Perley kept the boy for her during that stay.

Once out of detox she disappeared from view with Bobby in tow, for over eight months.

7.

THEN ONE SUMMER DAY, WHEN JOHN THOUGHT HE WOULDN'T hear from her, two years or more after the crisis on the reserve, she and Bobby appeared again. People said she was now erratic like her mother had been—obviously scatterbrained. And as crazy as an eel.

Even her old friends, and she had few, felt she was very different now. She communicated with no one.

She pulled the teakwood motorboat out, and began to repair it. She spent half the summer doing this. She had a friend of hers, Packet Terri, lift the engine out and place it on the big side table in the barn and there she worked, all day long. She had been taught enough mechanics by those people who loved her, taught how to cast a fly rod, hand-tail a salmon, shoot a buck on the run across the field. She did this not because she wanted to compete with men but because to her, this was a natural thing for her to do.

That teakwood boat, bought in the late forties, was going to be her escape. She and Bobby would go to their small cottage across the bay, where her grandfather used to go to hunt duck—they would stay there together all August. She would fish and dig oyster and clams.

That is what she told John in a phone call. The teakwood inboard motorboat was what could save her and Bobby. It was the only thing she had seen during her birthing pains. So the engine was worked on, manuals were brought out, people were consulted about the crankcase, about gaskets, about replacing the spark plug wires, and new piston rings, but she was determined to do the work by herself. And then one late night, about eleven o'clock, there was from across the grand manicured lawn the sound of the engine starting.

"Eureka!" she wrote.

And the next day she had that name put on the front of the boat.

She left a note, which said:

"Don't worry—Bobby and I know what to do to make this right."

And:

"If Doc wants his flip-flops, mail them to him COD."

But she did not get away until late, after four, and the swell had started.

They said the air was cold—the spray froze her face because the windshield had broken—and that she had a catatonic stare. (Or those who said they saw her, days later when people were questioned, did.) She put a blanket over Bobby and placed him up against the engine housing to keep him warm. It all looked to observers as if she needed help, and there was no one in the world to help her. So people gathered at the wharf to watch her go. Just as people have always done to those eccentrics during the cottage months when all people seem to have a more tenuous grasp on reality.

Yes, a great adventure to her grandfather's old duck-hunting lodge, where they would roast marshmallows, and he could bathe on the beach, and make sandcastles without being looked at.

She stood up at the wheel, looked over her handiwork, smiled and waved to those seeing her off.

"Bon voyage," she shouted to herself.

She was not much more than a child herself; Bobby hidden from everyone so no one would make fun of him. She had plastic pails and shovels, a beach towel, ten packets of Kool-Aid, hot dogs and hamburgers.

She arrived across the bay to the small family island about ten that night, and waded the boat in. The wind was from the south, the last bell-buoy light was faint, another five kilometres away.

She unlocked the small cottage door and unloaded the box of groceries and the beer and gin. Then she went to get her son, but couldn't wake him. His face was pressed toward the engine, and his arms had not been strong enough to move away. She called his name many times. She stroked his face.

There was no response. She looked at him strangely. The stars were now out, and it was August and meteors fell and dazzled the black night air.

She tried to find out what was wrong. Perhaps this sickness caused him to go to sleep.

"Bobby?" she said. "Bobby, dear Bobby?"

But he did not wake up.

Ever again.

There had been a leak in the engine that she had worked on, to get the boat in the water. She had been too stubborn to ask for help from one of ten mechanics she could have phoned. Yes, in her own way she had been too stubborn—too silly to think she must do it all by herself. As Packet Terri said later:

"The lady needed a good kick in the rear."

But that was for another time.

Bobby had died of carbon monoxide poisoning. He had just gone to sleep of a sudden—just like that, lying up against the engine she had worked on all that summer. She had put him aside the housing in order to keep him warm.

"Bobby died," she wrote. "I put him near the engine and he fell asleep. I held him in my arms for nine hours. I sang the *Big Rock Candy Mountain* to him, I am sure he will go there now."

Then in agony she was furious with herself—two dozen times people had asked her to let them help, and each time she was too stubborn—oh yes, she was going to do it all—and she hated herself now! And worse, the boy had trusted her, trusted her to know what she was doing when she really did not know.

That was the sting that in fact would never end.

But then there was another sting—so it became a triumvirate of stings—and it was this: Bobby knew in his own way that she did not know what she was doing, and yet was loyal to her to the end.

She placed him in the water and watched him float away from her. And then, lying on the floor of the boat, she remembered the Scottish writer who said:

"The cheapest way out of Glasgow is a bottle of Bols gin."

So she opened the pint up, and drank and cut her wrists.

She lay in the dark floating over the River Styx, right into the Canadian Coast Guard vessel *Cape Tormintine*.

She spent two days in ICU in Saint John. When she came out, she was driven to the police station. Why? Because it was obvious to everyone she had committed murder—and then tried to take her own life. Impossible not to think otherwise.

8.

YET SOMETHING HAPPENED THAT SEEMED FORTUITOUS FOR Mary Cyr's defence.

There had to be a scenario where the killing of her son, which seemed indisputable, was also acceptable. And her lawyer found it, and made it the *prima facto* of the case.

That it was tried in the public domain was, for her, at this time, looked upon as a good thing. The boy, especially among at least the more vocal, was a societal burden. He should not have been born. This thought was especially prevalent among certain quasi-freedom seekers.

Especially to one or two who sometimes travelled to the edge of moral obscenity in order to prove to others that they were free.

"Look how she suffered—forced into a pregnancy."

So the country watched and waited.

It began to take the papers by storm—it became for the majority a daily source of debate, titillation and entertainment. The farther one got from the centre of her little province the more unimaginable the theories were. In England, especially; where they called her the "Femme Fatale of the Forest." And the "Bitch in the Backwoods."

It was outlandish, slovenly and deceitful, but since these reports were supposedly from the "most hip and sophisticated" of British journalists in the most advanced places, it was taken as a given that these things could be said. So once more she seemed to be fighting the world on her own. Nan sang in the house for the first time in months. She was happy again. Not because she was vindictive but because she was vindicated— the girl was as mad as her British mother had been.

So she sang "Frère Jacques," and opened up all the upstairs windows to the sun.

But Perley reacted differently. In fact he was the only one in the family to think her innocent. He brooded over the case for two weeks, and then hired a lawyer—one of the sharpest in the country, a man with many roots in progressive positions to defend her. (Well, the Toronto lawyer had no progressive opinions—every opinion he held he elevated to the stature of being progressive.) He was short, he was rotund, he had a flow of white hair, he said bellicose things.

(What was more striking is the fact that many women took the lives of their children over the years because of depression or being driven mad, and were treated with compassion. But the lawyer said he was not looking for compassion, but justice—for Mary.)

Perley was not as sophisticated as he should be. He should have guessed looking at this lawyer that her defence would be a circus.

One of the reporters who came to report on this was named EL. He got the job for a Windsor, Ontario, paper because he was the lawyer's nephew. And for weeks you could see him in one of the little restaurants in town, staying at one of the small bed-and-breakfasts, taking notes and talking to the locals about making a movie of the week about the case.

So, and John knew this so well, what they first had to do was make her *guilty*—hope she would be *charged*—and then *defend* her *right to be guilty.*

It would be truthful to say she was completely innocent of it all, she had no hand in the death of a child she loved, but it was far better for all concerned to say they were defending her right as a woman to terminate the life.

So what Mary later called *the giants of social awareness* took over.

On one side the prosecution was saying what Mary Cyr herself would have said, that the child was a human life, while the defence was saying she had done what she would never think of doing, because she had been driven to it.

The entire country and in fact many countries took a position.

"He was not at all hopeless," the prosecutor said. "He had a good mind and a good heart and he loved the woman who betrayed him out on a cold bay at midnight."

"Yes, yes. Yes, I betrayed him," Mary Cyr said. "I betrayed little Bobby. I betrayed him and killed him, and I wish to die. Is there an electric chair here—could our good friends in the US spare one for a few hours tomorrow afternoon?"

(Unfortunately this very line was printed in New York and Paris, and was now reprinted in all its glory in Mexico.)

The boy was wrapped too meticulously, put in a position where it was impossible not to breathe carbon monoxide from the engine, for it to be anything but planned, deliberate and calculated, the prosecution asserted.

(This too made its way to Mexico, which strengthened the idea of poison in some people's minds.)

For the sake of the defence—she, Mary Cyr, pale and withdrawn, had no say. She was overwhelmed and burdened by this child. That she had taken it to Switzerland hoping to find a cure, but it was hopeless. And so everyone decided she was a young woman alone with a terribly impaired child—a woman who had an impaired childhood; the child coming, it was suggested but never stated, from incest.

For some months the talk of a trial, and when it would happen, filled the papers. The Montreal doctor she consulted was interviewed, and would provide evidence for the prosecution; the New York and Swiss doctors were interviewed, and would counter for the defence. And all would say much the same thing.

But on her twenty-fifth birthday a deal was struck. She pleaded guilty to negligence. She received one year of house arrest.

Garnet and Nan spoke for the many when they said:

"She has been a burden on us, but we still love her."

But after a time (and this was published in Mexico as well), the entire country of Canada became sick to death of her. Radio talk shows said that anyone mentioning the name Mary Fatima Cyr ever again would be fired.

The defence attorney was paid some $220,000.

Mary Cyr never spoke a word, for over a year. She collected all of Bobby's toys, all his clothes and gave them to charity.

She got involved with someone. She married someone in Halifax—some older gentleman, who liked to feed pigeons and was allergic to eggs. (This is how he was described in her diary.) He was eighty-six when they met. She told her diary:

"We were both on the rebound—he had met his first wife in 1918—in the trenches. Sadly she died of a queer little cough sometime in 1979."

She stayed with him until he died. She was terrified of AIDS and so perhaps married him because of that, looking as she said:

"For respectability."

That did not come.

By that time John had presented the results of his investigation into Bobby's death to the family. And this is what he said privately to Garnet, speaking about the inboard motor. It was damaged and she had never managed to fix it properly, but she had not planned to harm her child.

Besides, John said, she had packed everything to take for a child, to the beach. She had then unpacked everything and opened the cottage. She had started a fire in the fireplace in the boy's bedroom, to warm him up when he came in.

So in fact she had no idea the child was dead. Besides that there was one other thing: she had ordered the boy a dog—a little chocolate lab, which he never got to claim.

Almost three months after she came home from Halifax, Bobby's body was found. It was picked up by a herring net off Escuminac.

His tiny little body, frail and elderly, had not changed; the toy he had been holding was, amazingly, still clenched in his hand, green from the seaweed and kelp that kept in their grasp the body of a child and the secrets of their world.

She had recognized her flaw too late—the flaw that certain wilful women had, to show the world they could do things just the same as men—when in fact only certain men (or women) did those things and there was no shame in not doing so or in asking for guidance if you did do them. That was rebuilding an inboard motor.

But she was too stubborn to ask for help. She was going to show the world—and people like John Delano—but John did not need to have her do those things—he did not need her, or himself for that matter, to prove anything now. Her wilfulness to be a championship woman is what in the end caused her little boy's death. That one affectation she hated in other people, she exhibited on the dry teakwood boat.

All her life she would remember Packet Terri saying:

"Let me set that up for you, or at least show you."

And she, turning and smiling and saying:

"Never—I don't need anyone. This is for Bobby and me. So I will do this just by myself."

To her, no matter how brave she had been, she would be guilty until she died. So what did it matter when that death occurred?

PART TWELVE

1.

ANOTHER FOUR DAYS PASSED. THE MEN CAME, BY ORDER OF Mexico City, the department of mines, the department of justice, to excavate the cave-in at the Amigo mine.

No one had predicted this. But people in Oathoa felt it had to be because they wanted to charge Mary with these deaths too. That seemed the only logical reason.

Of course it was for an entirely different reason. That is, for almost two years there was a microphone in Mr. DeRolfo's office—and just on the off chance, the man who carried the engine to the garage and worked on Mr. DeRolfo's Mercedes was asked to bury a wire inside the back seat a month ago—just about the time poor Mary Cyr arrived.

Mr. DeRolfo, his wife, Gidgit, and Hulk Hernández had been taped for a long time. So even if Victor did not have a tape to give—Bara had one.

Few knew about this operation by the police in Mexico City, but it was related to the *CHUG A CHUG* of the drills going into the earth, the sad whir from the machine; the men watering the drill down, to keep it from overheating—flying in new expensive drill parts out of Canada and the US.

The dig had started slowly, with backhoes and dozers, and then more men came. And then someone came and asked DeRolfo for printouts of the levels—and at what level were the men most likely trapped. Then they asked him how difficult it would be to get down into this mine—where the safeguards had been put, and what walls and drifts had been reinforced. They asked how large the safety rooms were, and where were they exactly? And where was the money spent—perhaps it would be better to go down another way; if the levels were re-enforced like Amigo declared, it might be better to tunnel somewhere else into a safe room. And the more they spoke to him, the more they became certain that something was not quite right. (Of course the head of the recovery team knew this because he was a member of Mexican Special Forces, which had been after Mr. Hernández a long time.)

And then Mrs. DeRolfo had to go to the hospital because of stress— saying the accident and the deaths were terribly discomfiting to her. There was a picture of Mr. DeRolfo holding her hand, tears in her eyes, and a big bouquet of flowers, and a box of Kleenex near her sickbed.

2.

STILL TALLAGONGA CONTINUED ON, NOT KNOWING OF THE tapes, or the transcripts, and thinking that in order to indict someone, there only had to be partial truth. So now if the case against Lady Mary was partially true, with Mary Cyr now in jail it was not a long stretch to make it completely true.

"*Para la ciudad de Oathoa. ¡La Ciudad de Oathoa!*" Mr. DeRolfo would say, and he would raise his fist as he left his wife's hospital bed.

For the town of Oathoa.

When he came through the crowd, people would now clap.

"*Compensación por el sufrimiento—*" compensation for the suffering—he would say.

Then one day he said something that caught a nerve:

"Forty million. Or Mary Cyr stays where she is."

On the nightly news it played very well back in Canada. People, they say, only need an excuse to be outraged; they need it to satisfy the famine in their lives. A privileged woman, Mary Cyr, murders and tries to adopt. She comes to Mexico to steal a child. The man who tries to retrieve her is a corrupt cop who, let's remember, was suspected in his own adopted son's disappearance. Certain Greenpeace activists, Nigel Cruise's protege Ned being one, planned a major demonstration, yes, and acts of civil disobedience too.

Signs were printed.

"Forty million or keep her in Mexico."

They marched on Parliament Hill.

Yes, she saw it on Mexican TV.

Mary was exhausted, hot and tired. "It's snowing there—look we're having a late-winter storm. *¡Nieve!*" she exclaimed.

Then the op-ed piece in the *Toronto Star* spoke for many when it addressed her past, her relationship with Denise Albert, her flights of fancy—and, as the piece stated, no, they were not pointing fingers. The tide of opinion had long ago turned against her, it said. That is, the initial feeling over her right to do what she did with a horribly deformed and sick child some years before, and the sympathy this writer and her husband had always entertained for young women in general, who were the easiest ones victimized, had given way little by little to a sense of disgust, at her wealth and privilege and the sexual liaisons she must have had with her grandfather. This writer and her husband, the article did state, had a chance some years before to help this woman, but the help was unfortunately refused and Mary Cyr's decline started at that time.

The piece was written by the famed advocate for women, Ms. Rory Cruise.

And as many said, her name spoke volumes.

3.

FOR JOHN, THOSE SAME THREE DAYS OVER EASTER WERE eventful; visiting privileges had been taken away. He did not know why this happened. For a time the guards told him to come back in an

hour—or come back tomorrow morning. But then on the fourth day—
that is, the Tuesday after Easter—he was told he was not welcome.

"No visit," the man at the desk told him, waving his hand abruptly,
as if they had caught on to something deceptive that John was up to. "No
visit no more—no *más* visit," he declared, his tie immaculate but sweat
under both arms, one eye drooping.

Then as he was walking back to the resort a police car picked him
up and drove him back to the station. There, sitting in what was, he
determined, interrogation room four, he was asked questions for over
an hour. Did he see the body of Florin, did he know where Florin was.
Did he think he could outsmart the police of Oathoa, did he have rela-
tions with Mary Cyr. When he said no to that, Erappo Pole smiled
and said:

"Why not—everyone else has."

Then they questioned him about Señor Xavier—who was paying
him? And the Cyr family—were they a family of criminals like so many
people thought? Every time he answered a question they looked more
disturbed and positive he was lying. Then suddenly Constable Fey came
in and spoke to the two policemen in the room. He spoke quite harshly
and was quite impassioned.

They all went into the hall for a few moments. Then Fey came in, and
without looking at him said:

"You can go."

And so he did. But he knew by the way they obeyed Fey that he had
more clout than an ordinary policeman—so he must know something
more as well. And if he knew something more as well, then he must
know something about her innocence. And John began to remember
everything that went on since he arrived.

Certainly someone else is working on this, he thought. Certainly Fey
knows something very important he is not saying.

John went back to his room. He did not know what to do. He sent his
findings off to the Canadian embassy and waited for a reply. A standard
"Thank you for visiting Canada's website in Mexico" came back.

—

They came from the *tierra caliente*—the hot land—and now it *was* hot. It was too hot for John, who could not seem to function in it—the heat blazed down upon him, even when he wore the hat he had bought from a rack at the *supermercado*. It was too hot for Mary, who lay on the floor of her cell, silently as the hours seemed to drip away—remembering how she had in her rooms at the cottage all kinds of things she collected. Moosehead quart bottles that she spent her time shining, old CYR COMPANY OIL cans that she kept in immaculate condition—a porcelain British flag—a picture of Beaverbrook with Jean Norton at a spa. The picture of her dog, Muggy Muffs. The picture of Denise Albert that had by now become famous. The picture of her mother shaking hands with John F. Kennedy. The little jar Debby Dormey collected blueberries in; the autograph from Neil Young, which she cherished until his attack on her family's pipeline some years later. The knowledge that half or more of the people whose careers she applauded and championed, men she first helped get published or promoted and sometimes did benefits with, did not think her more than a frivolous rich girl. None of them came to her defence. Now, in silence, with the heat seeming to draw away the air, she realized this. She realized she treasured people, and gave money to their causes while they secretly scorned who she was.

She thought of Bobby and called his name softly and said:

"You are loved."

It was what some anonymous person had written her from Canada, after so much hate and glee. Someone had simply written and said:

"You are loved."

It was, as we later discovered, Beeswax.

4.

STILL SHE COULD SEE THE DONKEY, WITH ITS SAD BLACK EYES, and she could see a girl—she did not know it was Gabriella—go to it with a big carrot, only to back up—terrified—when the donkey hobbled toward her; throwing down the carrot and running back beyond the fence, and then looking at it.

The old donkey was blind, and little Gabriella would try to help it locate the carrot without getting close to it. This kept Mary busy also. For she would haul her crate up to the window, stand upon it, and she and Gabriella would communicate.

"*He perdido mi reloj*," Mary would say, pointing to an old, dusty stick on the ground.

(She thought she was saying, "Pick up the stick"—what she was actually saying was "I have lost my watch"—but Gabriella caught on, and using the stick, and stretching it as far as she could, she was able to push the carrot toward her enemy, the blind old donkey.)

And finally the old donkey put its snout to the dirt and fumbled with its mouth in the old tuffs of grass until it found the carrot.

"He got it," Mary shouted. "You did it—bravo, *señorita!*"

A week or more passed, and every day Gabriella came to the donkey, and some days Mary would give her money and she would go to the market and buy apples or carrots for it. Mary would wait for her to come back, longing to see her skinny little body.

Gabriella would talk to her. She would wait until no one was around. This was generally during the hottest moments of the day. Then Mary gave her some more money and said:

"Buy a bucket for water—for our donkey."

"Pardon?"

"*Comprar un balde de agua.*"

And so little Gabriella came back with the bucket.

Then Gabriella would stand by the cell, and speak slowly in Spanish and English, trying to get Mary Cyr to understand.

Everything would be all right—but Gabriella said Mary Cyr must swear and bless herself and spit if she had not done anything.

So Mary Cyr swore that she had not, and blessed herself that she hadn't and spit out the cell window.

Then one day she asked to make a phone call, for her cell phone, which they said she could keep charged, was dead. And Gabriella gave her, her own phone to call.

She phoned Xavier, and told him to phone her family.

"What do you want them to do?"

"I want you to tell them, 'Do not send anyone else down here—especially from the family or they will be arrested.'"

And Gabriella, with her hair as black and shiny as coal, told her that she had a tape.

"Give it to the right person—for my sake. *¡Por favor si usted puede por mí!*"

"*Sí, sí,* Mary Cyr," Gabriella said. "*Sí, sí*—Constable Fey."

5.

FEY HAD KNOWN SHE WAS INNOCENT FOR WEEKS. IF HE TOOK what he had learned and added it to what John had learned, he had a scenario that was fairly solid and simple. And it had nothing to do with the crystal cave. It had more to do with crystal meth, and the trafficking in stolen goods from the coast; and even the cartel. And this is what it had to do with and Constable Fey knew this.

You draw the curtain back enough and you found meth and cocaine, and a stable of innocent young girls transported to America. That is what you discovered—and no one in his office wanted to discover this.

Especially any scenario that implicated the DeRolfos. But it is what Ángel's father had discovered on his way to Los Angeles and why he was shot in the back of the head.

This was the trail that John without knowing found and Fey had known about. It concerned a man nicknamed Hulk, who used the coal mine to launder money, and who orchestrated the stealing of millions in funds sent down by Tarsco.

Did Isabella Tallagonga wish to discover this? Sure she wanted to. However, she knew she would be dead or at least ruined once she discovered it. Mary Cyr then had to pay, the price of cartels. But you see, knowing this the Mexican police and judicial system involved wanted it to happen quietly—they had wanted Tarsco to pay a great penalty; wanted Mary Cyr to be hustled out of the country after some months in jail. The tragedy for them is Tarsco refused to pay.

It was amazing that John had realized this. But really in another way it was completely obvious, and Fey knew it was.

As for John Delano, he was given his passport back. He was told to make arrangements to leave the country or he would be arrested.

He would be arrested of all things on the suspicion of murder.

"Whose murder?" John asked calmly.

Constable Fey did not answer. But really in a way, by not answering he had. And then John said this:

"I want to warn you—the DeRolfos are going to leave—but they are going to create a diversion so they can go—they know with the mine being excavated it is only a matter of days—so something will happen."

Fey said he would decide about the DeRolfos in his own time.

Then John handed him the Dutch doctor's report.

The Dutch doctor's report read in part:

Arseen worden niet ingesteld als de oorzaak van de dood. de oorzaak van de dood was een ernstige pak slaag door één of meer personen Ik onderzocht het lichaam post mortum. Ik ben ervan overtuigd en dus zal de wereld dat het hier een miskraam van Justitie.

Translated roughly, it said that arsenic was out of the question and that to charge Mary Cyr would be a miscarriage of justice.

The world would know this sooner or later.

And though Fey shrugged at this as an imposition, he knew this too.

6.

FEY, ALONG WITH MOST OF THE TOWN, ALONG WITH DELANO, and all the women who kept vigil along with tourists and the press, went to the funeral of Victor. The body had been held an inordinate amount of time because of the concern of Alfonso Bara. Alfonso Bara and his wife also paid for the funeral.

They had dressed Victor in new clothes—a decent shirt and pants with a small bow tie. What was his full name again, a newspaper reporter asked.

They asked his mother; that is, Lucretia Rapone. But she just stood looking perplexed and angry that they asked her something so annoying, so Gabriella said:

"Victor Gregario Sonora—aged fourteen years."

Mary Cyr watched it from her cell—she could see the procession wind its way down the hill to a graveyard; cameras from all news agencies were there too.

She stood on her crate attempting to hear people. Wanting herself to say goodbye. But there had been so many over the years.

"*Usted pagará por eso, señora Mary,*" a man said behind her.

She turned about, startled. There, his face exhibiting surprise at her beauty, was Erappo Pole, the policeman who blew bubbles.

Now he said it again:

"You will pay for that, Lady Mary."

He didn't think she understood, but was hoping the world heard.

She understood and no longer cared what the world heard.

That night twenty cameras focused on her as she was led down the street to once again meet with the prosecutor.

"*Sonríe por favor para mí si puedes—*" Sharon DeRolfo said.

Please smile for me if you can.

At that meeting Tallagonga asked her, in fact pleaded with her, to confess, to forgo the circus of a trial, and she would see that things would go easy. She also said that her brother, Perley, was threatening to appear and trade places with her.

"My cousin," Mary said in a tired voice.

"We are afraid for his safety," Tallagonga said. "It might be better if you say you are guilty."

"I have been guilty all my life," Mary Cyr said. "But I am no longer guilty—I will not be guilty anymore. You see, I saw more and much deeper than other people, so I was often accused of their crimes, but now I will be free."

"So the money was not to buy a child—maybe it was for drugs."

"Maybe it was to be given away to people you say you cherish," Mary said. "So if you feel you are lying about it, which one of us do you think is telling the truth?"

Mary had started going to Mass again—along with the other convicts. It was nice to sit in the seat, and have a sermon about forgiveness in a language most of which she did not understand. Everyone was at Mass—even Erappo Pole. Sometimes she was allowed to watch them set up the Mass; an altar boy brought in the chalice and set it on the white tablecloth. There was a little bell, and the water and wine sat in two little jars on the end of the table. The water looked purer than any she had ever seen, while the holy water in the little font was listless—still, she blessed herself with trepidation, hoping for her sins to be excused.

The altar boy was so tiny he had a hard time lifting the book for the priest to kiss.

I will be better able to cope—she thought, whenever she took the Host.

At least, she prayed she would be.

One night she fell asleep and dreamed she was in the great pine forest behind her house. Every pine she touched turned golden and the needles fell to the ground. At first she was thinking everything she touched turned to gold. Then she realized she had killed everything she touched. When she turned to walk back to her house, all the windows were open, and white curtains blew out into the sun. The sun as white as the Host she had taken that day, and the curtains were as white as the priest's white vestment.

She saw herself outside of her body staring down at herself. She looked over and Bobby was with her, holding the toy truck Maxwell—he smiled at her, as if to make her understand.

Ah yes, Bobby is dead, she thought, and so too is little Florin. So they must be together now. And Victor—yes—there he is, on the side of the cloud.

There were other people there too. Pedro and his wife, Alicia. Why she knew this she did not know. She only knew she would forget it once she awoke.

She held Muggy Muffs in her arms, and the needles covered him, as well—almost, she thought, as bright as flame.

PART THIRTEEN

1.

THE NIGHT SHE HAD DANCED AT THE BAR IN TRACADIE, SHE SAT alone. She drank tequila. She looked across the room when she licked the salt, drank, and then brought the glass back to the table with a kind of *clink*. She sucked the lemon and watched people come and go.

Princess Diana had died a few weeks before.

And that was where she met Lucien. He asked to sit. He lit her cigarette in the measured way of a new beau. He told her about his boat, saying: "I have to drive up later and check my boat, the *Marianne*—"

"What?" she said. "You actually have a boat?"

"Of course," he said.

"Can I see it?"

"Of course—do you want to come with me?"

The song was "Rock and Roll Hootchie Coo."

"I just don't believe you," she said.

The song was "Little Darlin'."

"Ah, a boat is nothing," he said. He sniffed and turned to look across the bar at the girl he was supposed to be with. The girl his boat was named after—the girl he was thinking of marrying.

When he turned around, Mary Cyr was looking at him, with her dark, penetrating eyes. It was as if he was naked. He became as weak as a rag doll—one of those tragic ones. The kind of effect women can have on men with a glance; to make them, as Layton once wrote, as weak as piss.

Lucien tried to speak, but only his lips moved.

The song was "Pour Some Sugar on Me."

They left together. And not a man could take their eyes off of her.

Not a man in the whole goddamn fuckin' place.

In so many ways, if she did not love so much, she could destroy them all.

He took her to his thirty-two-foot lobster boat moored in Neguac, and helped her down the ladder to the bow. She smelled tar and waves and was at peace. Inside he had a ship's log. He asked her to write in it:

"Ta da," she wrote, and "I knew Princess Di—she invited me to Kensington Palace."

They both laughed. What an absurd thing to have written.

He had regained his composure. She was impressed by him. He took off his shirt. He walked about bare-chested, his tattoo of the Acadian flag above his heart. And the night smelled of the warm salt air.

He spoke about his quota of lobster and how to get around it and take even more. That someday he would build a house. That he would have his own business.

"But aren't you engaged?" she said.

He shrugged, blushed then said:

"So what?"

"Oh dear me." She smiled.

He opened a beer for her. He sat back on the small swivel chair with his hands folded behind his head, watching her. He was Lucien, the boy—long ago—who had broken little Denise Albert's heart. The boy Denise had timidly asked to dance at the spring hop and he had said:

"No—go away, don't bother me."

Now Mary told him in a quiet, halting voice that her granddad once had a boat too.

"Oh—what kind?" Lucien asked.

"Oh, it's nothing like this," she said.

He turned on the FM radio, and piped the music through speakers.

" 'Five to one, baby, one to five. No one here gets out alive.' "

She smiled. It unnerved him, so she stopped smiling.

The night was soft. He popped another beer and then another.

She went to the wheelhouse, and looked out the broad window, and he turned the key so the auxiliary power was on.

"Oh," she said.

He came close to her. His breath was slightly laboured.

"I can teach you," he said. "Have you ever been out on the bay?"

He ran his hands over the sides of her breasts, pretending to be instructing her on how to hold the wheel. She thought of dear old Nigel.

"Me?" she said, smiling. "Out on the bay?"

He did not know who she was. And for a while she may have forgotten as well.

Then one day—it was in the winter and she had moved into a rooming house. She was working at Doyle's Meat Market. He had broken up with his girl—the girl who had called Mary Cyr names in the convent.

She sat in the rooming house, and stared out the window at the bay. So he visited her. He proposed.

"I have lots of money," he said. "See my car?"

"Yes, I did—it's wonderful—and almost new—I rarely had a car that was almost new."

"Well, there you go," Lucien said, proudly.

"I wonder if I could drive it someday." She smiled.

"Sure," he said. "I'll teach you."

"I wonder if I could ever teach you," she said.

"Of course—sure in somethings—" he said, looking around her room, the forlorn place with snow on the aluminum porch roof.

"What about Marianne?" she said.

He told her a secret—he was changing the name of his boat—and if she wanted it to be named after her, they had better damn well get married. How is that for news?

"Oh oh," she said, "dear oh dear."

She looked at him, gave a slight whimsical nod, almost gone tragic in the setting sun.

"Are we going to get married?" he said. "I have other women who want to, you know—I'm not hard up, you know."

2.

SHE HAD HIS PICTURE TAKEN IN A SMALL CUBICLE IN ZELLERS. She had him sign some papers. He signed his name:

Lucien DeCoussy.

Then they drove to a place near Moncton for the civil ceremony. He borrowed his brother's suit. He had big brown shoes. He asked about her family.

"They're a no-show," she said. "I think they are a little bit overcome by it all."

"Well." He smiled. "They have nothing to fear with me—you can tell them that!"

It was now springtime. There was still snow in the woods—at least down over the steep bank by the motel where he carried her through the door, to the smell of carpet and dark-pine wallboard. From the back window they could see the debris of a lost winter, the old wire fence.

The walls were grey and the television was blurry. He had bought some sparkling wine.

"Let us drink a toast," he said.

After a while he asked her why she hadn't unpacked. She asked him if they might go somewhere else.

"But what about the oysters I ordered?"

"Oh—oysters," she said.

She did not like the musty smell in the room, the smell of leftover sex from other people. He took out his big flat wallet, to look through it.

"Where do you want to go?" he said. He had blond hair and blue eyes and was trying to be kind. He waved his hand and said:

"I have three-hundred and ten bucks—but this here room is paid for."

She smiled at him sadly, almost full of love. He went to find the opener for the wine.

"*Aller gauche,*" she said.

He went to have a pee.

" 'Dream angel, where are you' " came the song. She then went and had a pee. She felt sorry for Marianne—the girl from long ago who had teased Denise Albert to distraction because Denise had wanted to dance one dance with Marianne's beau. Tragic.

Yes, she thought, grabbing some toilet paper to wipe herself. I have become tragic.

Lucien was waiting for her, naked on the bed.

"Oh sure," she said, as if she had forgotten why they were there. "Just a minute, please."

She went outside and spoke on her phone.

She wore now a little black dress, with no underwear. She was like that at times. But she didn't go to him. She went and sat on a chair.

And then a limo pulled up. And the driver got out and opened the door.

"Come along—dress—hurry up—*vite!*" She smiled.

"What is this?" he asked.

She sat with him in the back seat. She took his hand. She looked out the window when he asked questions. She remembered teaching Denise Albert how to waltz, so she would be able to waltz when he asked her. They waltzed in the room, when it was snowing outside.

"Ta da."

He now realized it was probably a joke his friends had played on him. He kept saying:

"Where is Hermanigile—wait until I get my hands on him. I'll ring his skinny little neck."

She patted his hand.

"Yes," she said, "don't be afraid."

"Me—afraid?" His chest heaved out. He smiled.

3.

IN THE SMALL AIRPORT—ON THE OUT-OF-THE-WAY AIRSTRIP against the soft spring sky—they waited. And waited.

"What are we doing?" he asked.

"Waiting," she said. She looked at her watch.

A sock hop too and the song "Endless Love"—a song that was for the summer, the trees bountiful and the earth gone sweet.

"Do you remember her—Denise?"

"Denise—no—well, I knew many Denises."

"Oh dear," she said.

They were silent for a long time. She smoked a cigarette, and then looked at him, quizzically.

"Would you ever light a dog on fire?"

"A dog on fire—no!"

"Thank God for that," she said.

When the plane landed, he became confused. His eyes got large and he looked all around to try to see someone.

"What is this?" he asked.

"My plane."

"Your plane?" he said.

"Yes, one of them," she said, remembering the artist's son, and the party she had begged Nan to let her go to when she was fifteen. (When she already had a child hidden at home.)

Now that little girl was a ghost.

And perhaps so was she.

She sat down in front of him. She took something out of her purse and handed it to him.

"What is this?"

"Your passport."

The shoes he had borrowed from his brother hurt his feet, and they flew away.

In Spain she went to bed early—after she said she could pee standing up. The night was gentle.

"Tomorrow," she said.

"Tomorrow what?" he asked, staring at her in a kind of deep fear.

"Tomorrow we look for Paco—and if we find him—well, I think you are strong enough to beat him up—you are Lucien DeCoussy?"

"Yes."

"Well, Lucien DeCoussy, I know you are no pussy." She smiled.

So they began their search. To the many Dénia bars and night places and drove all the way to Benidorm.

They did not find Paco either—well, they found twenty-four Pacos, and more than a few of them gigolos, but not any of them the right one. A Paco with the studious look of a lounge lizard smiled at them when they mentioned her mother, as if not only should he know her but they would find the stories about it amusing. But no, he was not the Paco either, though he started to tap his fingers on the bar quickly as if he was playing the bongos for them. Then he began to sing a Spanish lament so they would stay. But it did not entice them. A golden chain dangled from his neck, his hair was slicked back and peppered with just a tad of grey that he had tried to hide. The sun was going down over the red buildings when they left.

They drank most nights at the Blue Trumpeta. They would walk to it after supper—poor Lucien followed her about. He did not know how not to.

The bar was always lively, with many expat Germans, and a few Dutchwomen. Englishmen trying to be proper, the scent of their empire gone, their hair sticking up in rude little tuffs, their women willing to be seduced by young energetic Spaniards who pretended to be socialists and concerned for the world.

Then one evening she was about to leave. But turned around quite startled and asked the bartender, where in the world did he get *that* bottle.

He took it down and handed it to her. She held it for the very first time in years.

"We found that in the sea," he said. "It was washed up onshore."

"Where's the letter?" she asked.

"What letter?"

"The letter that said, 'You be a renegade and I'll be renegadier than you. Just you wait and see!' "

"How did you ever know that?"

"I am like that—at times."

4.

SHE WROTE IN HER DIARY THAT THEY WENT TO THE OLIVE grove that her family once owned. And she walked too along the back roads on a journey to somewhere, stood in orange groves when the sun came out. All of this was seen and known. But then one evening—when the sun was setting over the hills behind them, she wanted to see the place her mother wanted to buy. *¡Dios mío!*, which was far away up in the hills, secluded and empty with the sky pale and the farmhouse white and brown. It was cold, the sky a temperamental cooling pink and the wind smelling of the sea. She drove the small Fiat up to it, past the last of the night lights on the hills, and Lucien got out. She was, she said, trying to find things for him to do. He felt out of place—worse, she was filthy rich and that seemed almost worse than he being poor, because now he remembered all that he had bragged about and he felt ashamed. He felt shame as he said for—

"*Allumant sa cigarette avec un sourire.*"

Yes, she remembered his tossed-off, ordinary arrogance when he lit her cigarette with a smile.

Did she want him to feel this shame, she asked her diary. Did she or not?

No, of course she did not.

Still, it was a question the diary answered this way:

"Oh, little Denise—my favourite Acadian girl in the world must have felt shame when she walked across the room and asked him to dance— when her only friend in the whole school was the awkward *maudit anglais*, who had taught her to waltz against the Panamanian moon that desperate night so, so long ago so he would take the time to waltz with her. But you see—you see, he could have been so kind, two weeks before she died—but he said NO.

"Ah you see, people do not think I loved the French, but how could I not love the French when I loved her."

Then she added:

"And the Montreal Canadiens."

In her diary she said the terrible old farmhouse was a place of last refuge for her mommy. And so she wanted to see it, the one Paco had asked her to buy. It was still for sale, for 1.6 million pesetas. Or $160,000. That is how she knew the men she met named Paco were not the one her mother knew—they knew nothing much about this farmhouse beyond the town, in a small olive grove, overgrown and windswept in the hills. A place that Paco thought he could seduce some rich widow into buying for him, somewhere along the line. And gosh almighty, Mary Cyr was a rich widow as well.

They went inside. They lit matches and moved along up the flight of lonely stairs to the top attic, where looking out they could see the town of Dénia so far, far away, and all her dreams, that is, all her mom's dreams, seemed to crash against the shore in waves.

"Splendid," Mary Cyr said. She wondered if her mother had looked out this same attic window, on those days, when Mary was at Rothesay. And then came to the conclusion in her heart that she had, and that it was all, in space and time, only a second ago.

"Let's stay a minute here—and listen to the wind," she said to him. They sat for a moment and the night was sweet, sweet in the gentle breeze.

"Can I ask you something?"

"Ask and you shall receive," she said.

"Are you rich?"

"Do you know I am almost certain I am?"

"How rich?" he asked. He was trembling a little.

"Oh—" she said, looking at him and then looking away, "very rich, I think."

And so they went back down those narrow attic stairs and across the living room, with its huge old fireplace filled with debris; and an old, unhooked stove in the centre of the kitchen; a fridge that was unhooked, with a tattered, electrical cord. And then they opened the hatch to the basement, to see the foundation.

"I don't think we should go down there," she said.

"No—come on—come—" he insisted.

He went ahead of her, and lit his lighter.

"Come along," he said again, and reached out to hold her hand.

She took his hand, and their fingers touched, and she smiled at him in a kind of sorrow—perhaps mixed with a bit of her own stupid-ass self-pity. And then he took another step and disappeared.

He had fallen into the cellar's open well.

Harsh—impossible—terrible—but true. But the harsher moment was this: she held on to his arm for an hour, on her belly, begging him to lift himself out. But he could not. A car passed by on the road; she yelled from the cellar, but no one heard. She kept screaming for help, as every few minutes he would try to place his feet on the slippery stones and lift himself—but the broken stones gave way one at a time, and he would lurch downward.

"Oh don't do that," she would plead.

She could not see his face—except for a small sliver of it, when the moonlight came across the back cellar window and seemed for an instant or two to reflect in his handsome eyes.

A black rat crawled over her back, then crawled up and stared at her face, but she still held on to him.

"Ah—Mary Cyr," he said. "*Je suis fatigué—je suis fatigué.*"

And he fell. She heard his body hit the bottom with a kind of *thud*, and light splash.

Fifty feet into some black, filthy water seven feet deep. He called feebly.

Only then did she run to get help.

Again she had drowned someone, the rumour was.

But the great report came by way of the Mexican press about this. The drowning of Lucien DeCoussy—except, they spelled his last name wrong. There was an interview with the woman Marianne Gaudet, now married with two children, who spoke of the hellish woman who had bewitched her fiancé and carried him to his death on a broom.

5.

AND THEN TEN MORE DAYS PASSED. LISTLESS AND HOT, BORING and tempestuous.

People came and went, passing by her cell window. Women and men. Lucretia always came two or three times a day. Mary would be attentive with her. Once, she took off her silver watch and handed it over.

"*Para mi hermana*," Mary Cyr said, and smiled.

Lucretia had become more and more important. She said she wanted to find Florin, but she spent more time near the jail than searching.

Mary herself watched her with a rather penetrating gaze. A newspaper picture had been taken with Lucretia looking into the cell window, the caption: "A mother searches for the source of her pain."

In the morning Lucretia would wake with a start, as if something important would happen this very day. She would remember who she spoke to the day before—she would look at the date—the resort usually had the New York papers on Wednesday, Friday and Sunday—and three times her picture was in the paper.

How glorious was that?

Principia took her aside and told her she knew who Florin and Victor's mother really was, and it was not right for the memory of her or Pedro Sonora to speak like this and take over their lives. But Lucretia gazed past her as she spoke, and then stood and went through the beaded-curtain partition into her little section of the *apartamento*. For days they did not see much of her.

Lucretia would dress in mourning and head to the church, and ask Principia to go with her.

Once when Lucretia asked Mary if it was true that there would be a great reward given to anyone who found out the truth, Mary had said, "No."

"No?" Lucretia asked. "I could find the truth out for you—I could if you got me the reward."

"No," Mary said. "*Nada—nada. La recompensa no es para ti.*"

The reward is not for you.

She smiled. "*Ya tienes tu recompensa.*"

You have had your reward already.

And she turned away.

"Then I will dispose of you!" Lucretia had said.

"Only God can do so," Mary answered.

Mary was no longer well. Now after all this time in jail she was to the other prisoners just another one, who was not so special as to warrant special attention. But the young women still came up and asked her favours, and she would comply.

"Could you get me to Canada?"

"Yes, I will try."

"Are you going to order out today?"

"Yes, if you want and they let me."

"I need bus fare so my mother and son can visit—*por favor*—I have not seen my son in two months—he is a bebe."

"*Sí. No mas problemo.*"

And she would tell Principia to take the money and make sure the bus station knew a ticket was bought, at this end—and that it would be a return ticket. Then she would with the other women stand in line with her toothbrush, her towel and face cloth, waiting to wash. The women she once thought were so foreign to her were now her only companions. The women who once thought she was so foreign to them looked upon her as a somewhat endearing oddity. But they kept coming and going—some only for a few nights. She was the only one who seemed to stay.

Then she would be taken back to her cell and locked in. She wouldn't go to the window much anymore. She would sit in the corner in the dark with her knees up, her chin on her knees; staring out at nothing.

Lucretia would come to the cell window and look in. Mary could see her peering one way and then the other, shading her eyes.

"*Es de noche. No puedo decir*," Lucretia would say to someone.

It is dark. I can't tell.

"Hey, Mary," she would call. "Hey, Mary, *mi amiga—por favor—mi amiga—*"

But little Mary Cyr no longer answered her.

6.

THERE WAS A GREAT AMOUNT OF GRACIOUSNESS THE FAMOUS Mary Cyr could spend, and she had spent it willingly all of her life—but that was over now. And they did not even know.

How is it that I am alive? she would think. Why is it that I lived? Whatever was the purpose of me?

But things continued on, outside, to show finally why she had lived. That she had lived to show the falseness and tragedy of scapegoats, and that she had not known it, until now—and that others would recognize this in her, and then once again, as they had with so many through the ages, from Joan of Arc to Anne Frank, and with so many in camps and prisons and dark places of the soul, and with so many of our prophets to whom they would wail and beg forgiveness and forget they had ever played a part in their fate.

Then they would reduce these lives to *irony* and *absurdity*, like our favourite writers, and laugh.

Once, but only once, the women got into a fight over the money Mary had—and she saw two of them kicking and punching each other over a few coins that she had dropped. She had never known poverty like they had, but many who had known poverty would not have done this. Little Debby Dormey would never have done that, nor Gabriella or Victor or Florin.

The women grabbed at each other's hair and kicked, and one tried to rip the other's shirt off. And others stood around laughing at this, while an older prisoner yelled: "*¡Silencio! Ustedes dejarán de luchar.*"

Quiet, stop fighting.

Mary never knew what they called the peso—*lana, varos, plata*—a lot of names she could not keep straight. But she ran to her bed, lifted the sheet, ran back to the bars and handed them both a two-hundred-dollar Mexican bank note.

"*Hay no lucha*," she said. She smiled, tenderly, like a mother. Like the mother she wanted to be, and to have.

"*No lucha*," she said with such sadness that the two fighting stopped and looked at her a little spellbound.

"*Su culpa tuya la hemos hecho triste,*" one said to the other.

It's your fault we made her sad.

"No—*no problema*," Mary Cyr said.

And then she went back and sat on her crate.

Two days after Doc advertised he was giving an interview to *SCREW* magazine about his "two women" from the Cyr family and was to appear nude, Mary issued a statement that said:

"I don't think that is very nice."

John remembered that statement now. And the hilarity that accompanied it. Yet it was a profound statement—concise and kind, and whimsical.

The next day she was brought to court. There was a great deal of press from the United States and Britain, Canada and Japan. The sirens wailed and she sat in between two officers.

There was not a second where there was not a flash of a camera.

They handcuffed her hands behind her and led her into the courthouse. She was weak, and strangely, she found it difficult to take the steps. The courtroom of course was packed.

It was all in Spanish, and she kept looking around. John was there, and Mr. Xavier, and the Dutch doctor, Norma van Haut, and her husband, the big German, who had jostled people out of the way to make room for her. The Dutchwoman told the press in Amsterdam the night before:

"*Ze is geheel onschuldige, God helpen degenen die doen het niet zien.*"

She is entirely innocent. God help those who do not see it.

Then she told the story of her long association with Mary Cyr, a woman she had actually never met. She had wanted a pen pal, long ago when she was fifteen, and some young girl from Canada answered. She was thinking, Norma van Haut said, she would have a pen pal from New York or somewhere very special—but this young girl named Mary Cyr became the first to answer her. She lived in a small province far off in Canada. Norma van Haut was conditioned to like Canadians because of their helping to liberate the Netherlands. But it seemed for a while this girl Mary Cyr did not like the Dutch, and Norma said it took a while to convince her that the Dutch were not much like that man who insulted her mother. Once she convinced her of that, Mary became:

"*Ze was zo licht en zo vriendelijk is als een bloem.*"

As light and as sweet as a flower.

But Norma van Haut said it became obvious that she wanted to find something out about that man's father—"*And I spent my first year in university rushing about for her.*"

"*Je het erg,*" they asked. Did you mind?

"*Nee.*"

But, Norma said, the strange thing was, when she found all of this out, and could have brought it forward against the man who had attacked her family in *Der Spiegel*, Mary Cyr said:

"Let it be."

"Let it be?" Norma asked.

He will have to find out about it himself.

So you see, Norma van Haut said, "She can't be guilty—she just can't be."

"What else do you know about her?" the newspaper reporter asked.

"Oh, *zette ze me via medische school*," Norma van Haut said. "Oh—she put me through medical school—she does not know that I know."

"And what do you think of the coincidence of meeting her now?"

"It is the will of God," she said. "And I did not believe in God until just now."

7.

NORMA SMILED WHEN SHE SAW MS. CYR, HANDCUFFED BETWEEN two large guards, walking into the courtroom, and Mary smiled a little back.

She was formally charged with murder and indecency to a body, and the kidnapping of Florin Sonora.

Judge Entenda Jesus de Oliva Gabel looked very business-like, and matter of fact. As if this was simply his duty and he was not at all over-whelmed by the press, or the photographers or the television cameras from around the world, which meant he was trying his best not to be completely overwhelmed. But he was sweating and looked uneasy, and his voice shook just a little when he spoke—a tremor filled his voice, a kind of echo surfaced along the courtroom walls, a sound that dissipated in coughing and shuffling of feet.

Isabella Tallagonga did not look Mary Cyr's way at all. Tallagonga long knew there was a great deal of interest in this trial everywhere, and everywhere she now looked foreign correspondents witnessed the proceedings —so she had to appear very stern. And when she turned sideways, her eyes locked on those of a little Japanese woman reporter, who seemed terrified of her, so that is who she seemed to be speaking about:

"*Asesina, loca*," she said. And the young Japanese woman shook slightly.

And the evidence was of course irrefutable. In fact she did think: Bara will never trump this! And she knew that this is what it was all about. This trial meant her entire career, one way or the other.

This in fact was the one thing this trial was actually about: the fight between her and Alfonso Bara. She was worried for one other reason—something one of her friends in Mexico City had told her, that Bara had something spectacular that he was going to unload on the public within the next few days—a week at the most—that might trump her.

What would he be cooking up—just something to try to spoil her great national debut? And this is what she was thinking—but that thought drifted away, and she looked—glanced, really, toward the back of the room—and saw Principia, and her daughter, Gabriella, and son, Ángel, all staring at her with rather fixed expressions, Ángel's mouth moving just slightly as if a mute was trying to speak.

Estoy Bien no te preocupes por mí

I am fine, do not worry about me, Mary had learned to say whenever people said she looked ill.

They finally asked her what she would plead, guilty or not guilty.

"No. *Yo no soy culpable*," Mary said, but you could hardly hear her.

No. I am not guilty.

Tallagonga was worried.

Xavier remained firm, and told the family in New Brunswick it would be a plea of innocence.

"No," John said to Nan, who asked him if a guilty plea might be best. "She does not want to plead guilty. People have called her guilty all of her life—she will not plead guilty now. Not anymore!"

"*Mon Dieu, c'est à vous, un servant*," Nan said, with artificial outrage.

"Yes," John said. "It is up to me, a servant."

Tallagonga also had some shocking news about the case just hours ago. The defence would ask that the body be exhumed. Erappo made it clear that Tallagonga should try to stop this. But Tallagonga knew trying to stop it would cause greater suspicion internationally than she ever wanted to.

Erappo shrugged as he shed his bulletproof jacket, and sat down.

"What can you do with all this nonsense?" he said.

But there was something worse—something was wrong with Mary Cyr herself. She did not look well—she looked listless and uninterested and certainly unafraid. And Tallagonga had heard that Erappo Pole had been tormenting her—and this came to a head one night in an argument with the little guard—Constable Fey's fiancée.

So all of this had to be settled, and it all had to settle down. It was like a toothache—you let it go, let it go, and finally half your mouth is sore and infected.

"*¡No se atreve a tocar a esa chica otra vez!*" she said to him, as she left the big office and walked down the hall to the small cafeteria that almost no one used.

Do not dare touch that girl again.

They called Isabella Tallagonga "the spider"—because of the web she could weave around luckless people, but she was now casting a web that might swallow her.

8.

THE PICTURE IN THE *GLOBE* THE NEXT MORNING DID SHOW Tallagonga on those steps. It also showed Cyr getting out of the police car, while policemen with assault rifles flanked her.

"Mary Cyr goes on trial," it read.

After the not guilty plea Mary Cyr was led back to her cell. She was hobbling on her left side. The little guard, just as many others, did not notice, for she sometimes walked strangely since she was hit on the head as a child. She was, for a while, taken to be mentally disabled. Nor did she ever mind. That is, that they once thought she was backward. Today as she left the courtroom, she handed a note to Xavier; it read:

"Get him out of Mexico or lock him up until you can."

She was referring to John. It was too dangerous for him and nothing now could be done.

Besides, he knew her too well, and if he visited her again, he might find out that which she did not want him to know. So if he was out of Mexico, it would be better for her plans.

Mary Cyr was determined not to let anyone in on her secret. It was a secret plan to solve her problem. She did not want Perley to come down and take her place. And then she began to have dreams about her youth. Some of those dreams—some of them were so glorious—she had been so full of joy with her mom and dad.

But she had a vision now and again, of a dancing bear. The bear she and Perley had seen when they were children. She could tell the dancing bear had tried to put on a happy face, but it was all for naught. That was the month after her mom had left for Europe. She knew the bear's happy face hid so much sadness about its world.

A few weeks after Lent started she began to have a fever, and her dreams became intensely bright. There was a road, and it had snowed, and what— there was wind in the willows. She would run to the waves, but when they came crashing in, she would laugh and rush back into her father's arms. No, it did not take a lot, to be filled with joy—a few wisps of sweet air and a melancholy wave against the shore, that's all there had to be.

And then there was Denise Albert, standing so clearly before her, and Denise said:

"Well, Mary Cyr, ho hum to all that—I am expecting a hug."

And that filled her with joy too. And then there was Bobby. How sadly he looked at her when he realized he was not the same. How ashamed, and how she would give a hundred lifetimes to see him again. But then he smiled and shook his head playfully, and said:

"You must not worry about me—Mommy. And please no more fretting about the dancing bear—its name is Hobs and it is here with me. Safe and sound."

Well then—there you go. But then there were dark dreams too, one filled with soft dark waves, and endless clouds. And she heard her mother

crying in a room, and she couldn't get the door opened—it was supposed to roll on wheels and the wheels were stuck. And they remained
stuck.

But then her mother said suddenly at the end of that dream:

"Ah, my sad girl—I am right behind you—see, turn around."

Then she remembered how the years passed away and she became an
obstacle to everyone, and also to herself.

She woke almost always in the middle of the night. She was so weak—
well, what would it matter? She had not eaten in four weeks. All during
Lent. They thought she was fasting. She thought to herself—a poem she
had learned after Mr. Cruise went away. Yes, she had loved him deeply
for a time. She recited it again today, slowly, almost silently:

"Darkling I listen and for many a time
Have been half in love with easeful death
Called it sweet names in many a mused rhyme
To take upon the evening my quiet breath
Now more than ever seems it rich to die
To cease upon the midnight with no pain."

That is, there was another side to Mary Cyr, a modestly unobtrusive
side, a kind of darkish side that was not a fashion statement—that had
been a part of her for years—something that most others did not see,
but a side she exhibited during her piano recital, or her fights with the
tyrannical girlfriends, a side that *embraced* death. And now this side had
blossomed in a cruel holding cell in the small resort town of Oathoa.

Here is what she thought of:

One early evening she was sitting on a bench near Saint James Park—
or was it in the park—or just near it. It was after her second marriage,
and in the autumn, she thought, and she had managed to go away. It
was either that, or tell everyone about it, about Mr. Cruise—and she
couldn't. People came and went. There was commotion over something,
but she didn't notice. As she was sitting there trying to sketch the tree

in front of her, she looked up and a woman, surrounded by people, was looking over her shoulder.

"Ah," the woman said. "That is really quite fine—"

"It's a little bit fine," Mary Cyr said.

"Well, your accent—not American—why, you're Canadian?"

"Yes, and you are British—I could tell in an instant."

"Yes, my name is Diana—"

"I could tell that in an instant as well."

Diana laughed. Mary Cyr did as well. Perhaps it was a laugh that said both of them were cursed. But they seemed to like each other off the bat. Diana moved away, and then suddenly turned, strolled back, looked at her, and said:

"Are you up for a little visit with me?"

She wrote in her diary that Diana was wonderful—it was simply a paragraph three-quarters of the way along:

Diana invited her to a concert, and they partied with Sir Elton John. Diana became her friend, before she died. That is what she wrote in Lucien's logbook on the night when the waves lapped against the starboard side of the boat. The night she pretended she was not on the River of the Broken-hearted. And then there was this in the diary:

"Di was kind to me—she sent a car around to bring me to her. She introduced me to Elton John, and of course many others too. But I did not tell her what I knew. I could not tell her that the royal family was fascinated with how the United States manufactured fame and notoriety. That two hundred years after the revolution they had been adopted simply as cutsie-pie celebrities by the United States—a role they played to perfection. That the remnants of the British Empire were barking mad. That they had a grand palace with many rooms and in each one sat the remnants of a bad choice, India and the Irish. That they had done in the Irish in a miserable way. And yes the Acadians as well. I could not tell her because though we only knew each other for a year, I loved her too much. Besides, besides she already knew."

And then this entry, the last one about her friend:

"Oh, but why did she die on me—why did she have to go away too."

9.

SHE DID NOT KNOW WHEN SHE DISCOVERED THAT IT WAS TIME TO go. Maybe after her friend Diana died—maybe a long time before then. But when Perley said he was going to come down to save her, she realized she was a burden to everyone who she had ever loved. So she devised a plan—and a very good one.

She had placed the copies of those newspapers that had insulted her integrity for weeks, around her body, to look as if she wasn't wasting away. She walked back and forth in her cell, or sat on her bunk with her feet size five not quite touching the dirt floor, and looked an average a hundred and ten pounds. And under her loose top and underneath her ballooning pants that still made her look so young:

"*Mary Cyr es puta—diabla—asesina*" written large.

Pages and pages of "*Mudered no sólo los amantes sino su hijo.*"

Murdered not only lovers but her son.

Photos of her tossing the gold charm bracelet over Niagara Falls.

And pages of photos of her in chains.

Pictures of her estate in New Brunswick.

Pictures of the farm in Dénia, Spain.

Pictures of her husband and her mother's lover, Doc Swain, who turned up naked in *SCREW* magazine.

There were pictures of her sitting on Lord Beaverbrook's knee, a picture of her half naked walking into the sea.

"*Me wa amante—era salvaje y insashabe puta.*" EL

I was her lover—she was a wild and crazy bitch. EL

She had placed them around her body, layer by layer, until you got to the picture of little Denise Albert, which was placed next her heart.

They had given her the means with which to say goodbye. The little guard was kind enough to allow her to shower in private, at the resort. So she came and went to the shower with a robe around her body.

Under all of it she was skin and bones, and sores were breaking on her flesh. Sometimes—well, she could be so stubborn it was like arguing with a brick wall. And once she decided something—she did decide!

So there you go, ho de ho ho ho!

Even when she got a secret note from someone close to the prosecutor's office that told her if she pleaded guilty, she would be back in Canada in eighteen months.

"What is in Canada for me now?" she said. Yes, she sounded spiteful—and she was sorry—for decorum was the thing.

No—she had done what she had done, and she would now go away.

They just did not know it yet.

Debby Dormey's mother had taught her the secret without ever meeting her once.

For when you do go, you do not have to say goodbye. If you are brave enough, you just have to someday walk away.

Years ago the Miramichi writer who she liked but who she could never read told her that they both were the kind of people who did not belong. He said you couldn't fight that—ever, *for they will not allow us safe passage to the end of the night.*

Which meant, and he smiled: *"That you and I will leave them—so suddenly that it will take a while for them to catch their breath and realize we are no longer here—"*

Every time she closed her eyes, the world got farther and farther away. When she breathed, she was racked with pain.

"*Señora, ¿puedes darme algo de dinero?*" she heard softly.

Can I have some money?

"*Ah, claro. Dame un minuto y lo conseguiré para ti.*"

Just give me a minute and I will get it for you.

"*¿Nos amas?* Mary Cyr."

Do you love us, Mary Cyr?

"*Sí—toto—muchas mas.*"

And they would giggle at her accent and her choice of words.

And then they would talk about the love affair going on between two women in the cell at the end of the corridor and say:

"La de da da da."

She did not know what she handed over—it was almost fifty dollars. The woman looked at her, astonished. She nodded and said:

"I am sorry."

And her eyes closed slightly. She felt as if she might fall. The day was warm and mucky, and the donkey was lying down.

"*¿Estás enferma, mi señora?*" the young woman asked.

"No—no—no—" Mary Cyr said. "*Toto bien—toto bien—*"

10.

PERLEY WAS ON THE PHONE TEN OR TWELVE TIMES A DAY, TO people in Mexico City, telling them to act—and telling them that if anything happened to her, when she was proven innocent, it would come down on the heads of those who had put her in chains. A week or so ago he was put through to a man named Alfonso Bara. He spoke and Bara said:

"Yes—of course—well, what comes of it comes of it. Things may turn out if you are patient—now is the time to be patient."

Bara was interested in advancing his own career—and this had a lot to do with freeing Mary Cyr. But only at the right time. And he had much to weigh as well. For the idea was formed, over the past month or so—that the worse she was treated in backward Oathoa, the better it was for him in Mexico City when he freed her from those chains. Bara had learned something two months before from his own investigators, who were actually investigating Hernández and his relationship to a woman name Sonya "Little Boots" Baron. All of this had taken time, as it does anywhere—but Alfonso knew that the money given to Amigo to do upgrades was stolen, and that almost four million of it went to this woman, who ran drugs just north of Acapulco. So he knew very well, before Tallagonga had ever seen Mary Cyr, that the back-door way into the corruption of Little Boots was through Señor DeRolfo and his wife, Gidgit, and their illicit connection to Hulk Hernández.

And why did he first suspect corruption?

Because Carlos DeRolfo had built his wife a chapel in 2002.

"*Quien construye una capilla podría estar esconde un pecado.*"

Anyone who builds a chapel is hiding a sin.

So he had spoken to his wife's father, a man who was always optimistically energetic, the man in the white suit jacket who had walked by the cell carrying the outboard motor the first day John had arrived. The man worked at the garage, and had the best pair of hands as a mechanic that there was. He worked on Hulk Hernández's SUV and his *imported* cars. It was easy enough for him to plant small microphones in both Hernández's SUV and Carlos DeRolfo's Mercedes.

The information they received over the next nine months was fantastic.

People in his office asked him near the New Year if they should inform Tallagonga.

"*No, no—no es importante.*"

He was going to seek warrants from a certain judge.

So all of this was proceeding when the bump at the mine happened.

Then something completely bizarre occurred, with a woman named Mary Cyr.

"Bizzaro," Bara said, after the name of the popular American cartoon. He could not believe it. He did believe the initial story; that is, that she had come down with money (he suspected a drug buy but changed his mind), and had harmed a young boy.

Everything in his case was put on the back burner.

It looked very good for Tallagonga for a moment—and Bara with his plodding and his clandestine campaigns seemed to be overshadowed.

But after a while things came together; the coal dust, as it were, settled. He had one man working in Oathoa, who he could trust, and he relied upon that man—and that man was Constable Jorge Fey.

But you see, for his own political advantage he did not want Fey to stop the case, or produce evidence to contradict Tallagonga right away— the more headlines he saw, the more damning it was. That is, if he had not played this game, Mary Cyr would have been released in four or five days after her arrest. John Delano would not even have had to fly down.

But Bara also had to be certain that Mary Cyr was innocent, for she seemed so culpable.

"You want me to keep her here?" Fey had asked.

"Just for a little while," Bara had said.

So it put Fey in a terrible spot and made him play the role he detested. He had to say it was arsenic when he knew it was ludicrous. And he had to deflect the investigation by the Canadian officer, who was getting closer to the truth every day.

Also, the man in Oathoa—not Jorge Fey, but the military colonel sent there the day after the mine disaster—the man who had eight soldiers with him to guard the mine—to make sure that an investigation Bara was planning would not be corrupted, and who reported only to Bara— told him the morning after Mary Cyr was arrested that she was not the one who killed the child—or as he said, the children.

"Who is it?" Bara asked.

"We are not sure. But we think it might be Señora and Señor DeRolfo," the colonel said.

Even Bara was amazed at this. "Are you certain?" he finally said.

"*No, no, señor*—not positive. But we think so."

But again Bara asked them to wait.

"I have them, Hernández, Dr. DeRolfo, and yes—her, Boots Baron— only I need a few more hours—just a few more."

But then, just when things were going to be resolved—Mary Cyr freed, the embezzled money revealed—something like an act of God happened, and the communication to the town was interrupted and no one could get a message in or out. It was the *tormenta de Oathoa* (storm of Oathoa) that had come two months early. The harshest storm since, people said, the *asesinato de John F. Kennedy.*

This storm destroyed what they had all intended. That toppled two transmission towers so even the cell phones could not ping off of them.

And when that happened, Lucretia Rapone decided it was time to be the mother she was, and to kill Mary Cyr. Or she did not decide it; her new best friend, Gidgit DeRolfo, decided it for her. It was the only way Gidgit and her husband could escape, while letting Lucretia grab the attention. They would escape everyone, and Little Boots Baron said she had a place reserved for them.

As for Lucretia, who wanted a reward:

"No, you will get no reward," Mary Cry had told her, emphatically. "You have had your reward already."

And how strange this reward would reveal itself to be.

11.

THE NIGHT AFTER MARY'S COURT APPEARANCE, ÁNGEL HAD SET out to go to the gym. The old gym, a gym that had produced fifteen good Mexican boxers in the past thirty-two years—though no good heavyweights—was up off the farther end of the Calle Republica, in a nondescript building hidden away at a turn in the road. Only a simple sign marked it: a small pair of faded boxing gloves on a board that read *To Box*.

Ángel took a shortcut and walked by the jail. He saw the woman in the cell looking out at him. He walked toward her, staring at her, wondering what he could say to make her tell the truth. Moonlight came down on the white dust, the world was quiet—no one was around. He stared at her for a minute or more. It unnerved him and he looked away. He had never looked away from anyone in fear before. But now he had— why? She was beautiful, but that was not why. Or was it? The moon came down on her soft hair, her look was like a haunted little girl—but that was not why. He wanted to be angry with her and he could not be—her dirty fingers clutching the bars of the jail—her tiny hands told him she was not the *asesina* everyone said. Though how could he be sure? There was talk of people who were going to haul her out of the cell and kill her. Of course that was just talk he was sure. No good man or woman would let that happen. But it was even discussed on the local radio station here, the station that prided itself on being at the forefront of political disclosures, always telling the people of Oathoa who had and who did not have their best interests in mind. This radio station, the standard in socialist patronizing, told them of the Cyr dynasty, worth billions; told them of the pipeline in Canada that destroyed First Nations houses, and the destruction of great forests too. Angel had listened to all of this on the radio for days, his arms folded, shaking his head and tapping his feet, self-righteously condemning this woman, just as everyone did.

And this woman, this sad little creature, was supposedly the heart and soul of the Cyr dynasty.

The woman on the radio station interviewing Sharon DeRolfo had asked her about the mine, and the implosion and who bore the responsibility.

"Ah—the Cyrs as much as anyone," Sharon had said.

"Mary Cyr also?"

"*Sí.*"

Suddenly, however, Mary smiled at him, a wan, imploring and elusive smile, delicate and unashamed, blameless in its intangibility, and strangely he in turn smiled back.

He then turned and made his way gloomily along. And before he got to the gym he met Constable Fey.

"*Ven, Ángel—quiero hablar contigo,*" he said.

Come here, Ángel—I want to speak to you.

Fey told him that the ballistics on the gun he had carried had come back. Ángel looked at him, perplexed, not understanding.

"It has all come back," Fey said, somewhat angrily, as if something was Ángel's fault. But he was upset at himself—at the charade he was forced to play with the woman in the cell and the people he took orders from.

Because of little Victor, Ángel had taken the world on thinking he was engaged in a noble thing for noble people—but now this all seemed to be changing in just three or four days. He stared in perplexity, his brave open face shadowed, and the moonlight casting down into the white levels of dirt.

It is the gun that killed your father, Constable Fey did not say—he would not tell Ángel this until DeRolfo and Hernández were arrested. But he did say:

"It was used in a bad crime and they gave it to you to kill someone else—so you know who these people are now."

Constable Fey paused. Then he said:

"They wanted to blame Victor's death on you—"

"On me?" Ángel asked.

"Oh—they wanted to put the blame on your shoulders—if the boy had not made it into Mary Cyr's villa, they would have—Señor DeRolfo would have, without batting an eye—they would have blamed a murder on you. Maybe two murders. You would be in jail—and no one would care for you either."

"*¡No te creo!*"

I don't believe you.

"That is what they intended—so you could have been in that cell, and she could be back home in Canada—it was all the same to them. But that policeman from Canada, John Delano, has known this is what they intended now for three weeks. And he can prove it, because of the blood outside the villa—he says to me—*es sangre que ha fumigado, de alguien tratando de respirar*—"

It is blood that has sprayed from someone trying to breathe.

"Mary Cyr could never have the force to pick someone up like that—so our Canadian policeman is very smart."

Ángel looked at him. Then he looked behind him—down toward the jail far away. Then he looked at Fey again.

"*¿La mujer es inocente?*" Ángel asked, looking toward the cell again.

The woman is innocent?

"*Sí,*" Fey said nonchalantly. "She has done nothing—nothing at all."

So why was she in jail?

But Fey did not answer.

"I told you what I told you—and I was not supposed to tell you this yet—but I did."

Ángel watched Fey get into his car and drive away. Then he looked toward the cell. It seemed even from this distance, over three hundred yards he could still make out Mary Cyr's beautiful eyes staring right at him.

He continued on, in a daze.

That woman's innocence meant that everything in his life was about to change—and all his plans were ended. Just like that.

¡Todo lo que había oído de Hulk Hernández era una mentira!

Everything he had heard from Hulk Hernández was a lie!

12.

ALL THAT NIGHT ÁNGEL AND GABRIELLA AND PRINCIPIA SAT UP, wondering what to do. They believed, and quite appropriately, that they would be killed if they told about the toy truck.

"What if they are at fault—what if they are?" Ángel said. "What will happen?"

"So if it means the end, it means the end," Gabriella said, quietly, to Ángel Gloton. She was saying there was a sacrifice a soul must be prepared to make. And she added:

"If it is true, then maybe they didn't want me to go to university— maybe they are working for other people. Maybe Papá found out and something terrible happened to him." For Gabriella had heard the rumour that something terrible had happened.

Then thinking this about her sister, Lucretia, Principia shuddered.

That is, when just two days ago they could not move, they were paralyzed with fear lest they say something—all of them now knew they must speak. It was like a Pentecost came over them this week, and strangely it was the week of the Pentecost.

Perhaps this lick of flame came over him when Ángel had watched Mary Cyr trying to make it up those steps, jostled by the crowd. How could they sneer at such a delicate child of God? He had thought of her this way since the night before.

And it did not matter any more how powerful the DeRolfos were.

"*Decir la verdad y el diablo de la vergüenza*," little Gabriella finally said.

Tell the truth and shame the devil.

Far away, in Mexico City at the office of Mr. Bara, there was another tape. A more deadly one, which Alfonso Bara listened to as the day grew dark and night fell, and the buildings were lit along the square, and cars and trucks flew past, and the sound of music could be heard from their radios. It was the tape recorded from the conversations in the SUV.

He had turned the tape on a hundred times in the past two months. There was talk of prostitution, of marijuana exports, between Hernández and an unknown person—who had turned out to be Erappo Pole. Then there was talk about Carlos and Gidgit DeRolfo and how best to deal with them, because they were both greedy and untrustworthy—the idea of the mine was discussed, the idea of taking money from the sale of coal to make up for some kind of loss—the idea of pleasing someone, who must be pleased over a girl she saw named Gabriella, and the DeRolfos could be used in that regard. There were four tapes that he had, of these rather obscure conversations, the topics, many of them inconsequential.

Then Hernández took a trip—almost three weeks ago. They thought he was going to his summer house up the coast. (So he had his SUV tuned up. This is what John saw when he passed the garage. They put a better microphone inside the dashboard.)

And Bara had that tape as well. In fact as soon as the SUV was started, the tape was turned on in Fey's office, and these tapes were sent to him, Bara.

"There is going to be nothing here," he said when he received it.

And then, at exactly the seventeenth minute of the tape, a voice—sharp and clear, but musical and proud:

"*Quiero saber no errores como la última vez.*"

The tone very matter of fact, very concise.

I want no mistakes like last time.

"*Como estaba con los niños.*"

As there was with those children.

So, someone knew about those children. And it was a woman's voice.

Oh, he knew it was her voice. It could be no one else's. Little Boots Baron.

"Those two sicken me," she said.

And he believed she was talking about the DeRolfos.

Whose deaths they were talking about now, Bara could not determine—but it became clear that Little Boots Baron was ordering something.

It was probably the deaths of Gidgit and Carlos DeRolfo. In fact, he was certain that was what was being discussed.

Often Bara listened to this tape just to hear her voice—knowing every word that was said. In fact for the first week that he had this tape, Bara did not tell anyone—frightened lest he be wrong and worried about who he could trust. Now, however, with a new government in office, he realized he could bring this forward and order the arrests of at least six people.

What he was so furious about is that Little Boots, who always wore a certain amount of makeup, had delicate *crèmas* applied by a private masseuse to ensure her youth, was responsible for forty-three murders, mainly of men and children. Not one accusation had ever stuck, because supposedly she was a housewife who did designs and drew pictures for birthday celebrations.

Mary Cyr, who had done nothing, had been taken to jail in chains. Ms. Baron, the black widow, was aware of this, and completely fine with it.

There was one more thing: the video security camera at the resort Mary Cyr stayed at, which Fey had sent to him instead of sending it to

Tallagonga a month ago, showed someone throwing Victor Sonora out of a sky-blue Mercedes.

13.

IN THAT JAIL MARY CYR SAT.

Sometimes it was dark; then a car drove by. There was shouting, or laughter—then silence. Or sometimes the wall was illuminated, or a shade passed over it; or sometimes almost, it seemed as if she was being lifted up, and held in her mother's arms. They were in Spain, and she was a child, and the water was clear and cold. Her mother lifted her on her shoulder, and they both dove into the sea.

She was so frail now it would not take very much to lift her. She remembered how she had been talked into investing money in a *crème* that was manufactured to make women look young. It did not seem to matter much at the moment.

"*No soy culpable,*" she whispered.

Again and Again, and Again.

And then:

"I am going to die—strange that it will end like this."

Dawn might come, but so too would a terrible storm. It would knock out wires and transponders and lights—it would wash away sins, supposedly.

Mary lay in silence. She did not know that three people, Ángel and Gabriella and Principia Gloton, had listened to those charges at the courthouse, and were now determined to say something.

The three met Constable Fey and a man called John Delano. They began to speak all at once. John Delano had been ordered out of the country or he was to be charged with accessory to murder. But he did not go. This made Constable Fey like him even more—and though Constable Fey had been given authority to arrest him if he chose, he had not done so.

"*Necesito mostrar,*" little Gabriella said.

I need to show.

Then she ran the four dusty blocks to her *apartamento*, and came back, out of breath.

"Attend." Gabriella said. And she took the tape recorder out of her school bag and handed it over.

"*Escucha,*" she whispered.

"Listen," Ángel said. He looked at Fey and Delano. He knew his father was dead—and that he had been murdered. That was Ángel Gloton's biggest crime—the crime his ambition had almost—almost allowed him to make. The crime of allowing his ambition to negate the truth. It was like this: His father travelled with thirteen young women north to see how they would be treated. And he was murdered because he wanted to tell people in Oathoa what actually happened to those girls. And Ángel knew this would have happened as well to Gabriella. This is why he now looked ashamed. It was something that Gabriella would never know. No one would ever tell her. But he, Ángel, at seventeen would put a stop to it.

Everything he had ever wanted, hoped and dreamed of was destroyed by that

TINK TINK TINK.

That is why for a long time he pretended not to know.

"*Escucha,*" Ángel said.

They went back to Fey's office. He set the tape recorder down, and pushed Play. At first there was garbled talk, and much static. And then there was Carlos DeRolfo speaking. You could hear that in the distance. Then a siren. Then there was some machinery being moved. Fey kept looking at the tape, ready to say what in hell is this, when suddenly he heard absolutely clearly.

Tink tink tink tink

And again.

Tink Tink Tink Tink

It was from someone somewhere beneath their feet. A kind of prayer. That was it; it was a kind of prayer.

Fey's face turned white—even more so than John's at that moment. Because the real truth was this should have been known weeks ago, and the rescue attempt should have continued. Now he realized they had died in agony, while the hole above was covered over.

"That's nothing. *Nada*," Erappo Pole said, looking around at them disgustedly. And then he appealed to Fey:

"*Amigo.*"

His face in the light of the afternoon was course and his lips were grey, his belly was huge and his hands were thick. Once he was a child, and even now, there was a moment where Erappo Pole had a childlike look, where he stood like a boy in a schoolyard.

"No," he said, like a child. "NO no, no, no—" Hoping that the more he shook his head, the more emphatic the denial would seem.

But at that moment, Principia took out what John knew must have existed and could not find.

The toy truck.

Ángel looked at them, looked at John, then answered Erappo quietly:

"*Déjame oír esto otra vez.*"

Let's hear it again.

And so they did.

Then of course there was this story—the third story—the third part of the story, maybe. It involved when these things that were known would be made known.

Bara had known about all of this and more for a number of days. Though he did not know how the men had died underground, he suspected why the search for those men had been suspended. And he suspected much more. That is, he suspected where Florin had been taken, and was about to have the body removed. He knew his source— that is, the man who planted the microphones in the SUV was Pedro Sonora's cousin—and the thought of those little children dying, especially when people like Hernández still hugged him and patted him on the back, was destroying him.

But Bara needed all of his ducks in order. He felt he should wait one more day—or two at the most, he said. Even a Canadian girl can last in jail another day or two. Besides, we have given her, her own bigger cell, her fridge, and allowed her money. When we make the arrests, we will get the body of the child and she will be set free—with an apology, to boot.

"But," Fey said, "why not release her now? Everything has been proven or can be within a day—I feel and so does the Canadian police officer—that the longer she sits in jail the more dangerous the situation might become."

"First, you cannot without a court injunction—and another appearance before the judge. Second, I want to pick up Hernández and offer him a deal—I want Ms. Baron—all of this other stuff happened out of the blue. It is really secondary to my primary concern!"

And of course the third thing was this: he wanted to prepare a story for the press, which showed that parallel to Tallagonga's investigation was his own, more thorough one—one that did not rely on hysteria (he felt he could use this in Tallagonga's case) but on the simple, immaculate jurisprudence and adherence to the law—and that did sound very good. Besides, he deserved it. He had worked in Mexico City, in one of the endless number of judicial departments, looked upon as a provincial—but now was his *oportunidad* and he would maximize it for his own benefit. He would be able to make a case, without being self-indulgent, that the case against Cyr was begun because of her name and wealth and not because of the wealth of evidence against her. That Tallagonga's duty should have been to investigate vigorously, and not to vigorously impede an investigation.

But Bara did do something. And so Sharon DeRolfo's cell phone rang—the little country-and-western ditty she had put on it—and she picked it up, thinking that it must be New York or Toronto—two places where calls were supposed to be coming in from in the next hour—and she heard her old boyfriend's voice—the man who had married her cousin instead—the man she supposed now disliked her.

"Shar-on," he said. "*¿Cómo está, mi amiga—*" he said. "*Tengo una historia para ti, que te hará famosa.*"

I have a story for you, one that will make you famous.

Sharon would be like so many: when fame came, it came in such a devastating way it was no longer welcomed or wanted.

14.

EARLIER THE VERY NEXT DAY THE CLOUDS FORMED, AND A great storm was coming. Everyone was waiting for it, and as so happens, not a sign of wind for two hours, and the mugginess and heat clung to the sides of the buildings and the dark alleys. Motor scooters sat abandoned in front of buildings that seemed closed. Portals were drawn shut. Upstairs *apartamentos* faced the sea with a kind of belligerence and resilience. All was quiet. The donkey lay down in the dirt; its ears were low. Mary Cyr lay down upon her cot and tried to sleep.

She dreamed then of winter apples, the snowdrifts white, and apple seeds falling into the white powdered snow. And she held an apple in her snowy mitten, two bites taken all at once.

And then there was a small sound, far away—a church bell it sounded like.

Once she went to university. (She wrote in her diary.) She took English and history and psychology 101. One day they gave a test to students— mainly in fun—and she wrote in her diary: "I am not a psychopath."

All the questions were pretty standard—it wouldn't have taken much for any really good psychopath to fool the examiner. A definite yes gave you five points.

"Would you be sorry if your mother or father died?"

"Would you protect your brother or cousin if someone lied about them?"

"Would you care for a child?"

"Would you give up your life for a child?"

"Would you feel sad if you saw a dog tortured?"

"I am so happy I am not a psychopath—it is one less thing I have to worry about," she wrote.

She was drifting away, to see her father, and her mother.

A great storm seemed to be coming outside—the walls of some building seemed to crumble, or was that in her mind? Then it became terribly dark, like a certain biliousness in the waving trees of mid-summer. Or was she dreaming? She did not know anymore. Then there was a gigantic crack, from somewhere. Hailstones began to fall, and all the power went out.

"Hermana, te amo," she heard the woman she bought the bus ticket for say. But that was two days ago, or a week, she did not remember quite when. The thing about starvation—is that it would be almost impossible for her to eat now.

Then all the lights flickered and went out.

The little guard came to her cell, and spoke. She was quite worried, but tried to pretend she was not, and Mary knew this.

The police had gone because of an emergency at the hospital out on the highway; the soldiers who were at the coal mine had been called somewhere as well, and left in a truck. So they were suddenly alone, except for her, a little female guard and Erappo Pole.

The little guard said she would buckle up, and make sure things were safe. And so she went from cell to cell, woman to woman, to see if they were okay. Then she went upstairs and locked the big, big door. Oh yes, and then she took a pail and mop and tried to mop up the water already on the office floor.

"Mary Cyr can fool some of you for a while, but we who know her, and her family, realize she is a sick and murderous terror."

It was the last thing she had taped over her breasts just three days ago.

That made it really quite hard to breathe.

———

In Mexico City, Bara decided now was the time to arrest Mr. and Mrs. DeRolfo, and tomorrow at the very latest he would let Mary Cyr go.

But Mr. and Mrs. DeRolfo were packing—had three hundred thousand dollars in American money—and were planning to leave. They had their escape route planned and the diversion planned as well. The storm just happened to be a bonus. Those men they were to meet once they crossed the border would prove a most fateful meeting.

But they were going north on the road toward the border. It would get dark and windy, the car would rock, and signs would fly in front of them as they went—but they would make it outside of the danger zone the first night. Then they would place a call to a woman. They would say:

"Sorry to bother you, we are so sorry to tell you we can't for the life of us go any farther today—the storm is too bad—we are going to put up tonight here, and leave again tomorrow, can you tell the men to wait."

By that time a disaster would have happened in the town of Oathoa that would implicate everyone—tar them all with the same brush.

"Of course," Little Boots Baron would answer. "I will tell them to wait."

"We are forever in your debt."

"Consider it paid."

Their bodies would be found bound and mutilated in a dumpster in a small Texas town two weeks later.

PART FOURTEEN

1.

JOHN DELANO'S FINAL REPORT WAS WRITTEN FOUR MONTHS after he came back from Mexico.

Now, of course, with all that ruin people saw a different story emerge, but as so often happens, it was too late. Now the tabloids were shifting, but their moral outrage was to them as justified as always.

Why had they not seen it? Why did they not recognize Professor Cruise for what he was? What had Warren known that he, Greg, did not? And why did she go to Mexico? That is, the entire family's business dynamics were scrutinized by ten million Canadians, and by just as many British and Americans, trying to figure out what someone might have done to stop this atrocity against her.

The amazing thing was all that they had managed to find out after the fact. Was it always going to be like this—after the fact? Were you always going to say someone was great only afterwards, only after blood and darkness? And what about that man Pedro Sonora? Had he pinged his tin cup into nothing, like a man crying out to God, condemned forever to cry? Was he the final emblematic silhouette of man, banging a symbol to an empty sky?

That was peculiar, John said, but in a way as natural as any other tragedy of conscience. That is, those who yelled loudest against her when they had the chance did not now utter a word to ask forgiveness for themselves. They were very quiet now. The Cyr pipeline that had been damaged by those who drove to the pipeline in cars that used oil, and slept in houses that needed it, and wore clothes that contained it, now issued not one statement about her. The university profs as well who spoke of progress—and said that the Cyr empire was one of failure and disaster, sitting in buildings some of which were donated by Cyr money—did not now come back to reinvestigate themselves.

"But," John said, "it was in actual fact building for days—the idea to break in and take her out of her cell." He said this to the family as they sat in the big room at the front of the great house in Saint John. Fog rolled into the windows, and all around were the trappings of despair and darkness, even, or perhaps more especially, in this bastion of understated constant wealth and privilege. Nan sat at the back of the room; Perley sat in the corner on a chair by the window, his huge body almost obsolete. He was the only one brave enough, and willing enough, to trade places with her—the man picked on all his life. He had tried to fly down, but his family refused—so he had taken a plane to Toronto, and tried to get on an international flight. He was already to go. But he had no passport. He had not been able to find his. They told him he must reapply for a passport before he left the country. So Perley went back home. When he got home, he found out that John himself was going to be arrested for conspiracy because he would not leave Mexico.

"When did they come for her?" he asked.

"Oh—it was when they knew she was innocent," John said. "Because they knew she was innocent."

"What do you mean?"

"I mean in the most secret part of a mob and all that a mob is party to, they very often know the one they *accuse* is not guilty. So taking them out of the cell is actual proof that they are innocent—it is a strange thing—if you believe in heaven, which I do, and hell—which I still worry about; and the Virgin Mary, which I do, and Christ, who I do, though I am afraid I rarely go to Mass—if you believe in that, in that, then you will see the scapegoat in the little donkey, and Mary Cyr clutching the bars of the cell and looking out on the empty street, as the crowd gathered—there is something awesome in her look—something forever luminous and determined, something forever part of our Canadian soul."

"Was she brave?"

"Yes, I think she was," John said, reaching over and taking a package of cigarettes from the pocket of his coat and lighting one. "And you know what else?"

"What?"

"She went to Mexico because she had to—she wanted to find out about the mine—that is why she went down—she was taking money down to give to the poor, but soon after she got there the implosion happened—so she stayed because she wanted to find out why it had happened. The idea of dropping an earring in order to meet Victor was a calculated gamble. Our sister was smarter than any of us—but she didn't let on."

"Our sister?" Nan said.

"Is that what I called her—our sister—well, there you go. At the end Norma van Haut was her sister I will tell you that."

It was all over now—all of it. That is, the protesting against her had all but stopped. And now among her adversaries there was only silence, accompanied, if they thought of it, by shame.

When they finally came down the stairs and along the corridor and got to her cell, the little waif was sitting on the clothes crate, looking out at them with her luminous eyes. The weather had made it dark and rain swept into the cell. The lines were down. Great mad waves of water washed the streets, and here and there sparks flew up from broken wires.

The police force had gone up to the highway to rescue people there— at the hospital, and a busload of tourists had overturned. The group of army cadets had been placed on the roads. And the streets of Oathoa were empty, except for a dog or two scurrying half mad on hind legs kicking up against the wind.

"The main street passed the resort—narrowed and narrowed, but it finally led to the jail," John said.

Far down the street a little girl watched without a sound, looking over at them in awe. This was in fact Gabriella. Why was she in awe? Because, the world had stopped, and some other thing had taken hold of men.

People had mistaken Lucretia as Florin's mother and no one would be able to tell anyone different. Even as Gabriella followed behind and shouted pleadingly that she was not the mother. She became the mother—she became at the moment all mothers in the world—and now because of this, she had to act it out.

Lucretia was carrying Florin in her arms along the street. A crowd of people surrounded her and jostled her. There was now such rage forming against *the lady in the cell*. Mary Fatima Cyr was therefore alone; except for a little female guard, in a big hat, and Erappo Pole.

Gabriella ran back to her apartment to find Ángel.

"You have to help her."

"Who do I have to help?"

"The lady—in jail—no one will help if you do not."

"Why?"

"Because you have to," she said.

Erappo Pole had taken this madwoman to the child. Behind her great clouds swarmed in the sky. It was so dark that the flat sea looked angry and vampire bats with their pig-like noses skirted the heavens.

The crowd gathered as the storm gathered. Norma van Haut and her husband ran to the jail when they saw the crowd gather. Mary Cyr was looking out at them from one side of the cell, they were looking in.

But the crowd was too, too enraged. Constable Fey was five miles away, where the bus had overturned twenty minutes before. The heavy rain poured down over the brim of his hat. He heard his cell phone buzz and then go quiet.

Every time the little guard tried to phone his cell phone there seemed to be nothing but a busy signal or dead air. She tried ten times.

Worse, John Delano himself had been placed in the cell above Mary Cyr that morning.

So there were few if any people to help.

Still, when they tried to get to her, the big German tossed people right and left and right again, but finally went down under their assault—tried to stand and was kicked in the face until he lost consciousness.

"*Puta, puta*," they screamed.

Mary came to the cell window, just as Ángel parked his little scooter across the street. The wind howled and the scooter toppled over. He looked at it, and then turned his attention to the crowd. He seemed to be very calm as he watched them.

Drawing nearer he saw the face of Mary Cyr. She seemed to him to be a dove beating its broken wings against some wire cage.

People would write for months—even years—that Ángel was captivated by her beauty at just this moment, that he could have at this moment said as the poet declared, that *beauty was truth*. But suddenly all the rumours he had heard about the DeRolfos became clear. He looked and saw Florin's little body in a heap near the old donkey.

They went to tear her—as they said: "Tear her by her tits out of the cell."

He followed behind them.

He turned and was only a few inches from her face. Her beauty overwhelmed him, some said, and he protested:

"*¿Usted es una mujer inocente?*"

He asked this as a great lightning bolt flashed far away, and she could hardly make out his words.

"You are an innocent woman?" he had asked her. His face was sad, and drenched with rain. "Please tell me you are."

"*Sí,*" she said. She smiled. Like a foreigner trying her best to understand some stranger on a train.

They said she sat in the cell, at the last holding a comb—no one knew if it was to protect herself or comb her hair—and perhaps she did not either. She could hear them coming, and every time a door banged she trembled slightly, just as those men had trembled when they heard the clang above their heads.

The Dutch doctor stood at the cell window, trying to fend people off. But she had no hope of doing so.

The little guard suffered too; she ran the length of the cells and let other women out, to help her—while trying to use her billy club to protect who she thought was a vicious woman but still and all a prisoner to be protected with her life. She was Constable Fey's fiancée. And all the while the mob got closer, and then closer. The women in the other cells came out, yelling and screaming for the mob to show decency—to show decency. They tried to protect her as they grappled with the mob along the corridor. Plants and chairs were overturned. The two women lovers came from their own cell, both with belts in their hands to swing. It did no good at all.

Ángel followed behind, hands in his pockets, still not sure what crowd he was part of.

However, darkness was everywhere. And very suddenly they all stopped to look in at her. She simply stared at them all—all of them. There was nothing more to say.

Lightning flashed and *¡Viva Cristo!* was illuminated. Then hailstones the size of golf balls fell.

Some palm trees were uprooted, telephone wires came tumbling oddly down, and live wires flashed and bobbled on the streets. The donkey bayed against the onslaught, looking as if its hair was going to be ripped off. She felt sorry for the donkey, as it fell forward onto its head, and could not lift itself again. That is what she had been looking at when she first saw them coming up the street.

At the end there was a gash and blood coming from Norma van Haut's face, flowing freely—that was the picture in the *News of the World*. And in the Spanish paper this headline: "*Intentó protegerla con su vida.*"

And yes, that was true.

Norma van Haut had tried to save her, yelling:

"*Cometes un error.*"

"*Lo siento—por todo*," Mary Cyr said, when they forced themselves into the cell.

I am sorry—for everything.

"*Tú no estás perdonado,*" Lucretia said.

She had to say it. It was her moment.

You are not forgiven. Or in a more personal way: I do not forgive you! She wore the designer sunglasses and the watch Mary had given her—in fact, she had combed her own hair to be like Ms. Cyr's for her picture that would appear two days later in *Gringo Magazine*.

"A mother finds her child."

Greg ran most of the business now. He had much to deal with. The protests against his company's plans to build a pipeline had come to a head during the crisis with his prodigal cousin. It had caused much of what Greg called "sour press." The protesters had destroyed six of his trucks and had tried to sabotage a rail line. That was when they could say that Mary Cyr was a deplorable human and link her to the Cyr Corporation. (Greg took measures to distance himself from his cousin, just as he had always done—and he didn't think she knew.)

He was sorry for that now. They were all sorry for that now. In fact, he was sure some might plan to write a book in order to exonerate themselves.

Or perhaps not.

He looked over all the files. He looked over the mounds of newspaper reports—the idea that a hurricane had happened so the police were busy elsewhere; that the streets had flooded so mad people were left to their own devices.

The barber had closed for the day, and had run into the street with a pair of scissors, which he would never have done if the man whose hair he was cutting had not jumped up to see what the commotion was.

The power went out.

Was that an act of God? He wasn't sure.

Greg would have to get in touch with the Dutch doctor and thank her for doing what she could. Of course Delano too—yes, why hadn't he thought too much of him? Both of them had risked death protecting her. Delano, who was suffering from a bad heart, had stayed when he was ordered to leave.

And that young Angel Gloton! Was that his name? Strangely you hear of people you would never have known existed—but there he was. He punched three men silly and then hit a fourth and almost knocked him cold, before he was thrown down and booted unconscious. It was as if he hadn't made his mind up until the very last moment what side he would fight on.

What had started it all—Greg was trying to determine this. But all he remembered about Mary Cyr was the leaf that had fallen into her auburn hair at sunset, when snow fell and the sky in the distance was pink over the black tree line. He should have helped her, held her in his arms, and taken her home. But of course he did not. He was unfortunately not like that.

So this is what happened.

Earlier that day Lucretia was driven in a car to the DeRolfo house. Gidgit had prayed all night in the chapel. There was a smell of sweet flowers and the chapel lights were on. And she blessed herself.

When she heard the car pull up, she left the chapel with her dark kerchief over her head. She met Lucretia in the foyer, and grabbed her with both hands.

"We have found your child," Gidgit said. She said it quickly, almost indecipherably, so that Lucretia, spellbound at being here, did not understand.

"*¿Perdón?*" Lucretia said.

Gidgit kissed her suddenly and told her, with tears in her eyes, to prepare herself for another tragic day.

"*¿Dónde está mi hijo? ¿Dónde está mi hijo?*" Lucretia said, looking around in sudden terror.

"*Ven te llevaremos a él,*" Gidgit said.

The rain and wind had started, when Lucretia was taken to the dump. She was confused because she wore her best shoes and dress. She looked at them in sudden contempt.

"*No aquí,*" Gidgit said, tears in her eyes. "*Por favor.*"

Lucretia was taken to the dump.

There, amid seagulls overhead, and rats running across the garbage, the wind coming up, and mounds of garbage ready to fall and slide into the ravine where desperate people made their homes, she was shown the boy's tiny body, covered in rat bites.

"*Mi hijo*," she whispered.

There was silence as she carried her child, decomposing and filled with rat bites, back over the streets. She was an ancient mother, a mother in the age of Boadicea. And those that gathered about her as she laid the child down near the road to the jail were silent.

The rain was so vicious it was difficult to make out one person from another. The wind broke limbs from trees. Lucretia suddenly seemed naked within a flash of lightning.

Over the severe, desperate wind people could hear her wailing.

No one could silence her, and no one could comfort her anymore.

"She is not the mother," Gabriella said. "She is not the mother." But no one wanted to hear, no one cared.

Men told each other they must take action. They must, or be damned for being cowards. They started toward the cell grim and determined, their bodies exhibiting a kind of hysteria. Mary Fatima Cyr looked out at them, her shining eyes wide and curious.

Mary Cyr's middle name was Fatima because Nan had insisted on it. And Elaine had said of course.

Mary had visited the shrine where the children had spoken to the Blessed Virgin, who had promised a miracle and so made the sun move to touch the earth so that thousands of people, intellectual and ironic and sophisticated, who had come to jeer, fell to the ground in terror.

At Fatima Mary had said a private prayer—many private prayers to the great Lady in the sky. She asked forgiveness.

It was after she had lost her grip on Lucien.

She said the Our Father.

She wanted forgiveness now.

They all walked up the street, their bodies strangely illuminated in the storm appearing and disappearing in the wind and rain, coming for her like spectres out of her childhood dreams.

They started toward the cell.

"*No te perdono*," Lucretia said, looking in at her, while men and women cheered her on to say something to the whore. Say something to the whore!

I do not forgive you.

The week before—or about a week before, when she knew she would die—she had phoned Garnet about Perley. Garnet was very surprised to hear her. He asked her how she was.

"I am fine," she said. "But you must do something for me—you must go into the linen closet—the one up on the third floor near Bobby's playroom—there is a small leather chest—it is where your son, Perley, keeps his passport. You must take it and throw it away, so he cannot come here. And," she added, "do you think you have treated him well—I mean—as well as you should have?"

"I—I don't know."

Yesterday morning she woke to a faint smell of some Mexican flower and farther away a haze and the smell of diesel and the *thud, thud* of a great excavator at the mine site. The clanging and the monotonous *thud* of the excavator had come into Mary's cell. It had started over a week ago.

She stood on her tiptoes to better see and listen to it. It certainly sounded foreboding to her.

"What are they doing?" she whispered, to one of the women.

"Oh," the woman said, trying to sound formal. "Oh, they are proceeding with a plan to recover the bodies."

"The bodies?" Mary asked.

"Oh my dear—the bodies buried there seven weeks ago."

So yesterday the paper *Gringo Gazette* reported that the two million Mary had on her was all the proof they needed that Tarsco was guilty of trying to bribe someone to stop an investigation.

Ca Cug went the machine. And the men with oxygen tanks and helmets with giant lights began to work with security ropes attached to each other and walk downward, slowly—so slowly they looked like robots from some strange movie long ago.

But others heard the *Ca Cug* as well. And one was Gidgit DeRolfo.

The house was in shambles—doors were open, hallways were blocked with clothes, rugs rolled up, paintings were taken down and laid against the wall—trunks moved out—yet most of this would have to be left behind.

"Spring cleaning," she said to anyone who asked.

Neither she nor her husband knew of the dozens of documents in Bara's office that condemned them, and exonerated the woman in that jail cell. Nor did they know a microphone was finally placed in their car. Or that Maxwell the truck was now with the police.

They still believed it was simply a matter of them doing one more thing to make their own innocence sacrosanct.

So they had Lucretia driven to their house. Señora DeRolfo looked into her eyes, startled by the black roots that intertwined within her blond hair, and her coarse mouth, and said:

"I know you as a mother who has suffered like me."

This was exactly what Lucretia was waiting to hear—though for the life of her she did not know it until that moment.

"*¿Quién es esa mujer?*" Little Boots Baron asked in a phone call three nights before. "*¿Es ella la madre?*"

Who is that woman? Is she the mother?

"No," Gidgit said, "she is insane."

"Well, show her the body—it will make the whole town hysterical—" Little Boots said. "Then you two leave town and go where I tell you to."

"And no suspicion will fall on us," Gidgit said.

"Of course not—you have my word on that—" Little Boots answered.

The DeRolfos sped away toward their appointment. Everything they said now recorded, even the unfortunate sudden shock when they learned they were trapped.

———

What was curious is that Fey and John had discussed sneaking Mary Cyr out of town the night before. And it almost happened. Norma and her husband were there as well.

"I will take her—and I can get her across the border—I will have someone help us—you must help us—before it is too late," Norma had asked. Fey said okay. Then he spoke to his fiancée, the little prison guard, and became worried for her sake. For her sake he did not know what to do. If Mary Cyr escaped, his fiancée would lose her job—she might go to jail herself.

He went back to his office and telephoned Alfonso Bara. He had Principia's tape in his pocket. He told Bara what had transpired.

"It is time to let her go," he said.

Bara was looking out the window at the giant square—the evening lights were on, the sounds of buses rounding the circle and stopping, in the distance with the sunlight casting over it, the historical waterway that existed from the time Mexico City was an Aztec domain.

He paused. Then he said:

"No, it would alert Hernández and Little Boots Baron." And that is who he was after. "Everyone would start to scurry away."

Alfonso Bara told him to put John in jail until the case was solved. "It is for his own good—too many people know he is here."

John was in jail when Norma van Haut stood guard with a little stick. He was in jail—and looked out on the trial about to take place. His face was cut open because he had fought to remain free. And that was that. They put him in protective custody and informed the Canadian embassy that he would be leaving Mexico on Flight 967.

2.

NOW IT WAS JULY. IT WAS EVENING IN A HOUSE OUTSIDE SAINT John. Still fog had settled in, and John had the remnants of a struggle— a hand that had been badly broken, and a mark across his right temple ending just above his ear—both in the process of healing away, but leaving a silver-white energetic question mark that seemed to pose a futile question to the world.

John told them that sometimes the script for a great actress is not the one she desires, but the one she deserves—or more to the point, he decided, the one she cannot escape. For weeks Principia begged Lucretia not to pretend. Lucretia did not know her final scene would be carrying the decomposing body of a child she never liked up the street as trees and power lines toppled. She had no idea that this would become her greatest scene.

At first no one paid attention to her. But little by little as the wind wailed against them they gathered near her. When they tried to take the child from her, she pushed them away, and continued.

"*¿Quién va a hacer algo con esa mujer miserable?*"

Who is going to do something about that miserable woman?

But Tallagonga, whose office was in the building next to her—just across the street from the café where they stood—came out and tried to reason with them.

"You must let the law decide."

She pleaded—but the script had already been written, and she had been instrumental in acting her small part. She called as well for the police, but they were gone. So that, too, was futile.

As futile really as the little stick Norma van Haut held in order to prevent them from advancing.

"*Mary Cyr es inocente,*" she screamed over and over, and over.

Half the men, who broke into the cell, knew the child was not Lucretia's. But it was a child and the mine disaster made up for it. If they only had waited one more day, they would have realized the mine disaster was not her doing either.

" 'Render unto Caesar that which is Caesar's,' " Mary Cyr said, when she saw them coming, as the mob got closer to the jail and John tried to get the guard to let him out.

"*No es posible,*" the little guard said, looking at him strangely. "*Usted está bajo mi protección.*"

(It is not possible. You are under my protection.)

"'Render unto Caesar.'"

John heard.

For a long while John wondered why she had said this.

"What then does Caesar have—what does Caesar own?" John asked them back in Saint John. All of them were silent. Fog rested against the window. Then in spite of it a small bird cried—a bird on the wing going somewhere.

"Nothing," John answered for them.

"Caesar owns—nothing—not a thing."

3.

ERAPPO POLE OPENED HER CELL DOOR GRAVELY—AS IF, EVEN though he had been ordered to obey the law, law had its limits and honour was honour. The human condition is one of deceit punctuated by moments that overcome it. It is what Little Boots Baron knew—as she spread her deceit into the town of Oathoa nine years before with her friend Hulk Hernández. So the Amigo Company was doomed. If Mary Cyr had not come by, they were planning to take Gabriella that autumn—now that she was old enough to go.

Mary Fatima Cyr held a comb in her hand, looking at them, sitting on her little bed, her feet on its crate.

"¿Estás luchando?" one of the men said,

"Fighting back, are you?"

Aghast that she would dare.

Haul her out onto the street, they said.

Puta.

Cunt.

Fucker.

Cock licker.

Slut.

Whore.

All of the things most of them wanted a woman to be.

When they turned to take her, Ángel Gloton was there.

He looked at her. She was holding Plu, her childhood comforter, in her arms. She smiled.

He did not know what he would do.

Great lightning flashed and down the street the whole cement floor of the fish market was now under water up to the stalls, and dead mackerel floated and live crabs scuttled away.

Mary Cyr looked at Ángel with a sweet kind of curious ambivalence, thinking he was the Angel of Death. She looked up at him, and then looked at the two men holding her, as if she was awaiting a discussion to take place about her future. Until one of the men took her Plu and threw it down. Ángel's expression changed. He began to hate them, and what they had done to her.

"*Dejarla con nosotros, amigo*," one of the men said to him.

Leave her to us, friend.

He said, "*No!*"

"*Debes dejar que vaya*," they said.

But again he said, "Let her go."

They simply decided to drag her by him, but he stood in the cell door. He threw a hard right hand.

One man went down—and then he got his right hand high on another's forehead and drove him across the cell, breaking his hand— then another, he hit hard with his broken hand, and that man's two front teeth broke and he fell. So Mary was free from them for a few seconds. He smiled tenderly at her, and held her under her left arm.

He began to haul her away from them, thinking he could get her to safety, but she turned and said:

"*Una momento*," and tried to find Plu.

Ángel looked away from Erappo Pole.

Erappo Pole was standing in the corridor. The man he had trusted walked up behind him and hit him four times with a billy club. He tried to grab the club, but after the first blow he was almost unconscious. He fell, blood gushing from the back of his head. He was not yet seventeen years old.

"Help him," Mary said, trying to bend down and pick him up out of the water that was now coming into the cell.

"Where is Plu?" she asked. But she had it in her arms.

Ángel had left his scooter across the street. He had worked extra days to buy it. That was over now.

"*Muere por la belleza,*" Erappo said. "*Los Glotons—están todos en él.*"

He dies for beauty. The Glotons are in on it.

Lucretia was standing outside the cell door, looking at Mary as she was being dragged. She still had Mary's sunglasses on, but her new blouse was soiled with live maggots from having carried the dead child.

The little guard, Constable Fey's fiancée, took her revolver, and came down from the upper cell where John Delano was, as the men proceeded dragging Mary along the black hallway.

But they had locked the side door, and she had to try to find the keys in the back office under that stairwell. Then, when she finally found them in a cup in the cupboard, she had to find the right key and rush back.

They dragged Mary Cyr into the field near the donkey. There, as far as the reports went, they held her down. She said nothing—at all—as a bunch of men clipped her hair with a pair of scissors the barber brought from his shop. It is said the wind was so strong that the hair flew up and up in the wind, as it was being snipped away, and one could see her bald head, rough and bruised, looking like the inside of an orange peel.

None of this is verifiable.

"Wait," Lucretia said. "Leave her alone. I am not the mother—I tell you *I am not the mother!* You know me. You all know me. I made it up."

But no one paid any attention to her. In fact they turned on her and told her to get the fuck out of the way.

Then a man ran to Ángel's scooter, which had been tossed up in the wind, and took the gas tank that had been broken off it, and ran back to her.

"Pour it over her—get that rag of hers and soak the whore with it—"

They poured it, holding the gas tank up, with the spigot opened, and gas flowing over her body and the man's white long nervous fingers.

Lucretia started to back away.

"No," she said, "NO."

The priest who had given Mary Cyr Communion very early that morning, and spoken of courage in the face of evil, watched from the far end of the churchyard, beside himself and without the courage to act.

Everything was quiet as they tried to get something lit.

They kept complaining about the wind and the rain.

"*¿Por favor?*" Mary said, as a plea. The only plea she would make.

Then ten of them (as were indicted in the murder charges filed by Tallagonga) finally got a newspaper with a picture of her on it lit, lit her old childhood comforter, Plu, and managed to set her afire, then chased her around, continuing to sprinkle the gas on the burning blanket. Then her whole body was smoking, but some hair and clothes began to burn. It did look very strange.

"The bitch smokes more than burns," someone yelled.

"There is nothing we can do—it is the weather."

Mary staggered, tried to find her way forward, and stumbled to her knees, rose again, and began to walk toward her tormentors with her hands out, as if seeking someone to hold her. But one man pushed her in the direction of another and then another tossed her, going back and forth in a circle. All or most of them shouting and laughing.

"She's starting to burn better now," Erappo said, rather stoically.

Some were terribly silent. Smoke and flame billowed from her clothes and sparks came off the tuffs of hair left on her head, which she kept trying to put out. There was a smell of burning skin.

Now and then good people shouted from buildings:

"For the love of God, leave her alone. Someone help her to stand— look she has fallen again—help her, someone."

A man came out to help her, but they threw him down. John kept yelling to her—that he would come and help—he would come and help. But he knew he couldn't get out.

She turned and looked at him—up, toward the sky—for a second—and he saw that her left eye had been beaten shut.

Then suddenly Mary began to run around again. She was trying to escape the circle, and the flames started to creep up against her pants.

Lucretia watched as Mary Fatima Cyr ran, waving her arms in the air like a young girl as if looking for something. She kept running and running round in circles, trying to get the sparks out. But the flames grew.

The little guard had by now opened the door, and heard:

"Snow."

It was Mary Fatima Cyr's last word.

She fell sitting up, her childhood blanket on the ground beside her, still waving her hands for a while. Then she fell backward, her right leg really trembling. Plu was burned to a crisp. She still held it.

When it was over, Erappo Pole said:

"The gringo officer in the cell—he wants the same, let's give him the same as her."

He started toward the jail again. He stoically carried the billy club with which he had beaten Ángel Gloton.

The little guard, with her big hat and a revolver in her hand, walked up to Erappo Pole and shot him in the head. He gave her a startled look, as if he was a child once again, then fell.

She arrested the men who were there.

Subdued and terrified, no one said another word.

Not for a long time.

John told the family this. He did it because he had to. Because it was in the papers anyway—on the *News of the World*.

Then he said:

"He who wrote *A Discourse on Inequality* left his five children in a foundling house—"

He did not know why he said this. It seemed he had to.

4.

PEOPLE IN TOWN TURNED AGAINST HERNÁNDEZ. THEY SPOKE about Little Boots and the evil she had done. Then the bodies of the DeRolfos were found. They died two days after they had got to Texas. Little Boots told them to wait in a safe house there and she would send men to help. The money they had on them was gone. Little Boots stood only five feet two, and was defiant to the end.

"A criminal empire," she said. "I am a housewife who plays bingo and works at church suppers."

But she was extradited to the US in 2009 and now sits in a Texas prison.

After a week or so, people found out all about the mine.

Not a new timber had been put in place.

They found the men, three weeks later.

Pedro Sonora was lying by the statue of Our Lady, near Gabriella's boyfriend—the rest of the men were sitting or lying a few feet away from him.

Pedro had kept tapping his spoon to the end. He died with it in his hand.

Autopsies showed some of the men had lived nine days.

Mary Cyr's autopsy showed she died of smoke inhalation. That is, they felt she had become unconscious in thirty or forty seconds.

When they undressed her in the morgue, they found all the headlines. Not one of the papers had burned too too much. They unravelled them carefully—one after the other—her whole life of scandal stapled to her chest—just like the Bob Dylan song said. The last one, before they reached her breasts, was the picture of Denise Albert.

The one closest to her heart.

"My friend, I made you famous and you didn't even thank me," she had written.

Underneath all of it her naked body was shiny white.

Victor's body was exhumed. He had died of a crushed larynx. Little Florin still had a french fry coupon on him.

Lucretia is awaiting trial in the Prisión del Rayo. No one protests her innocence more, and she is known to cry all night, while being taunted by other women.

Principia and Gabriella received the money that Mary Cyr had promised.

They could charge Hernández with half a dozen crimes, including murder and the rape of the Spanish woman.

John told the Cyr family all of this. They kept staring at the scar across his forehead, where they had struck him down.

Sharon DeRolfo moved out of the house, moved away from everyone.

Left her girlfriend and lives alone.

The chapel Carlos had built his wife was removed.

John read all of this meticulously in his steady, steely monotone. But they all listened.

The real problem for Alfonso Bara is he did not allow her to go free weeks before. That was always going to be a problem for him. Now that she had died it was worse. He should have let her go—Constable Fey had said she was innocent the day after John Delano arrived.

He had written this: "There is a Canadian policeman here—a bothersome sort in a way, none too outgoing, but do not underestimate him. He has been here five days; he knows the boy was not murdered by this woman. He is certain adults were involved, and that it had to do with the mine implosion."

He had sent that off to Bara. But Bara still hesitated. The trap was too exquisite to spring without catching whom he wanted.

Afterwards Bara was clever enough to say he could not chance giving away his position to people who were brutal enough to do what they in fact had done. That the death of Mary Cyr was mob related and no one could have foreseen that—that he had started the excavation in order to free her, and not to condemn her. He became an under chief justice, just as his wife had hoped.

Constable Fey was made captain, was later promoted to district superintendent. He married the young woman who was Mary's guard and friend.

Tallagonga continues to this day to be prosecutor in Oathoa.

EL did finish his book. In it, he had gone to Mexico to help Mary Cyr, and was thwarted at every turn—and he used much of John Delano's research, saying it was his own.

People said they were going to build a statue to Mary, right in the square of Oathoa. In fact Tallagonga was one of the statue's major supporters. But still there are kidnappings of tourists now and again, farther along the coast, and scams are set up to injure tourists and force them to pay huge amounts at the hospital. In fact, Norma van Haut has written on this for *Der Spiegel* just recently.

Add that to the fact that Nan is still alive and still has enormous power and has decided to donate a church in Mary Fatima Cyr's honour.

Mary was famous now—more famous than any of her accusers—and all the talk against her just went away.

It was easy enough, really, to find out who it was. His name was on the park bench—written that long-ago November by a hopeful young girl.

"I like Mr. C.—Mary Cyr."

Generations of children sat on that bench, the evidence beneath their bums.

It was too late now. For forgiveness or recrimination. He had forgotten about the poem. He had forgotten much about her. He would simply fade away.

After that Perley resigned from the paper. All papers, all things, forever. He hardly speaks a word to anyone in the world. But that wasn't the best of it. No, the best of it was he was seen in the company of a beautiful woman—they danced in bars and clubs, went skinny-dipping in the ocean, and he never once apologized again for who he was or how he looked.

People said he cornered Doc one night and beat him unconscious. Just like that. Not one bit frightened anymore. That was the real secret, unknown and untold, unrehearsed and unfettered; our Perley Cyr was as strong as an ox.

Poor Doc couldn't go out of his house for more than a year.

"Me?" he said. "Why are people so angry at me—I'd like to know?"

Then he promised he would change—promised his grandmother he would do better. And so far, he seems to have improved.

Ernest Vanderflutin has a part interest in a bakery. He has remarried, to a Jewish woman.

Paco died of booze in 1988.

Father Ignatius was beatified in 2010.

Mary's diary was returned to the family.

And John Delano would go on, in his own tragic way, and have at least one or more great cases, and like Mary Cyr leave us too soon—but that is a tale for another time.

ACKNOWLEDGEMENTS

I have, as always, far too many people to thank. My dear editor, Lynn Henry. My agent, Anne McDermid. My publicist, Shona Cook. Peg McIntyre, wife, Harley partner, world traveler, by my side for more than fifty years. My granddaughter, sweet Blair Alice, who thinks her Papa has written all the books in his study—but will someday, I hope, realize he has written one or two good ones. Her father, John, and her Uncle Anton know that my love is unconditional—and whomever says the contrary is a liar, fraud, snatcher of souls.

ABOUT THE AUTHOR

DAVID ADAMS RICHARDS is one of Canada's preeminent writers. His novels *Crimes Against My Brother* and *Incidents in the Life of Markus Paul* were nominated for the Scotiabank Giller Prize and published to wide acclaim. Among his other recent novels, *The Lost Highway* was shortlisted for the Governor General's Literary Award; *The Friends of Meager Fortune* won the Commonwealth Writers' Prize for Best Book; and *Mercy Among the Children* won the Scotiabank Giller Prize and was shortlisted for the Governor General's Literary Award and the Trillium Award. Richards is also the author of the celebrated Miramichi Trilogy and has written four bestselling books of nonfiction: *Lines on the Water*, *God Is.*, *Facing the Hunter* and *Hockey Dreams*. In 2017, he was appointed to the Canadian Senate, representing the province of New Brunswick.